Demon Raider
The Death Stalker

By
David Andrew Crawford

Synopsis

Now with the first leg of his quest over, the second book, Demon Raider, the Death Stalker, starts out with Dark finally finding himself in the Dwarven City of Duergar, an instrument of revenge, seeking redress for wrongs done to him and his family as he begins to set his plan for vengeance in motion. Aided by the powerful artifact, the Eye of Dagda, he enters the city under the guise of Giacomo, the Jester and sets out to destroy the Halflings' Guild and its leader Sneak Longfoot, the Grand Master of the Guild.

Dark, using all his skill as an assassin and his powerful arsenal of magical items, causes murder and mayhem throughout the fortified City of the Dwarves. One by one the leaders of the Guilds and their followers will pay for the injustice carried out to his parents. Then and only then will Dark have peace in the knowledge that his parents have been avenged and all those responsible have paid with their very lives.

Darkness will fall upon the Kingdom of Duergar and one lone assassin will rise up against the sinister forces who have gone, as of yet, unpunished. On his quest for vengeance, Dark must face his first of many terrifying tasks that poses as much risk to himself as it does to his targets. Any doubts he may have he will bury with the dead as he puts into play a plan that will have him hunt down his numerous adversaries and in the end his shadowy blade will drip with the blood of his enemies.

Only there is one slight problem with his perfectly laid plan. For starters, the Döckálfar, a dark skinned sub-race of the Elves has entered into his one man war, and bringing with them their hated and sworn enemy the Elven Witch Slayer's of Eldred to resume their age old conflict. With the aid of the Dark Elves and the Lycans, Kalifen begins conspiring to establish a New World Order under the control of the Illuminati and the one true god, the Shadow Lord.

Having obtained the first two evil relics of the Lich King, Shaddai Var, the Fleshweaver, will arise, and through his knowledge and use of the dark arts of a Necromancer, to summon the spirits of lost souls and amass an army of undead, the likes of which the mortal world has never seen before.

This book is action packed with ancient secret rituals, black magic and secret societies where prophecy and divination collide…inside are pages filled with werewolves, vampires and a seventy foot zombie, Oh My...OH MY!

Assassins Inc.
Carleton Place, Ontario
Canada
www.davidandrewcrawford.com

ISBN: 978-0-9876773-4-1

Design: Dedicated Book Services, Inc. (www.netdbs.com)

Dedication

To my Mom, through her all things are made possible

I

Now...where was I...ah yes I remember now.

When Dark awoke the next day, it was just dawn, the time that marks the beginning of the twilight before sunrise. The faint red and yellow slivers of sunlight had crept slowly over the land of Sommerset and as Dark made his way down stairs he saw his grandfather resting peacefully in his favorite chair. The tall dark figure sat there motionless, his deep set eyes black beneath his great brow. Dark knew Mephisto must have stayed up all night without any sleep. It almost seemed impossible that the old Mage could be rested at all, yet he rose without stretching and still somehow the grim face of his grandfather looked relaxed and alert.

"Are you ready for this?" Mephisto asked at last.

"Just tell me the Styg was able to get me the information I asked for," his grandson replied anxiously.

"He has indeed," the old magus declared shortly. "And I think you will be quite pleased at what he has obtained."

Without warning Mephisto took hold of Dark's arm with urgency and propelled him through an opening in the cave wall that magically manifested itself upon their approach. Together they hurried through the still glowing stone archway and down a long hallway lined with magic sigils and symbols that glowed a deep red. They continued down the long, high corridor of his grandfather's cave and up a winding staircase as the walls echoed with the rapping of their boots on the worn stone floor. Finally, when at last they were atop the stairway, he found the entrance was surrounded by a litter of blackened rocks, and what stood closed before them were two gigantic wooden doors, with no apparent handles or visible locks of any kind. They featured a pair of beautifully carved ferocious looking dragons, set here to guard what lay beyond. They crouched on clawed feet underneath enormous coils, their scaled sides slightly gleaming. Their large leathery wings were folded and their huge heads rested on their wooden perch as hooded membranes were closed over ancient eyes. Smoke curled from blackened nostrils, and as Dark watched, the two dragons both exhaled a ribbon of blue flame. All-seeing and ever alert, the dragons awoke and slowly they peeled their heavy heads from their wooden confines and both turned in unison to stare directly at the two intruders.

"Who dares to approach us?" The dragons gave a grating hiss, swaying over them, crested heads erect, as their golden eyes flamed and smoke shot from their nostrils.

"I am Mephistopheles, the Silver Dragon," he shouted triumphantly. "Now let me pass and open the door, then rest your weary heads and slumber once more."

Immediately the dragons obeyed and retreated. Spurting flecks of foam and smoke, they lurched back and both resumed their initial position on the huge doors until at last they were still, and slumbered once more. Mephisto's great library opened slowly in front of Dark; he stared guardedly at the dragons, but both lay motionless as the flames in their eyes now burned out. After some hesitation, the young grandson of the Silver Mage moved forward and entered the massive chamber, his elven eyes quickly noting the ancient austerity of the library as he moved into the multi-colored light that slid down tired streaks through a mass of large stain glass windows. Nine wide marble steps led down to the gallery floor. On each side of the staircase, Greek and Latin letters described the life of one Mephistopheles, the ancient silver dragon.

"Is that new?" Dark exclaimed.

"Sure is," was his grandfather's casual response.

"Nice touch," his grandson added thoughtfully.

"… Thanks," he smiled faintly in the darkness.

Along the inner walls, four recesses contained female statues of solid gold representing wisdom, knowledge, intelligence and virtue, eerily each one turning their head in procession, as stone eyes began to follow Dark's every step. The vaulting, two-story gallery was lavishly decorated with ornate ornaments and carvings. The floors and walls were faced with colored marble with low Ionian pillars supporting small reading tables.

"You going to tell me any time soon what we are doing here?" snapped Dark irritably.

"Patience my young impatient apprentice," his grandfather advised lightly. "All in good time."

They walked through another set of double doors, separated by yet another corridor where rolled up manuscripts were stored in square niches along the inner walls. Down a narrow walkway they came where stairs in this cavity lead to the upper level. In here, the upper level contained a collection of fine paintings and artifacts, a pair of confidantes with matching arm chairs and a large circular rowan mountain ash tree table with a specimen marble top inlaid with the Silver Dragon's Coat of Arms.

They moved past numerous clay tablets and dusty leather bound books until they stood at the far end of the room under a glittering tapestry. What was depicted on the hanging was a fool wearing black and gold parti-colored garments with a matching eared and belled hood. The jester's hosiery was footed with exaggerated curling points at the toes; he played a pipe and rode a sort of hobbyhorse with a man's head. In the fool's hand he carried a bauble with a small head on a thin black rod and concealing the character's features was a black expressionless mask.

"This is what you needed to show me!" Dark exclaimed in disbelief. "I don't even know what this is..."

"This is what I spent all night waiting for," his grandfather continued quickly. "This is the only known historical record of Giacomo the Jester and it lies, not in a library and not even in Ravenherst its last known home, but in my own specially-built... personal...library..."

"I'm going back to bed." He started to move away from his grandfather.

"All right get back here, I'll tell you what this is." The Silver Mage motioned for him to come back, then he began to speak. "Reputedly he was the first court jester in the Northern Kingdom of Ravenherst. He is by all accounts a devil character responsible for a number of deaths during his time at the King's court. Some say he is even responsible for the murder of Sir Conall Kernach, famed Knight of the Red Branch Order. One of his ideas of a 'joke' was directing anyone asking for directions to Ravenlock towards the hidden quicksand and bog marsh by the River Esk. Some realized in time, while many did not and were never seen again."

"And what exactly does this have to do with me?" he questioned.

The old sorcerer frowned and shook his head, a look of consternation registered on his hardened face.

"This is your passport into Duergar and your way into the Assassin's Guild. On this wall hangs an extremely rare embroidered tapestry done entirely by hand from the world renowned weaver Ficini, whose skills and trade have been passed down from generations. He used an ancient technique that attached gold and silver threads on magically infused backing cloth and decorated it with real jewels and gem stones. His tapestries are quite rare and exclusive to only royalty and the very wealthy."

Dark opened his mouth and glanced questioningly at Mephisto in objection but was cut short.

"The reason the Styg picked this particular scoundrel is for two reasons. The first, Giacomo has already been chosen worthy by the Black Council to gain membership into the Assassin's Guild in Duergar, a feat not so easily gained. As you know, the Regent or Head Guild Master only allows ten new hopefuls to join the Guild each year."

"And the second," Dark asked curiously.

"Giacomo is famed for never removing his mask, not even for Kings or Queens. In darker circles they say you will never see what lies underneath his fool's mask, but when he does remove it, it usually means death is nigh for the viewer.

His face has never been seen by a living soul able to tell the tale...until now."

The wise wizard slowly brushed his right hand gently against the gold and silver threads of Ficini's magnificent creation. Only then, after the briefest of moments, did he speak the arcane words that activated the spell.

"Ficini I ask of you with all my might, can Giacomo come out and play this night?"

Immediately after the magic words were spoken, an opalescent glow quickly spread across the intricately hand-made tapestry, imbuing it with a pearl-like sheen. The weaving was so spectacular that the scene within it came to life until it became a living wall that allowed both of the anxious onlookers to see the play unfold before their very eyes. What played out before them was a mixture of various tricks and slight of hand, skilled juggling with extraordinary feats of acrobatics and tumbling routines. At the very end of it all was the final act where the jester dismounted his human horse, strolled straight up to the pair, bowed gracefully for the expected applause and finally removed his fool's mask.

He stared at it with great wonderment, as everywhere there were touches of color and life and with wide anticipating eyes Dark spied Giacomo's true identity and was disappointed almost immediately. Physically, the jester was hardly an imposing figure. He had short, plain brown hair with no distinctive marks or features of any kind...he was perfect. His plain features made it much easier for him to play the part of a faceless servant, to become one of many figures in a crowd or to escape notice in any city on Eorth.

"Are you not pleased my boy?" the tall mystic asked quickly.

The dark assassin nodded his satisfaction, as a slow smile crept briefly over his lips.

"He's definitely the one," his lean face stared steadily back at Mephisto. "But just one question; if Giacomo's face has never been seen by a living soul, then what about Ficini? He must have seen his face or how else could he have captured his features in this enchanted moving picture?"

"There were rumors of course, but only rumors," his grandfather answered slowly. "Sometime shortly after his gift was presented to Giacomo, Ficini disappeared without a trace and was never heard from again."

"And where is this Giacomo now?" Dark urged a moment later.

"According to the information given to the Styg, you should be able to intercept this dark fool at a place called King's Crossing, just northeast of Innsbrooke, near the City of Carnac," the Silver Mage responded quickly. "You'll have to leave soon if you wish to locate him in time. *Alba* already awaits outside ready for you and your command."

The half-elf assassin nodded solemnly, as both exchanged quick glances at one another in silent agreement.

"Wait...just one more thing before you go!" exclaimed the excited wizard incredulously, motioning for him to follow.

Mephisto stopped and murmured briefly under his breath; an ancient bowl made of solid gold taken from the tombs of Scottish Kings was now found sitting on the large circular table in his private library. The tall, dark figure of his grandfather mechanically raised his right arm until his tightly clenched fist was in position directly over the golden artifact. The outstretched hand of the old mystic began to take on a bright bluish hue that quickly faded to a barely perceptible aura that now surrounded it. Tiny floating silver clouds instantly whirled into existence and as his hand slowly began to open, tiny droplets of rain started to fall until finally letting loose a drenching downpour. The water that gushed stopped almost as suddenly as it began, filling the bowl only inches from the rim. Then he offered the bowl to his grandson and Dark stared down into the water and saw nothing but the shimmer of the fold that held it. He bent even closer until shapes began appearing in the gilded depths; before his eyes a miniature city formed itself in the clear liquid. A fortress city, massive and aerie, graced with high glass rooftops and dozens of slender towers fringed by green forests and surrounded by mountains. Within seconds the City of Duergar faded from view and new shapes formed into the tall reeds of Sommerset and lapped by the gentle waters of Dragon's Mouth Lake. Entranced by the vivid imagery Dark bent closer still, until his face touched the cool magical water.

At that very instant, it seized him. Down he went headlong into the water amid roaring laughter that filled his elven ears and darkness his eyes. He struggled slowly at first, as one would when waking from a dream; he pushed against rolling waves; his mouth opened and he tasted the fresh water of Dragon's Mouth Lake. As quickly as he was caught, he was now freed. His head broke the surface once his feet found solid footing again. Gasping for air, he quickly wiped the water from his eyes.

He stood chest deep in the lake next to his home he had seen in the bowl, facing a sandy shore fringed with green reeds and the *Albatross* only a few feet away. Instead of wading ashore, the wet assassin instead blinked from existence and when he did so, he saw not watery shafts, but the stone walls of his grandfather's library.

"Have you lost your mind old man!" Dark sputtered angrily. "What would make you do such a thing? Look at me, I'm soaked to the bone!"

"Just hang on one second and hear me out and I'll explain everything," he promised amid bursts of laughter.

Mephisto watched his grandson's reaction for a moment and then continued. "You're about to embark on a very serious undertaking and who knows when or if we're going to have a laugh at your expense ever again," he smiled. "In all honesty, I just wanted to add a little levity to the situation... that's all...just have a little fun...just in case."

Dark Solus shook his head once again in disbelief, the anger now gone from his eyes and a faint smile played over his tightened lips as he looked up at his grandfather.

"How can I stay mad at a face like that," he shrugged shortly and nodded, then quickly folded his wet frame around the old man. "I didn't know you were so worried about me."

"Me worry...why should I worry?" he mused mockingly, pushing away the wet child that now clung to him. "It's your neck out there not mine. Now come along my boy, we really should be on our way. Duergar is a long way off."

The grandson of Mephistopheles bore a look of confusion. "We old man?"

"You didn't think I was going to let you have all the fun did you?" the old mystic responded quickly, with a faint smile. "Besides who else are you going to get to pilot your cloud castle to Duergar?"

Dark looked back at his grandfather sharply, studying the serious face and for a few moments he fell silent as he slowly mulled the prospect over.

"Well, it's not like I have a choice."

"You don't," the tall mage added. "I'll be there in less than a fortnight. Now get out of here and be careful."

"Don't worry, I will," Dark promised quickly, a pool of water already formed about him.

"Before you go though, be a dear would you." Instantly in his outstretched hands were a bucket and a mop.

Dark sighed heavily.

Upon quick inspection of the now dry floor, his grandfather nodded his approval with a smile and the two said their brief farewells with mixed emotions and parted. Mephisto had already gathered up a few belongings; quickly grabbing a rather large leather bound manual and a few rolled up scrolls and a moment later was traveling through the skies above Dark Manor Castle.

So it was that on an autumn morning, after changing into his dry armor, he left under bright skies alive with racing clouds and sailed on towards Duergar. With a brisk wind at his back, they glided through the protective veil of Sommerset and soon reached the blue waters of the open sea. Steadily northward the *Albatross* flew, past the string of seemingly endless islands that made up his homeland of Faëroes. Past towering mountains that framed the highlands, past misty meadows until finally they soared out over the vast great ocean. Out over endless waters his faithful flying friend flew, quicker than the spring wind on the backs of tall mountains. Far across a plain of blue they went, until the Islands of Faëroes dwindled to tiny specks on the horizon and vanished altogether.

On the ride towards Duergar, he had fallen asleep, but now awoke and peered out from the concealment of his warm cloak. He saw the clouds racing around him and far below he saw the gray and rippling eastern sea. The *Albatross* sped steadfast over the unfamiliar waters and never slowed until they saw a light, which appeared to shimmer off the high headland on Duergar's western coast. The bright light lit their way, guiding them through a thick blinding mist that drifted aimlessly in the windless air. As they came to a rocky shoreline, the fog dissolved, drifting away in gray tatters to reveal a rolling landscape dotted with white huts of fishing villages and where sheep and cattle grazed. Crumbling walls showed where great forts of old had once been and close to their walls stood a castle that was little more than a stone watch tower now. Dark called down, but no sentry answered; the fortress stood silent and shuttered, apparently deserted.

As Dark traveled the late hours of daylight before the evening sky embraced the lonely night, he watched below those people who braved the late hours to travel the open road. Some were merchants who followed a circuit of markets and fairs, their pack animals and carts laden heavy with furs and fresh hides. Some were troubadours and jugglers, with minstrels and bards who performed from court to court. There were soldiers going to or returning from one of the innumerable wars going on at the time. For an hour or more he traveled through high mountains, until he eventually reached the border region where green forests swept into the distance as far as the eye could see.

By the time Dark arrived at King's Crossing, it was sundown and the faint rays of the late afternoon sun only barely lit the dark forest and evening crept into the western sky in blue and purple streaks. For several long minutes they circled around the large stately elm tree that served as a signpost for the intersecting cross roads. The marker tree guided all travelers alike pointing the way to the locations of the greatest kingdoms on Eorth. The worried assassin had risen slowly to his feet and began scanning the land about them for any sign of Giacomo.

"Damn it!" he growled, breathing heavily and shaking his broad horned head. "Where is this little bastard?"

It was becoming dark too quickly and the jester had carefully erased all signs of his passing, leaving a number of confusing false trails for anyone who attempted to follow. Less than an hour of sunlight remained and the coming of the night would help to hide the little fool from any stalking assailants. Dark found it difficult to surmise where this trickster might be, but decided it would be unwise to stay here for much longer. If Giacomo reached the gates of Duergar and gained the protection of the guild, his plan for revenge would be over before it ever began.

Dark moved quickly now and with great purpose and reached eagerly into the dark interior of the demon's mouth on his armor. The black-garbed assassin removed his hand and withdrew the large Gem of Location and a moment later asked for the whereabouts of the elusive jester. A blue glow spread outwards as the Son of Solus brought the power of the magical stone to life. Then the shimmering star stirred and from its mist rose and shot upward and disappeared into the air.

"Let's go *Alba*," he ordered quietly.

The highway they followed quickly dwindled to a common tinker's trail, where a man would have to stand aside when a horse-drawn wagon passed. He found himself sailing over a rolling moor when the sun dipped into the west and the tall trees threw long shadows across the ground. The air grew still and cold as darkness fell, causing the armored assassin to pull his hooded cloak tightly around him.

The darkness that blanketed this part of the world in those days was a little hard to envision now, but through this sparkling tapestry they smoothly sailed guided by the light of the radiant moon. When it was full, even the smallest blade of grass on eorth shone sharp and clear. When it waned or was obscured by dark clouds, a man could not see his own hand in front of his face. The night sky was an ebony canopy crowded by a retinue of stars and banded by the Milky Way. Off in the distance he spotted a pale sliver of light, a point of brightness so familiar and easily seen like a beacon for sailors. It was the Lighthouse of Duergar.

They were quite close to the borders of the great city now, and once he reached this point, he knew he would have to find his new friend quickly. He traveled on through lonely roads, hills and woods, rendered lightless except for the pulsating glow from the gem that suddenly lit bright. There in the distance, Dark saw the jester's outline at midnight and heard, floating through the air, the voice of his intended target, singing a merry little tune. He was extravagantly bedecked in black and gold as a court jester would and bejeweled as a sultan.

The *Albatross* dipped down towards the unsuspecting entertainer; Dark caught himself abruptly, afraid he had given himself away, but a mirror on Giacomo's carriage had. He paused with the thought left hanging, when suddenly the jester, now wise, urged his team of horses faster. He set off after his prey moving steadily through the air, neither rushing nor pausing, but always gaining on the fleeing fool. The huge black shadow of the *Albatross* suddenly fell over the rapidly moving carriage. In an instant Dark had used the power of his necklace and now settled himself beside the masked rogue. Giacomo felt a chilling fear surge through him at the sight of this demon-like being, feeling bewildered by the sudden appearance of this creature, but still he abruptly turned to face the strange newcomer.

"Just what manner of creature might you be?" the jester stammered fearfully, as the cruel red eyes of Demon Raider passed quickly over him, his courage gone.

The black-garbed assassin snatched the hapless clown by his front tunic, pulling him close, until their faces were only inches away.

"I am Death," his words were spoken in a barely audible whisper. "And I have come for you."

A blinding blue glow spread outward just as Dark uttered his last word. Too late the horned assassin saw the master fool bring the power of his mock scepter to life. A bolt of shimmering light streaked from his outstretched marotte, striking Dark with crackling energy and sending him crashing backwards into a thick and sturdy maple tree. Giacomo had slowed his carriage and brought it to a stop and was already leaping down to the forest floor, his eyes fastened on his attacker, studying the being closely for the first time. Then his blackened eyes went wide in astonished disbelief. For this horned creature was not so easily finished as Dark began to stand, the surface of his body crackling with tiny bolts of energy.

"I see you are versed in the black arts," his voice pierced the distressed mind of the jester. "So am I."

The conversation was brought to a sudden halt and Giacomo suddenly felt something had changed in the forest. No birds sang, no breeze blew in among the pine needles or even rustled the fallen leaves. His eyes went large with fear and he stopped all movement and stood as still as a statue, all except for his trembling hands that clutched at the talisman around his neck.

With the ancient words still on his tongue, a flash of light and a roar of fire wrapped Dark's steel hands with wisps of black flame. An instant later the area surrounding the two combatants became sheathed in barely perceptible yellowish-orange flames. With a mighty explosion, the flames burst into a fiery wall that exploded skyward with such a brilliant radiance that it bathed the area surrounding them in a flaming tongue of fire as bright as sunlight. The hot uneorthly black fire crackled and hissed and from this magical flame emanated the smell of molten metal and sulphur.

"We wouldn't want you to wander off now, would we?" Dark's voice rasped menacingly. "Who knows what possible terrors could await you out there. It's best to keep you here… safe…with me."

While still bewildered at the sight of this demonic fiend, Giacomo abruptly remembered the object he clutched so dearly held his means of escape. About his neck on a fine chain of steel hung a platinum amulet, sculpted to resemble a shining star. It was embossed with golden symbols and intricately engraved with ancient Elven runes. Dark was already moving forward, his searing red eyes narrowed and began to smolder with a formidable look of anger. At that moment, a divine power began to radiate from the jester's talisman, which started to glow and pulse with a soft golden light. The pulse quickly began to steady and brighten into a constant flow of brilliant yellow and within seconds Giacomo disappeared.

Dark suddenly stopped and slowly looked around; then both demonic faces smiled grimly. There was no movement anywhere. The assassin's sharp gaze moved robot-like from one area inside the curtain of fire to the next. A sudden movement to his left snapped his attention to an area only a few yards away, making a quick study, then a moment later he was back to his search. For a few moments no one moved, then abruptly the unwise fool took a step forward.

"Watch and stare my final coming of might," Dark began to invoke the powers of the Plane of Shadow. "Under a full moon, between both worlds we fight. For when light is fleeting, you become a shadow of eternal night!"

Immediately, a shifting, whirling field of semi-solid shadows began to rise around him, like trained snakes with an innate link to his own shadow, compelled to do his will, for the darkness was attached to his very soul. A creeping darkness began to spread, streaking outwards like the night that overcomes the day, cloaking the ground and filling the area with these wisps of writhing blackness. The shadow flickered, moving in an aggressive and independent manner; it stretched out passing through any and all objects that impeded its path. The dark gray haze appeared around the invisible jester, surrounding him in an aura of shadow, leaving Giacomo trapped in a patch of strange shifting darkness. Dark quickly pointed a single clawed finger at the enchanted talisman around the fool's neck and the bauble he held so firmly in his clenched fists. With a simple command the transparent tendrils reached into the very shadow of the fool. They seemed to grasp and tug at the objects until finally tearing them away. Within seconds, Dark had stolen the two artifacts, recalled the shadows back into his own and stored the items safely away inside the forged demon's mouth.

"Real magicians don't need wands to perform magic," he announced curtly. "Now fool, any more parlor tricks up your sleeve?"

Giacomo, now visible, stood silently on shaking legs, his blood turned to ice, his usually keen senses were now raw and distorted with horrifying terror, the last vestige of his courage now gone. There was no where left to run and like it or not he knew this was a battle to the death.

"Just one!" Left with no other choice, Giacomo removed his belled hat and with his right hand placed it inside, quickly unsheathing a long sword at his side with lightning-like motion, then crouched down ready to attack. "I am Giacomo, the incomparable. King of Jesters and Jester to Kings and I will not die this night!"

The muscular form of Dark moved forward a few paces at the same instant, then darkness surrounded his hand, turning it into a deadly weapon. His own shadow began to coalesce into the shape of a long sword, its shadowy form darkened as if perpetually in shadows.

"I know this sword and only a being from the pits of Hell itself could construct such a weapon," Giacomo muttered almost inaudibly.

"Then you know about its poisonous blade," Dark's voice broke out of the growing darkness. "And how once delivered, the poison takes only a short time to exert its lethal effect. This venomous substance enters into one's bloodstream and then is quickly carried throughout, slowly turning the victim's heart, body and mind to a black...lifeless...ash."

Out of sheer fear the jester attacked with surprisingly blinding speed, but the deadly horned assassin was not to be so easily finished. Parrying the death blow dealt, he lunged quickly to one side. Before the attacker could find his target for a second assault, the nimble form of the half-elf assassin was upon him. Dark dealt the jester a savage blow that sent him tumbling backwards onto the hard ground. Giacomo, still on his knees, was holding his blackened visage in pain, trying desperately to recover as blood streamed steadily down upon the red stained ground. His black mask had fallen off, separated into two pieces, and just like his disguise, so was his ordinary face, split perfectly down the middle from his forehead down through his chin.

"Die you black faced emissary of the devil!" the jester roared in anger, his wild eyes widened, his own blood ran in small rivulets down his pale face and into his soaked garments.

Climbing unsteadily to his feet, the flamboyant jester retrieved his fallen sword and trying desperately again, he rushed forward trying vainly to strike a solid blow. The two-faced fool was determined to finish his demonic foe, thrashing and swinging madly over the leaf littered battle ground. Giacomo cried out in fury and struck wildly at the black-garbed assassin, but his blows were parried easily with wisps of shadowy tendrils constantly following Dark's weapon as it moved about. With a devilish grin and moving as fast as thought, Dark began to flash through the conduits and pathways of the ethereal plane, manifesting into multiple locations. Faster than the eye could blink, this unsuspecting attack came from behind; Giacomo tried desperately to turn around but it was too late. The stealthy assassin reared back his shadowy blade and with a forceful lunge shoved the sword completely through the man's caped back and out through his chest. Giacomo shuddered horribly, turned almost completely about, then slid slowly to the blood soaked eorth and sank to his knees. Dark brought forth the fiery rage of the dragon wand, his blackened body was instantly engulfed. The swollen flesh split and shredded so that the bones showed through until finally the bones themselves crumbled. With no more than a faint cracking and pattering, the curtain fell for the last time for the fool and the body of Giacomo, the incomparable, was at last, gone. When the fire died, all that remained was a charred outline of the man, and a small handful of black ashes remaining. Dark stood motionless, the wall of fire abruptly ceased and the battle was finally ended; the last assassin standing stood positioned like a statue in the silence and emptiness of the bloodied battleground.

II

Dark firmly grabbed the leather reins and flicked the long stiff shaft of his new coach whip over the horses' flanks. The long lash made a loud crack that caused the animals' ears to flatten back against their heads and they suddenly jolted away, charging forward as fast as the wagon would allow. The woods were a wall of concealment surrounding him on either side of the narrow path; the giant black branches seemed to reach out waving blindly about under the moonlight. The sky above barely showed through the thick boughs of the great trees in patches of bright silver broken only by a few distant stars. The horses flew over the uneven terrain. Above the thunder of their horse shod hooves, he heard the occasional cry of some faraway creature. They rode as swiftly as the wind, so that small shrubs, tree branches and small pockets of fields flashed by in a dark blur.

The forest was quite large and it took him almost three hours to reach the other end when he finally pounded through and out the other side. When he reached the Northern entrance, he could see wide open plains stretching northward, and beyond there was yet another mountain range which appeared to run toward the east. The weary traveler pulled out onto the smooth floor of the plains, then, raced out across long watery meadows, sending up squawking flocks of sleeping fowl, as he moved on toward the walled and towering City of Duergar.

The famed city was surrounded on three sides in a horseshoe fashion by mountains and the sea that opened out to the west. Apparently, even in the fall, these plains were very green with well-tilled fields full of life in the endless expanse of this open country. It was so vast that Dark could see the actual lateral line of the horizon where the sky fell to the green eorth.

It was close to the witching hour when the exhausted half-elf drew within sight of the great lighthouse and tall towers of the fortressed City of Duergar. It had taken him almost a full day of constant travel; his hazardous battle with Giacomo the Jester had taken its toll on him and now all he wanted was for this night to end. He knew this was a moment in time that he had waited for so long and now at last it was here. His time for vengeance was now at hand. His body was worn and sore; his normally keen mind numbed by lack of sleep and constant travel, but his spirit rose with excitement at the sight of the majestic City of the Dwarves.

Dark called a sudden halt to his team of horses, realizing he needed to don the disguise of the jester before he got any closer to the watchful eyes of the sentry that stood guard at the gate. A moment later he brought forth the Eye of Dagda and held it in his open hand. The huge gemstone was of a rich red color, unfaceted and convex. With only a thought, the stone of nobility began to slowly rise and took a position just above the assassin's horned head. The energy of the ruby was intense and vivid. When held up under moonlight, it lost its deep red tinge and became the color of a burning coal.

"I sure hope this works," Dark spoke to himself, trying to sound confident.

Before Dark began again, he looked upon the distant towers of the city with mixed feelings. Since the murder of his parents, he had trained for years and longed for this day. He had studied hard under his grandfather's careful guidance and learned the secret of assassination from his teacher, mentor and now friend, the Styg. He asked for this, wanted this, by his own choosing. His grandfather had asked him not to, pleaded with him and even tried bribing him to reconsider his decision. But it was too late. He had already decided; he was not to be swayed, not by anyone…not ever.

Dark's eyes narrowed and a strange feeling of doom settled into his thoughts as he looked down on what would be his new home. The Son of Solus, still to this day, felt a deep sadness for the loss of his parents, but his thoughts took a dangerous journey as he remembered how those responsible deliberately and vindictively turned against them. All at once Dark was in a rage and there was real hatred in his eyes. He quickly grabbed the whip, striking out in the air, the crack echoed like cannon fire and the team of horses surged forward. He was about halfway as they neared the fable city, its vast mass sprawling and shadowed against the night horizon when he began to notice the magnificent detail of the majestic dwarven city.

A riot of architectural styles and designs played throughout the city's remarkably impressive skyline. From its deepest foundations to its highest spires, Duergar beautifully displayed the history of the Dwarves for all to see. Heavy stone Dwarven architecture provided the basis for most of the city; this ancient stonework reached back to a time when humans did not yet exist on this continent. Most of the city was decorated with engraved images inlaid with precious metals and set with gemstones. Though most of the gold, silver and gems had long been stripped away from the stonework, enough still remained to show the vast wealth commanded by the Dwarves who once lived here. Among golden domed buildings and the flowering trees rose shadowy spires of enchanting beauty, surrounded by mesmerizing lights that looked like dancing multi-colored lanterns. Gently arching stone walkways bridged the different levels of the city's open spaces, creating a magnificent stone web of thoroughfares. The centerpiece of Duergar was the legendary School of Magic, an ivy-clad, silvery stone tower used as a center of studies for all the arcane arts. Surrounding the host tower of the Arcane were seven more towers enchanted to float around, like celestial beings orbiting the sun.

Dark had swung his tired team from the tall grass of the plain land onto a broad cobblestone roadway. The road wound straight ahead towards the lighted high walls of Duergar, looming black against the horizon. He was close enough now to make it out in better detail; the sprawling city and the movement of archers on the stone ramparts.

The entrance through the towering outer wall was brightly outlined by torchlight; the massive wooden gates standing open on oiled hinges were guarded by a large number of blue-garbed sentries. The disguised assassin peered carefully ahead watchfully, moving at a slow crawl, and pulled within a few feet of gaining entry. Moments later he reached the mammoth gates of the outer wall and was immediately approached by four armed guards that quickly stopped him.

The disguised assassin made no effort to hide his masked face as he waited for the four armed soldiers, his keen elven eyes casting about in undisguised apprehension. Each of the sentries wore sleeveless tabards in a deep, rich, blue velvet, the front and back hems a pointed v-shape with splits in the sides up to their leather belts. The design of a circle of black thorns with a black scaled venomous snake entwined throughout was embroidered on the front. Under their tabards were long sleeve mail coats with matching leggings made from the same chain mail. On their heads they wore close fitted sallets that extended and formed a pointed tail with a steel bevor, worn in conjunction and used to protect the wearer's jaw and neck.

As the four soldiers came to stand in front of Dark, their broad swords at the ready, he noticed one particular guard hurriedly abandoned his post and disappeared into the streets of the city beyond.

"This is a strange hour for travel my friend," the gate commander asked questioningly. "Now state your business, and be quick about it. I don't have all night here."

"I am Giacomo, the incomparable," Dark insisted quickly, trying his best to play the part with an embellished bow. "King of Jesters, and Jester to Kings."

"So, what would bring Giacomo, the incom...incompra... that word you said," he stuttered dumbly.

Before the masked assassin had time to even answer another annoying question, one of the four guards that most resembled a donkey's ass shouted out, "That's quite an outfit you've got on there," he mocked loudly. "Where did you get it from...a doll shop?"

The other three guards all chimed in with only slight laughter, because the joke wasn't really all that funny. One actually commented that his daughter had a doll that looked just like the black and gold dressed jester. Dark had to laugh in spite of himself. He knew that this was more or less a shake down, where he would have to open his purse wide to gain entry into Duergar.

"My hosiery is made from the finest silks of the Far East," was his boastful reply. "And my cape is made with fur from the great white wolves of Vandringar, my beloved home to the North."

"So again I ask you jester, what would bring Giacomo the incom...incompra...the incompra...that word you said, this far away from your homeland?" the crooked sentry asked while working his way outward from Dark and his companions in a widening circle, his shadowed eyes looking at the jester's carriage.

A moment later the Sergeant-at-Arms was back at the concealed assassin's side, an unusually worried expression now clouded his broad features, his head tilted slightly as he looked up at Dark.

"It seems to me we've got us some real trouble here, Giacomo my friend," he announced solemnly, resting his hands determinedly on his hips, his steely gaze raised to meet the masked fool. "I think what we have here boys is a smuggler. And we all know what happens to smugglers here...don't we boys?"

For a moment no one spoke; no one moved; no one even breathed as the two parties scrutinized each other in the torchlight gloom of this serious situation. Dark already prepared himself for an alternate plan, when the Sergeant of the gate made a quick motion towards the disguised assassin. The four sentries moved forward hastily, snapping the sharp tips of their swords up to Dark's masked face. Suddenly a door burst open from one of the gate houses and a frizzled veteran appeared, staring at the magically altered traveler and the four guards. He gave a short, loud command, and reluctantly the soldiers sheathed their swords and backed away a few paces. Dark had not moved and gave no indication that he even had any interest in what was happening around him.

"Commander Grellner," the soldier exclaimed in greeting, his head bowed briefly as he came to attention and saluted his commander. "We were just..."

"I know what you and your men were...just...doing!" the captain began speaking in a slow fury. "Do you realize that what you...and your men are doing is a hangable offense?"

"But sir," the gate Sergeant urged a moment later. "He travels alone at this time of night... and he's wearing a mask...and..."

"Silence!" the infuriated commander of the gate roared, grasping the ass's front tunic in anger. "Now get out of my sight and never let me catch you and your men doing this ever again. Now go...all of you! And, I'll deal with you later... private."

Captain Grellner released the man in shocked silence and spat on the ground before turning his grizzled features toward the late visitor.

"Y...y...yes my Lord," the soldier stuttered and nodded eagerly, then he and the three other guards turned, and all disappeared back into the gatehouse, while an impatient and angry Captain of the gate moved closer towards the disguised assassin.

"You're late!" the eager and impatient voice of the commander cut into Dark's thoughts, then cautiously looked at the man he believed to be Giacomo the Jester and handed him a square piece of blackened parchment and half a playing card depicting a man wearing what might be a jester's hat; he carried a bundle of his belongings in a stick slung over his back.

"Now take this, it will tell you all you need to know...Now go!"

Without waiting to see the Captain's reaction, Dark again started toward the towering gates of the outer wall. The gate itself was constructed using the rare blue lapis stone with alternating rows of relief dragons and aurochs. It stood nearly as high as a Frost Giant and at least twenty feet wide, with two sheltering towers solidly standing erect on either side. In seconds he reached the tall, metal bound gates, then immediately the heavy bars were drawn back and the gates slowly swung inward to admit one.

Dark passed beneath the shadow of the great gateway, under the watchful eye of her many stone guardians, carved gargoyle statues in the form of fantastic grotesque figurines. Their monstrous stone forms seemed to hang in the darkness above him serving as co-protectors for the city, and warding off any evil spirits that came to corrupt Duergar. The gates themselves were made from massive timbers that had clearly once ruled the heights of a lofty forest, for the sturdy beams exceeded the height of any on earth. Strapped together by bands of the blackest iron, hammered in place with spikes the size of a man's leg, the massive portcullis was made of blackened steel bars entwined with barbs as thick as a man's arm and were raised to allow passage through to the processional. This grand avenue of the free city was the thread that truly bound its citizens together. It was lined with walls covered in gold chimeras on glazed bricks. Also marking its route and offering their protection were statues of Dwarven deities and monuments to great deeds of old, now long since forgotten.

Dark followed wordlessly as he stared in wide-eyed amazement at the craftsmanship and artistry of these truly wonderful works of Dwarven art. During the daytime, the street would be teemed with carts and wagons alike, pedestrians and riders, even the occasional shepherd or herdsman driving some of their stock before them. His stolen horse drawn carriage mounted the wondrous route, paved with stone and entered through the gates of the inner wall to the pillared courtyard that loomed just ahead. The pillars were believed to hold up the sky and were painted a vibrant blue with hundreds of stars to represent the night sky. Once more the guards stared openly at the masked face, but none moved to stop the late traveler from entering. Dark seemed to shrink in size as he proceeded down the King's Way Road, the main city thoroughfare, his dark form wrapped ominously in the fur cloak, his black mask glinting and exposed under the moonlight. But at last that evening when the whole City of Duergar lay locked in sleep, horses steel hooves clattered noisily on the cobblestones of the street.

He traveled down the grand avenue of the free city which more or less ran straight north, past many of the city's grandest buildings, to its final end at the gatehouse of the Grand Citadel. In his hand the small black piece of ash paper had already began to animate, producing a glowing blue arrow that suddenly changed direction. He obeyed immediately and steered his carriage accordingly; the arrow directed Dark through the now empty streets, taking him past shops that contained the wealth of the world; silks from the far East, their colors still brilliant under the light of the silvery moon, rare and costly spices that promised delights to one's own palate. In moments he crossed through the heart of the Low Marketplace and finally onto the High Marketplace. The roadway split around a vast oak wood tree, once used for hanging criminals and so forever after was called the Hangman's Tree.

Beyond the tree, past tall multi-colored buildings and small shops and taverns, the arrow directed him up a man-made embankment that carried him gently up to a small hostelry with a well-lighted porch and lively sounds of laughter coming from within. A sign that read "The Golden Eye Dragon" hung over the entrance and the onion domed towers of the sprawling inn, with their wide bases and high narrow stain glass windows made it quite unique among the buildings of the Dwarven city.

Dark quickly stabled his newly acquired team of horses and carriage in the tavern yard, then quickly wheeled about and proceeded on toward the doors of the inn. He never paused, but reached for the huge iron ring fastened to the wood and pulled the door open. The instant the heavy wooden doors swung inward, closing behind him, the laughter stopped and for a brief moment there was no other sound as the masked assassin in disguise stood momentarily in the well lighted entrance. Then a low voice from the back of the large room called for him to come over. Dark moved toward the voice without even a backward glance at the silent patrons that stared gawkingly, his eyes focused only on the thin man who now motioned for him to come over and sit with him.

Inside he found it most satisfying. The interior of the well aged building glowed brightly in the torchlight, the dancing flames catching the splendor of the colorful murals and paintings that decorated The Golden Eye Dragon Inn. The warm firelight brightened the gay colors of finely painted storage chests and gleamed on hanging copper pots. Set in a series of deep window embrasures were several beeswax candles that shone steadily.

Then the darkly disguised assassin stopped near the back of the elegantly furnished chamber and placed his half of the torn tarot card on the table in front of his new contact to the secret, occult-like guild of Duergar. The thin man was blonde and clean shaven, his thin figure was cloaked in a long purple robe with the strange symbol of a great horned owl.

He was several years older than Dark, but held his tall frame erect in the same manner as that of his grandfather. Another curious feature about the man that his keen elven eyes almost missed was that he had very faint criss-crossed scars over both his cheeks. The disguised assassin knew immediately that this man long ago had an unfortunate run in with his father and he was not to be trusted.

"You're late!"

Dark made no move but stood silently before his new acquaintance, saying nothing, his eyes riveted on the thin man's face.

"Oh yes, I almost forgot," the agent for the Assassin's Guild said placing the missing second half of his tarot card with the other missing half until it was finally whole once again. "Now please, sit down."

His eyes followed the cloaked jester, looking cautiously about. For Dark there were too many doors, too many places that could conceal one's enemies and for his liking too many eyes that could see too much.

"Allow me to introduce myself," the deep voice seemed to rise up out of the depths of the eorth. "My name is Pinnister Blackadder, but you may call me Pin for short."

"I am Giacomo the ..." Dark's speech was cut short by a movement just to his left as four young travelers came into the tavern and seated themselves just a few feet away.

"There is no need to tell me your name, Jester," Pin began again. "I know exactly who you are."

"How wonderful for you then," the masked assassin responded quickly. "Meeting me must be quite a unique thrill for you."

"Yes indeed…a real, thrill of a lifetime," was his mocking response. "Now I am to be your liaison between you and the Guild as well as your guide, if you so wish, to the city. Anything you may want to know, you come to me. The enchanted parchment you hold will guide you to a safe house where ..."

"I don't think so," Dark interrupted quickly, igniting the enchanted paper over a flickering candle flame. "I'll find my own accommodations thank you."

"As you wish," Pin responded quickly with a smile. "Now our meeting here tonight will be a short one as I have other matters to attend to, but tomorrow I wish you to go to the Grand Bazaar and find a man named Mr.Fekkish. Give him this coin. He'll know what to do, and he'll give you all the information you will need."

A bullion coin, made entirely out of gold, was placed on the table, which Dark quickly picked up, then like a street magician, he held up the coin, openly displaying it between his fingers and thumb. His empty right hand came across slowly, mechanically, taking the coin between his right forefinger and right thumb. The magician took the coin away and held it firmly. Dark held the gold sovereign out for Pin to examine, showing the coin was now in his other hand and that his original hand was clearly empty. With a quick gentle puff of the Jester's breath, he turned his hand over and began to rub his fingers together, slowly opening his right hand to reveal...the coin had vanished!

Outside the inn the wind rose with a howl; the horses stamped and whinnied, then the door blew open. The patrons inside all turned quickly at the sound and were astonished at the sight it heralded. Eight small, child-like figures all clothed in green and black garb stood in the entrance.

"Do you think you could have found a more crowded place?" Dark exclaimed sarcastically.

"Just ignore them like I do."

The annoyed assassin nodded soberly, a sudden premonition springing into his alert mind. For Dark knew that these little evil creatures were trouble just waiting to happen. Soon a growing crowd of the tiny revenants clustered around the young couples' table, muttering threats to the men and several innuendos towards the women. Just then the door flew open again and the hostelry became suddenly quiet, as if all inside shared the same guilty secret. A larger than average halfling, his features dark and gloomy, walked in out of the night. His eyes were wild and his movements almost convulsive. All but Dark avoided his gaze, as he swore at anyone who dared look upon him. Even the tavern owner and his staff avoided looking at one another in the eye. Everyone left him alone to his devices, for it was well known the little man had a violent temper.

"Another friend of yours?" the masked jester spoke darkly.

The thin man was silent a moment before speaking. "His name is Fetch," the answer came at last, as a quick and silent nod was exchanged between Pin and the leader of the pack. "I would stay away from that one if I were you."

"A fitting name for a dog," the disguised half-elf growled irately.

"You have no idea," Pin replied quickly.

The four young travelers, their faces flushed red, now all rose and turned and left the tavern swiftly, vanishing through the large wooden door. Immediately after, one of the smaller halflings came scurrying towards their leader; he was almost crawling in fear, until his mouth was placed next to the other's ear in silent whisper. All at once, with nothing more than a simple whistle from the stocky halfling's lips, the rude pack of halflings obeyed instantly and followed them outside. Fetch's expression was set and impassive as he came to halt directly in front of Dark, his thoughts intensely concentrated on the jester. The disguised assassin's head moved slightly, fully aware he was being studied and his deep green eyes fastened on the small figure facing him.

"Don't look at me...don't ever look at me!" the rude hobbit exclaimed shortly. "I really don't like it when your kind even look at me!"

Just then, mustering the little courage he had in reserve, Pin leaned forward carefully putting himself between Dark and the intrusive leader of the pack and flaunting a shiny, silver signet ring. "Please leave…now."

The word had been barely spoken in an audible whisper. When Fetch saw the seal engraved on the ring of the high ranking guild agent, he froze in sudden shock. Along with the heraldic crest, his eyes reflected a ferocious determination, a fiery strength of character, and an inner conviction that reminded the halfling of the chain of command, demanding his attention and his obedience. Slowly he raised his face until the torches inside the inn fully revealed his dark angered features to the watchful men and responded with a faint nod, his face stony and impassive. Taking a glass of hard liquor from a nearby table, he slowly turned and walked back across the wooden floor to the waiting halfling bartender. He handed the now empty glass to the little worker after one quick gulp, mumbling something incoherent, then turned abruptly to the door. Turning back the large hobbit waved slowly to the jester, speaking garbled oaths and phrases, a faint smile of satisfaction on his broad face and then disappeared into the darkness.

"Please don't tell me he's really leaving?" Dark cut in mockingly. "He's so much fun, just like a tiny, little animated children's windup toy; I just want to pinch his cheeks and tickle his plump little belly."

"Shall we continue then?" was the slender man's only response.

The slow, low voice of Pin cut into his thoughts, drawing Dark's attention back to his midnight meeting with the representative from the underworld. The young assassin agreed and nodded quickly. In brief, clipped sentences, the thin, purpled robed liaison spoke again of the next day's meeting at the Grand Bazaar, then finally offered Dark a few parting words of caution. He explained the manner in which the Night Watch would be arranged, noting the pattern in which the guards would be posted about the city. He told him to look for the markings of Moloch, which would undoubtedly lie throughout the streets of Duergar and on all buildings run by the Guild. He further explained that at all costs, he was to avoid speaking to anyone about Guild business and finally, he was told to stay away from Fetch, the leader of that particular Halfling pack.

Dark quickly nodded his agreement, though he was keenly disappointed that more was not divulged about his initiation into the Guild and his enemies within. The meeting ended shortly thereafter and a tired and hungry Dark Solus walked out of the inn still lost in thought. Outside the tavern the air was crisp as moonlight glittered on frosty windows under a black and ominous night sky. As he wrapped himself in his cloak, he paused momentarily, his keen elven ears alert and his black eyes open and watchful. Then out of nowhere he heard the deep, haunting sounds of wolves howling. Then there were sudden footsteps on the cobblestone streets behind him, and a small, lithe form came to stand silent under an archway in a dark alley. Long, scruffy hair shadowed wide eyes that looked up at him momentarily then leapt away into the darkness beyond.

Dark gave chase, shadowing the creature through the city's avenues and byways, his cloak shrouded form gliding quickly and stealthily out of the cover of the black shadows cast. He moved cat-like, his footfalls muffled by his magic boots as he raced steadily forward. The trail ended some moments later in a quiet cul-de-sac. He heard the women's trembling screams long before he reached the place and among those screams he heard the sound of bestial laughter. From the shadows behind them, the dark assassin gazed down on the grizzly scene, pensive but unperturbed. What he saw, what he witnessed, and what he experienced deep within his mind that night left an indelible imprint on his memory that would stay with him forever. The night seemed to pass in slow agonizing minutes and long endless hours, for what he found was a nightmare. Amid a litter of blood and bones lay the mangled bodies of the women and their male companions. He witnessed a pair of wolves burrowing their noses deep into the bodies, feeding on the flesh even before the victims were dead. They fed in a manner of all wolves, gorging themselves until their sides were swollen taut and they could not eat a single morsel more. A person less of courage might have recoiled in horror but on this night, in the gathering gloom, he lurked, silent, still and menacing. In the darkness he waited and watched no longer and out of the shadows Demon Raider stepped.

"Leave us!" Fetch's voice pierced the air in a shrill command, then wiping his mouth on the sleeve of his shirt, he feigned a belch of contentment. "We have just killed and we are strong, so leave now or I might wish to kill again."

There was no movement from the demonic assassin, no sound but the wind blowing swiftly across his masked face as the horned figure stood restrained. Then he seemed to rise and moved forward as silent as the shadows all about him, he began to walk slowly forward towards the pack's leader, his shadow blade held tightly in one hand. He froze in mid stride; in one fluid motion he easily deflected several thrown daggers, then at once he rose to tower over their owner. One steel-like arm gripped the fellow's throat before he could escape. Before the small halfling had a chance to defend himself, the swift blade of Dark's shadow sword came down sharply on the exposed throat of the struggling halfling, slicing from ear to ear, and the lifeless body crumpled to the earth.

With unbelievable fury the large hobbit drew his sword, and without pausing, raced toward the glowing red-eyed figure. Heedlessly, he knocked everyone in his path aside, his broad face grim and terrible, waving his drawn weapon with grand circular flourishes. The enraged hobbit was very fast, and closed the gap between himself and Dark in a matter of seconds. Shrieking with fury and frustration, he threw himself at the masked man, swinging wildly with his sword. As the leader of the pack reached the Son of Solus, his sharp weapon raised and for one terrible second hung poised above this new enemy of the pack. The black-garbed assassin struck back with his own blade, with wisps of shadowy tendrils following the sword's every movement. Then it fell. This instrument of shadowy death was buried to the hilt into his large chest, a terrible whiteness flooded and contorted his features.

"I really hate you filthy, little bastards," Dark whispered softly, smashing his fists into the creature's face, feeling the sickening but satisfying crunch of his foe's bones breaking beneath his gauntleted fist.

The stricken pack leader fell heavily, knocking him back roughly against the far wall, as blood bubbled from the creature's mouth. For a moment there was silence once more. Dark stood silent, staring coldly at the wounded hobbit as he tried vainly to stem the blood that flowed freely from his open wound.

"You think me unarmed," Fetch's voice rose sharply, his words harsh as he struggled painfully to his feet, blood streaming from his mouth, his chest bleeding freely. "You think me helpless. Do you honestly think I am so easily defeated... so long as I have breath in these lungs, I am neither!" The halfling's broad figure was bent slightly from pain, his left hand held over his chest that was bleeding profusely. The valiant little humanoid was tiring rapidly growing steadily weaker from the massive loss of blood. His face pale and drawn from the great effort it took to stay on his feet.

"How dare you expect to destroy me, something that is not even mortal, but only a spirit of death, a race of deathless existence embodied now in this physical form."

"Who?" chided Dark, grinning with fanged teeth.

The halfling, barely standing, flung his head back like a jackal, then viciously began ripping his bloody flesh and tore at his clothes. Screaming he dropped to his hands and knees. He writhed in the filth of the city streets, gasping and foaming at the mouth; as he writhed, his body lengthened and changed. When he rose again, he was in the form of a sizable werewolf. Yellow eyes now glittered, and with sharp fanged mouth slavering, he launched himself at the shadowed stranger. Bursting forward he roared, yet Dark stood his ground. The beast came closer still, swelling up until it finally stood taller than a man. On its foul breath the monster carried the reek of blood it had shed, the stale stench, the rankness of its immortal sin, in its cold eyes were reflected scenes of past carnage, diabolic creatures tearing at flesh, its victims impaled on the points of sharp unforgiving teeth. At that moment the lycanthrope lashed out with both clawed hands, slashing at the demonic looking assassin from head to waist. But the beast's sharp nails glanced harmlessly off the dark enchanted armor causing sparks to fly about them. The creature opened its jaws as wide as the gates of Hell and prepared to swallow him whole.

Violently, Dark now moved as fast as thought and as if removing the head of a dead rose, he plucked out the heart from the monster's heavily furred chest. With glowing eyes, the dark assassin stood unspeaking before the corpse. What previously had been a werewolf, fanged, furred and clawed, was now only the small body of the pack leader, his ravaged face transformed back by sweet death. He laid still and smiling, suffused with a saint's tranquility.

Dark now turned his attention onto Fetch's remaining pack members. The animated demon face of his armor growled aloud, its eyes glowed crimson as savage jaws snapped back with a hunger of its own.

"There are still ten of us and only one of you." One of the creatures bravely rasped in fury, as he and the rest of the pack twisted and convulsed into their furry forms.

"Who said I was alone." The challenge did not go unanswered.

From behind the pack the surrounding shadows seem to shift, as shadowy shapes began to form. Phantasmal images of nightmarish creatures, ghostly images that began to rise silently, waiting to wrap themselves around them, then violently falling on their unsuspecting targets, in a field of shadowy energy that would cloak their entire bodies and trapping them in Hell's perdition...forever.

"Now...who's next."

III

At the cock's morning crow it came, from the under belly of the city, where only the fowl were stirring at dawn's first light. When the raucous cry from an old woman sounded, the Night Watch were roused and soon gathered around a grizzly scene and found an appalling sight.

The first man blanched and turned quickly away. The back alley was a charred house of horrors. Swaths of blood were painted on the walls and spattered about on the cobble stone floor. A disgusting gray mass of matter adhered limply to one wall; the contents of someone's smashed skull. In a darkened corner, a disembodied eye stared eerily upwards from the ground.

One of the Watchmen moved several feet closer into a growing number of birds and peered carefully ahead. A moment later, he wheeled about, calling out loudly, and motioning sharply to his watchful commander. There was a furious rushing of raven-black wings accompanied by a frightful shrieking of disrupted scavengers as the black flock turned suddenly skyward rising reluctantly as they scattered into the early morning sunlight. What was found was the rest of the body from the smashed skull, bitten, clawed and cruelly distorted and flung across a pile of fresh horse dung.

"Looks like there's been a horrific battle of some sort," a young guard still in his early teens spoke solemnly, his tunic and shield bearing the crest of the Red Branch Knights. "This one is definitely dead Captain."

"Sir Merrick!" another sentry announced curtly, lifting up his steel visor slowly. "You're going to want to see this."

The Captain of the Night Watch, Sir Merrick Arawn Morgan, moved forward toward the grisly scene from what he quickly surmised was a theft gone horribly wrong. He was a hulking man, standing well over six feet tall with piercing green eyes, an aquiline visage and straight graying black hair that he kept tightly bound in a long braid. His skin was red and weather worn with the first wrinkles of long exposure to the night winds, and signs of middle age were beginning to appear on his whitening bearded face. As Captain of the Night Watch, it was his sworn duty to augment the forces of law and order during the hours of eventide, for when darkness falls, the Royal City Guard turns the city streets over to them to patrol and even make fearful those who might visit Duergar with dishonest intent. They were granted their charter by a Directorship of wealthy merchants who wanted to curb the rapid growth of crimes being perpetrated at night and the ever growing distrust in the people's constables under Lord Blackthorn's reign.

Finally Captain Morgan halted in the middle of several headless bodies, charred and lifeless, sprawled carelessly in death, their burnt discarded carcasses still baking slowly in the white heat of smoking red embers. Bright bits of light glinted in patches from blackened blades of swords, some discarded by fleeing men; still others were clenched by the dead hands of their fallen owners. The Night Watch commander choked as the smell of smoky death struck his nostrils, his ears caught the sound of flies buzzing busily about the blood soaked naked form to his far left. He looked back and smiled grimly. He knew the young recruits under his command had never before seen death like this up close and it would be a lesson they would soon not forget.

From the still smoking headless corpses and the single concentration of men, except for the lone body torn to shreds, the Knight quickly surmised in his own mind that it had been a short, vicious struggle to the death. There had been no quarter asked and definitely none had been given. He recognized immediately the gnarled charred bodies were still somewhat distinguishable with their small stature and unusually large feet for their size; these child-like beings were definitely Halflings. But it was not until he had looked closely at the lone mass of mangled meat that he recognized several still very legible tattoos. A golden eyed dragon to be exact; this was the bloodied remains of Fetch, leader of a Halfling group known as 'The Pack'.

A sudden movement out of the corner of his eye snapped his attention back to his companions who were about to walk into the scorched remains of a large magical ring of fire with fiery sigils that quickly ignited around the inner ellipse, then faded almost as quickly as it had begun. From the now dormant flaming circle, the Red Branch Knights heard a hissing sound, barely discernable above the sharply played song from a pair of large wind chimes that were playing their song in a gentle breeze. Then they saw a sight none has ever seen since. Five heads began to bob up and down, heaving ever so slightly above the ground inside a lightly glowing pentagram. The floating heads gobbled and snorted, taking in mouthfuls of maggots along with large, juicy grubs as they fed hungrily. Undisturbed, the severed heads continued foraging as sticky loops of saliva dribbled from their greedy maws.

"Hold Sir Merrick!" the loud command rang out sharply. "This is no longer a concern for the Night Watch; this matter is now to be turned over to the people's constables, the Royal City Guard."

The battle hardened veteran, still bewildered by the sudden appearance of these ghoulish apparitions, lowered his sword and abruptly turned to face the familiar grating voice behind him.

"There hasn't been a royal guard since the demise of the only true monarch of this city..." he paused, with his words left hanging, unspoken in the silence. The giant commander stopped suddenly, his loyal regiment hastened quickly to their leader's side, each one peering past his broad frame as a dozen or more armed guards hurriedly made their way towards them. Each one wore black on black tunics and tabards emblazoned with the intricate insignia of a circlet of black thorns with a black scaled venomous snake entwined throughout. There was a man who accompanied them, a tall, thin man, black haired and cleanly shaved, his gaunt figure dressed in a black tailored, high-collared coat and cloak with a thorny pattern embroidered throughout. He was an articulate persuasive man, with an alert air and anxious brown eyes. He bore no insignia of office save for a large medallion that bore the likeness of a horned owl that dangled from a long silver chain about his neck. Even though he was several years older than the big knight, he still held his frail looking frame in a regal manner, with both hands clasped loosely behind his back. This was Lord Blackthorn.

Captain Morgan moved several steps forward, saying nothing, his eyes riveted on the regal man's lean angered countenance. The stoic knight made no move but stood silently before this Napoleon, staring at the familiar smug expression, his eyes giving off an undisguised glint of burning hatred. He held back not just recent memories and events, but even more he held back his tongue.

"You are relieved Sir Knight," Blackthorn's chilling voice echoed off the white-walled buildings that were now stained red with drying bloodied remains. "Take your men and leave this crime scene...now!"

Merrick knew it was pointless to argue the matter, like he had so many times before to no avail, and at last conceded, too tired from a long night's duty to contest. The Captain of the Night Watch turned abruptly to face the throng of soldiers still faithfully following him and threw his hands in a command as the tall figure addressed them.

"You heard our Lord and Sovereign," the proud voice rang out in the light of the rising morning sun. "It seems our services are no longer required, so let's make our way back to the barracks to a warm meal and soft beds to rest our tired weary bones and leave this bloody mess for these garbage men to clean up."

Without waiting to judge the monarch's reaction, Sir Merrick Arawn Morgan wheeled about and proceeded through the open gates and under a giant archway to the streets of the city beyond.

"SERGEANT!" the loud shrill command of Lord Blackthorn cut into his soldiers' thoughts drawing each one's attention back to being obedient servants to the Crown. "Try and use that fat pudgy little brain of yours and attempt to ascertain what exactly took place here last night!"

"But my Lord," the rather rotund Sergeant-at-Arms stammered fearfully, "Surely Sir Merrick, who is widely known for his skills of detection would be more suited for such an endeavor?"

The tall Dictator of Duergar snatched the hapless officer by the front of his black tunic, dragging him close and raising him well off the ground, until each one's face was only inches away from the other. "I gave you an order Sergeant Caine." The flushed angered face seemed gigantic and distorted and his fierce eyes were narrowed with rage. "Disobey me once more and I shall roast you over an open fire like the fat little pig you are."

But he would never know what his response would have been. For as he hung there in midair, struggling helplessly in the unnaturally powerful iron-handed grip of the lean Druid, the hovering heads rose from the ground and flew, light as a bird towards them. They began to quiver and gyrate in mid-flight, their cheeks ballooning, their tongues snaking out from between empurpled lips. Their eyes burned a sickly scarlet. The hair on their heads rose and rippled, transforming into a mass of eels, writhing around in a whirling frenzy as if they had just been caught in a net.

Like a pack of wolves on the track of a wounded deer, the corporal heads flew at the ashen-faced men of the Royal Regiment of Duergar, streaking straight for their unprotected throats. Several unsuspecting guards were silenced before they even had a chance to defend themselves, their throats savagely ripped out. One sentry got off a quick cry for help and slashed wildly at one of the heads, cutting off an ear; that seemed only to enrage the beast further, as he too fell lifeless onto the cobble stone streets amid a growing pool of his own warm blood. Another of the decapitated heads had clasped onto a soldier with super human force, drawing the man's tongue into its mouth until flesh could stretch no further. Then with a surge of uneorthly power, the creature pulled the tongue out by its roots, gouts of gushing blood spurt forth leaving a bloody gaping hole.

As the bald, portly officer hung in midair, struggling violently in the powerful druid's iron-handed grip, five black shadows suddenly fell over them as the death-like forms descended from the early morning skies. Lord Blackthorn, still angered, but now confounded by the sudden appearance of these demonic creatures, lowered the corpulent conscript to the eorth forthwith and turned to face the strange beings. Sergeant Caine stood on shaking legs, his blood turned to ice, his senses were raw and distorted with terror, the last remnants of any courage he may have once possessed were completely gone. There was no time to run, no chance to defend, as he was rooted in horror, feeling a chilling fear surge through his quivering obese body at the sight of these five deadly apparitions.

Great red eyes swiveled in his direction, their jagged jaws battered onto him, tearing savagely at the helpless man's large limbs, until streams of crimson blood came billowing out amid a barrage of oaths and obscenities. Rivers of blood spilled out into the street from raw, open wounds, his arms ripped clean from their sockets and both legs removed at the hip. The slender overlord of Duergar, while still bewildered at the sight of these flying abominations, was not in the least panicked. Showing no signs of fear, he turned headlong to face each of the evil entities, a broad, devilish grin spread slowly over his lean countenance as he extended his arms in gesture. In the next instance the glowing eyes of the dark druid began to smolder, as bolts of searing red light erupted outward from steely fingers, just as the heads turned hurriedly to him. Bolts of burning fire flashed menacingly, slicing through in a powerful, blazing surge of arcane energy that reached the black figures and beyond. The magical energy struck the rapidly moving craniums with a sharp crackle, holding them fast, draining the nocuous spirit from its mortal shell as they writhed in wailing agony, loathing the power that was destroying it.

Slowly they fell to the eorth, blackened skin crumbling into dust as it descended until finally they were gone and only small piles of black ashes remained. The flame abruptly ceased and the battle was ended; only Lord Blackthorn and one lone soldier survived the frightening incursion alive, positioned like statues in the silence and emptiness of the blood-soaked ground.

Covered from head to toe in blood and guts, the young sentinel didn't move, still stunned by the sudden appearance of the disembodied heads and the violence that ensued shortly thereafter. He stood staring hypnotically as if waiting for them to rise and somehow come back to life, cautiously prodding the ashes of the burnt remains with one foot. The Sovereign of Duergar turned mechanically to face his last remaining escort, his eyes wandering amongst the dead trying vainly to grasp what had just transpired.

"Find the Captain of the Guard and apprise him of the current situation; I expect his full attention on this matter. And one more thing, inform Captain Caine that his blubbery mass of a brother is no longer with us...and clean up this mess!" Lord Blackthorn declared coolly, his dark eyes coming to rest directly on the battered and bloodied face of the newly promoted serviceman. "And congratulations... you've just been promoted."

Without a backward glance at the silent guard, the black-garbed magnate took several long strides, his flowing cloak billowing out behind him as he walked. Through the ornate archway he passed, until finally, he was no longer in view.

IV

Within the private chambers of the new Ruler of Duergar all was dark and silent. Amid the silence were small black forms that crawled wearily about the stone floor of the silent room, easily startled, their forms hunched before they would scatter back to the safety of their homes. It was a single black chamber with the south face open to the dim light of the breaking morning sky beyond and the seemingly endless stretch of structure and buildings that formed the Kingdom. In this cavernous room the sunless walls were wet and cold to the touch; an evil aura permeated the somber air like a black shroud of death.

In the center of the room was a large pentagram crudely etched into the floor with several small burning black candles placed at every point within the large star. A gaunt figure knelt just outside the circle, silhouetted against the flickering shadows, a man bereft of hope, but not of longing. His features once handsome, now his face was no more than parchment-like skin stretched on a frame of white bone, and his eyes were dark and empty. His desolate whimpering and weeping cries sounded of unforgettable agony, drifting slowly out across the great room and beyond.

Sick with desire, he rose, moving slowly from candle to candle offering a few drops of blood from a cut freshly made to the palm of his hand. Within moments he stood alone, his eyes black and shining, deceptively placid, like two pools of water that were hiding something evil and destructive. With boney hands he now gripped a twisted black staff that bore strange ancient runes, each one etched in a different language. It seemed to hum with an evil glee in the hands of its master. He firmly placed it upright; instantly the power of the staff steamed hotly and flared with a raw chaotic energy. Atop the evil artifact, and within the blackness of the skulls' hollow sockets, tiny glints of flame flashed spark-like with an insatiable hatred. The floor about him became charred and black and the damp air smelled sickly of decay.

The Staff of the Lich King's glow began to brighten. Almost at once the glow intensified sharply to a pale green color that silhouetted the hunched form of the entranced wizard against the darkness. He raised the staff high over his head and one of the skeletal heads opened its crooked mouth and shot out a thin, brilliant arc of fire that flew into the center of the large pentagram. One by one the power held within the glowing runes of the nefarious relic flared up. As the last of the foul symbol's light finally faded, a conduit to one of the Nine Planes of Hell opened, drawing its elements into the world and igniting a black ring of fire on the ground. Howls and shrieks of unimaginable agony spilled forth from the impenetrable blackness beyond. Dark and frightening shadows began to ooze out of the floors, the walls and even from the very air surrounding him, filling the area with wisps of writhing blackness.

Suddenly a cool breeze stirred in the stifling stillness, as if somehow wrenching free of the rancorous space that now held it. In the dim light, Kalifen discerned a thin thread of smoke uncoiling from the center of the magic circle. The wisp of vapor rose lazily toward him. He watched transfixed as the faint luminosity resolved itself into near human shape. He began to see the pale oval of a face, indistinctive at first, yet it seemed to regard him steadily with kind eyes. The image grew clearer as the power of the staff was further invoked until it gathered slowly into material form. The image was that of a young woman, drifting in the air just a few scant inches above the floor.

She was as lovely as the dawn. Her long hair was a halo of shining reddish-gold, her cheeks were softly flushed and her slender body was as quick and bright as a sunbeam. She smiled upon the gaunt man and regarded him with gentle eyes. A sweet familiar voice eddied around the dark magus and when he heard her mellifluous words, his inexpressive face grew tight and turned light in color as a single tear slid slowly down his hollow cheek.

"Nora...I have failed you..." his words were cold and frozen and filled with deep regret. "I wish I could take back these words I say to you now...but I cannot." The concentration he had to maintain to keep the portal open wavered, his arm that held the staff lowered slightly. "I can only beg your forgiveness and pray you hear my words...I promise you one day we will be reunited once again...somehow...someway."

"My Liege, Lord Blackthorn approaches!"

The sudden interruption came from one of the vigilant sentries on guard, just a few feet outside the chamber doors. The unexpected disturbance behind him caused the faceless cowl of Kalifen to pause and turn slightly. He was not ready yet, and with a low oath, the sorcerer hurled the silver bladed athame he used in the clairvoyance ritual to the floor in front of the closed doors. And as if the ringing of the metal on the stone had been a summons, the large ornate doors to the massive chamber flew open as Lord Blackthorn surged into the room. Kalifen looked back abruptly to see the intruder, then quickly back to the ghostly image of the comely woman still floating in the air. It faded even as they watched.

The Sovereign of Duergar rocked slightly on his heels. Awkwardly he turned his gray eyes fixed coolly on the great Druid. Lord Blackthorn came forward a pace and stopped. Just then, the two sentries on guard rushed into the room to stand silently, awaiting their master's attention.

"Leave us!" Without turning to face them, Kalifen gestured abruptly toward the open doors facing north. "We are not to be disturbed. Go now, and wait for us by the boats."

Without hesitation, his two soldiers obediently shuffled awkwardly back across the dark chamber until they reached the doorway, which they quickly went through, closing the doors behind them as they did so.

Kalifen's gaze shifted slowly to meet that of his advisor's. "Don't just stand there, help me you fool."

The Druid did not look surprised.

"Help me..." he began again, then sagged downward, barely catching himself in time to keep from collapsing.

The tall man instantly moved to his master's aid, but immediately stopped as Kalifen's boney hand came up in warning.

"Bring me something to sit on you fool!"

Without another word, the dark figure of the Druid bounded toward an oval table and brought back with him a sturdy wooden chair. Kalifen weakly sat down, pain and frustration lining his jaw.

"I see you have been using the staff once again," Lord Blackthorn spoke softly. "I feel it is unwise..."

"Hold your tongue sorcerer, and remember this. I allow you to live as long as you serve me." Kalifen's face was dark, his eyes filled with anger as he struggled to rise half-way out of his seat. "Betray me...and I will joyfully send you back to rot in Hell...Xuchia."

The dark Druid spoke firmly as his master slipped back into his chair. "Of course my Liege." He bowed slightly, a faint mocking smile passed quickly across his lips. "I implore you to pardon this intrusion Lord and Master, but I must speak with you."

"Then speak dog!" Kalifen winced in pain, his voice hard and bitter.

Blackthorn stood his ground. "There is an urgent matter that demands your attention. Some members of the pack were murdered earlier this morning, and I fear this may be a harbinger of things to come."

"This is a matter for the Halfling to attend to," the dark magician sat rigidly in his chair, cold hands still gripping the shaft of the black twisted staff. "He is their leader is he not, so let him be the one to take care of those filthy beasts; besides there are more important issues that demand my immediate attention."

"But Sire, it is imperative..." the large Druid pointed out suddenly, but was quickly cut off.

"It is imperative that you obey my orders, if you wish to live!" Kalifen exploded, rising slowly he came forward threateningly.

The chamber grew still and silent. Master and servant stared wordlessly at one another, their eyes locked.

"Yes, my Lord." The black-garbed figure of Lord Blackthorn stood rigid, his face expressionless and hard. "I live only to serve the greater glory of your name."

"You forget your place Xuchia," the dark Lord of Duergar's impatient voice cut through the momentary stillness with a biting sharpness, as the darkness of the massive room seemed to deepen. "See to it that it does not happen again, for next time I will not be so lenient. Now tell me, have all the arrangements been made for our voyage?" The worn face of Kalifen was drained of color and his dark eyes stared blankly at the silent form that stood in front of him statue-like.

Resolutely the tall Druid met those staring eyes with undisguised hatred and disdain for his master. Fighting down the urge to cut out the evil mystic's black tongue, he forced himself to remain outwardly calm before speaking again. "The ships and crew are ready to launch. Your captains have all gathered in the war room and await your orders," he continued evenly.

Slowly the Ruler of Duergar moved to stand at the foot of the etched pentagram, a faint smile creeping over his dark face. He paused momentarily, and then directed a withered glance at the wily Druid who waited patiently behind him.

"Excellent, we shall set sail in one hour's time," his rage slowly began to subside and within the darkness of the hood he nodded in satisfaction. "Inform Longfoot of our departure and while we are away, if he has any unforeseen problems, he is to consult the witch immediately; she will advise him well. Make sure your servants keep a watchful eye on our fat little friend; he is not to be trusted..."

Several steps away, Lord Blackthorn watched as his cloaked master suddenly stopped talking, his eyelids drooping heavily, his breathing slowing, his form turning statue-like in the dim candle light of the chamber. He still held the black staff in both hands before him, with the blackened skulls at the end, their eyeless sockets gleaming brightly. One of the engraved runes began to glow hotly. Then suddenly Kalifen rose sharply to his full height, a terrible whiteness flooding his worn and haggard face. A dark force coursed through his pain-racked body, his boney hands closing firmly about the ancient evil relic, gripping the black staff until his knuckles turned white with pain. Then the staff slipped from his hands, his eyes glazed over; with a long exhalation his lean frame crumbled, lifelessly to the stone floor.

With leaden steps, the stone faced Druid made his way over to reach his master's side and knelt beside the self-proclaimed Ruler of Duergar. The fallen dark mage was still alive, his shallow breathing harsh and his eyelids twitching sporadically. Grimly the slender Druid reached down and cast the wicked artifact of antiquity away, then raised the wounded man upward; abruptly the eyes opened for an instant. Kalifen spoke softly, a barely perceptible murmuring, and then he drifted back into unconsciousness once again.

Quickly the Druid stripped aside the unconscious man's black robes to reveal that his undershirt was deeply stained with fresh blood. That too was pulled back to reveal a gaunt and skeletal body with withered flesh stretched tight across horribly visible bones. Patches of rotting skin began to wither and turn to dust, falling from his dying form like ash as his decaying body broke apart. The long aged scar on his neck seemed dark and sickly and a freshly new etching of another of the evil symbols had been superficially carved into his fragile skin. "You shall not die just yet Kalifen," his words were quiet and composed. "Unfortunately I still have need of you."

The Druid did not hesitate now; his tall sparse frame rigid beneath the fur cloak, his face became hidden within a growing shadow. There was a thunderous rumble that seemed to echo within Xuchia, his eyes glazed over as a surge of arcane energy exploded and four draconic heads sprouted from his shoulders. Green and yellow sparks flew off his body as a light breeze suddenly picked up loose debris lifting and swirling it around with a faint howl. His flesh hardened and his eyes gleamed red. A sinuous barbed tail grew out from the base of his spine and a pair of great black leathery wings burst from his shoulder blades. A quick build up of icy blue energy began to center on his outstretched hands that rapidly became an enormous bubble of frost that washed out over the motionless wizard.

The blackness began to fade and turn his parchment-like skin almost transparent, then slowly to a pinkish hue. Kalifen opened his eyes and stared up at his servant from the cold floor, his cowled face lifted against the screen of the light from the candles that now burned low. For a long time he laid still, motionless, save for the ripple of cloth garments in the light breeze from the air still swirling about them. When the Druid finally spoke, his whisper filled the quiet with deep, sudden bluntness.

"I have seen to it that your body remain in this suspended state for a few more weeks, but you will need my sustaining magic if you wish to live. The Staff of the Lich King has given you only its curse, only the Shadow Lord can provide you with what you so desperately desire."

There was a long pause. "Once again you have proven your worth to me sorcerer," the awaken mystic responded. "Continue to play your role as Lord Blackthorn and you shall have what it is you so desperately desire demon...your freedom."

The movement of the Druid's head was barely perceptible. "Thank you my master."

"Now leave me." Gathering his robes about him, he sat forward, face bent toward the floor in his chamber. "Let me rest awhile and gather my strength. We leave in one hour."

Lord Blackthorn was silent for a moment, and then reluctantly nodded his head once again, bending slightly forward with his response. He turned quickly and started towards the set of double doors, cast a withering glance at Kalifen and stalked away from his master's chamber without a word.

The Ruler of Duergar sat in silence for a time, glancing periodically toward the hastily discarded Staff of the Lich King. His stricken face was pale and drawn and a fear never before seen reflected brightly in his eyes. His face remained lowered for a moment showing a look of sadness and resignation, and then slowly, he lifted it once more to speak aloud. "Nora...forgive me." The only answer that echoed back was that of his own voice.

V

When Dark awoke, the night sky was gone as the first early morning rays of light from the East signaled the approach of dawn. For a moment the tired half-elf rested quietly and studied the finely furnished chamber in silent leisure, allowing the cloudiness of sleep to disperse and his well rested mind to awaken fully. There he laid, still wrapped tightly in the warmth and solitude of his large, plush bed, unwilling to acknowledge that the day had already begun without him. He saw that his demonic set of armor was lying on a large chair near the bed and on an ornate wooden table rested the red jeweled Eye of Dagda.

Suddenly the large set of double doors to his royal bed chamber burst open and a huge creature furred and clawed padded noisily toward him. It was Baron, his pet Chimera. He greeted the monstrous hybrid fondly, rubbing the black mane around all three of the beast's thick necks, stroking softly the large bat wings arising from the creature's back. He had been with Dark for several months; almost fully grown, he was quickly becoming closer and more faithful than any man could have been.

"Hello my boys," Dark muttered cheerfully, as sloppy tongues began licking his face relentlessly.

Just then, Renfield the invisible manservant and personal aide to the head of Dark Manor, gently knocked on one of the open doors before silently walking inside.

"May I serve you breakfast my Lord?" Renfield asked his young master in an all too serious, and forthright manner, holding out a cotton housecoat that Dark drew slowly about him, belting it loosely around the waist. Another of the unseen attendants quickly crossed to the large and lavish hand-woven curtains that draped the far wall, drew them aside and proceeded to push outward several of the floor-length glass doors that opened onto a massive stone balcony. Light flooded in softly from the early morning sun as a cool breeze from the North warned that the winter Solstice was close at hand. Renfield was busily moving about, lightning scented oil lamps to chase the pungent smell of blood and human remains from his master's dark armor. A floating apron appeared carrying a silver tray of steaming food and drink. The ghostly apparition hastened outside with Dark's meal and deposited it on a round clothed table and urged him to eat while it was still hot. It seemed the serving cook stayed herself from leaving just yet, lingering until Dark had taken a first bite and was satisfied of the response.

"Excellent as usual Mrs. Crocker," Dark responded hastily, covering his full mouth with his hand. "Each meal is only surpassed by the next."

"Thank you my Lord," the aproned specter curtseyed then turned away and went out again. "But please call me Betty dear."

There was the faintest sound from falling footsteps in the hallway beyond the chamber doors, instantly alerting the Baron of Dark Manor, who was crouching down ready to pounce on his unsuspecting victim. Moments later, the tall form of Mephistopheles entered the room, dressed newly in flowing robes of the clearest white, his long regal garb shining bright in the glowing light of the new day. Instantly the impatient Chimera lunged forward like a predator on its prey.

"Get off me...you're too heavy," the old wizard spoke, his voice loud and commanding as he fought to push the over-zealous beast down. "Get off me you big piece of meat!"

"I see his training is going well," came the quick sarcastic response, finally wrestling one large clawed paw away from his face. "He's so much more...obedient!"

"I've tried having Renfield teach him to be more submissive to authority," Dark remarked with jovial mockery. "But for some reason he just doesn't seem to pay him any heed."

"Yes...that is quite strange," he seated himself on the chair next to his grandson and motioned for him to continue eating. "Morning Renfield."

"Good morning Sir," the steward of the cloud castle approached the pair with his master's soiled garments hovering in the air, held by invisible hands. "I shall have these items cleaned immediately my Lord, and if there is no more need for my services, I shall take my leave."

"Yes, of course, Renfield. Thank you."

The unseen manservant turned abruptly and exited the bedroom chamber, closing the doors firmly behind him. Baron had wandered over to Dark, his snake tail wagging quickly side to side, then dropping down next to his master, his heads resting comfortably on his enormous paws, black eyes closed contentedly.

"You do know that cute and cuddly creature here will transform into a ruthless predator in just two year's time?" Mephisto interjected, then, fell quickly silent as he saw his grandson frown in annoyance.

"You know that small pendant of my father's you gave me," Dark broke in quickly, his head lifted sharply. "Well it's malfunctioning or something because I keep getting shot at...a lot."

"If you had been paying attention when I presented it to you at the time," Mephisto cocked his head, then, looked at the Lord of Dark Manor sharply. "Then you would know that it only works against non-magical weapons...right."

"Any word from the city?" he asked quickly changing the topic of conversation. "Maybe something in the local news... maybe?"

"Indeed there is." A touch of impatience revealed itself in Mephisto's dark face as he simply stared at his young grandson. "Now, I already know what happened, so don't bother reading it to me."

"No please, come and join me," Dark smiled coldly, deftly kicking a chair out to accommodate the angered wizard. "I insist."

Deposited directly in front of Dark was a newspaper called 'The Guardian'. These broadsheets sold on the streets of Duergar and contained various types of reading material, anywhere from the news of the day to ballads and political satire. On the front page, printed in bold lettering was the day's headline news with the caption that read 'Rise of a Demon'.

"They have me intrigued already," Dark responded with a mocking tone lifting his head slightly to smile at his grandfather. "One Hundred and One Nights, a new book of Arabian tales. And look, priceless manuscripts have mysteriously gone missing in Timbuktu."

"See anything else?" His grandfather asked evenly, slowly seating himself.

"I do see an article about ten fantastic facts and legends of Edinburg Castle in Scotland." He paused for a moment, his eyes studying the many headlines as he tried to narrow down the possibilities.

"Keep looking," the ancient magus responded quickly, tonelessly, while dipping a chocolate biscuit into his tea then mechanically depositing the softened portion into his open mouth.

"The remains of Richard III have been..."

"Oh do get on with it!" Mephistopheles the Silver Mage shot him one of those angry looks that dismissed his grandson as an idiot incapable of understanding anything of any real importance. "I don't know why you always have to be such a smart ass."

Dark laughed mockingly. "All right, all right, old man, calm down or you'll get those thick, padded under garments of yours in a bunch...and trust me when I say, nobody wants that."

His grandfather's tall frame went rigid; his hands gripped the edge of the table until the knuckles went white as he leaned forward sharply, his eyes black with rage and disbelief. "Vanora, that bitch!" the angry magician was on his feet, shouting. "She promised me NO ONE...WOULD

EVER..." He trailed off sharply, halting at last as he waited for Dark to stop laughing.

"Nobody told me...She never told me anything you old fool," Dark responded slowly, trying to restrain himself from laughing any further at his grandfather's expense. "Nobody knows, nobody needs to know and I'm sure as hell that nobody wants to know...all right there Lucky...and I mean nobody."

"It's all that damn caffeine in that damn herbal tea!" the white robed elderly wizard muttered as he sat back down again, slamming his clenched fist against the table. "And I have been under a lot of stress you know."

"Well don't stress yourself out too much there, all right Lucky," Dark replied vehemently straightening his paper as he did so. "Besides, Renfield just had these chairs re-upholstered, so relax...have some water instead, and let me finish reading."

"Yes, of course, you're right," Mephisto agreed with a faint smile. "Please, continue."

Dark shook his head emphatically, folded the newspaper in half, then almost sheepishly the familiar broad smile returned as the young half-elf brought his gaze back and resumed his reading.

"A strange, horrific scene greeted the Royal Guard of Duergar in the early morning hours of the waking sun... blah, blah, blah...here we are; witnesses gave a description of that frightful event saying a supernatural being standing a full two heads taller than the tallest man, its terrifying form churned out a blackness that swallowed the light, as large eyes glowed red within its own skull. The demon then spat gouts of fire which writhed about him. Then the dark shadows that surrounded the beast finally swirled and faded...and with that, the demonic fiend was gone."

His grandfather listened quietly to the long tale; his lean bearded face remained remarkably, for the most part, an inscrutable mask, broken only slightly by several perpetual half smiles, a few absent nods of his head and a couple stray looks from sharp blue eyes. He recognized quickly enough why his grandson had invited him for morning tea. This was the payback for him ordering Renfield to leave the flaming remains for Baron's master when he arrived home late last night. Moments later Dark finished his story and waited patiently for Mephisto's response.

"So let me get this straight. The only reason why you asked me here this morning was so I could listen to the same dribble I've already read earlier today," exclaimed the ancient mage in sudden understanding. "All because I made you clean up that foul beast's burning dung?"

"Yeah, that's right," Dark acknowledged approvingly. "And the humiliating part, well that was just a bonus."

"Hmmm...is that so...well you know that humiliating little problem of mine...it's hereditary." He trailed off for a moment, then sipped gingerly at his aromatic Asian beverage, poured himself another cup and passed the teapot to his grandson who accepted it without blinking. "More tea, Lucky?"

It was almost noon when Dark entered the bustling City of Duergar, concealed in the midst of dozens of traders and travelers from all over the globe. Black robes were wrapped tightly about his muscular, lean frame and the hooded traveler's cloak was pulled even tighter about his head so that none of his facial features could be seen save for narrow eyes that shone dimly like a cat's. He noticed immediately that there were soldiers everywhere patrolling the streets and wide treed lanes of the city. There were huge numbers stationed at the main gates and throughout the megalopolis, all bearing Blackthorn's insignia and apparently they were the only activated units in all of Duergar. The citizens of the city were understandably frightened by what had happened the previous night. Word of the slain and the circumstances that surrounded their deaths, along with the strange occurrences thereafter, spread like wildfire. Snatches of conversation about headless bodies and flying goblin heads were heard from whispered lips and hushed voices.

He passed without hesitation through the metal-bound gates to the Garden Quarters into the broad streets; he could feel the sentries of the City Guard staring at him. Dark continued moving forward without a backward glance at the silent guards, his eyes instead peered into the shadows about him where he quickly discovered a few well armed guards taking a bribe from a few well groomed men.

It was a busy hour with people pushing and shoving their way past small shops and boutiques that lined the grand avenue and ran inward toward the Grand Citadel. He marveled at the many stately houses and mansions in this quarter, all screened by trees and hedges that carefully bordered manicured lawns and fragrant gardens. Duergar was a city set apart from the rest of the world, with thousands of travelers passing through its gates every day. Generations of immigrants from all over had settled here and made the city synonymous with commerce and cosmopolitanism and its status as a beacon of culture was symbolized by the legendary Lighthouse of Duergar that stood over four hundred and fifty feet tall. For the most part, the people here seemed content with the government that ruled them and the way of life provided for them.

The well concealed assassin maneuvered his way through the crowded streets. It seemed every public thoroughfare in Duergar was teeming with carts and wagons, pedestrians and regal riders, even the occasional herdsman or shepherd during the day could be seen driving some of his stock before him. He turned west onto another roadway called the Grand Avenue, where along both sides of the broad street were rows of merchants that sat on wooden divans in front of their stalls. Each of them tightly grouped in a space of about six feet in width; their most precious merchandise was not on display, but kept hidden away in locked cabinets. Only clothes were hung out in long rows with a picturesque effect. Here prospective clients sat casually in front of a dealer talking with him, drinking tea or Turkish coffee in a totally relaxed way.

The day was still warm as Dark hurried past other travelers on their way abroad until finally he walked quickly through the tall iron gates that lead into the Grand Bazaar. The market place was unrivalled amongst other markets in the world with regard to abundance, variety and quality or rarity of the goods for sale. As he entered, he saw the High Market was a maze of elegant awnings, genteel art galleries, courtly gentlemen, gracious ladies and money...and lots of it. If you are seeking exquisite artisanship, exotic ingredients and unique styling, the Grand Bazaar is the place. In the bazaar there are eighteen different entrances, each one bearing the name of the sellers of a particular goods, and all eighteen gates open each day in the early morning and close in the evening. The number of known shops amount to a number well over four thousand, plus another three hundred were located in the adjacent Hans, a large three-story building called the King's Road Inn, a place where travelers could rest and recover from the day's journey. The inner Bedesten hosted the most precious of wares, jewelers, armors, crystals and magic dealers all had their shops there; and that is where the silent moving assassin headed to next.

"Gather round, gather round!" a loud booming voice rang out from behind a growing throng that quickly assembled closely together. "Ladies and gentlemen, what you are about to see has intrigued scholars and audiences like yourselves for centuries."

Dark's first inclination was to keep going to meet with his rendezvous, but instead he paused momentarily and pushed his way through to the front of the forming circle, his dark form wrapped ominously in the black cloak. The growing crowd swelled from a few dozen to several hundred as a short, stocky eastern man stood holding a black cloth bag next to a small Indian child who sat on a large woven basket. The man was dressed in a multi-colored cloak and a vest of blue and pale yellow, his large frame moved around the boy and basket with the graceful ease of a cat as he held the bag up high for all to see. He wore a blue turban that held a giant sized ruby that matched the color of the red dot in the middle of his forehead. He had a long black moustache and an even longer slender beard that hung down to his sandaled feet, his eyes were shadowed and mysterious, his gaze almost frightening.

"Hear me good people of Duergar," the magician spoke as flashing fountains of fire erupted from the sandy floor around him. "I am Naseeb the Great, magician, conjurer and Lord of illusions. I have traveled far from a land of exotic mystique...where magic originated from...home where the purest, minimumalist and mystical of magics still exists, a land where magic not only intrigues but dazzles the senses... India!"

Taking the small jute bag and having first shown that it was entirely empty, he then put his hand into the black sack and upon withdrawing his hand again out came two small game cocks. After the wild roosters put on a fight for the intrigued spectators, they were then covered with a large piece of red cloth. When the sheet was removed, the two cocks were magically gone and in their place now pecked and pawed two gray partridges that quickly began foraging for insects to eat. The Eastern magician covered again and the medium-sized game birds now became writhing black snakes; they were immediately covered again while the bored boy whisked a bothersome fly away from his lips, yawned and wiped the sweat and dust from his face with the hem of his shirt. When the sheet finally lifted for what Dark hoped was the last time, there was nothing. The venomous reptiles had simply vanished from view. The large crown seemed completely unimpressed by the tricks done by Naseeb the Great and were thoroughly unamazed by his ability to make common animals appear and disappear. Several of the unbaffled spectators remarked that it was not even magic, some even laughed, and their laughter seduced new onlookers into the group. Boredom finally overtook Dark and slowly he turned in motion to leave, but hesitated as Naseeb stepped forward holding what appeared to be a long, thin rope that was knotted at each end. He wiggled the device around for all to see; he pulled and stretched on the rope, even so much as biting it with his teeth.

"The Old Indian Rope Trick!" he proudly announced with accented English words. The blue-garbed conjurer set the rope on the sandy ground and waved his hand over it several times as he said the magic words, '*Yantru-mantru-Jâlajâlâ-tantru.*' He then lifted the long rope again, turning slightly to face his audience fully, carefully holding his arm straight out and parallel to the ground. "I will swear by any god that I have gleaned this ancient knowledge from Muslim murshids and Tantric sadhus," the magician began again. "I have gained these powers from both the tombs of Islamic saints and from the burning grounds of the Hindus!"

Even though the massive crowd of onlookers did not know it, Dark knew that Naseeb the Great, by the way he stood, by where he placed his props, by the direction in which he looked and by many innumerable other subtle slights and unnoticed strategies, had indeed arranged his crowd. All eyes were focused on the Indian Fakir as he clutched in his right hand one end of the coiled rope, while he held the other end with his left. With a vigorous shout and great bodily exertion, he threw it into the air in a perfect vertical line. It fell. He threw it again. Each time it somehow seemed to have gone higher though it fell several more times. All the while the holy man kept muttering, whining, imploring, crying and gesticulating in an exaggerated theatrical pantomime. At length he warned the spectators who were crowding upon him to keep the circle as wide and broad as it was at the outset. He gathered the rope once more into circular coils in his right hand and with a supreme effort and a wild shriek, threw it up at a great height toward the cloudy sky. Then all of a sudden, he pulled on the dangling rope with the greatest of violence two or three times if not more. It did not fall but instead it somehow seemed tightly fastened.

Up and up rose the silk cord, the knotted end growing smaller and smaller the higher it traveled, until it disappeared from sight altogether. To all appearances it had sailed up until it reached the nearest stratum of clouds and receded behind it. Even Dark could not see the top of the rope, which had gone out of sight into the white mist, while the other end hung down on the ground. The next thing the on-looking assassin witnessed was the small Indian boy rushing forward; leaping upwards he began climbing the silk cord. He went up very quickly, climbing higher and higher and was soon lost from Dark's field of vision.

"Babu!" the magician called out angrily. "Come back down here...Babu! You naughty boy!"

Several more times the eastern conjurer would call back his boy assistant and, on hearing no response he became even more enraged. The portly magician, now furious, armed himself with a long, sharp knife and ascended the rope himself duly armed with intent on carving the child as he might carve a turkey. With blade in mouth, he climbed, first with one hand then with the other, his stubby legs equally agitated and acting, he rose higher and higher until he too vanished out of sight into thin air. An argument was heard far above the crowd, followed by the most agonizing screams of pain. A few moments later, pieces of the small boy began to rain down in fragments while shocked spectators cried out in horror, their gazes went wide as they looked back and forth at each other.

First a leg fell to the ground followed by an arm, then the other leg and arm together, until finally the remainder of the boy's body and decapitated head. The Indian Fakir reappeared, covered in his assistant's blood as he began his slow descent down the erect silk cord towards the many gaping mouths and silent shocked faces of the crowd. He quickly collected the limbs and put them into the empty wicker basket and replaced the lid. After a few brief passes over the lid with his hands, the boy miraculously leapt from the basket fully restored, somehow reconstructed out of a heap of disjointed limbs and miscellaneous organs. Naseeb the Great returned proudly to center stage and grandly bowed with theatrical grandeur to a great chorus of cheers that erupted from the exuberant audience who were full of unrestrained enthusiasm. The magician's assistant, now complete again, was busily collecting scattered coins tossed by the awestruck and astounded observers, his small felt fez filling up quickly.

Without further delay, Dark threw a solid gold coin, wheeled about and proceeded on toward one of the northern gates of the Grand Bazaar, his black cloak still wrapped tightly about him. The High Market's overall architecture and styling was not unique to any nationality and did not differ from other large covered market places, but if it is your make up to haggle, then this is a place that will hold and arrest your complete attention. It also offered a myriad variety of products from trinkets and souvenirs, spices and sweets, precious jewelry and beaded tapestries, magical tomes and artifacts along with the finest armor and weaponry in the free world. The endless variety was confusing to first time visitors especially with the constant persuasive and persistent cajoling by the strategically positioned sales people that man the outside of each shop.

Following the directions communicated to him by Pin, his liaison to the underworld, Dark finally arrived a few minutes before twelve noon at his destination. What stood before the black-garbed assassin was the most ingenious of mechanical contraptions he had ever seen. Standing twenty feel tall, this fantastic device for telling the passage of time took the form of a large, gray elephant with an Indian driver seated cat-like atop its massive neck. Positioned on the back of the great beast of burden was a howdah, a hand carved wooden carriage that was beautifully decorated with expensive gems and precious stones. Two red Chinese dragons were twined around a silver arm that hung above a Muslim scribe who sat on a gold disk. The number of hours since sunrise was shown on a black and silver disk at the top of the clock, and an Egyptian phoenix was perched on a golden dome that shone like the sun. As Dark soon found out, every half hour, the bird on the polished dome would whistle and spin around; the man sitting on the balcony lifted his hand up as a small ball fell from a falcon's bill into the serpent's open mouth. The snake then slowly lowered the ball into a brass vase on the right shoulder of the elephant; the handler immediately began thrusting at the elephant's head with his axe as he lifted with his other hand a staff that he used to beat down on the large mammal's thick hide. Finally the white ball exited out the creature's chest falling loudly onto a hanging bell that announced another half hour had passed.

Dark glanced apprehensively at the clouded noon sky, his lean face still hidden behind the cloak pulled tightly about him. His black eyes suddenly focused on the lighted canopy of the large tent before him that silhouetted two men moving within. The assassin's keen eleven ears listened to snatches of the conversation between the two, trying to remain inconspicuous while at the same time able to get close enough to hear what was being said. But their tongue was completely foreign to him and what little he did understand from the garbled speech, consisted of only useless information.

Before Dark could get any closer, two Persian looking men exited the large tent. Both were dressed in scarlet red caftan cloaks that reached down to their ankles, with expensive silk headgear, known as a saraband, which was folded into a fan-shape at the top of each man's head. The trained assassin knew that these long and lavishly decorated garments were given as rewards or even as a mark of favor from important dignitaries or sovereign. The splendid and specific decorations, colors, patterns, ribbons and even buttons indicated the rank of the person to whom they were presented. And from what Dark could tell, it was the man on the right with the long beard and moustache that he had come to see. Something else caught his sharp cat-like eyes, two faded crosses scared both his reddened cheeks. Undoubtedly a parting gift from his father, and it was meant as a constant reminder, that this person was not to be, nor should they be trusted...ever.

A giant cloud bank moved solidly in position over head, hanging ominously between the light of the sun and the black shadow that crept over the tented bazaar. The man with the large dangling moustache gazed expectantly at this black-garbed appointment with intense gray eyes watching the assassin's every movement. At last the two Muslim men shook hands and parted company. The Persian vendor, without further delay, made his way forward until he came to stop abruptly before the dark cloaked patron.

"A fine piece of Muslim technology," declared the Middle Eastern proprietor. "Only one of many ingenious devices designed by the polymath inventor Badi Al-Izz Ismail Bin Al-Razzaz Al-Jazari."

"Yes indeed, it truly is a charming timepiece," came Dark's coded reply. "What type of currency would you accept for it?"

"Only gold sovereigns," the round calculating face stared steadily at the impassive half-elf.

"Will this do?" the words came out slowly as the assassin held up the gold coin given to him by Pin.

Without so much as another word, Dark was led through the open front of the lighted long tent, his dark form still wrapped in the black robe, his cowled head slightly bent against a steadily rising wind. They entered into a cavernous multi-roomed warren, filled with antiquities of a diverse multi-cultural background. The interior was extremely dim, lighted only by a few ceramic oil lamps molded in floral designs. The low lights cascaded down onto a set of long tables with a layer of scattered dust covering various odds and ends from ancient manuscripts to a few engraved swords and matching daggers along with a large cache of tankards and other tarnished trinkets. It looked as though at one time these items may have been for sale, as each bore an antiquated yellowing tag whose value had long ago faded from even the keenest visions.

"As I am sure you already know, my name is Mr. Fekkish," the Persian proprietor spoke with a thick Middle Eastern accent, his covered head slightly bowed. "Now if you please, I must have your name."

"I am Giacomo," finally came the young assassin's reply, cocking his shadowed head slightly. "King of Jesters, and Jester to Kings."

"Ah yes, I recognize that name." For a brief moment the Muslim vendor panicked, abruptly realizing who it was that stood only a few scant feet away. "A jester is a person who is meant to be a funny man, someone who entertains and makes us laugh. You do none of these things. You are a bad man...a very bad man."

"Once again I see that my reputation has preceded me." In one fluid motion he moved to tower over the unsuspecting man, Dark's vice-like hand griping the fellow's throat, cutting off the cry for help before it could escape. A sharp blade from a concealed knife came forcibly down into the Persian's meaty belly. "I shall cut the fat off your belly and cook it for my supper if you do not tell me what this coin can buy me."

"Yes Sayyid, right away Sayyid!"

There was no mistaking the chill feeling of terror that ran through the eastern man's pudgy body as he moved breathlessly in the shadows, his pounding heart beating loudly enough to hear. The elderly merchant smiled with a single glinting gold tooth and held back a tent flap in the rear of his shop with one hand while he ushered the cloaked assassin inside with a slight bow and wave of his other arm.

"Peace be upon you," the old peddler muttered as he closed the large flap and backed away quickly. "Peace be upon you."

With the Persian huckster gone, Dark found himself standing in front of a round table behind which sat a young pretty Gypsy girl shuffling a deck of playing cards. Without so much as a sound, the tiny girl held out her delicate nymph-like hand, seeking payment for services not yet rendered. The black-cloaked assassin obliged, tossing the marked gold sovereign, bouncing it deftly off the table and into her outstretched palm. Upon receiving payment, the small child produced a golden globe topped by a diamond encrusted cross that boasted eighteen rubies, nine emeralds, nine sapphires and three hundred and sixty-five rose-cut diamonds.

"What, no reading?" the disguised half-elf asked mockingly.

Without an upward glance, and again without uttering a single word, she casually began shuffling the deck, and then she turned over three cards in succession. The first card was the Fool, a depiction of a beggar wearing ragged clothes and stockings without shoes, leaning on a staff. The second that Dark saw was the Devil; in his right hand he gripped two chains, and each one was attached to a collar that hung around the necks of naked human figures. The last of the Tarot cards he knew all too well, Death. The card portrayed a skeletal figure, as the skeletal bones are the part of the body that survives death, riding on a white horse carrying a black standard emblazoned with a white flower. Surrounding the reaping skeleton horseman were dead bodies and dying people from all classes, including kings, bishops and commoners alike.

"You are going to die." Her tiny voice whispered in sad response.

The assassin stared at her expressionlessly for a moment, then nodded slightly.

"I know...but not today."

The black-garbed assassin shoved the gold orb into a pocket beneath his long robe and with a slight nod of his covered head to the slender young Gypsy, he ventured back into the interior of the large tent. Dark froze in mid-stride and uttered a low oath, for standing directly in front of him was the Muslim shop owner between two towering armed sentries, their huge black bulks unmistakable even in the poor light. Mr. Fekkish slowly wagged his finger back and forth mechanically, obviously still angered as his eyes alone reflected a hatred that now burned within.

"I told you did I not, you are a bad, bad man... a very, very bad man. How do I know this you ask?" the fat man exclaimed in anger. "You played at a wedding one day, a long time ago, for an Arab Prince named Sahib Ahad Bahadur and for his lovely new bride. This man was my nephew, and even before the Walima, the marriage banquet was over, several guests, including my nephew had somehow mysteriously died that day... and by Allah, I know it was you who murdered them all. And in my country, you will see that bad men pay with their lives. But before I take your life I shall have that which was given to you by the Gypsy girl, and whatever else of value you may possess. Consider it payment for the death of my nephew."

"Well what can I say," the cloaked imposter jested. "I guess the bride just didn't wish to marry someone so fat and revolting."

For a moment no one spoke; no one even moved so much as a muscle as the two parties scrutinized each other in the dimly lit gloom of the large tent. The silence was broken when the first arrow flew from the assassin's hand crossbow with a sharp hum, striking dead center to one of the large sentinel's exposed forehead. A second and third black bolt scored solid hits to the other Islamic guardian, striking him squarely in the chest, then he too fell lifeless onto the carpeted floor. Abruptly, there flashed a fourth steel-tipped projectile piercing the Persian shopkeeper's fleshy quadriceps muscle of his right leg. In a roar of mingled pain and rage, Mr. Fekkish dropped to his knees, clutching the injured leg with both hands. Dark fired a fifth arrow that embedded itself into the kneeling man's left shoulder, spinning his husky form completely about so that he crashed uncontrollably into a pair of priceless vases. The wailing Muslim got off a quick cry for help, turned sharply back and slashed wildly at the shadowy figure with a curve dagger from his waist. With maddened terror the Middle Eastern merchant tried to fight back, slashing frantically with his hunting knife at anything he could reach. Dark caught the dull flash of the sweeping blade as it whistled by his unprotected abdomen, as his own steel-like blade came down to ward off the blow. Their eyes locked momentarily, but the Persian man could only meet the assassin's piercing stare for an instant, as he felt it burn right into his frightened heart.

Then in an instant, with blinding speed, the black-garbed assassin struck out with the long sharp blade of his shadow sword, severing both hands at the wrists of the estranged Mr. Fekkish. The wounded man let out a loud, haunting howl of pain that echoed throughout the high market, alerting every city guard to the cry.

"The removal of one's hands is a proscribed punishment in Islamic law for thievery, is it not?" Dark muttered at last. As he wrapped his long cloak tightly around himself, he paused momentarily and smiled grimly at the frightened shopkeeper, a faint smile of satisfaction on his lean face. The disguised half-elf placed his hands together in prayer, bowed deeply and spoke a few last words before disappearing into the darkness. "Peace be upon you."

VI

A broad cluster of cotton-like clouds slowly crossed directly in front of Dark, as the cloaked assassin wearily made his way to the front gates of his castle home. The day was still warm and in the west, the late afternoon sky was deepening into a soft golden haze, obscuring the clarity of the majestic skyline.

The tall iron gates were slightly ajar when the Lord of the Manor walked quickly toward the large front doors of his fortified stronghold. With weary elven eyes he strolled through the sunken garden, a large fragrant courtyard within the protected walls of the floating citadel. The garden was laid out with hedges and vines, containing deep lotus ponds surrounded by symmetrical rows of cypresses and palms. It was beautifully proportioned and well balanced for a more classical appearance, adorned with sculptures, statues and graceful gothic fountains that contained water jokes which sprayed jets of water at unsuspecting visitors. Raised flower beds were laid out in squares comprised of the most vivid of reds, yellows, blues and pinks flowers and sub-tropicals from the four corners of the world. He was still approaching the stone threshold at the front of his home when the heavy oak doors opened from within and standing there, unexpectedly, was his grandfather. He was dressed in a multi-colored cloak and vest of white and silver etched with ancient symbols that moved about slowly. His lean tall frame moved with the graceful ease of a cat as he made his way down to the stone path when he caught sight of his grandson. The old wizard stopped short and a moment later his eyes went wide with surprise.

"Dark my boy!" Mephisto exclaimed sharply. "What in the name of hell...you startled me!" He moved quickly to his grandson and gripped his shoulder warmly. "You just getting back?" his grandfather said with a smile.

"Yes and no," Dark growled angrily. "I've been back and forth from the city to here, here to the city, so many times today...I don't know where my head's at."

"Make a list," the old magus broke in. "I always tell you to make a list and then you won't forget." Mephisto started to smile, then thought better of it and changed his mind quickly as he caught the mood reflected in his grandson's joyless expression on his face. "Well some dinner and a hot bath are exactly what you need. Come, you can tell me about your meeting over a few fingers of brandy."

Once inside, Dark directed the servants to prepare a feast and draw his bath, and he was led off to warm welcoming waters that not only soothed his muscles but his mood as well. An hour later, and a new change of clothes, he joined his grandfather in the great hall for a dinner fit for a king. As they ate, Dark related to Mephisto the strange encounters he had made at the wondrously entertaining Grand Bazaar. He described in detail the mysterious Indian rope trick performed by an Eastern magician and his assistant, a small boy called Babu. He told of his noon meeting with the marked Mr. Fekkish, a little Gypsy girl and the object he was given and finally of the unfortunate accident that befell the Persian vendor upon his leaving.

Mephistopheles, the Silver Dragon, listened quietly to the long tale, manifesting no visible surprise in his grandson's recital of the day's events until the part about the severing of the Muslim man's hands with which he appeared immeasurably displeased.

"Did you really have to cut his hands off?"

"Maybe not," continued Dark slowly, inwardly musing over the question in his mind. "I suppose not..." he trailed off for a moment to reflect upon his actions, then sipped gingerly at his brandy. "I have to say in my defense, I only cut off his hands..." He shook his head and grinned openly. "It's not like I killed him or anything."

"No, no, of course not." Mephisto reached over and gripped his large hand around the bottle of aged spirits and poured another round for himself. "But why stop at just the hands? Why not cut off the tip of his nose or maybe his ears, or even his tongue for that matter?"

"Damn it," the jovial assassin exclaimed loudly slamming his hand hard against the large dining room table. "Why didn't I think of that? I could have really done some justice to him."

"Dark!" his grandfather growled angrily, almost spilling the contents of his crystal snifter. "I will not tolerate..."

"I'm only joking." Dark took charge quickly, light-heartedly he shook the old wizard by his shoulder. "Besides, the crooked Persian shyster was obviously marked by Dad for a reason. So let's just move on to the next subject or should I say object."

Dark quickly produced a large leather pouch from beneath the table and then poured the contents into his open palm. The golden globe sparkled brightly in the candle light; its ornamental glow, a deep and rich one filled the large chamber with wondrous bejeweled images. Amid the flickering lights of the flames, the ancient wizard's eyes went wide with excitement upon seeing the regal radiant artifact.

"It's beautiful," he acknowledged approvingly. "I can't remember the last time I've seen one."

"To be honest with you I didn't have, nor do I have any idea what it is," admitted his grandson reluctantly. "I only knew that you would know what it is...so what is it?"

"It's a Sovereign's Orb," the venerable old scholar snorted. "This is a piece of coronation regalia. The Orb represents Faërie sovereignty over the Eorth to be held in the monarch's left hand during his crowning at the coronation. The jeweled cross which surmounts the gold ball reflected the King's title as Defender of the Faith and Supreme Ruler of the Faërie folk."

"That's great," came the familiar mocking voice of his grandson. "So what do I do with it?"

He paused for a moment before speaking again and watched as Dark placed the gem encrusted gold ball into the pouch and gently placed the leather container onto the table in front of him. The young assassin sat quietly back in his chair, staring blankly into his brandy glass, obviously deep in thought.

"I don't know, but we'll figure it out...we always do."

Mephisto poured himself another glass of brandy, then passed the swan like carafe to his brooding grandson who accepted it without blinking. The pair then stayed up nearly half the night and finished off two more bottles of the fermented liquor before retiring for the night.

When Dark awoke, the night had quickly clouded over; the sky was a mass of heavy, rolling blackness that settled ominously about the misty castle. His head was aching and his body weary from the previous night's drunken debauchery, yet he somehow remained awake and upright. The Orb was only the first step in his long journey for revenge that might possibly go on forever if he wasn't able to solve this golden riddle. Even though Dark knew eventually this perplexing conundrum would be explained by his ever so clever and wise grandfather, just how many more hoops must he jump through before he could get close enough to his enemies. Close enough to either destroy Kalifen and the Shadow Lord or be destroyed himself. Until then, there would be no going back to Faëroes, to the home his mother and father had built, a place where he used to feel safe and secure.

The truth terrified him. In the silence of his bedroom, Dark Solus was alone in his crusade, a one man army against impossible odds, and deep within himself, he fought back against a deep rising fear of terror. What if he failed? But coming from far below, from a depth located near the outer boundaries of the most evil of grievous intent, burned only one intense and innate emotion. Hate. It fuelled the fires for vengeance, a violent revenge on those who had brought harm to the people whom he loved the most. It consumed him with an uncontrollable rage, a poison that long ago permeated every pore and every fiber of his being. This very strong and powerful force molded him, shaped him and now drove him to seek retribution on those responsible for the death of his parents. He took quite a long time to finally dress, then walking back to his sitting chair he lowered himself slowly. His head seemed to have cleared a bit, but his movements were still those of an old, old man who himself had consumed a small tub full of alcohol. Baron moved over in front of him and the motley crew of fanged faces stared sympathetically upward at their young master. Dark sighed and moved his hands tiredly to the creature's heads.

"Let's see where the old man is shall we?" he muttered. He rubbed each fiendish head slowly, then rose awkwardly and continued on toward the grand stairway that led down to the lower level of Dark Manor. Greeting him at the bottom was Renfield his faithful servant, with a full tray of food that had barely been touched and a dirty brandy glass that was used to dump someone's pipe ashes into.

"Master Mephistopheles is in the library, refusing to retire," the invisible manservant spoke slowly. "I've tried persuading him to sleep, even for only a few hours...but still he refuses."

"Thank you Renfield, I'll see what I can do," Dark promised.

Within the massive grand castle library, a room rich with murals, stained glass and row upon row of antique books, was his grandfather. Mephistopheles the Silver Mage looked up wearily as his grandson entered the dimly lit library. Dark studied the old wizard's fatigued face momentarily, reading the sorrowful failure that was written there. The exhausted sorcerer pushed himself back from the reading table at which he had been seated all night and rubbed his tired gray eyes. On the book littered table, an untouched tray of food had been casually pushed aside; candles burned low, their hot wax dripping into long white vertical lines. Scattered about in large piles lay the books that the ancient historian had spent the night studying intensely, undoubtedly putting himself in that familiar hypnotic trance as he carefully examined every possible reference on the little known ancient artifact.

"No luck?"

"Nothing," Mephisto grimaced as he looked up at his grandson.

All Dark could do was shake his head, lost again in silent thought of sheer helplessness.

"This was our last hope," Mephisto angrily pointed at the leather-bound book that lay open on the table. "And it contains only a single reference about the Faërie King's Orb...and that information was useless."

The ancient tome was one of more than a thousand volumes of the history that formed a small part of a larger work kept by the Elven Kings and their trusted scriveners from days long ago now lost in myth. These learned works were worn and old, even though they were carefully bound in leather and polished brass, then sealed in bees wax, all served to protect them from the ravages of time. They contained, in its entirety, the known history of the Faërie and Elven people. Millions and millions of transcribed pages were all carefully hand written and recorded down through the years by expert Elven historians and chroniclers alike.

"I have read through every one of those books, studying every passage that could possible apply."

All Dark could do was nod as his exasperated grandfather looked up at him again.

"I'm completely at a loss." He rose clutching his sore aching back, slowly stretched and walked over to the leather pouch that contained the golden sphere in question. The weary magician opened the bag, carefully removing the royal treasure within and held it aloft in the palm of his hand, his now blue eyes carefully looking the object over for something he could have possibly missed in his previous examination. "If only we knew someone who could possibly..." he trailed off sharply, looking at his grandson who suddenly came to the same epiphany. But before either could respond with the common cognizance, Renfield entered carrying a long splendid leather case, which he promptly placed gently on the reading table in front of them.

"Pardon the interruption my Lord," the ghostly figure formally addressed his young master. "Master Teigue has arrived."

In the next instant the comely faërie, dressed in a coat of bottle green, fluttered in on wings that shimmered and shone like fine jewels. Dark straightened up with the thought left unspoken, his attention now given over to his indentured servant of whom he quietly beckoned to his side. He crisply directed Renfield to prepare a bath for his grandfather and set out some fresh smelling clothing before getting breakfast for the trio. It was only a few hours after dawn and they had not eaten since the previous night.

"Teigue!" Mephisto shouted, with a quick glance at his grandson. "Just the faërie I wanted to see."

"Really, little ole me?" the tiny enchanted creature of folklore exclaimed excitedly, laughing in delight that quickly turned to mistrust and skepticism. "What do you want old man?"

"Tell us all you know about this item." Mephisto once again held the Faërie relic high in the air, its golden shell shining dully in the dimly lit repository. "Or more to the point, just what in the hell are we supposed to do with it?"

"That's a Sovereign's Orb." The small winged faërie darted back and forth, to and fro, staring meaningfully at the item of antiquity for a moment, glancing quickly at the curious pair who waited respectfully in the background. "It's been a long time since I've seen one though. How did you ever come by such an item as this?"

"That's not important now; I'll tell you all about it later," Mephisto responded quickly. "What's its purpose?"

"It was a symbol of Dagda's dominion over the world held under the protection and authority of the unearthly ruler," Teigue responded in turn as he came to rest on a rather large volume of ancient Faërie history that lay closed on the grand reading table. "It was created for the true coronation of these human monarchs to be placed in the left hand at the end of the ceremony with scepter and the imperial..."

Both Dark and Mephisto turned to look at each other, then quickly brought their attention back to the small humanoid being.

"What's its real purpose, faërie boy?" Dark pursued the matter a bit further sensing the faërie was withholding information. There was a long moment of silence.

"Dark...Mephisto, it's just that Faërie law prohibits..." Teigue's usually steady voice shook as he tried to interpose a quiet explanation to his young friend's question.

"Teigue!" the cranky old conjurer interrupted quickly.

"All right...all right!" he glowered fiercely at the angry mystic before continuing. "You don't need to shout; I'm not deaf you know. Now in the beginning of time, when the world of mortals and spirits had not yet grown asunder..."

"Oh do get on with it man!" Mephisto shouted angrily causing Dark to give him a warning nudge.

The winged woodland creature tried to say something unkind in return, but Dark, once again, moved quickly in front of the pair before speaking himself.

"Do continue, Teigue."

He stood close to his exhausted grandfather, glancing at him every so often in warning, making sure he did not interrupt again.

"Yes, of course, Dark anything for you," Teigue continued without changing his tone of voice, glancing slyly at the now seated Mage. "Well, after these earliest days, as country villages swelled into towns and they had risen to great cities that began to dot the landscapes, did humans begin to domesticate their world. Then, during the days when the land held many Kingdoms, came newly self-proclaimed Kings claiming both land and title, causing the natural world of Faërie to shrink and with its inevitable decline, the powers of its spirit denizens faded and shrank from the clamor of a burgeoning humanity. So they retreated into the remaining tatters of the wilderness, then shed their expansive ways and became as elusive as shadows. During this time, both Faëries and mortals, though separated, were still bound in a web of needs and wanted desires and given the thinly veiled disorder of the world, it was not surprising that the ungovernable realm of Faërie remained powerful and intrusive. It was then that the High King of the Tuatha Dé Danann reached out to these human lords in bold defiance of their alien nature. A golden gift was bestowed upon each ruling mortal monarch on Eorth, a magic talisman that held within its metal shell a dark secret, an even darker purpose. The term Dagda did not refer to the Faërie King's virtue, but instead only legends of gluttony and savagery clustered around him. It meant that he was the most powerful among that race of powerful faëries and in his heart he felt no love for these ancestors of the Gaels, these mortal invaders who conquered and now ruled his land."

"So again I ask, what's inside?" Dark asked quietly.

"This splendid object charged with magic holds within its golden confines a diminutive creature, a familiar to the court of the High King," the faërie continued. "Caught and imprisoned by powerful enchantments and ancient primordial forces was the inner umbra of a Faërie's shadow."

"You mean to tell me there is a little Faërie trapped inside this thing?" came the lean assassin's curt question.

Both Teigue and his grandfather shook their heads no.

"I am familiar with this part, however," Mephisto interrupted quickly. "As long as you hold a faërie, you can command its shadow, but you must imprison the mythical being in a glass casket made from the creatures own tears. A further sacrifice must be made to appease the High King of the Tuatha Dé Danann; the cutting off or removal of one's own body part to be made as a form of penance or apology."

Dark cocked his head slightly as if considering the implications, staring back at the seated sorcerer incredulously.

"Your grandfather is quite correct I'm afraid," Teigue turned back to Dark. "In three day's time, upon receiving these precious gifts of regalia, the human Kings who supplanted the Dagda as ruler of the Eorth would soon have a small shadowy spy hidden amongst them. These tiny vessels of enchantment became the eyes and ears for the Ruler of the Seelie Court, showing the same malice toward humankind that would be displayed by their master."

"Three days...with only two remaining," the assassin flushed. The anger and frustration he had held inside was working its way to the forefront. "Just tell me what I need to do so I can be done with this. And might I remind you, I do not have three days."

"You must break the curse that has its shadow trapped in the service of Elven magic," Teigue replied. "But beware, no mortal can predict or control these beings of the first world; their spells were charged with formed patterning that have to be worked through before the grip of magic is released."

Dark waited a moment for the tiny woodland historian to continue. He did not. Instead, the faërie simply stood there staring curiously at the gold Orb.

"Let me finish the rest for our little preoccupied friend here," Mephisto broke in, leaning forward. "These challenges issued by the old world were, in fact, tests of human character, actions that averted or undid the enchantment. And some of these trials placed mortals in terrible jeopardy, meant to test the most basic of human virtues in their perilous age... courage, character and honor. In most cases, these challenges were usually individual affairs, sometimes taking place on small farms or in isolated villages or hills that lay among the humble folk of the world."

"Sometimes?" Dark responded with frustration. "Then this place could be anywhere."

"Not anywhere..." Mephisto bent forward to open the pages of the book the small faërie was standing on, quickly picking up the Emissary to the Faërie King and gently placing him on his shoulder. The iron gall ink used in this particular manuscript had turned brown with age, especially after it had been sitting around for a few centuries. The script was of an ancient style of handwriting, the parchment had stretched and buckled with parts of the paragraphs faded, but the words were clear enough to read.

"Deep within a regal vessel of might that rides upon a sea as bright as sunlight. Trapped and sealed and bound quite tight, hidden under a bold starry night lay your heavenly guiding light. Set on the Isle of the Ancient, the old, the just and the right, shall you meet your unfortunate plight."

Within moments of reading the antiquated passage, Mephisto lowered himself back into his chair, studied the book for a moment longer, then wordlessly closed it. The tired old magus rose once more and reached out to extinguish the candles on the long reading table, briefly hesitating for a second, then suddenly his weary eyes lit up. The wise wizard quickly scooped up the Sovereign's Orb and with a steady hand delicately placed the golden globe warily above the candles flickering flame. Instantly the round regal sphere rose a few feet into the air and the wide eyed trio were treated to a visual extravaganza as a stunning light show brought the area to life.

The walls became a spectacular canvas of light, bathed in a changing display of brilliant optics that transformed the library into a kaleidoscope of colors. A projection of stars illuminated the coffered ceiling, creating a perfect illusion of an incredible night sky. Than a brilliant flash erupted from the candles flickering flame and from this flash appeared an island landscape of about forty shades of green consisting of blue lakes, canals and winding rivers. Sandy beaches fringed the island's pure shores with rugged mountain ranges that dominated the skyline. Atop the Orb, the gemstone encrusted cross began to faintly glow, the power locked within flared up immediately flooding the area with a dazzling blue light. Within seconds the brilliant light of the crucifix streaked outward across the rolling hills of the pleasant green land until it came to rest in the center of the island.

"This is a map of Ireland," Mephisto exclaimed assuredly. "And if I'm not mistaken, the spot where the cross has come to rest upon is known as the Mountains of Conmaicne Rein in Connachta, and that is where you need to go."

Dark grinned in agreement and clapped his grandfather on the shoulder, feeling a measure of gratitude and relief. In the next moment, the brightly shining stars and magically made island disappeared and were gone as the impatient assassin quickly removed the gold Orb from its lofty perch and placed it once again back inside the large leather pouch.

"Oh, I almost forgot the reason why I'm here," Teigue exclaimed finally. He rose, then quickly flew over to the forgotten case and opened it without hesitation. "A gift from the High King of the Faërie to help aid you in your quest."

Dark stared with child-like eyes and saw a pair of marvelously crafted matching daggers that gleamed with a bright silvery sheen. The shimmering blades were made from faërie steel that had been chemically silvered and an inscribed moon glyph that glowed with a soft white light. The hilt was ivory inlaid with more silver wrapped in black silk and capped with a crescent moon made from a single cut blue sapphire. The wide-eyed assassin studied the enchanted artifacts carefully for a time, then lifted the twin set of shining weapons and examined them further. He noted both the light weight and perfect balance of both blades before carefully replacing them back into their wooden case.

"They're beautiful Teigue," Dark declared thoughtfully. "You must thank His Highness for this most splendid gift."

"Of course," Teigue assured him. "I will give him your kindest regards and most gracious appreciation for this wonderful present."

"Splendid," his grandfather burst out, a hint of satisfaction in his voice that elicited excitement. "We've solved the riddle of the Sovereign's Orb and you have a new weapon to aid you in your battle against the Lycans. I suggest we all get a good meal into our bellies before Dark travels to Ireland. I am feeling quite famished."

They stepped out of the dimly lit library and made their way across the large marble hallway floor to the large dining hall that held a table laden with enough food for a small army. Each one ate until their bellies were full and their appetites satisfied. Teigue quickly related a few short stories about the Land of Faërie and warned Dark about consuming any faërie food or drink. He gave an example and told that the fruit from an apple tree was of such vast power that any mortal who ate it would never hunger again, but would always be drawn to the Land of Faërie. He also warned that when a day passed in his realm, though it be but just a day, a full year would have passed in the mortal world, so again he was reminded of the quest he was about to undertake.

When they had finished, they made their way outside where it was still raining and a storm approached from the south, its dark skies were heavy and laden. Dark led Mephisto and the tiny faërie to the stable paddocks where *Alba*, his magical flying vessel, lay resting quietly. The young half-elf stood silently before the large *Albatross*, then lifted his hand and stroked her satin neck slowly, gently, before bending forward to whisper into the giant bird's ear. With a final word, he swung upon the enchanted beast's back, his tall form wrapped in a black robe, his cowled head bent slightly against the steadily rising wind.

"I think it wise that you take our little friend here along with you," the tall mage ventured after a moment, pulling his own cloak closer about him. "I think we may have finally found a use for him. He can speak in the ancient language of Faërie." He stopped abruptly and faced his grandson. "You watch yourself and keep an eye on trouble there, you know what he can be like."

"I'll be careful Grandfather, but I don't think there is much to worry about," Dark replied jokingly, with a quick glance towards Teigue. "I've got back up with me this time."

They said their goodbyes quickly, their faces exchanged uneasy glances, then Teigue and he were riding away and it was not long before they were out of sight of Dark Manor. They sailed with speed, seeing little on the limitless and rolling great sea except for the occasional pod of bottlenose dolphins and the flash of leaping fish. From time to time they heard the blowing of the whales and slapping of the water's surface with their tail stock. Then there came a space of a few hours that they made no landfall at all and traveled in a thick cloud of mist that was broken only occasionally by streaks of pale and watery reflected sunlight.

Soon after they spied in the distance a thick woodland covered coastline fringed with huge stretches of golden sand. The *Albatross* steered for it, spread her giant wings and slid quietly into an estuary of bluish-green water so clear that the travelers could see the silver sands at the bottom and the darting scarlet salmon that swam there. The shores on either side were fringed with the greenest of trees Dark had ever seen and from their shadowed midst poured the carols and festive songs from unknown birds. Within seconds *Alba* took to the sky again, this time passing over several small shires and townships as well as high castle walls and long farm fences until the mountain of Conmaicne Rein loomed ominously before them.

The *Albatross* glided softly across a large body of water and within seconds grated onto a small sandy beach, her massive wings now at her side. The unlikely pair were at the edge of a wide loch that pierced the shore of a thick harsh pine covered country. "So my little faërie friend," Dark finally spoke. "Where do we go from here?"

"Well...we need to start looking for signs of faërie life in the forest," Teigue said finally, after a quick survey around him. "We are looking for a circle formed on the ground by mushrooms, or one formed by bent stalks of grass. These are Faërie Rings, each one marks the boundaries between our worlds. No more than a trembling leaf or a faint glow near or on the ground might betray the presence of my tiny cousins."

"I just hope we're in the right place," Dark paused to observe the crimson path of the slowly setting sun. "We don't have much time left."

Just as the sun touched the mountains of Conmaicne Rein near the loch, the waters began to churn, and in a shower of glittering spray, an armored knight, riding a white charger, burst through the surface. Trailing behind him was a ghostly crowd of children and maidens who danced to the haunting music of ringing silver bells. They followed the warrior across the water until finally disappearing with him into the mist that surrounded the lake.

"Yeah, I'm pretty sure this is the right place," the little faërie nodded his head wonderingly.

The air was crisp and cool as the small company set off into the foreboding forest. They headed north, pursuing narrow paths guided only by his small companion who followed trails and signs only a true faërie could see. The forest was so uncharted, so crowded with bodiless voices and unknown beings that the Irish gave the place the name of Cunnartach or Perilous.

As Dark wandered under the dark canopy of evergreens, he was startled when the waning day seemed to brighten suddenly. In the next instance, the landscape was transformed. The skyline of crags and ridges, as well as the rough highland was still familiar, but the mountains and meadows seemed distant and ghostly as if a heavy mist had somehow descended. Just then a busy twittering filled the air around them as if a flock of finches had settled in the trees ahead. Both paused and listened intensely until finally the singing grew into intelligible voices that somehow Dark began to understand. His features quickly became grim.

"They are warning us," Teigue smiled gravely at his half-elven companion.

"I know," the black-garbed assassin spoke quietly. "Let's just keep moving."

When the pair finally cleared the woods on that chilly afternoon, they halted almost immediately. Before them a river ran through a deep ravine. Near its opposite bank stood a magnificent island castle bristling with black towers. A long stone causeway bridged the cold water to the fortress and walled on either side were rows of blood-encrusted pikes which pierced the shredded flesh of the necks from a score of helmeted heads. These were the remains of knights who once had dared enter this place before. Standing at its center, braced on widespread feet was the sentinel of the causeway, a giant of a man, armored in black plate-mail with a surcoat stained scarlet.

"None shall pass!" the strange knight's grated voice howled through the cold air and echoed in Dark's ears.

"Wait for me here," the young assassin spoke with urgent purpose as he strode towards the black knight, his shadow sword quickly forming in his gauntleted hand.

He was met with a roar, and within seconds the two combatants were locked in a battle to the death. They lunged and feinted and swayed on the stone bridge each grunting and cursing amid the clang of sword on sword. Again and again they would collide and fall apart lurching toward each other over and over, their great swords scything in the cold air about them.

The giant guardian was much bigger than any knight the Elven assassin had ever encountered before. He stood on two large tree trunk-like legs, more than 10 feet tall, his huge body covered head to toe in long barbed spikes. His face was covered by an intimidating great helm depicting the devil with gold gilt eyepieces and a pair of large ram horns that extended from either side. He cautiously stalked the new intruder, both gigantic hands securely grasping a massive great sword with a broad black blade with two lethal sharpened edges. He stood for a time, his tall form black against the stone rampart, poised to defend himself. Several times the giant sentinel gestured tauntingly for his undersized assailant to approach but was given only silence followed by a wicked smile.

Finally, Dark flung his black cloak aside and came forward. He closed the distance between him and the sizeable combatant until there was no more than a few feet separating them. Quickly, he began to reach into the vast Plane of Shadows and drew forth a dark conjuration. With a grin he began to draw the supernatural umbra into himself.

A shifting, whirling field of semi-solid shadows and tiny rifts in the air began to rise about him. They wavered and shifted eerily, partially obscuring his lean form in a faint caul of black membrane. Suddenly the crisp air exploded with sharp shadowy tendrils that sliced through the mammoth man of steel like blades.

The titanic knight staggered backward, seemingly stunned by the sight of his own blood as it poured forth through gaping holes in his armor. Taking advantage of the sentry's momentary incapacitation, Dark willed his own demonic shadow to stretch forward until it reached behind the wounded watchman. Within the blink of an eye he fell into his own shadow where he stood, and instantly rose from it at the other end. At last, with a gurgling scream, the custodian of the stone causeway fell silent. The assassin stood victorious over his lifeless body, while at his back the fortress gate swung open letting out a stream of blinding golden light.

In its arch was framed a garden in full bloom, where trees flowered and birds sang, even though the year was dying and in the Perilous Forest the leaves were dry and brown. The blackened gate swung loose on its hinges as both Dark and his faërie companion moved forward through the gate. An empty cobbled street stretched out before them. Crumbling houses lined both sides, huddled close against the city walls. Aged doors stood wide open as warped, broken shutters banged loudly in the wind. At the end of the street, a vast palace stretched high and pale into the gloom of the gathering dusk.

An unsettled voice hailed him from on high as both he and Teigue looked wearily up. Deep darkened windows lined the palace wall above their heads. Occupying each embrasure, a torchbearer stood silent. These foreboding creatures wore black but the dim and flaring lights they bore revealed skull-like faces and their empty, burning eyes. They sang songs of death and called for Dark and Teigue to join them. It was the tiny faërie who cursed them and pushed them on until he found a way that led into the palace hall.

There a new enemy awaited them, standing huge and silent in the shadows. He had a man's shape, yet Dark knew this was no man. Light from another world glittered in his darting black eyes. Gathering in his will, the confident assassin crafted the cold ink-blackened shadow blade and shouted his challenge. The creature gave no answer, nor did it move. Just then a battle axe, whirling in the air, sailed toward the young half-elf, its sharp edge bit deep into his armored shoulder, causing streaks of blood to ooze from the gaping slit. He paused momentarily, pulled the axe from his wounded shoulder, and smiled grimly at the little frightened faërie.

A second axe followed, then a third, fourth and finally a fifth. They circled hovering around Dark's head, slicing viciously toward his horned helmet and swooping down upon his sword arm. For a brief moment there was silence once more. Without making a sound Dark stood still in the Palace hall trying vainly to stem the blood flow from his slashed shoulder. Then he heard the sharp sound of voices high up above him in the dimly lit windows of the hall, the ghostly torchbearers now facing the interior, gazed down grinning with deathly grins.

"Time to end this sorcerer!" Demon Raider whispered harshly, the shadow sword still tightly clenched in his hand.

The voices grew louder now, seemingly coming from more than one direction. Swiftly, wordlessly, and aided by magic, the black-garbed assassin dashed forward and thrust his black blade into the sorcerer's chest. All too easily the man had vanished into hushed darkness. Released from command, the hovering axes fell harmlessly to the paving stones of the hall. Then the shadows gathered themselves into a dark shape, and an armored figure, mounted on a horse that spat gouts of fire, loomed tall over Dark.

"That's no sorcerer!" Teigue's words died into the darkness as the creature's piercing stare burned right through his frightened little heart.

Dark began moving toward the perimeter of the grand hall, his weapon held ready as a cold sense of determination gripped him. Wicked eyes fastened on the young assassin, their depths drawing him closer to the reddish glow that burned within; an open invitation to death. With slow cautious steps, horse and rider began to make their way toward the motionless half-elf, the creatures breath rasping with every step. It drew closer and closer to the spell bound assassin. He wanted to call out or cast a spell, move away, do anything but stand still, yet the strange burning eyes held him transfixed. He was finished, he thought.

In a flash, Teigue flew in front of Dark, yanking him around with a slap to break the spell of the creature's terrible gaze. Dazed, Dark stumbled backward and fell clumsily on his boney posterior. The creature stopped several yards from the fallen assassin, its fiery glowing eyes hidden behind one raised disfigured clawed hand. Its breath sounded in slow, harsh grating rasps as its cruel eyes rested on the tiny faërie that stood between it and the dazed assassin.

"You are a fool to oppose me!" the voice hissed from deep within the creature's formless face. "Now half blood, you shall feel the wrath of my power!"

At last Dark rose to his feet, as silent as the shadows that surrounded him. With a dramatic sweep of one lean arm, he gave a single chilling command that sent the tiny faërie quickly towards an open staircase inside the main hall.

"The power that flows through your veins demon was born of the pit...and that power...is mine to command!"

As Dark performed the final gesture of the ancient spell, a surging power from deep within him began pushing out from all sides. His body exploded with a blinding radiance that bathed the area around them in a white aura that had a silver scale pattern overlay. A sickening stench exploded in the air. The assassin's shadowy assailant shrieked in excruciating pain. Then before the young half-elf's eyes, the demonic warrior and mount dwindled and sank to the palace floor until finally dissolving into a stinking, spreading pool of black liquid. At that very instant, the torchbearer's burning lights went out.

Trembling with fatigue, the black-garbed assassin, his breathing heavy, waited in the darkness for the next attack. But there was none. Just then, two points of light appeared in the shadows, growing brighter as they slowly approached. Dark soon found they were made by the jewel-like eyes of an enormous serpent that swayed back and forth towards him. Rising from the stone floor of the darkened hall, it enfolded him in its massive coils. Its eyes stared into his; its tongue flicked delicately towards his masked face. The viper locked his immense frame vice-like about the body of its struggling victim, his straining muscles slowly crushing the life away. Dark's held fast arms clutched vainly for something to break the hold that was killing him. For a moment it appeared to the wide-eyed faërie that his companion was surely doomed. He was torn by the desire to save his friend, but was held spell-bound by the titanic struggle between the two powerful beings. The two blackened figures were immobile in the center of the Palace hall, like statues frozen in place, displaying the great strain of their battle. The strange serpent's thick muscles heaved with exertion, its long fangs snapping in fury at its victims guarded throat only adding momentum to the assault. The young elven eyes grew heavy; he swayed and sank to his knees. Summoning one last desperate surge of power, he invoked the horrid words of the Nine Planes of Hell. Suddenly a small haze began to form at the corner of Dark's bulging eyes. A fiery glow wreathed around his enchanted armor leaving it with a deep red luster. The magical hell fire exploded outward in a furious burst, lighting the area around them in a reddish glow. His wet scaly foe let out a massive howl of pain, as not only did its skin catch fire, but the creature's cold blood quickly boiled in its veins. The once great beast was now nothing more than a pile of smoldering meat that lay lifeless on the Palace floor.

In that same instant, as Teigue lay frightened and shaken on the blackened stairway, with flames rising higher and higher around him, Dark was on his feet, shadow sword in hand. A moment later his black blade fell and severed in two the still flaming carcass of the huge viper. Holding one piece of the severed snake, the steel-eyes assassin gritted his gleaming teeth and reached deep inside. Then with a yank, the weary half-elf pulled out a tiny glass box shaped like a heart, and quickly smashed it with his clenched fist.

"You are Dark Solus, son of Elim and you have won me my freedom and proved your worth." Blackness pressed upon the young assassin's tired eyes, and he fell, absorbed into the darkness.

He awoke in sunlight, stiff and sore, but yet somehow still alive. He lay in the cockpit of the *Albatross*, whose wings were already stretched out ready for flight. There on the bank, Teigue stood and next to him a faërie woman who was regarding him thoughtfully. She seemed clothed with the dawn, for her drapery was the color of rose petals, and she was crowned with a cascade of fiery red hair. She met Dark's stare with green cat eyes, as shy as any woodland creature. And in that instant, the assassin knew his tiny companion was lost, for every thought of King and country had faded into that gaze.

"I am Gwendollyn, protector of this forest, or at least I was" she began speaking when she saw that her savior had finally awakened, "until that vile brute's evil magic stole my shadow and imprisoned me here. Your courage has sent his guardians from this world; your bravery has freed me. You will never be forgotten."

"Do you know who did this to you?" Dark voiced the question quickly.

Gwendollyn nodded her head emphatically. "He may have used my own shadow as a tool for espionage, but the same spell binds us both as one. His eyes and his ears were as my own. I shall provide you with a means to locate his lair and gain its entry, but before I give his name, I beg you once more for aid. My sister has also been trapped by this sorcery. Where her prison is, I know not. I ask now for a dark knight, such as yourself, to challenge this enemy and restore life to my imprisoned sister."

Gwendollyn stared at him wordlessly for only a moment, then sank her head onto Teigue's shoulder. Tears ran down from her eyes and she shut them tightly.

"Of course he will!" ventured his faërie companion abruptly.

Dark stared at him incredulously before bringing his attention back to the weeping faërie woman.

"You only have to tell me his name my lady."

Finally she spoke again, her words whispered. "Mordecai Richelieu."

Dark paused, he had heard that name once before a long time ago when he was only a child. "I will free your sister, and I swear the prison I place Richelieu into shall be eternal." He reseated himself. His face was expressionless as he stared back at the tiny faërie. "Teigue will see you home safely. Farewell and may next time we meet be under better circumstances."

But this time Gwendollyn did not answer him. Her hands lifted to her fatigued face and wiped away streaking tears. Her green eyes opened and settled on her new retainer. Without speaking a word he held out his arm to the faërie girl. She came quite willingly, as Teigue lifted her to the saddle of a tiny white stallion that was magically manifested with a word and a gesture. In a language Dark could not understand, the Emissary to the King whispered to the animal, which obediently turned. With her faërie companion pacing alongside, horse and rider threaded their way through the trees and into the sunny meadows that lay beyond.

VII

The cool autumn wind whipped around the body of the *Albatross* like a hushed whisper as it headed eastward. High above the enchanted craft three small songbirds rode the bright air and sang without ceasing. The first guide was blue with a crimson head, the second one scarlet with a head of green and the last had many colors whose head shone like gold. On the bank, stood Teigue and his new consort, the tiny, red haired faërie. They neither moved nor spoke, but they watched Dark steadily. When *Alba* finally reached open water and gathered speed, the weary assassin turned to look one last time. What he saw was a solid sheet of mist rising from the waters at the emerald island's shore and creeping swiftly up sandy banks, curling around the trees and rocks until at last it blanketed even the tops of the tallest oaks.

The mist eventually dispersed into coiling white ribbons that drifted on the surface of the sea; eventually even these ribbons disappeared. And where the island had been was now only empty water. The black winged sailing ship pushed high into the clouds, filled with a billowing faërie wind and sailed steadily eastward. Still above her, the three birds flashed and tumbled and sang their songs of serenity. In the boat, the Son of Solus lay sleeping. He woke only when the singing had ceased and the city had come within sight.

Within moments, under a spell of flight, Dark left the company of his magical ship, closed the eye of his Ring of Invisibility and set out to reconnoiter. Like a baby bird who had straggled way behind the flock, he quickly caught up to the small cluster of birds and soon was passing overhead the famous seaport of Duergar. The Colossus of Duergar, a hundred foot tall statue of a handsome god crowned with the shining aureole of the sun, stood ever vigilante over the entrance to the city's many harbors. Ships from all over the world were busy loading and unloading either passengers or precious cargo, making it the largest port on Eorth. His feathered guides took him to a quiet street nestled in the Business District at the northern edge of the city amid a cluster of similarly constructed buildings. This small private quarter of the free city was considered one of the most peaceful, with the surrounding homes belonging to successful adventurers, merchants and even some minor nobles. Its major feature was, of course, the shops and guildhalls for many of the hard-working craftsmen and women who dwelt here. Most of the customers recognize each other and the proprietor of any given establishment, is usually the owner. The street that surrounded the house was not particularly busy this day, but it was seldom empty either. The City Watch, while it did not have a great presence here, was not neglectful of its duty and could quickly be summoned if the need arose.

The houses here were not small by any means, but were crowded uncomfortably close together. There were hall marks on the front of the house of some of the trades people; an ornately carved balcony and railing for a woodcarver; a complex sweeping staircase for a carpenter and even an imposing facade of granite for the stonemason. The home he stood in front of was neither the smallest nor the largest of homes in the area. There was nothing to set this particular house apart from any of the others. Most people passing by wouldn't find the principal reason for its selection. The owner obviously did not want to call attention to himself.

It was a single two-story stone structure built for privacy and security, having no windows installed on the lower level. Each one was fitted with thick glass and a thin lattice of strong steel bars to keep out any unwanted visitors. The roofs to the house were steeply canted, made of thick cedar planks covered with black slate, making it extremely slippery and unstable, even for the most dexterous of burglars. Seemingly, the only visible entrance to the single abode was a tall gateway with a simple rounded arch standing about twenty feet high. Thick walls flanked either side of the arch and a well constructed wrought-iron gate stood fastened with a complex series of locks and hidden levers. On the courtyard side were two heavily reinforced doors, more than likely barred from the inside. A bell pull was placed to the right of the gate allowing callers to announce their presence to the occupants inside.

The song birds, no longer silent, now fluttered and flashed around the bell pull, as each one began pecking out a magical ring with the skill of a trained percussionist. Suddenly their gentle tapping ceased and the birds no longer rapping on the bell took flight, becoming three bright specks in the sky and headed for home. The last of the sounding notes acted like a key opening up lock after lock in procession like falling dominos. Then, the gate opened slightly, followed by the reinforced wooden doors that also opened up to the inner courtyard.

He moved quickly, closing both the iron gate and thick doors behind him. The walls surrounding the courtyard were quite high, again securing privacy for the owner. The sweet smelling area had a cobblestone pavement that was slick with wet leaves and mushy fruit from a row of apple trees that ran down the inner court's left side. A small stone building sat back in the far corner of the northern wall next to a lush garden of fresh flowers, herbs and vegetables. Standing majestically in the center of the grounds, surrounded by a ring of ornamental shrubs, was a huge bronze statue of a roaring lion.

Dark moved as silent as a shadow, making his way across a short flight of stone steps that led up to the front door. Suddenly, and quite unexpectedly, a rather large cat made from a clear smooth glass, its tail flicking leisurely from side to side, sat still in the yard, alert and unblinking. He stared at it. As if divining the young half-elf's own thoughts, the clear cat arose and sauntered casually toward him, stopping just out of arm's reach. From the reflective whiskered triangle of its face, a soft and soothing voice spoke clearly.

"Who are you?" it said. "And what are you doing here?"

The invisible assassin was too taken aback to reply, and for a brief while he could not. The glass cat seemed to feel no need to continue, so it sat back on its haunches, cool eyes gleaming in the afternoon sun. It closed its feline mouth in that ever perpetual prim yet eerily haunting smile, and said no more.

Dark stared back at him wordlessly, his hand toying idly with the Ring of Invisibility, pulling at it, twisting it. Finally he opened the eye and its magic suddenly ceased to be and he was visible again. "How is it that you are able to see me, when others can not?"

The cat's response was a look of infinite boredom. It sat and said nothing.

"I am Giacomo," he paused, glancing about restlessly before continuing with a slight bow. "Jester to Kings and King of Jesters."

"Why didn't you say so in the first place," the feline familiar answered. "Follow me if you please. I will take you to my master." Without another word, the large tom dropped to all fours and loped away toward the front entrance, magically disappearing through the high, covered door of the house.

Somewhat to his own surprise and impelled by this curious cat, the disguised Son of Solus did exactly what the furless feline asked. Though seemingly unoccupied when he first entered, the home was fully furnished and showed signs as if someone had been living here recently. The glass cat did not offer to explain what had become of the owner, nor was he going too. He simply entered the household as if it were his very own, moving through the darkness of the living room to a flight of stairs that led to the second level.

"Such a fine stately home for one such as yourself," he asked his question from behind a beautifully detailed black and gold jester's mask.

"Ah well...we have many such homes," said the cat, then gestured up the stairs. "My master awaits."

The transparent cat moved silently up the wooden stairwell and Dark fell into step directly behind him, pausing only briefly to read a thick mat embroidered with the words 'Welcome to the Hallow's End'. He stepped cautiously onto the upper landing and peered into a low lit room beyond. The disguised assassin quickly glanced in several directions for any sign of hidden sentries or possible surprises, but the hallway showed nothing unusual and the animated figurine motioned him ahead.

Reluctantly he was led into a large circular room of the two-story brick home, his masked face lowered in grim determination. Through the latticework of a large oriel window, Dark could see the garden and statue that decorated the grounds of the Hallow's End and the sunlight fading in the cooling afternoon as evening approached. The cat now squatted on its haunches by a small lighted fireplace, as it began to groom its transparent tail of spun glass with a rasping tongue. The flickering flame cast a dim orange glow over the room, causing long shadows to dance along the plain white walls. An elaborate oriental rug covered most of the stone floor, and sitting next to the fireplace was an overstuffed sofa. A magnificent round table stood in the center of the chamber, with several high-backed chairs surrounding it. Among the items on display gracing the table were freshly cut flowers, presumably from the garden outside and a dimly glowing sphere with magical lights dancing within, grasped by a demonic looking hand carved in stone. What was even more curious than the latter, was a glass container filled with a clear liquid that seemed to be preserving two living eyes that quickly swung to look in Dark's direction.

"I must say I am quite surprised to see you here so early... Master Giacomo," the disembodied voice eerily sounded out from behind one of the high-backed chairs. "We weren't expecting you so soon."

"I'm surprised you can see anything at all," Dark's own voice sounded steadily back.

"I spied you the instant you first entered the Hallow's End, or rather my fragile looking friend here did. I see you've already met the Marquis de Carabas."

The fire crackled, the wind blew outside; the cat, its glass paws tucked snugly up under its transparent body, purred and when his master spoke, he flicked an ear to him. The cat sank into a deep sleep and spoke no more.

"Come, please have a seat, we have much to discuss."

The stranger quickly replaced his eyes into their empty sockets, then stood up courteously, towering over the disguised assassin as he came up to him. There was a moment of awkward silence as they faced one another for the first time. The stranger stood well over seven feet tall with darkly handsome features, framed by long black hair that fell well below shoulder length. He had deep set eyes, which showed only as black slits in the shadows beneath a pair of heavy brows. Two small horns protruded ominously from his forehead; his skin was a shiny pale red, but slightly pointed ears and yellow fangs marked him as some sort of a demon. Swathed in regal finery, he seemed dangerously charming and he spoke with such eloquence and grandeur that Dark thought him a devil, not a demon. What was most striking to the young imposter was his digits. He had six steely fingers on each hand and his legs ended in cloven hooves.

"My name is Mordecai Armand Richelieu, but you may call me Mordecai," he announced quickly, extending his hand with a powerful grip, then nodded to the jester. "Please have a seat."

His skin was cold to the touch and felt like metal and he smiled with what Dark could swear was a mocking grin. He moved slowly past the demonic man to a vacant chair where he seated himself, his keen elven eyes still on the stranger. The dark man beamed with pleasure and nodded in satisfaction to the seated assassin as he signaled for a serving cart filled with assorted alcohol that moved forward unmanned.

For the most part he sat in silence as the conversation between he and the stranger lengthened from polite pleasantries to a more intimate discussion on the function of the Hallow's End as a sort of safe house and contact point between he and the Guild. They then moved to a more whispered and more intimate discussion of the people and happenings of the city. Dark found out quickly enough that this employee of the Assassin's Guild was actually quite subtly trying to draw out information on the masked entertainer.

"If we're done with the formalities," he broke in quietly, "I really would like to get started."

The dark face of Mordecai nodded as that familiar mocking smile crossed his red lips fleetingly.

"Of course Giacomo, of course, though I am not surprised that you would be so eager to begin. You see I know who you are; indeed, I know you very well."

Dark froze and was so dumbfounded at the demonic man's reply that he was unable to respond and sat staring at the dark stranger. Mordecai raised a clawed hand to his chin to stroke a small triangular beard, staring silently at the masked man who waited uneasily for him to continue. There was a long moment of stunned silence, with his heart beating rapidly, as the disguised assassin could only stare in speechless amazement. Dark's open mouth reluctantly began framing the inevitable question, when the stranger finally uttered a deep loud chuckle that caught him quite by surprise.

"You see, you're exactly like me, no time for any frivolous chit chat, just straight to the point. I like that; you'll do well in this organization, very well indeed."

Mordecai loudly snapped his steely fingers twice and instantly the slumbering cat, now wide awake, bounded up and out of the room and quickly down the stairs. Within moments, the glass feline reappeared; it trotted in, its tail erect and clear eyes bright with interest. The strange familiar carried in its maw a rolled up parchment which it set beside the cloaked jester. Then it shook itself and finally slid over to sleep upon the sill of the large window.

"This is the first of three tasks you must complete if you wish to enter into the service of the Assassin's Guild of Duergar." The dark face turned towards him and a slight smile played across the strange man's devilish features.

Dark edged his chair closer to the table and leaned forward to take a closer examination of the rolled up parchment. Upon opening the scroll he knew immediately what they were. These were elaborately decorated vellum documents offering numerous images and outlining in detail all the personal data associated for a targeted assassination.

"His name is Cui Tie Q'ill, or Q for short." He settled back in his chair, easing his tall frame away from the table, his large arms slipped silently down into his lap. All the while his dark eyes stayed locked on those of the jester's. "He is known in the underworld as a debt collector. His exploits in this field excel all others, and it is said there is no debt he cannot collect. At a moment's notice, if so ordered, he would be ready to liquidate even someone close to him without a second thought. Always faithful to his mission..."

"Until now," Dark grumbled, glancing casually towards the door way of the room.

Mordecai paused, and let the remark pass, his fiendish face lifted slightly. "We have used every means available to us to find this man, from our vast web of known contacts and costly bribes, to location spells, all to obtain the whereabouts of this collector, but to no avail. In your hands is all the intelligence my agents have; his last known location, his most frequented hangouts, his habits, his friends and even any accomplices Q may be known to have."

"What did this man do that would make the Guild so desperate for his demise?" the seated assassin interjected suddenly.

"He was sent to collect a coin cast that was stolen from the Royal Mint of Duergar." The strange man's voice turned hard. "It has been well over a fortnight since he was last seen. I suspect he is either dead and therefore the cast may very well be lost or, perish the thought, stolen once again. The last and more probable solution is our friend has stolen the coin cast for himself and is awaiting such a time as to broker a deal on the open market for the valuable item."

"And now you want me to find this man that you yourselves cannot find, eliminate him and bring that which he has stolen back to you." Dark followed quickly. "Anything else?"

Mordecai's face seemed to close in about itself, becoming dark and secretive. "There is something you need to be very much aware of," he leaned forward, his dark visage suddenly expressionless in the firelight, creased in black shadows. "As I am quite sure you are well aware, beneath the underbelly of this monolithic empire lies a collection of extremely powerful and organized families from the rich and elite of the upper class. Altogether thirty-three families make up this syndicate of crime. Each family has been given a specific region within the empire to both work in and control. A single family, in truth, usually dominates each one of these empires, but being the Head Family is no guarantee you stay there forever."

Mordecai sat slowly back into the high backed chair, his dark expression did not change. "In this world all deaths are seen as opportunities and powerful men have rivals, and these rivals tend to send killers, such as yourself, to remove these men. So over the years, the blood being spilled between the families has transformed from business and survival to an all out war. A secret battle now rages, fought in quiet shops, backend streets, darkened alleys and even lonely roads leading to the city. It is called The Whispered War. Most of the good folk and the like, know nothing of it. The battles between families are usually small and over quickly."

"What about the bodies?" a touch of impatience sounded in the jester's voice, his head lifted sharply.

The tall man cocked his horned head reflectively. "The bodies, if ever found at all, are usually just written off as random murders, a dispute between feuding thieves, an unfortunate accident, or mere banditry. And of course, the other Guilds of the city all watch with great interest. For whoever has the ear and attention of the Sovereign at any time will have an unfair advantage and much to say about what will happen in this clandestine War."

"Who or what is the Sovereign?" Dark asked quickly, remembering vaguely hearing about such a person.

He looked at the disguised assassin sharply. "Even though most of the families remain independent, they are all bound to, and must yield to a higher authority. And that power lies in the hands of the Council of Thirteen. At the head of this black council sits the Sovereign. This Grand Master of Assassins has sole uncontested authority among this syndicate of crime. If the Sovereign decrees something shall be, then believe me it shall be."

"You said most families?" Dark interrupted suddenly, his gaze was steady, as his eyes met the dark man's own.

"Tired of their position in the hierarchy of the organization, some of the families decided to acquire some outside help in their quest to rise within the ranks." He trailed off momentarily, his eyes narrowed as he stared down into the fire. Then he looked suddenly back at Dark. "This is when the Döckálfar or Dark Elves entered the city in secret. Their mysterious presence brought with them the Spider Plague, a horrific pestilence of evil that was used against members of the ruling families. There were lumps that formed on the victim's body within a day or two. They would soon turn black, split open and begin to ooze puss and blood. It was possible to recover if found in time, but more than likely death would come quickly. The sickness would befall when the sores, filled with tiny spider eggs, would hatch. This species of arachnids would consume their already dead prey. The victims would usually be found in the morning among thousands of baby spiders who were busily spinning new webs around the drying bones of the infected carcass. Today, they are a dangerous tool to be used in the political games of the nobility, and those who have had dealings with the Drow wisely tend to keep their mouths shut."

"Thanks for the history lesson..."

Mordecai cut in quickly, the tone of his voice was sharp, almost angry as he leaned forward once more. "The lesson here is not to get involved with the Whispered War at all, for once you do, you become part of it...forever."

Dark sat silent, saying nothing, only waiting. There was a long uncomfortable silence as the two strong willed men faced each other. At last the dark man began again. "Anyway, if you complete this assignment successfully, you will be one step closer to joining the Assassin's Guild."

"And if I fail?" his head lifted slowly, almost methodically.

"Just see that you don't," Mordecai declared bluntly. "Any further questions?"

Dark studied him wordlessly for a moment, then shook his head.

"All right then, best of luck." The fiendish face managed a brief smile.

The black cloaked assassin rose wordlessly, his true expression hidden behind the jester mask's false facade. He walked away from the table several paces before abruptly stopping then slowly turned back again. The Son of Solus held his gaze steady. "I'm afraid your spy will no longer be of any use to you." His voice now became hard and insistent. "You see I have freed the faërie; neither her nor her shadow will ever serve you again. And Mordecai, I expect no more prying eyes because next time you will not see me coming...I promise you this."

Now it was the dark man's turn to be silent. Dark quickly turned away and made his way outside. At the curtained window stood Mordecai, his face turned dark like a concealing black fog, his eyes now seemed to glow red like a burning flame.

VIII

The afternoon was almost gone as the last of the sun's light faded into an intense orange and red glow that filled the surrounding sky. This unique atmospheric condition was created the moment the trailing edge of the sun's fiery disk disappeared below the western half of the horizon. Dusk soon followed the darkest stage of twilight, which at that point the sky became completely dark. Under the black canopy of nightfall, Dark moved with slow, mechanical steps, threading his way through a band of river men and passed unnoticed by the guards at the Cargo Gate and entered into the River Quarter.

This particular section of Duergar had a rhythm and pulse to it that seemed to increase when the sun went down. The area just seemed to come more alive when darkness would overtake the city. This most boisterous of districts, the first of what would be many stops this evening, was known as the Jetties, a sprawling collection of large, older houses shoved together and connected by a maze of dimly lit alleyways and dead-ends. Most of the business in this quarter centered around entertainment, so naturally it was a safe bet that rouges and scoundrels kept a sharp eye out for an easy target, willing to relieve a traveler of his heavy load of treasure. With its taverns, whorehouses, gambling dens and worse, the River Quarter at night was a shadowy land of flickering torches and blazing lamps. And whether it be day or night, it was always teeming with drunks and ruffians and pedestrians scurrying in the street as the loud shouts and laughter of revelers filled the night air.

Aided by the power of the eye that rested just above his head, he adopted the disguise of a common person; just a simple man in simple garb. With black hair and near olive skin, he dressed in dark woodland colors and hidden beneath his green hooded cloak, he carried the Gem of Location. Much like the Guild's efforts to find Q, Dark also found the magic of the powerful artifact was unable to locate the elusive debt collector, so the use of other means of finding this man must be implemented.

The dark detective moved past a motley crew of fishermen and local merchants who were still milling around their respective booths and stalls, yelling loudly at the last of the perspective customers. He witnessed beggars and street urchins wandering from person to person, their dirty hands held out asking for any crowns or scraps of food that could be spared. Ever so often, he would glance about and see the occasional outlander traveling aimlessly from place to place with the watchful eye of every unscrupulous person on him or her.

Hours quickly passed; the light from the street lamps began to diminish, their oil almost consumed as the dark hours were sliding towards morning. Now restless and hungry, the demonic assassin of the dark flitted through the shadows from tavern to inn and brothel to bordello in search of the elusive debt collector. In this commoner's disguise, he looked in every dusty corner bar and pub, every disreputable gathering hole and every dark and sinister backroom that was thick with shade in the infamous district. Alone on the cobblestone streets walked Dark, his footsteps gave no sound on the cold hard ground and his breath steamed white in the cool air. All was quiet. The road before him stretched out white as the winter moon was ending its long journey across the heavens. No one was around him, but before he could make a decision whether or not to return home, a song swelled from the rooftops and lingered hauntingly in the air. The lone assassin recognized the sound immediately. Those chilling noises were the tiny chorus hoots of the Pack, signaling its members to rally together for what he assumed would most likely be the start of a hunt. At the loud doleful cries, the young half-elf paused and froze where he stood.

For a long moment, for a single tempting heartbeat, he considered abandoning his quest and beginning his own hunt of the Halfling Guild, starting this night. Even as these seductive thoughts raced through his mind, a more sober voice advised him of only one conclusion. Reluctantly, and with great effort, he gathered himself and engaged the magic of his Ring of Invisibility. Retaliation against these dogs of dark alignment would have to wait for at least one more day.

The apprentice of the Silver Mage quickly began to concentrate and finished his spell in a whisper. The magic, now enhanced by his strong willed voice, gave its strength and potency and with that he uttered a final word of power, "Fly."

Light as a feather, the invisible assassin now soared high above the street signs, stone statues and church spires. He flew silent as a shadow through the city streets, where a moonlit landscape spread out silver before him. He flew swiftly, as swiftly as the wind, so that rooftops, tree branches and people all flashed by in streaking blurs. And among them, among the clattering of horse's hooves on cobblestone boulevards, he could still hear the frightening wail of the wolf's cry.

He slowed at last after several minutes of flying and found himself on the east side of town, near the main thoroughfare of Duergar. Still cloaked in invisibility, he arrived at his last stop for the evening, the Gentlemen's Noose. It was a dark little establishment that lay huddled near the oldest quarter of the city. A long barred window looked out into the street offering a great view of the foot traffic going by. The sign above the door displayed the illustration of a richly dressed man hung around the neck from the branch of a large green tree.

Possessed with every weapon of stealth and subterfuge, Dark was also formidably skilled in the grand art of illusion. The Eye of Dagda, still hovering above the assassin's head, appeared only briefly, glowing brightly like a burning star before fading into invisibility. What he created was a literal invention for his planned operation of deception. A magical mirage, a vague, translucent shadow of his body's form bearing an exact resemblance to its living predecessor, but filled with a life that was not its own. This exact duplicate twisted and undulated in response to the conjurer's silent commands and finally moved forward to carry out the elaborate pretence of being a real traveler.

In the wee hours, well after midnight, Dark made his way out of the courtyard and into the Gentlemen's Noose with his paranormal partner just out of sync with his own motions. Laughter echoed within the opulent house. Within seconds the door of the tiny inn opened and only Dark's projected illusion stepped quietly into view. He entered into a white-walled room; a great hearth at the end of the hall leaped to life with a roaring fire and around the walls, candle flames danced and glowed. The Gentlemen's Noose had a wide variety of clientele, ranging from local merchants and businessmen to cut throats and robbers.

The young magician's alter image stood before the innkeeper, a tall man clad in velvet and boots of Spanish leather. He smiled and greeted the stranger kindly, his voice when he spoke was one that somehow sounded familiar. "Allo govna," he said in a working class accent with a twinkle in his eyes.

"How can I help you?"

"It's been said that there are a number of dark dealings within the Gentlemen's Noose," the hushed voice was that of the invisible assassin, but it echoed from the mouth of the conjured image. "And that if anyone needed or required anything, that this was the place to find it, provided that they were willing to pay the right price."

The innkeeper paused and looked up at this strange apparition of a man, appraising the enchanted illusion curiously, his eyebrows were raised. Within seconds, Dark's unseen hand placed a small purse of gold coins in front of the man, which he quickly picked up and deposited into a strong box that he locked even quicker. "If you be looking for work, you've come to the right place," the tall man stated abruptly.

"Yeah, why is that?" retorted the magical manifestation.

"The people of Duergar are about to rebel," he stated simply.

"Go on," Dark responded dryly.

"There are two bidders for a man of your sorts," the innkeeper announced in a hushed voice, almost like a whisper. "Lord Kalifen, the soon to be crowned King and Fell Foehammer, the last legitimate heir to the throne of Duergar."

"What legitimate heir?" the assassin replied questioningly. "I thought the only true heir to the Kingdom of Duergar was Dwaric Duergar, son of the Dwarf King?"

"He is and always will be," the owner of the Gentlemen's Noose responded slowly, "but the people feel abandoned by him and Fell's father, Thoradin Foehammer who was King Duergar's closest advisor and last general of the Dwarven army. He stayed while the others dwarves left us to be ruled by a couple of power mad tyrants."

"I'm not here to join any war; my only need is information," Dark's twin mimicked his movements and it shook its head.

"Information, what sort of information?" he began again after a moment's silent thought.

"I'm looking for a man named CuiTie Q'ill," the invisible assassin stated simply. "This fugitive may also go by an adopted alias known as Q."

The velvet dressed owner paused, his association with the debt collector was given away when he slyly looked over to a man sitting next to the fireplace. "My apologies Govna, I've never heard of that man, but I'll keep me mince pies open for sure and you have me dickey bird on that. Now how bout a pig's ear, on the house of course."

"No thanks," the abrupt declaration came from the phantom lips of Dark's doppelganger. "I'll be back." Motioning a friendly wave to the innkeeper, the bewitched duplicate then made his way outside, a group of new patrons parted to let him pass through the front door and out across the street.

The tall owner of the small inn watched the illusionary image go without speaking another word, his eyes fixed on its departing silhouette until it was lost from sight. Then he turned to the strange man seated in the corner of the inn. As the ghostly form of Dark's doppelganger faded from existence, still invisible, he turned on his heel and made his way to a darkened area of the small establishment. He watched with black eyes, still clinging to the shadows for secrecy, as the large innkeeper moved quietly to a small table at the rear of the room and spoke in hushed conversation with the man seated there. The stranger was sitting quietly with his back to the rest of the bar, his face slightly bowed and turned away from Dark. After a few moments, a set of wide double doors near the serving area swung open and a husky, towering bald-headed man appeared from out of the darkness. He strangely wore a collection of thin chains and sharp hooks embedded through the skin around his thick neck.

"Q," the hulking man gestured for the stranger to come close. A quick smile of satisfaction crept over the lean countenance of the demonically disguised assassin. He had found his debt collector, and thought himself one step closer to fulfilling his quest for vengeance. CuiTie Q'ill took up his glass of spirits, offered a mock toast, placed it to his lips and drank, downing it with a smile, then set it down on a nearby table. With a slight chuckle, he strapped on his sheathed blade. The pair remained standing for a few moments longer as Q looked around a second time at the faces of the patrons of the Gentlemen's Noose. Without further comment, he moved quietly away and proceeded to the set of double doors and pushed through them to the room beyond.

Outside the inn the wind began to rise; a lone wolf howled once and the horses tethered to their posts stamped and whinnied. Just then, the door to the Noose blew loudly open. Some men turned quickly at the sound, and standing on the threshold was a slim, almost shadowy figure garbed in a loose-fitting cowl and cape. In the light of the moon, he was dark and forbidding, his facial features hidden beneath the depths of the charcoal gray cowl about his head. He surveyed four men seated just beyond him in the darkness, then closed the door and slowly walked over to them, smiling slightly beneath his cowl as he approached.

Black robed figures, their faces too were concealed in deep shadow, all were crowded around a circular wooden table plucking with cold hands at the leftover remains of what had been their dinner. These men were clumsy with laughter and flushed with drink.

Gazing carefully around, the invisible assassin studied them a moment with great care, trying to make out their faces, but his position gave him only brief glimpses of the men. He tried listening for a few minutes, but found it almost impossible to decipher what was being said over the noise of the crowded bar. Cautiously, his movements soundless, he moved slowly to where he might be able to make out what the group of dark figures were saying. Dark paused his progress abruptly, halting as he sank down into a crouch beside a vacant table.

In the sudden stillness he thought he heard an unfamiliar murmur from one of the hooded strangers, in a tongue he did not wish it to be in. He began to creep forward toward the source, and again he heard the low murmur, but this time he was certain. The variety of speech was Elvish in nature but different from the standard language. This was the dialect of the Döckálfar, and these men were Dark Elves. They were speaking with a fifth figure, the newcomer to the inn, his clothes clearly marking him as a woodsman.

The crouching assassin knew there was no time to ponder any further the mysterious meeting he was accidentally witnessing, but still he lingered a moment longer as one of the hooded elves brought forth a large item covered with a heavy cloak. There were several words exchanged, and Dark caught only snatches of the brief conversation, including something about payment in full. Then the silent assassin, still lurking in the darkness, saw something catch his keen elven eye. One of the stranger's legs escaped from beneath the long heavy cloak. What was revealed were tight-fitting breeches with the curve of her slender thigh and hip that drew Dark's eye despite himself. Dumbfounded, an astonished Son of Solus wiped away the weariness from his black eyes and stared. It was a woman! Why would a woman be speaking to a group of Drow?

Quickly crossing the small room in silent measured steps, and still lost in wondering thought, he dropped noiselessly just a few feet away from the group. He lay motionless as his ever alert eyes caught a dark, scarlet-cloaked figure moving slowly into view. The stealthy figure glanced quickly about the room and then turned his attention back to the unsuspecting woman.

The strange hooded female's outstretched gloved hand rested loosely on the large bundle. Then with lightning-like speed, the man in scarlet struck. The mysterious female figure was pulled backwards, her slender arm raised defensively, while her other hand securely held the unknown package. Her attacker reached up and quickly pulled back the cowl of her cloak to reveal that this was no ordinary woman. She was strikingly beautiful and that beauty seemed to weave a spell about the young, unable to be seen, assassin as he found her irresistibly seductive. He noted the telltale signs of her elven features immediately. Pencil-like eyebrows lay atop two pools of the bluest eyes deep with life. Light colored skin covered the finely formed features of her angular face, with just a hint of slightly pointed ears beneath long lush strands of blonde hair that fell past her shoulder and lower.

For a moment Dark gazed at her in a half-conscious trance-like state, then her angelic voice brought him back to his present situation and the grave danger that still lay before him.

"Get your filthy hands off me you damn, dirty Döckálfar." Her alluring face was emotionless, but there was undisguised hatred in the menacing tone of her voice that cut quick to the bone. Her sentence ended in a constricted gasp as the man in scarlet seized her roughly by the throat and began to slowly squeeze. He stared coldly back at her; she met his gaze with steadfast resolve, her own elven eyes furtive and filled with extreme repugnance for this race of vile creatures.

"What have we here?" the evil face stared menacingly at her, and a fury shot into his widening eyes. "Looks like my dessert..."

He was never able to finish. Only a slow mocking smile on the young female's face betrayed her intent. Before anyone could act, she wrested her lithe form free from her captor's iron grip and from an inner pocket of her cowled cloak she withdrew a dagger which she quickly put to use by impaling the scarlet garbed man in his upper thigh. The small dagger struck a second time into the shoulder of the cloaked figure as he clutched his new wound in sudden pain.

She quickly pushed aside the injured Dark Elf soldier and began running swiftly back in the direction of her escape, pulling frantically on the door to the Gentlemen's Noose. The lissome form of the female Elf finally pulled the door open and was fast slipping to freedom when one of the Dark Elves, now standing, held a slender knife dripping with black liquid and hurled it wildly at the fleeing woman. It struck the Elf's exposed shoulder deep to the bone causing a scream of pain to echo off the dark walls of the inn.

"After her you fools!" shrieked the maddened Drow commander, shoving the rigid form of one of his men. "And I want her alive."

Apparently cowed into obeying their commanding officer, the four cloaked Drow fighters sprang into action, and within seconds they were out the door followed by the scarlet man in step directly behind them. Dark watched the dark figures of the Elves move away from him in pursuit of the fleeing woman into a heavy morning fog, still undecided if he should intervene. There was no time to be sidetracked just to satisfy personal curiosity even if it meant saving a beautiful elven woman. The thought flashed through his impetuous mind, and in that instant the decision had already been made. Dark had to rescue her. Turning, the invisible assassin moved hurriedly over to the open doorway, pilfering a large shank of lamb along the way, a faint smile of satisfaction on his broad face, and disappeared into the darkness.

The female Elf felt the first drops of rain strike her face as she ran, with the thunder rumbling ominously overhead and the wind beginning to grow in force. Occasionally, she looked over her throbbing shoulder through the veiling clouds of thick fog for some sign of her pursuers, but she saw nothing. The girl raced at breakneck speed across the slick cobblestone streets, charging like a wild black mustang through the deep heavy haze. Large droplets of sweat began to flow down her face and ran into her blue eyes blinding her, forcing her to slow down. She paused momentarily to wipe away the perspiration mingled with rain. Abruptly she stopped, panting heavily, the poison that coursed eagerly through her veins slowly began to manifest itself.

Abruptly the four Drow henchmen appeared out of the misty murk behind her, their voices speaking in low whispered murmurs. For a moment there was nothing but the dark gray fog and the now steady rainfall. Then she watched a moment longer as the four shadowy figures moved closer, moving steadily toward her place of concealment. She clumsily threw off the cumbersome hunting cloak, already beginning to be soaked through by the downpour of rain. Hurriedly, fighting through the nauseating effects of the unknown toxicant, she withdrew the bright blade of her sword clear of its leather sheath.

The advancing Döckálfar were almost on top of her when her elven blade struck out of nowhere with a sharp hum, striking the exposed throat of one of the Drow henchmen. In a gurgling scream of pain, he dropped to his knees, clutching his throat in a futile attempt to stem the flow of blood. In that instance of shock and confusion, the elven woman launched a second assault, scoring a solid hit to the unarmored abdomen of a second member of this dark hunting party. He too clutched in fruitless vain, as he stumbled wildly away, crying out in a long loud piercing scream from the pain.

The female Elf forced herself to continue breathing in steadied, measured intervals, even though her heart was racing wildly. Then suddenly, the bent figure of the scarlet-cloaked male Elf slid noiselessly into view. When her attacker was only several feet away, his lean ashen hand slipped beneath his scarlet cloak and slowly emerged, gripping his own long, elven blade.

"Not this time whore," the male Drow growled menacingly. "You won't be lucky twice in one night."

The poison now raced through her slim body as her vision went blurry and she struggled to draw breath. Despite the ill effects, she managed a valiant smile but still sagged downward and kept on her feet only through sheer willpower. This time the scarlet dressed Drow did not pause and with a cat-like attack subdued the slumping girl, striking her sword hand in a stinging slap from his blade. Stepping quickly forward, he threw himself at the elven female, dropping his sword to the ground. He seized the front of her silk shirt, his cold dark eyes surveying the face of his captive. "Now I poke you with my dagger." The Dark Elf jerked her sharply, snapping her lean face close to his own.

Roughly he threw the injured girl into the arms of his remaining men and ordered them to take her to the ground. "Hold her down boys." He lay on top of the now unconscious Elf, his pants down around his ankles as he began tearing at her clothes piece by piece. "It's time for dessert."

Then a shadow fell over everything. The leader of this band of dark elven delinquents was so intent on having his dessert that he almost failed to notice the huge black horned shadow that seemed to rise up suddenly, as it seemed to detach itself from the deep hazy fog. The dark figure loomed up before them like a black, horrifying presence that threatened to swallow them whole. With a startled cry of fear, the Drow commander leapt to his feet, his leather pants still gathered about his ankles, his right hand gripping a long thin dagger.

For a long moment everything was silent. With black elven eyes he glanced about uneasily and watched as a wraith-like apparition appeared out of the mist, then disappeared into it again. Framed in the entry way of the dimly lit back alley stood a fiendish form that stared back at him. Tiny glints of red glimmered once in the thinning gray mist and vanished. A cloak the creature wore crumpled and sank emptily, falling to the damp floor in a pile. An instant later a cold commanding voice floated out of the darkness, its face still masked in shadow. "Now is that anyway to treat a lady?"

The strange voice stopped and the forbidding black form stood silently in the shadowed moonlight and slightly clearing haze. The leader of this group of Dark Elves could now see glowing red eyes following him as he edged closer to the unwanted intruder. Slowly the fading pale moonlight penetrated through the thinning fog and began to etch out the stranger's features in vague lines and obscure shadows.

"Piss off scum or die!" the Döckálfar shouted angrily, moving forward with cautious steps, his dark eyes catching a glimpse of what he thought was the stranger munching slowly on a rather large piece of cooked lamb.

"Well that's a small threat," a deep voice laughed mockingly. "That's a very small threat."

"Why you filthy human scum!" A savage rage welled up inside the scarlet clad Elf, his voice icy cold with anger.

Pulling up his pants, he quickly yelled orders to his men to stand ready and armed. Then suddenly the Drow commander lunged with terrible swiftness, his long cruel dagger trying vainly to stab at the shadowed interloper. Dark easily managed to evade the Döckálfar's initial lunges, then in the same instant, he brought the heavy piece of lamb and bone across the man's unprotected skull. Instantly the Dark Elf crumpled unconscious in a heap to the cold cobblestone floor. The demonic looking assassin, now visible, stared at the two remaining faces with mindless disregard, his lean fierce features fixed with a look of maligned intent. For a moment no one moved. Terrified, the dark faces of the Dark Elves could only stare blankly at the silent form that waited statue-like just a few feet away. The stalemate was over quickly as the courage of both of the Drows seemed to waver. Abruptly, they desperately charged down upon the demonic looking stranger, their swords held ready.

Dark met the rush with a ferocious counter assault that carried him into the very midst of his assailants. It was an uneven contest from the beginning as the two remaining elven men were silenced before they had even a chance to defend themselves. With a lightning-like assault, the exposed black flesh of their throats was cut away, and they too fell lifeless onto the muddied eorth. And for a moment, there was silence once more. Unmolested, Demon Raider passed quietly through the carnage, moving steadily toward the still form of the fallen female Elf. She was still alive, her shallow breathing was harsh and her eyelids twitched sporadically. Grimly Dark reached down and swept the limp form up onto one shoulder, and with his free arm he pulled the unconscious commander to his feet with superhuman effort.

The mist closed about them almost at once, then, in the blink of an eye, they all disappeared and the grizzly scene that was left behind faded into it.

IX

Haggard and worn, Dark stood in the entry of the manor house doors amid a rush of wind and rain. He moved down through the darkened room, his black armor glistening wetly in the dim light, trailing water onto the marble floor as he walked. He reached the castle foyer and there he halted as he heard the sound of running feet that echoed loudly from an empty corridor. Just then Baron came running in, excited to see his master's safe return. The monstrous beast welcomed his owner home with thundering glancing paws that scratched against his armor and eager whining followed by excessive growls and yelps.

"Baron, watch this one," he spoke commandingly as he forcefully threw down the Drow Captain to the ground with disgust. "If he moves…bite him."

The husky Chimera obediently obeyed and stood guardedly over its new black prey, all four beastly mouths, each one dripping with saliva, eagerly hoping to satisfy their early morning hunger.

Quickly Renfield, his faithful invisible man servant, arrived and made his presence known by ringing a small personal silver bell he kept in his pocket. Gently Dark laid his tiny consignment on the polished floor and stood quietly over the slim, blonde haired elven girl. Her hands and face were covered with welts and bruises, her soiled and torn clothing hanging damply from her limp body. Her ashen face lay against the cool marble tile as she still breathed in shallow gasps.

"Renfield, take her upstairs and tend to her wounds," he said finally keeping his voice low with an effort so as to not waken the rest of the household. "She's been poisoned, so you'll need the Cup of Wonders."

Hurriedly, the invisible chamberlain of Dark Manor rose, drawing up the elven girl's slender inert form in his arms. With slow steadied, almost mechanical steps, the chief male servant carefully climbed the ancient stairway, then moved beyond into a darkened corridor. Dark's grandfather arrived shortly thereafter, as he slipped down the stairs soundlessly. He was almost to the bottom when he saw Dark.

"I see you have finally brought a friend back to the house," the old wizard muttered curiously.

"Two actually," was his grandson's quick response. "The girl is upstairs; Renfield tends to her now."

"And what is this?" Mephisto urged a moment later, picking up the large bundle still wrapped in wolf skins.

"That's the reason he's still alive," the lean assassin spoke slowly.

Dark moved to his grandfather's side, as the Silver Mage untied the leather thong bindings and reached eagerly into the dark interior. He removed his hand and held a long bow shaped from a large block of darkly oiled and almost gleaming cutting of dense black wood. The dark wood was vibrant, as if somehow still alive. A grip wrapped in black dragon hide intricately covered the staff, providing its user with a firm grasp. Its narrow limbs were engraved with intricate runes of arcane power, the markings shifted and changed subtly. The tips of the weapon were made of magically hardened obsidian, set with a small ruby at either end and joined by a taut string made from a semi-solid black shadow that somehow allowed the wizard's fingers to pass through ghost-like.

"Do you know what this is?" Mephisto grinned at his grandson as Dark looked closely at the magical weapon.

"It's an Elven longbow," Dark spoke out suddenly.

"It's an Elven longbow," the ancient magus repeated mockingly. "This is not just any bow my boy, but the greatest Elven bow ever created, and quite possibly the greatest in all of antiquity."

Woodenly Dark reached for the ancient artifact, his fingers closing firmly around the intricate grip, a feeling of his Elven ancestry curiously welled up inside him. The black surface gleamed in the faint light with a deep luster, the bow's shaft flawless as if the legendary weapon had never been used in combat. It was unbelievably light, a slim perfectly balanced bow of extraordinary workmanship. He paused. Slowly, steadily, he began to hear voices whispering softly in his native Elven tongue. The whispers quickly became chanting angry omens, speaking a terrible vengeance on all Dark Elves it came near. Mechanically, and without hesitation, the assassin turned to face the still unconscious Drow. His grip tightened, his armed raised as the Elven archer directed his aim. He tried repeatedly to draw the string fully, but to no avail. Each attempt failed just as his grandfather's before him, with his fingers unable to catch hold of the semi-opaque fiber.

"Let's have that back shall we," Mephisto quickly reclaimed the Elven relic, his grandson's trance-like state faded as fast as it had come. "This is the long bow of the Black Fox, and those whispered words of blasphemy spitting vile curses into your ears were warnings that the Döckálfar are near."

Dark's grandfather glanced over and observed the little blackened form that lay idly on the marble floor of the castle. Then the old enchanter stepped forward menacingly and bent close to the Dark Elf's thin angular face.

"So who is our rat faced little friend here," the ancient magician rose slowly to his feet, turned and walked back to stand next to his grandson.

"I don't know," was Dark's quick response.

"And the girl?" his grandfather paused with the thought left hanging, then he turned and stared at his young apprentice. "Do you know who she is or what her involvement is with this treasured heirloom?"

"Again, I don't have an answer for you," he answered shortly. "Not yet anyway."

The demonic masked face turned toward him and a slight smile played across his lean monstrous features. He paused before speaking again. "Just why is this bow so important anyway?"

Mephistopheles smiled briefly at the question. "What do you know about the plight of the Black Fox?" His grandfather glanced down at him sharply, cocking one dark eyebrow in wonder.

"Well, if I remember correctly, he was an Elven archer of great notoriety and highly revered among the race of Elves," ventured Dark a moment later, then shook his head unable to recall any more of the legend.

"Well, that's more then I thought you would know," the ancient historian acknowledged. "But he was a she, and only one in a handful of elite archers in the ranks of the Elven army. She greatly excelled at her craft and soon became one of the finest archers in the world. One day she arrived home and found that Drow marauders had attacked her village and mercilessly slaughtered her entire family. With the slain body of her own child cradled in her arms, she made her way to stand in front of an altar amid the ruined temple of her Elven deity. She gently placed the dead body of her young daughter upon the religious platform, a sort of sacrificial offering to the gods. Then she swore an oath, sealed in blood, vowing an unceasing vengeance upon all of the dark skinned race of the Döckálfar, never resting until all of the Drow and their Spider Queen were expunged from the Eorth. Her wish for revenge was granted and to aid her in her crusade, she was given this divinely crafted weapon." The old historian paused and looked down upon the black bow with reverence. "Heartstriker is one of the two great relics wielded by the ancient Elven folk hero; the other being a quiver of black arrows, with their tips being made from very rare and unique Dragon Shards."

"Dragon Shards?" Dark asked quickly. "What are they?"

"Dragon Shards for starters are extremely uncommon," Mephisto began again with a quick look over to the still unconscious form of the Dark Elf prisoner. "They are fragments of living crystal imbued with magical powers.

This incredibly solid substance is almost weightless and essentially indestructible."

"Then shouldn't this bow be in a museum somewhere?" the demonic armored assassin asked after a moment.

"It was or so I thought," Mephisto conceded. "You see, the Black Fox was consumed with her quest to root out and destroy the Dark Elves, never laughing, never smiling, never stopping until Lolth and all her followers were destroyed. Then one night, a night that lay forever in infamy, she was finally slain in battle against the hideous Demon Queen herself. And after her passing, the bow she had carried was lost for centuries, locked away in the vault of a Drow Priestess. Your grandmother, the Queen of the Elves, began a campaign to recover the fallen archer's black bow. The Queen's own daughter, your mother, ventured alone into the subterranean City of the Döckálfar. She struck swiftly from the shadows with unmerciful accuracy; never allowing herself to be detected by either sight or sound, Leynorr slew every Dark Elf that stood in her way. Your mother succeeded in the recovery of the black bow and quiver, then from out of the dark bellows of the netherworld, she journeyed back home toward the City of the Elves. Afterwards, the Bow of the Black Fox was kept safely on display in Eldred and in the most prominent of all the museums in Elven society."

"Then how did this vile piece of garbage get his filthy black hands on it?" Dark finally asked, his voice edged with harshness.

"I don't know," the tall magus grinned at Dark and peered over the broad shoulder of his grandson at the now awakening Drow prisoner. "But what I do know is that our little friend here has the answers to all our questions."

Dark Solus looked at the little creature with a strong injurious look, his features twisting into an expression of disgust. Finally the Dark Elf tried vainly to rise several times, but the watchful Chimera, breathing heavily and bearing its fangs, gave a low guttural sound of hostile intent that forced the small being to cower back in fear.

"Move again and I'll let my pet have his first taste of dark meat," Demon Raider growled angrily.

"Let me go you cursed beast!" the Elf cried venomously, his eyes showing a momentary flicker of recognition as he caught sight of the horned intruder. "You have no right to keep me held captive! I have done nothing to you; I'm not even armed! I will tell…"

"You've done nothing," the demonic figure instantly moved over to his side, the leather-edged voice sounded menacingly in his pointed Elven ears. "Tell that shite to the girl upstairs you just tried to rape you piece of garbage."

In one swift motion he raised the squirming, twisting body of the rat faced Dark Elf, his scrawny neck held fast in the iron grip of the dark assassin. The gnarled black body appeared almost child-like as the hapless Döckálfar was raised well over a foot off the ground; the little humanoid was beginning to choke violently from the powerful grasp. Mephisto, seeing the prisoner's plight, at last motioned for his grandson to release his hold and lower his victim down.

"That's not our way," Mephisto urged a moment later. "Please don't go there."

"That's not our way," the tall half-elf repeated slowly. "That man has information we need, so one way or the other he's going to talk."

"What about the girl?" Mephisto declared abruptly, his lean hand pointing in gesture. "Surely she must know something, saving this creature endless hours of enduring pain and unbelievable agony."

The horrified Dark Elf could only dumbly watch, as he stared his two captors with unblinking fear, his large eyes wide as he awaited the answer to his fate.

"And what if he knows nothing, no…I can see no reason for permitting him to live, let alone go free" His grandson answered menacingly. "Maybe I should just cut his throat out right here and now. Then none of us would have to worry about him any further, how about I do that?"

Mephisto did not believe his grandson was serious, but from the sound of his voice, it did seem that he was in deadly earnest. The terrified Elf, not ready to face and endure any more pain, held forth his hands in final desperation for mercy.

"I beg of you, don't kill me," the now frantic Dark Elf pleaded, his wide black eyes shifting from face to face. "Please, please let me live…I swear to you I know nothing, just don't kill me!"

Dark started towards the little figure involuntarily at the unexpected plea for mercy; his grandfather tried to put a restraining hand on the assassin's wide shoulder but it was quickly brushed aside.

"And I swear you'll tell me everything I want to know," the icy voice of the demonically disguised assassin sounded out sharply as he ignored the Dark Elf completely. "By the time I'm done with you, you'll be squealing like a little pig."

With a few short words of power, translucent black chains seemed to coalesce from thin air and flew from Dark's outstretched hand to wrap tightly around the Drow's slender form. The iron chains wrapped around the Elf's body until he was fully encased and even his wry smile was bound by iron.

"You cannot do this," the mystic pleaded with his grandson, stepping forward, showing a firm determination in his face. "There has to be another way!"

"There is no other way!" Dark sputtered angrily, suddenly erupting into a fit of rage. "I will not allow anyone or anything to stand in my way, including you old man!"

Mephisto seemed to smolder in fury for a short while, fighting to control his own quick temper, then calmly he looked at his young grandson and shook his head in disappointment. "Listen to me," he said quietly. "The things we do now help shape our pre-determined destiny, and taking this course of action will only provide you a fate from which you cannot escape. Don't make this your destiny."

"And sometimes the hand of fate must be forced!"

There was a long prolonged silence. The tall wizard turned away from his grandson in a furious rage, his hands clasped angrily in front of him. After another brief moment, he wheeled back around again. But Dark had already turned, and with one great arm, lifted the struggling form of the Drow Captain over his shoulder and made his way to the far side of the castle wall. With several archaic gestures, these massive stone bricks gave way to reveal two large doors that were laced with a lattice work of intricate locks and steel metal bindings. He paused before the securely fastened enchanted portal; his iron bound prisoner had lapsed into a series of incoherent mumblings that were not completely muffled by his shiny metal gag. The Elven Commander gazed helplessly with wide and rolling dark eyes at the mystic who glanced back uneasily at the little captive.

Dark, ignoring the small muffled cries, uttered only a single word of magic, and the solid metal doors slowly swung silently open. A forbidding stillness settled over the great room, broken only by the expectant heavy breathing of the confined prisoner slung over his shoulder.

"Welcome to Hell on Eorth," Dark's voice was deep, becoming only a whisper in the stillness.

X

For a moment they remained framed in the doorway, then slowly Dark stepped forward into the stone chamber, his feet coming to rest on the damp floor and stopping short. The Dark Elf lay helplessly atop his captor's shoulder, his freedom barred as he shook his head in stunned disbelief. Then came the sudden grating of steel on stone, as the great metal doors began to close, swinging ponderously inward, its ancient hinges groaning slightly as they took the full weight of the great doors. With the opening closed, the intricate set of complicated locks and bolts slid heavily into place with the screech of metal against metal.

Finally there was only the sound of their own breathing in the deep silence of the castle dungeon. The pair moved forward into the inky fringes of the dark corridor, the air about them dead and silent. When the heavily chained captive glanced back, he saw the same blackness that lay all about him in heavy, impenetrable layers. Magnified amid the deep, hushed stillness were the hollow echoing of Dark's own footfalls along the smooth passageway. The cold that settled into the aged stone over the centuries of constantly cool temperatures seeped quickly through the little form of the chained Drow warrior that left him raw and shaking.

The air around them began to crackle with magical energy as the demonic-looking jailer finished uttering the last syllables of his spell's formula.

"In tenebris ad lucem."

Almost immediately, they heard the sound of falling footsteps approaching slowly from the distance. Far ahead they discerned a faint glowing shape that grew firmer in outline as it approached them. From the same direction as Dark faced, emerged the ghostly figure of a man bearing the grisly marks of a violent death. This spectral image that came towards him was legless and at first glance, headless as well. Steadily, the torso floated past, bearing in its long arm a hellish lantern fashioned from the remains of a human skull. The shadowy lamp had a slow flickering flame that crackled like plodding footsteps, creating a shadowy, mystical illumination that gave off a soft, continuous unearthly glow.

As the grotesque specter moved back down the corridor, the terrified Dark Elf saw that its head was, in fact, dangling by a thread of skin upside down between its own shoulder blades, the phantom eyes gleaming with an unnatural hatred. When it had finally drifted in the air past them, the burdened assassin crept forward from the shadows to follow it. It paid them no heed, its neck glistening in the eldritch light; the pair lagged many paces behind the dismembered apparition as it glided ahead guiding the company deeper into the dungeon.

Quickly each man became aware of huge still forms rising up on either side, images carved into the stone with faces and bodies that were not human, but indescribable other worldly beasts. These stone sentries stood vigilantly in the deep gloom, their twisted faces scarred by time, their eyes coming alive, fixed carefully on the two mortals who walked the ancient hall they guarded. Then at last the horrified faces of the stone creatures began to fall and fade away, leaving them alone once again with the ghostly torso as their only guide.

They kept moving, winding through a series of long twisting passages with their ghoulish but silent cicerone floating noiselessly in the lead. As they moved forward in the graying fringes of the dark passageway, the chained Dark Elf warrior became aware of other creatures in the darkness. At first, they were just a vague awareness in his mind, but then became soft cries of voices wailing and howling in utter despair of any hope for salvation. The terrible sound washed over him; the voices growing in despair and climbing to shrieks of unimaginable horrors of inhumanity. At last they appeared as living bodies of flesh, touching softly with flinching fingers the black flesh of the Döckálfar. He screamed in panicked frenzy knowing that somehow he was no longer in the world of the living, but one of death where these beings wandered hopelessly in search of escape from this eternal prison.

Finally they came to a stairwell cut into the rock wall, winding out of the stone floor and downward into blackness. Above the entryway, carved into the rock, were several words of a language centuries old and long forgotten. It served as a warning to all those who would enter that this was the house of the dead, for no one leaves here alive. Slowly they moved down the stairway with Dark's bound prisoner still in tow, held firmly in place over the assassin's broad shoulder. The Dark Elf's black eyes, uninhibited by any blindfold, keenly picked out several words inscribed into the stone surface of the stair wall. Only a few still knew the meaning of the words, but one word, the last word, the Drow knew its meaning instantly; '*Marwolaeth*', a word taken from an ancient Elven language. It meant Death.

Dark, still following his ghostly escort, slipped down the stairs soundlessly. He was almost at the bottom when a flicker of torch light cut through the darkness in the corridor ahead of them. They walked toward it, watching intently as Mephisto's tall form materialized out of the shadows.

"Stop, I beg of you!" the Mystic exclaimed, the black robes flowing gently as he approached, his fierce dark face resolute. "You must stop this madness; if not, I fear you will be heading down a very dark path that will lead you to a place of no return. You are not a butcher of men; you are an assassin."

"You just don't get it, do you old man!" Dark shouted back in anger, his pent up rage and frustration finally coming to the forefront at last. "I am a stone cold killer, and I seek vengeance. I am cruel, vile and wickedly savage, and if I need to be a butcherer of men such as this, then a butcherer I…WILL…BE!"

Dark's grandfather stared at him wordlessly. He hadn't allowed himself to consider that his grandson may have already ventured down a path of despair, one that held him trapped already like a rat in an endless maze. The old wizard motioned like he wanted to speak but the booming voice of the manor rang out amid the silence and gloom.

"Her Highness Queen Vanora has presently arrived."

Dark stood frozen in his tracks, his heart beating wildly as he awaited the confrontation he knew must come between them. He had been the one insistent on the choosing of his own path, a path he knew would not be that of the lawful Silver Mage.

His grandfather stood solidly before him, deep gray eyes burning with mixed feelings of both rage and frustration, his shadowed face a wall of granite. When he spoke again, the words were frigid and sharp.

"You know I have to go because if she were to find that poor Elven girl upstairs…well only the gods would know what she would do. So go and become that which I know you to now be…a monster."

Without waiting for any response, the magician turned and moved quickly up the stone stairs and disappeared into a black blanket of darkness. The last sentence was said with such a conclusive icy finality that even Dark felt a shiver of regret course through his body. Together, with his dark skinned captive, he raced back down the passage after the phantom light bearer, the soft glow barely visible in the distance. He turned left down another corridor and passed through a massive chamber filled with a wide selection and assortment of weapons and armor. At the end of this final passageway was an iron door fixed to the wall of the castle dungeon by bolts and cross bars. There the apparition paused, its severed head swinging ponderously against its back. As Dark drew back the rusted bolts and metal bars and pulled open the heavy iron door, the ghoulish figure turned and floated away until it was swallowed by a swirling gray fog and vanished.

They entered into a most diabolical and satanic chamber, specifically designed to evoke fear in the victims that bore witness to it. The underground room was windowless; it featured several trap doors in the floor which could be activated to throw prisoners into deep dark pits of water or live coals after long, lengthy torture sessions. The skeletal remains of incarcerated detainees were strewn on the floor while others were still held within cruel devices for confession. The walls of the prison seem to hum with a harmonic response before the room began to light up with a sickening red glow.

"This place is known as Ashoka's Hell," Dark's voice was sharp and wintry, his demonic penetrating eyes turned on the chained Döckálfar. "According to accounts contained in the Ashokayadana, the architect of this chamber was inspired by descriptions of the five tortures of the Buddhist Hell, and not just the design of the torture chamber itself, but the methods and devices he inflicted upon his victims."

The confined Döckálfar was then placed high upon a long two-sided hook, the same type used in butcheries to hang up meat or the carcasses of animals such as pigs and cattle. From this lofty perch, he bore witness to this Hell with his own black eyes. Torches blazed at its corners, shedding a lurid glare into the darkness, the shadows dancing across its flickering light. The images, no longer a conjuring in his mind, were truly frightening to behold, as he fearfully gazed about. The chamber was filled with a gruesome selection of cruel and barbarous devices specifically designed to extract information through excruciating physical pain. These instruments the Dark Elf knew all too well, from the simple instruments such as the pliers and hot irons that hung on the wall, to the complex devices like the rack that lay just below his dangling feet that was used to stretch the victim's back until the joints were painfully dislocated. And in the far corner, a fiendishly device rested, the Iron Maiden, an upright sarcophagus with spikes specifically positioned to penetrate the eyes. However, one machine of malice caught his eye and kept it, one that was truly frightening to behold.

The primary aspects of the Döckálfar society is a significant need for hierarchy and absolute control. For nearly a thousand years, the Cranic Wheel has been an instrumental part in their legal system. It was a regular part of the Dark Elves' political process, believing torture to be the only way to get slaves to confess their master's crimes. This was because Drow law strictly forbids the torture of its citizens, leaving the slaves of the suspected criminals to be the ones to endure tortuous persecution.

The Drow captive stared timorously at the mechanized nightmare of a machine, his own worst fears, he thought, would soon be realized.

"Terrifying isn't it?" Demon Raider looked at the hanging creature while he spun the giant wheel with little effort. "I acquired this instrument of torture from one of your kind, a Dark Elf, like you. He claimed to be a famous weapon smith, an artificer on inflicting pain." As he spoke, he continued to keep the wheel in constant motion. "Upon its final completion, its creator vouched for his workmanship with a formal promise and assurance of its specified quality and durability. He pledged on his own life that the deadly apparatus would perform perfectly the first time and every other time after that for at least a thousand years. So bold was his claim, and made with such swaggering bravado, that I asked him to prove his audacious declaration himself. He lies there now below your feet, his guarantee he kept in life as well as death."

Dark turned back to the hanging captive sharply, but only stood there staring into the unfortunate Döckálfar's horror-stricken face. "Now it's time for you to learn what our friends here already know," he announced menacingly, his eyes flaring red with fire as his right clawed hand grasped the Elf's black throat. "Don't be frightened by the machine or even its maker, but instead be afraid of the one who controls it. Be very afraid."

At that moment a high-pitched shriek sounded from the Drow prisoner, the chains rattled while his body was visibly shaking violently. There were a few more muffled cries of terror as the bound prisoner began thrashing within his metal bands until Dark finally loosened the chains about the creature's mouth.

"No, no I beg of you, don't kill me!" the frantic Elf pleaded loudly, his wide black eyes fearfully shifting from the wheel to that of his captor. "Please, please, I'll tell you whatever you want to know. I can be of great use to you…I can help you…I can…I can, I can tell you about the bow!"

The grim features of the demonic-looking assassin relaxed briefly and a faint smile played across his lips as he still eyed the quivering confined Dark Elf. The demon's mouth of his magical breastplate wolfishly smiled as well, with a grating growl that echoed eerily off the thick walls of the chamber.

"First tell me what you were doing with the Elven girl at the Gentlemen's Noose?" Dark urged a moment later, his voice icy.

"I am…"

Before the Drow prisoner could utter another word, the black-garbed assassin lashed out with a lightning-like strike with the back of his gauntleted hand. The forceful blow was like a hammer that broke the man's teeth and made his lower jaw ring with pain. The Dark Elf's angular face snapped sharply to one side as blood flew sideways from the violent impact. The thick red liquid gushed freely from his mouth and fell to the stone floor, his eyes sagging slightly.

"It doesn't matter what your name is!" the smile was gone from the horned executioner's face, his features hardened as he spoke, his voice angry and menacing once more. "Answer the question!"

"We were there…we were there to…we were there to sell the Black Bow to a potential buyer," the Elven Captain sputtered, his face covered with flecks of his own blood and an open cut on both his swollen lips. "And we had no idea that the person who showed up would be a woman, let alone an Elven one."

"What house do you serve?" Dark urged a moment later.

"I am a soldier for the noble house of De' Sade," he answered eagerly.

"Malice had a hand in this?" the lean assassin spoke slowly, his eyes shifting away. "But why would she risk…"

"Not Malice…her daughter, Ever Syn De' Sade…"

The small Dark Elf paused and looked fearfully at his masked captor, as the bound prisoner seemed to undergo a sudden transformation at the sound of his suzerain's name. Within seconds, squeals of agony filled both their pointed ears. The Drow's eyes began protruding from their sockets, his skin cracked like stone. From his gaping mouth he vomited forth a mass of hidden hairy arachnid denizens, each one dripping a thick yellow venom from sharp fangs. The surface of his body erupted into a rolling chaotic blanket of long jointed legs and small reflective black eyes. Impossible clusters of tiny spiders surrounded him, swarming over him, engulfing him, each creature biting, cutting, tearing away at his dark flesh. Sheer anguish and torture raced throughout his body, as the warm poison coursed painfully through his veins. Yellow and red ichor stained the ground and splattered the walls, his lithe form gushing his own fluids. The Döckálfar's eyes were still open, but with a glossy reflection as blood poured from his chest and dribbled down from the corner of his open mouth.

Dark could only watch in awed silence, bearing only an expression of surprise and horror before the Drow prisoner was finally buried under a rolling sea of writhing flesh eating anthropoids. Unmolested for the moment, the resigned assassin raised his left arm upwards and unleashed the power of the Dragon's Breath wand. Instantly the dragon's head emerged and sent a burst of red flame and blasted the spiders and Drow body with its discordance.

When Dark returned to the Grand Hall, it was beginning to grow brighter outside; the rain was falling in a slow steady drizzle through deepening gray skies. The steady rain beat tranquilly on the stained glass windows that let in what little light there was into the huge room. He glanced around the finely furnished chamber; quickly he spied both his grand parents who sat leisurely around a long burnished wood table, their faces strangely smiling at one another.

As he approached the idly chatting pair, his grandfather turned, and as he rose to stand, he loudly began to clap. "That was quite a performance, my boy, quite a performance indeed."

"Thank you, thank you," replied Dark as he bowed gracefully back, setting his horned mask down, grinning reassuringly at his uneasy grandmother. "What can I say; I have a gift for the dramatic art of acting."

"I must admit you almost had me fooled," Mephisto continued his praise without pausing. "If there was some award for theatrical stagecraft, let's say some small statue of a gold or bronze sculptured man, and presented at a ceremony honoring that person's study of dramaturgy, then you sir would win that award."

"Again, I thank you sir," responded the assassin, cocking his head and nodding to them in a courteous manner.

Vanora said nothing, but appraised them both curiously, then looked back at Mephisto, her eyebrows raised. "What are you two on about now?"

"Oh, it's nothing really, just that Dark here has a Döckálfar prisoner that has some information we need," Mephisto informed her shortly, then quickly turned his attention back to his grandson. "So what happened to our little friend; did he finally spill his guts, so to speak?"

"Oh he's dead." Finally he sat down next to his grandmother, leaning over he kissed her affectionately on her cheek.

"Good," she spoke curtly, obviously disgusted by the whole subject. "They're nothing but nasty little creatures anyway."

"What?" the old wizard sounded worried. "What do you mean he's dead? Quickly now, tell me everything."

For the next several minutes Dark recounted all that had occurred deep in the dungeon. He explained how the Drow soldier had been brought to the Cloud Castle and he went on to relate the mysterious girl, carefully refraining from mentioning the part about her Elven heritage and possible connection to the Witch Slayers, knowing full well what his grandmother's response would be or the gods forbidding, her actions against the girl. He went on to disclose the information he was given and the strange way the Elven man met his violently sudden and untimely demise.

"Well why don't you use those new found Thespian skills of yours and act like a good host and bring us some tea will you," advised the Queen of the Witches.

"I will go and fetch her Majesty's favorite beverage." The deep voice of Mephisto rang out in the hall as he rose commandingly to his full height. "You chat with your grandmother; she came a long way to see you." He paused and looked at their faces in turn, a half smile playing over his thin lips. His deep set eyes twinkled beneath his brow. He then hastened toward the open doors and went out, closing the large doors quietly behind him.

"Good, I thought he'd never leave." His grandmother stretched forth a slim ivory hand to grasp his own in warm greeting and slapped it lightly in affection several times. "I must admit Dark, I have come to you with purpose," she began again quickly. "I've come in search of Fane."

"You shouldn't have come to Duergar," Dark exclaimed, looking up at her. "There may be slayers in the city; it's just not safe for you to wander the streets looking for this person."

"This is very personal to me, my boy," Vanora responded quickly, raising her hand to stop him from continuing. "This person to whom I gave my trust has treacherously betrayed me. He was the one who pushed me into studying the Dark Arts. He taught me the ritualistic practices and rites of passage into the blackest of magic. He's also the one who convinced me that separating from the rest of the Elves… and even from your grandfather, was the only course of action to take." Vanora stopped abruptly and looked up at her grandson, watching curiously as to what his reaction would be. "So I need your help." She smiled at her grandson and he smiled back.

The sentence died away, unfinished. Dark felt a sudden pang of sympathy, his head coming to rest on her shoulder. "Of course I will help you; why would you think otherwise." Dark looked certain, his head slightly shaking. "Now tell me what your spies know."

Her hanging head lifted, as she took a moment to recover her thoughts. "They had followed his trail to here in Duergar, where he has taken up residence in the Old Quarter at a place called The Castlerock Arms. But unfortunately, over a week ago, one of my spies was compromised somehow and found dead in Fane's room. Now he's disappeared and we can't find any trace of him, and for this reason I have come to you."

"I'll find him." He gave her a smile which negated her own sense of uncertainty, then took her hand firmly in his. "And when I find him, what would you have me do with him?"

The Witch Queen paused, staring at the lighted stain glass windows of the Grand Hall. Her fragile features turned suddenly hard, her eyes flared with furious rage and a hardened resolve. "Bring that little rat bastard to me." The sharp command cut through the stillness, causing the bent figure of her grandson to snap upright, her voice cold with fury.

"Yes, Ma'am." He glanced at her quickly and nodded, smiling encouragingly.

Vanora changed the subject abruptly. "Now there is one more thing; I wish to give you something."

"You don't need to pay me."

His grandmother shook her head. "Look at it as more of a present than a payment," she paused. "As you know, there is a price to pay for the way we use ourselves. It's one of nature's laws, even though often we chose to disregard it. And when we use powerful magic, that price for a spell-caster is doubled. By using these supernatural forces, it is extracted from the very essence of the user by draining both strength and being. Some of that arcane essence that is lost can be recovered quickly, but sometimes, depending on the type of spell and will of the person, recovery can be very slow. There are limits that cannot be exceeded, and some limits can even shorten one's own years."

"This doesn't sound like a good present," Dark frowned worriedly.

"You silly little boy. I'm going to teach you a magic unsurpassed by none." The Witch Queen shook her head slowly, a growing smile played over her ruby lips. "This is a spell your grandfather would never instruct you in, for the consequences of its use are grievous. I'm going to teach you the formula for stopping time."

Dark hastened to nod his agreement, but Vanora stopped him.

"You cannot tell your grandfather I have taught you this," she began again quickly. "This is to be used in only the most dire of emergencies. With each use the caster forfeits a year of his life for every minute that passes."

The young assassin regained his composure, his smiling face suddenly became serious, and nodded his willingness to allow his new teacher to continue.

"Very well," the other acknowledged. "Let's go outside into the garden and I shall tutor you in the black arts."

The pair looked at each other and nodded in agreement. Vanora rose silently, gathering her cloak carefully about her small frame. Dark rose with her and stood quietly as he looked down at her. One delicate hand reached over to grip her grandson firmly around his arm, and for an instant bound them together as one person. Then they turned away and left the Grand Hall together.

For the rest of the morning and for most of the afternoon, Dark spent this time in secret study, being schooled by his grandmother in this black magic. Before the sun set she left them with a wave and a wink and left in a puff of black smoke and ash. Weary from the previous night, the young half-elf went to turn in for much needed rest. He tried stopping by the room where the elven girl was being kept, only to be told by his grandfather that she was still asleep and should not be disturbed.

By the following afternoon, the Lord of Dark Manor was awake; the rain was still falling in a slow, steady drizzle through deep, gray skies. He saw a dry set of clothes lying on a chair near his bed. He quickly rose to dress, noticing the strange absence of Baron, then was soon out through the door of his royal bed chamber. In a flash he reached the door to the elven girl's room when suddenly the door opened and an invisible serving woman appeared, carrying a tray of empty plates and dishes. He moved past the open doorway and upon entering, he instantly saw Mephisto and the young woman he had rescued the previous night, refreshed and dressed in a flowing gown of brightly mixed colors, her long blonde locks combed and shining even in the gray light of the heavily clouded day. Easily she was the most stunning woman Dark had even seen. He left the door open and moved beside his grandfather who was standing over the girl as she stood next to the large paned glass windows that gracefully let the light through.

He was not surprised to discover, and somehow very nearly missed seeing Baron, lying sprawled out behind a large elaborate bed, complete with a richly embroidered ornamented canopy. The mocking smile of his grandfather flashed briefly as the old conjurer began to speak.

"This young man is my grandson, Dark." Mephisto's voice floated like a joyful note on the air. "He's the one who rescued you from the Döckálfar soldiers."

She glanced at Dark, who smiled at her awkwardly. She was small even for an Elf, her body slender but athletic with her skin slightly red from the sun. Her long blonde hair fell gently down to her waist, shadowing an almost doll-like face, both innocent and beautiful at once. Her eyes flashed kindly at Dark's own, eyes that were clear, deep and blue and so full of life.

"It seems I owe you a debt of gratitude," she smiled, her voice was soft and lovely.

"Think nothing of it my Lady," was Dark's humble response.

"I am Aurra Greyfell, daughter of Ollen Greyfell, Ruler and King of the Elves." The young woman stretched forth a slim hand to grasp his own in greeting. "If not for your courageous act of bravery, I might never have seen him or my home ever again, and for that I am eternally grateful."

"Just tell me what you were doing at the Gentlemen's Noose the other night," he asked quickly, raising his hand to stop her from continuing.

The elven girl briefly hesitated, then began to speak. "As I already explained to your grandfather, I came to this city in search of my sister, Nysarra. She has been missing for quite some time and her true whereabouts, as well as her fate, remains a mystery to me…it's like she has completely disappeared from the pages of history. Duergar was her last known location and from here the last of her communications to me suddenly stopped…" she whispered, but the words became caught in her throat.

"Take you time lass," Mephisto spoke calm and steady and it seemed to brush aside her sadness. "We're in no hurry and besides we don't know what's happened to her so let's not jump to any conclusions just yet, shall we."

She nodded her head slowly. "So I took it upon myself of dispatching two of the best men from my own personal guard to follow the trail, if any, that was left by my sister. I first sent them to seek out a man I knew to be loyal to the Crown, a tailor and arms maker, Bodekker Stitch."

Both Dark and Mephisto quickly glanced over at one another, the same wry smile crept slowly upon their faces.

"You know him then?" Aurra stared at them both wordlessly for a moment.

"No, but he is someone I intended on seeing very soon," was Dark's response, even though she believed he was speaking almost to himself. The young assassin looked back at her, turning quietly. "And for me there is no better time than right now."

"Then you will need this," her hands lifted to her stricken face and wiped away the tears that began to spill down her reddened cheeks. Her blue eyes opened and she came forward quietly, her face expressionless once more as she slowly removed a signet ring of the House of Greyfell from her right finger, then handed it to Dark. "Give the tailor this. It is a symbol of our family's absolute authority; he will do whatever is asked of him."

"I'll be back as soon as I can," Dark replied graciously and taking the ring he slowly turned away.

Then he was gone, disappearing silently through the chamber doors, leaving Mephisto and the Elven Princess staring after him in the dull gray light of the bedroom.

The sun was still above the horizon when Dark stepped through the front door of Bodekker Stitch's tailor shop. Once again with the aid of the Eye of Dagda he was in disguise, this time as a handsomely dressed Elven aristocrat. His clothing consisted of a fine coat of blue silk with a surcoat and mantle of scarlet satin and a cotton cap trimmed with peacock feathers. As he made his way through the curved archway, he noticed several sentries were on watch, each one nodded in greeting as he passed. He found it strange that the City Watch would be put in place to protect an Elven shop for constructing clothes, even if it was a highly specialized one. A sudden apprehension swept through him.

As he came near a long wooden counter, he saw that a young Elf in a slim tailored suit was pulling closed a pair of hand-woven curtains that draped the far wall. The slim form shifted uneasily and his eyes refused to meet those of Dark. The young attendant ignored him completely, moving silently about extinguishing the lit oil lamps and candles that served to illuminate the large boutique. With his patience wearing thin, the disguised assassin spotted a small dusty bell next to a sign on the counter that read 'Ring for Service'. Without a second thought his hand came sharply down upon the bell push which moved the small metal clapper to forcefully hit the silver gong which caused a ring so loud that it pierced the ears.

An instant later, the short, unfriendly looking male Elf of an uncertain age trudged slowly over to the richly dressed bell ringer. As he came up to the counter, Dark noticed that the little Elf was limping badly, and a strong smell of wet dander assaulted his senses.

"Yes, can I help you?" asked the tiny elven employee of the tailor shop, his tone held a slight hint of mockery and contempt.

"Yes, I would like to speak to your employer, Mr. Stitch," Dark replied quietly, then brought forth the signet ring and presented it to the store clerk. "I wish for the couturier to make me a garment that is tailored to meet my specific requirements."

For a long moment, Bodekker Stitch did not respond, but stood rigidly in place, his cold staring eyes fixed solidly on the speaker. "Actually I am the couturier and proprietor of this establishment," he said at last. "I'm sorry but we're closed; besides we have a policy of no bartering, especially for worthless trinkets. I'm afraid we take only the King's Crown as an acceptable means of payment…so good evening to you."

There was a long moment of silence as the two faced each other. For a second Dark hesitated, his blue eyes studying the surly face of the other man, scrutinizing him. At last he nodded. "You should have taken the ring," the half-elven assassin managed finally.

Bodekker Stitch stiffened slightly, his face incredulous. "What?" His head shook slowly, dubiously. "What are you talking about?"

"I said you should have taken the ring." His voice was forceful and commanding, his eyes bore straight into Stitch's and the elven tailor found that he could not look away. "You see, when someone adopts a disguise for deceitful purposes, they tend to believe that their façade is perfect and nearly impossible to penetrate. And that's because most people are willing to believe their own eyes without question. However, they do not gain any insight into attitudes or opinions, their customs or even their culture. Anyone who had spent even a small amount of time among the Elves would know that when any Elf is shown a Signet Ring from the King's Court, your obedience is not just required, it's demanded. But that's not even how I became aware of your pitiful subterfuge. It's the fact that you smell like a wet dog's arse that gave you away…shape-shifter."

"Kill him!" roared the imposter quickly, recovering his wits about him.

It was then that the doppelganger saw the true face of the demonic being that now confronted him. A chilling fear surged through him at the sight of this deathlike form, but the living double of Bodekker Stitch could only stare at the black creature in shock and surprise as the broad, devilish grin slowly spread over the demon's dark countenance as it raised one arm, then attacked with blinding speed. The imposter was hurled through the air, powered by Dark's strong right arm, striking the frightened shape-shifter directly in the face with an audible crunch, and sent him crashing to the ground with a thud. Dark was already leaping forward, his incorporeal sword swung downward toward the creatures throat. But the deadly impersonator was not so easily finished. Somehow, recovering from the blow, it parried Dark's weapon with one arm that he had quickly transformed into a slender double edged sword. Before the black-garbed assassin could strike again, the soldiers on duty let out a blood thirsty battle cry and charged toward Dark, their long swords gleaming dully. The silent black bolts from the demonic assassin's self cocking hand crossbow dropped two of them in midstride before the remaining two swarmed over him like a pair of savage beasts. Dark stood firm as his shadowy blade cut their heads clean from their bodies with two swift sweeps. In the end, the soldiers all lay dead on the shop floor, their bodies forming small bloody heaps amid the shadows and dim light.

Seizing his opportunity, the shape-shifter turned to flee and began to run. Dark bounded towards him desperately trying to stop the imposter's escape. When he found his way outside, the Doppelganger suddenly changed into the form of a swift hare for fleetness of foot and headed out across the cobble stone grounds. And it was in that split second the masquerader's true appearance showed briefly the imitator's own small round, beady eyes that gleamed with malice and a triangular shaped soul patch that lay crooked just above his non-existent chin. But as he leapt away, he was unaware that far above him, mounting in easy spirals, was a great long-winged hawk. In an instant upon seeing the large, long eared rabbit, it attacked, rocketing towards him, talons at the ready.

The wary assassin stood motionless for a time, waiting for something else, something more. But there seemed to be no further sounds or strange noises, no movement of any kind betraying the presence of another living soul. He was alone for now, so resolutely he moved forward. Dark, no longer in the guise of an Elven Lord, seemed little more than a shadow. Moving soundlessly the assassin secured both the windows and the doors, drew the curtains closed, then turned back into the candlelight. Within seconds, he stood at the door that led to the back room. There he paused momentarily while he listened at the door. Finally satisfied he opened the door and stepped through.

He stood where the journey-men and apprentices would be working together, threading needles, drinking and sewing, sitting cross-legged on the long work benches. There were several overly large windows behind the work stations, indicating the importance of a strong light source. Huge rolls of wool, linen and silk lay on huge racks that lined the walls with an assortment of poseable mannequins that had fabric covered torsos.

He walked slowly to the back wall and began to skirt the base of the stone wall, his keen elven eyes studying every crevice and jagged line. Finally he stopped, his hand reached deep inside a mortarless portion of a stone brick and felt what he thought was a button and touched it. A portion of the stone wall swung inwards, revealing a cleverly concealed dark passageway. Quickly the black-garbed assassin slipped through the small opening as the stone slowly sealed itself behind him. There was nothing but total blackness, but he allowed his eyes a moment to adjust before he moved forward again. The passage stretched out and away before him; he saw the faint outline of smoothly-hewn steps cut into the hard rock floor, disappearing downward into more darkness.

The smell of sweet pine filled his nostrils, making him smile in remembrance of the foliage that surrounded his parent's house. The passageway finally ended at a massive iron door. Dark paused and studied it closely, his eyes examining the heavy iron bindings. After a moment, he called to Sleek, who quickly changed his form and opened a complicated combination of metal latches and tumblers. The door swung open and he cautiously stepped through.

Dark emerged into a huge circular, cavernous chamber with a narrow iron spiral stairway that led upward onto a suspended platform that hung precariously beneath a semi-circular stained glass skylight. It was in a sunburst pattern, radiating its splendor in golden shafts across a blue-paned window. There were several native Elven art features throughout the round space. In this room the walls and even the floor were covered in a mosaic of small, brightly colored tiles. Along the ring-shaped wall were twelve Elven warrior statues, hand crafted metal sculptures dressed in fine and fanciful plate armor, all standing at attention with their blades drawn upward in noble salute. Along the left portion of the wall, an Elven warrior was depicted, garbed all in black and trimmed in fur, wearing a dark mask with the likeness of a fox. Wielding the infamous bow, bestowed to her by the gods, the Black Fox could be seen wrapped in a magical aura of pale light doing battle with a horde of her sworn enemy, the Drow. An image of a giant spider with the torso of a female Dark Elf locked in mortal combat with the archer took up the entire wall to the right of Dark.

Without a backward glance, the silent assassin moved forward toward the center of the room. Dust lay everywhere like a soft thick carpet. Cobwebs fell from the ceiling and walls in long white threads telling him the area had not been used in quite some time. A cluster of stars winked into view and silvery tinges of starlight filtered through the high skylight window in thin ribbons that touched softly upon a statue of a proud and unyielding Elven King. With a few words of intonment and a wave from his hand, the torches that hung dormant for ages suddenly burst to life illuminating the giant chamber in a warm orange glow. The dancing firelight burned through the haze of old musty air that seemed to hang motionless throughout the secret room. The metal effigy glinted images of fire as the torchlight struck its untarnished mirror-like surface. He stepped noiselessly down into a sunken study, the inner walls lined with recessed bookshelves of old fraying leather bound books, the color of their bindings long since faded.

Dark glanced about the room with a mechanical routine and moved to get a closer look at the sculpture. Placed upon a plinth of heavy marble, the imposing statue was erected depicting the monarch astride his horse emerging into the daylight of legend and romance. On the front of the base was a bronze relief panel which read, 'A great warrior, leader and diplomat, King Tor Min Ra, united the warring Elven clans into one royal Kingdom after years of conflict. Destined for greatness from birth, legend prophesized that a light in the sky with a large, brilliant silvery plume trailing behind it, would signal the birth of a great King.'

Instinctively, he moved to the base of the statue and began running his hands lightly over the marble stone. After a few minutes of searching, his fingertips came across an unusual crevice. He reached in slowly, and lowered his head in concentration, his thumb firmly in place against what felt like a faceted gem stone. He pushed on it. At first nothing happened, then suddenly a bright blue glow spread outward from the metamorphic rock and ran quickly through the mosaic tiles like veins through a living body. An instant later, the two scenes on the curved walls began to play out like a vivid lucid dream. Finally the two rather theatrical performances came to their grizzly end and the glow erupted in a soundless blue fire, then they were gone, replaced by a beautiful scenic forest near a sparkling clear blue loch.

He moved to a portion of the forest scene where the warm rays of the autumn sun strained through the tree branches, illuminating a small double door of white oak and iron with handles of brass. A huge lock secured this magical door. He paused, then cautiously turned his head to glance suspiciously at the statues of iron that still stood in silent watch. Once again the assassin produced Sleek and placed him in the lock like a key and turned it twice. The ancient mechanism creaked loudly in protest, its inner workings rusty with lack of use but the metal bolt drew back. With a turn of the brass handles, the doors opened and he stepped inside and closed them behind him. The room he entered housed a metal smith's workshop; the corners were each supported with archways that were built into a hemispherical ceiling. Along the right side was the Blacksmith's bench with a variety of tools, tongs and jigs, as well as a large drawing of armor, most likely used as a guide by the Smith. The air here was not just stale with age, but the dark chamber was also filled with a putrid odor; the whole room smelled unspeakably vile. Then he spotted a rotting corpse on the cold stone floor next to a furnace of stone and brick. Vivid red stains were left where he fell. It was the rotting remains of Bodekker Stitch, still clutching a leather-bound book elaborately engraved with gold.

Dark reached down and carefully removed the thin tome from the dead man's hands. On the cover was the same seal, showing the same stylized anvil and hammer inside a silver wreath as the iron statues had displayed on their shields. A few moments later he rummaged through the corpses tattered remains and produced a large silver and gold ring with the same crest etched upon it. He immediately noticed the seal on the cover began to glow in unison with the ring as he brought the two items near to one another. He quickly opened the book. It was in good condition, the leather still soft and pliable, with the edges of the pages sharp and the binding solid. Instantly, blank pages began to fill with delicate script and line drawings. He leafed quickly through the journal, turning the pages of Bodekker Stitch's daily routine, his face bent close to carefully examine the inscribed writings.

His elven eyes lifted sharply and he listened intently to the deep silence. He sensed a trap. Just the mere thought triggered his sharpened and refined instincts, a sort of a sixth sense of warning. There was something definitely wrong and he knew it was time to go. He stood for a moment and still in the disguise of Demon Raider, the demonic assassin, and with the tailor's signet ring still in his own hand, he teleported into the previous room.

Not twenty feet beyond stood a slender figure swathed in black robes with a mantle of raven feathers draped around the shoulders. Dark froze and stood face-to-face with the strange newcomer. Cruel yellow eyes passed quickly over the black-garbed assassin, burning into him, somehow probing his thoughts. Dark, while a little bewildered at the sight of the cloaked creature that seemed to be waiting all alone, was not in the least bit panicked. He turned fully to face the strange feathered being, his cruel red glowing eyes passed quickly over the dark figure as he raised his hand and pointed to the ring in warning. "I have no quarrel with you," he spoke sharply. "So I suggest you let me pass or I shall set my steel minions on you, and you don't want that."

"So the rumors are true," a low female voice broke into his thoughts. "You are real."

Almost immediately, he saw that there were others, as he lifted his black eyes and gave a partial glance to the other side of the chamber. The door flew open as several dozen Halflings rushed over to their mistress, like black wraith-like forms they seemed to be all around him creeping even closer. They edged steadily closer, trying to encircle him from both sides like wild animals waiting for the time to strike.

Dark watched them circle closer, creeping about and engulfing him by the dozens, savoring the prospect of his death. It was a death that seemed assured for the necklace around his neck was cold and dead, as if the power it possessed was no longer. Something was definitely amiss; it seemed as if every spell he would use as a means of escape was nullified somehow. Alone with his magical powers seemingly neutralized, he would not be enough of a match to stop them all. They would eventually change their form and attack as one, lunging at him from all sides, their bites tearing him to shreds until nothing remained but bones. Then the heavy wooden door ahead slid closed, as the last of them entered the fray, cutting off in a sliver of light his only visible means of escape.

He glanced over quickly at the woman who stood just beyond the circle of her minions, her dark gaze still fixed on the lone assassin. She removed her cumbersome cloak with an almost casual arrogance, a winged feathered cape billowed out slightly behind her. Dark could see the strange girl more clearly now, and a quick scrutiny of her revealed that she was definitely human, or so she seemed to be. She was a long raven haired buxom beauty with light skin; a stunning woman dressed in a form fitting beautiful gown, wearing ornate pieces of jewelry with a raven motif. In her slender hand she carried a rod constructed of black metal inlaid with arcane symbols made from deep blue precious gemstone with golden inclusions which shone like shimmering stars.

Just then, a low mewing sound came from behind cloaked faces, as their small hands began to curl and a rumble issued from their throats that gave a sense of what was to come. Blood veined eyes began to roll, bones painfully began to snap and break. Their tiny bodies started to twist and turn, as each fell to the floor in uncontrollable convulsions. Their ears became long and pointed; their features twisted with savagery; their mouths had become monstrous jaws revealing rows of sharp, pearly white fangs. Now transformed, these creatures with yellow eyes stepped closer on all fours their large muscular bodies all covered in a neatly groomed brown and black fur.

"Surrender to me or die. My friends here are hungry and in need of a quick meal." Her words were a chilling echo in the deep unbroken silence, the magical rod she held in her hand began to glow. "You are completely surrounded with no possible means of escape. You are outnumbered, outmatched and you have clearly been outwitted…you are all alone…it is over."

Just then the pack leader edged closer and lifted his grizzled black head and made a sound that was part groan, part growl until finally a rather high pitched howl sounded out, setting off a series of frenzied howls that erupted terrifyingly from behind to answer his call in return. The doleful cries of the werewolves rose sharply, a long wailing sound that reverberated off the circular chamber walls, echoing hollow and shrill through the stone room. Their haunting cries slowly died into a quiet stillness, as their long, sharp claws raked the marble floor breaking the momentary silence as they inched their way forward.

"What say you now demon?" the Lycan leader stepped forward menacingly until he was into the pale fringes of the assassin's shadow.

"That's Demon Raider," Dark whispered with a devilish grin, his glowing eyes bursting into a red fiery flame. He stepped closer and bent forward, nearer to the leader's furry face. "And who said I was alone."

For a moment no one moved as Dark clutched the glowing ring close to his muscular frame. In the changeling's eyes there was a momentary flicker of recognition as he caught sight of the bright, bluish color shining in the slowly rising hand of this so called Demon Raider. The black-garbed assassin yelled wildly raising his fist forward towards his attackers, praying for the ring's strange power to aid him now. "Elven warriors, I call upon you to serve your master and defend me now!"

Nothing happened. He quickly tried again, this time concentrating on the power of the glowing ring in his gauntleted hand, calling upon the magic that he knew was contained somewhere deep within it. Again…nothing happened. "Ah shite!"

The yelps and barks of the werewolves broke sharply through his thoughts as he saw the encircling pack come directly toward him. Dark saw them all as if they had been frozen in one single instant in time, struggling as he did so to free the power that he thought lay locked within the ring. Then the huge pack leader attacked with blinding speed. Powered by his muscular hind legs he leaped through the air and struck the black demonic assassin in the right arm with a sickening crunch. Before his attacker could strike his target for a second assault, he seized the big black leader as the creature leaped for his throat and with one gauntleted hand knocked the Lycan sprawling. But the deadly cursed creature was not so easily finished. Recovering from the strong blow, it lunged quickly to one side, narrowly missing several bolts from the assassin's hand crossbow. In the next instant the huge form of the werewolf was upon him again, bearing the demonic stranger heavily to the floor.

Again Dark was not quick enough, as sharp fanged teeth viciously ripped through the metal of his armor and tore into his flesh. Searing, agonizing waves of pain wracked his body and right arm; his face became contorted with every piercing bite. The black furred Lycan attacker, with an animalistic brutality, shredding Dark's body further, his dark armor soaked with his own blood. How could any man resist such strength; no normal weapon could do the beast harm. Its ancient power and cruelty were beyond any measure of human experience. Acting more on instinct than his training, Dark's attack came in a blast of fire with no more warning than an erupting volcano. A burst of white hot flames sprang into existence from the open maw of the dragon wand, swirling and twisting dangerously, surrounding the pack leader in a searing burning flame of fire. The werewolf cried out, writhing in pain; it howled and whined trying desperately to pull away. But the demon's mouth on the assassin's breast plate seized hold of the enemy's front furred leg, twisting as the leader pulled frantically.

Finally with the sound of cracking bones in its demonic jaws, its white teeth tore through the flesh of the massive shoulder; gouts of red blood spouted as the leg tore free. Wailing in anguish as its life drained away, the beast stumbled backward and fell silent amid a growing pool of its own blood.

Staggering to his feet, Demon Raider stood bleeding from numerous wounds swaying slightly, the demon's mouth still holding the now human Halfling arm of the pack leader. The sorceress shrieked in anger, spewing forth oaths of fury and her readied rod came up. In a powerful surge of energy, red hot bolts blazed the length of the chamber, scattering the maddened werewolves as it streaked toward the wounded assassin. The light struck the dark horned intruder directly in the chest with a sharp blast, as he screamed his loathing of the power that destroyed him. The black body crumpled into dust as he sank. In another second, the assassin known as Demon Raider was gone, only a small pile of black ashes remained.

For several long seconds no one moved. It happened so suddenly and so abruptly that the leaderless Lycans ceased all movement and just stared at the blackened ground. Their cries died into silent stillness, still stunned by the sudden finality.

The illusion only lasted a few seconds but it was still long enough for Dark to escape the circle of death that almost ensnared him. With the aid of his mother's black baton, he was instantly propelled skyward and now raced up the stairs toward the skylight. His subterfuge was shattered when he smashed open the large round window above their heads. Already the werewolf pack were after him, bounding up the vertical stone walls like wild animals, their immortal cries thick with bloodlust. Dark turned to face them; his breast plate's gaping mouth was matted with their leader's blood.

The raven haired enchantress raised her magical rod once more and the devastating bolt streaked toward the fleeing assassin. The rod's magic flared up all about him and burst apart the hanging platform, tearing it apart from its iron bindings. With a shudder, the whole of the apparatus collapsed, falling down upon a large group of Lycans, crushing them under its immense weight. Dark managed to evade the devastating blast; dodging quickly with a single powerful extension of the baton, he burst through the open window and was gone.

XI

A chill wind swept through Dark Manor as Dark stumbled wearily into his castle home, now shrouded in a deep hollow silence with the occupants sleeping serenely in their beds. Something darker than the blackness of an early dawn appeared writhing and shuddering with the force of some kind of strange entity. Howls and shrieks spilled forth from within the troubled assassin.

"Mephisto!" The sound of his voice broke the stillness of the night air. He was stooped over clutching his stomach, his movements hampered by the pain. "Grandfather! GRANDFATHER!"

Still in deep sleep, both his grandfather and Aurra Greyfell were resting quite peacefully when another loud shout brought them both around and fully awake.

"Renfield, bring me silver…be quick about it man!"

Together the tired magician and their royal guest, the Elven Princess, quickly dressed and hurriedly made their way toward the main manor stairway. Mephisto and the tiny woman stared in surprise at the sight of the black-garbed assassin as he stumbled to a weary halt, his face and body bleeding in long streaks of blood. Dark stood frozen for a moment, his eyes on his grandfather's, his mind still dazed with shock. There was desperation in those eyes and on his fearful, blanched face. His voice strained with his attempt to emphasize the urgency that was driving him.

"Stay back, both of you…Stay back! You must!"

"What's wrong Dark?" Mephisto asked worriedly, as the figure of his grandson moved closer and he saw that he was indeed wounded. "Tell me boy!"

Dark slowly and awkwardly stepped forward into view, laying his hands upon the marble stair railing for needed stability. He glanced upward expectantly, searching for the first beam of moonlight that would fall upon his soon to turn form. Then abruptly, more out of fear, he drew back.

"The light…can't you see…it's changing me." Dark seemed badly shaken and his face reflected his dismay as he contorted his body, apparently in great pain. "The change, the change! It's happening, it's happening…I can feel it! The curse...The CURSE!"

For a moment no one dared move, then Aurra moved over to join him, but Dark quickly shook his head motioning for her to stay where she was. "Don't come any closer…I've been bitten…by a werewolf."

He caught his breath, twisting his head to again glimpse briefly out the window to see the light of the moon shining upon him before turning quickly back again. The bloodied assassin fell heavily to his knees and began stripping off his black, demonic armor, scattering the magical articles haphazardly about the marble floor. A bewildering confusion swept through his naked body as he fell to all fours like an animal and began to howl madly.

"Oh do shut up!" his grandfather's angered voice sounded sharply in his pointed elven ears, and the youthful face looked apprehensively upward at the enraged wizard. Both the magician and Aurra stood and stared at the naked kneeling assassin with blank expressions. "Have you lost your bloody mind?" Mephisto's voice rasped in fury at him, his eyes wickedly fastened on his speechless grandson. "How many times do I have to …you are of Silver Dragon descent, and are therefore immune to the Lycans curse. Do you understand this? You are part dragon; for all I know you may even have the ability to breathe fire…your mother couldn't, but who knows, sometimes it skips a generation or two."

Dark opened his mouth to speak, but could only stare at the old magus wordlessly. Mephisto's face froze rigid and stern.

"Now if you're done for the night, some of us would like to get back in our beds and go to sleep…I suggest you do the same." Mephisto ceased his chiding and relaxed his tall frame slightly, momentarily revealing his carefully masked true feelings. A second later it was gone. "On second thought, go mend your wounds in the healing pool. And for God's sake, cover yourself man!"

"Good night assassin," Aurra laughed aloud, her bright eyes dark and mischievous as she moved toward her bedroom.

Dark nodded, his throat tightening. Disregarding the pain from his injuries, he pushed himself up to stand, touching his wounds gingerly and winced. Slowly he started toward the door, his hand almost on the latch when his grandfather called out after him, his voice slightly anxious. "And take Baron out with you. He smells as bad as you look."

Dark stopped and looked for the big piece of beef he called his pet, whistled him to his side and led him out. The door closed softly behind him and the large chimera.

An unknown creature came for Dark through the lucid haze of that unique phase of sleep characterized by random movements of the eyes. It was a faceless creation of his dreams that rose up hauntingly every night since his childhood. From the blackened depths of his subconscious arose a thing of unimaginable terror, a thing that lurked somewhere in the deep dark recesses of his mind where all his deepest fears lay hidden. Each night it came for him, invisible with stealth and cunning. He could never see it coming; he never could. He screamed soundlessly for help, his parent's help, but they never came. There was no one, he was all alone against this faceless evil entity...

He came awake with a sudden start, abruptly lurching upwards from beneath his covering to a sitting position. The air in the healing pool room was cool on his ashen face. Beads of sweat ran down his face from his forehead and he could hear the sound of his own heart as it pounded wildly within. For a moment the weary assassin laid back quietly and allowed the sleep to disperse, and his mind to awaken fully. He saw a set of clothes lying on a chair near his bed and was just about to rise when the secret door opened and in walked Aurra, the young woman he had rescued. She looked well and refreshed, dressed in the same clothes, now mended, cleaned and dried, as when they first met and her long blonde tresses combed and shining. She was easily the most stunningly beautiful woman he had ever encountered. She smiled as she moved gracefully to his bedside.

"You look surprisingly well, for a werewolf," she smiled again. "The rest and healing pool seems to have cured you completely...and I don't see any fangs or thick clumps of hair anywhere...nope you're fine."

"Funny." Dark looked back with a sardonic smile. "What are you still doing here Princess? Shouldn't you be on your way home by now?"

"I came to thank you." She seated herself on the bed next to him. "If not for your heroic courage, I may not be alive today or worse. So for that I am, and shall remain eternally grateful...So thank you."

Dark threw his blankets aside and slowly climbed out of bed causing the Princess to rise with him in surprise and astonishment as she tried to hide her excitement, her face blushing red.

"You're welcome," he exclaimed, reaching for his clothes. "But you didn't come down here just to thank me, did you?" He paused just before putting his pants on, suddenly realizing the young woman with him was staring at him open-mouthed in stunned silence. She shook her head negatively and turned away to the door abashed so she couldn't see him changing.

"I wish to know if your sword is for hire?" the question came at last. "I would pay anything for it."

"That all depends. What do you want, a throat cut?" Dark asked, dressing himself quickly as he paused momentarily, his eyes fixed vacantly on the young woman's slim back.

"I want you to rescue my sister," asked Aurra slowly.

"And where is your sister now?" the assassin responded rather sharply. "Besides we don't even know if she's alive. Turn around, I'm dressed now."

The young Elven Princess turned back obediently and watched him curiously as he put on a pair of fluffy white slippers that resembled two long eared hares. Dark stopped quickly and looked up at her a little embarrassed. "What? They were a gift."

"I believe her to most likely be somewhere in the Land of Chaos," her words were fearful and spoken with a timorous apprehensiveness. "Most likely in the hands of the seller of the Black Fox's legendary bow."

"Let me get this straight; you want me to travel to the Underworld and rescue your sister from the clutches of the House of De' Sade!" Dark exclaimed angrily. "What do you take me for, some kind of fool?"

"Then she is alive!"

"I'm not saying that, but if she is alive…and that's a big if, then she would be there." He nodded soberly, a sudden premonition springing into his alert mind. If the Grey Elf was still alive, she would soon be subjugated to a life of slavery at the hands of the Drow. "I'm afraid Princess that going after your sister would be nothing short of suicide…it's just too dangerous." Dark trailed off into ominous silence. Hopefully the listener now understood the nature of the situation and the enemy they would be facing. The odds were just too great to overcome.

"I thought risking your life was your profession?" The moment of silence was broken as her final words seemed to echo back with a ringing sharpness.

"Risk, not throw away," Dark replied in almost a whisper.

"What's the matter?" Aurra spoke suddenly. "Is your sword not big enough for the task?"

"Nothing in life is free Princess; if the price is right my sword is yours." The question formed on the assassin's lips. "So then, what am I to be paid?"

"I am an Elven Princess from the House of Greyfell," exclaimed the tiny figure before the question was even completed. "Our coffers are deep with gold, or maybe one of our fine elven metal smiths could create weapons or armor for you. These are master craftsmen, their skill unmatched by any here on Eorth."

"That's not what I had in mind," he smiled roguishly, a little of his father's brashness crept out. Although he could not see her bowed face fully, he was certain she was blushing furiously.

Aurra became silent a moment before speaking. "All right…anything you want, but only for one night," the answer came at last.

"All right," he added. "The life of your sister for one night with you, but I expect my bounty perfumed and pretty."

"First the task."

His thoughts faded with Aurra's soft voice. She seemed small and vulnerable as she waited, her face beautiful and anxious. Without waiting for the elven girl to be led, Dark took her arm and propelled her through a magical opening of the weathered stone wall to a long stairway beyond.

Together they descended the carved stone steps into the inky blackness below. As they proceeded toward the large cavernous great room, Aurra asked Dark how he happened to be in the Gentlemen's Noose on that very night, but the guarded assassin responded evasively, still unwilling to tell anyone about his true plan. Instead, he explained that it had been a fortunate stroke of serendipity for his presence in the seedy tavern. She accepted his story without question and he found himself feeling a little guilty for lying to her.

Mephisto sat alone in the seclusion of his giant study, devoting his time and attention to a list of matters that required his immediate deliberation. Fatigue still lined his face and his eyes squinted wearily in the light of the candles that sat atop his wooden work desk. He rubbed his azure eyes, then his face, and when he took his hands away again, he found himself staring at the far end of the chamber, his eyes once again gray. A magical opening appeared and out strode Dark and the tiny Princess, their faces hidden in shadow. Aurra was the first to come forward, walking several paces ahead of her companion.

"Did he take the bait?" A faint mocking smile passed quickly across the old wizard's lips.

The small Elven Princess paused and regarded her new suitor coolly. Aurra only stared slyly at him for a moment, then shook her head with slow disdain and gave a final look of deserving scorn. "Hook, line and sinker," she replied smiling wickedly as the words rolled past her tongue. "What did you expect; he is a man, is he not?"

Dark did not know how to respond. All he could do was stare at the conniving woman and her collaborator wordlessly. Against a large bookcase, Baron raised his multiple heads and yawned loudly.

"I suppose you're in on this too…traitor." He glanced over briefly at the Chimera, who was laying sprawled out across the room sleeping soundly. Aurra had sauntered over and seated herself next to his grandfather just in time to hear the last comment. She smiled as he came up to them, her eyes dark and twinkling mischievously.

"Not to change the subject, but I took a look at the Necklace of Teleportation for you," Mephisto broke in. Then brought forth the small amulet and handed it to his grandson. "I have restored its magical properties for you; it should work as good as new."

"Then you figured out what spell she used to stop my escape?" Dark asked shortly.

"No, it wasn't a spell," his grandfather remarked quietly. "It would be something more powerful, something able to absorb multiple spells at once."

"Like a Rod of Absorption," the young half-elf exclaimed a moment later.

"Yes, I suppose," the tall magician responded slowly. "But such an item would be very rare and extremely sought after. And if a person does possess such a weapon, you would be well advised to take some precautions against such a foe."

"That's great advice old man. Why didn't I think of that." He mused mockingly. "Not to change the subject, but did Renfield bring my armor?"

"Oh yes," his grandfather smiled knowingly. "It's over there on the chair by the fireplace."

A moment later, Dark stood leisurely beside the magical items. He pulled the demonic breastplate out of the pile and dropped it on the table before the others. Dark grinned at Aurra and reached eagerly into the dark interior of the demon's fanged mouth. Suddenly the assassin removed his hand and poured the contents onto the open table. The others stared at the cache, Aurra especially looked at the item with great curiosity.

"It's a gem," declared the Princess after a moments consideration.

"It's not just any gem, it's a Gem of Location," came Dark's quick retort, his voice edged with a harsh note of disdain. "This is what's going to show us where your sister is…that is if she's still alive."

Aurra Greyfell opened her mouth angrily and then hesitated. She wanted to learn the truth behind her sister's disappearance, and if this object could find Nysarra's whereabouts, then she would hold her tongue for now. She stared momentarily at the Silver Mage, then turned back to Dark. "Show me please."

The half-elf hesitated briefly, then reached for the large blue diamond. He picked up the mystical stone and placed it gently in the palm of his hand. Perfectly cut, its color a deep brilliant blue with lustrous crystalline orientation, flashed sharply in the firelight. Aurra bent forward regarding it solemnly, then she looked back at Dark again.

"Find me Nysarra Greyfell," he spoke aloud.

As always the instant Dark finished his sentence, the Gem of Finders Keepers sprang to life in a blue glow that spread outward, then suddenly began pulsating rhythmically. Like clockwork, from within its crystalline core rose a shimmering white star. Instantly it flew higher and higher towards its new intended target, trailing behind it a translucent tail of white light. It steadily ascended until finally disappearing through the cavernous stone ceiling.

"Well, she's alive," Mephisto broke in, putting his pipe to his lips and lighting it.

For a long time the Princess didn't say anything. She just kept staring up towards the heavens, watching where the graceful star had vanished. When she finally spoke, it was only a whisper. "Thank you." She looked at Dark; she seemed like she was about to say something more, then thought better of it. She smiled openly, the first genuine smile he had seen from her.

They spent the next hour preparing for their journey and even ate a light breakfast. With little more than an hour remaining before noon, all three made their way to Dark Manor appearing outside the castle near the stable paddocks. The warmth of the autumn sun filtered through a mass of cotton-like clouds; the sunlit sky looked clear across the whole of the western horizon. Only to the far south lay a vast impenetrable blanket of blackness where the skyline was filled with thick dark mist that rose upward like heavy smoke.

Suddenly a great huge form soared out from a cluster of cloud cover, shimmering brightly in the warming noon sunlight as it dipped downward and came towards them. Aurra stared with wide eyes. It was truly the largest creature she had ever seen in her life. A gigantic feathered seabird with a wingspan of almost fifty feet, with a large strong bill with sharp edges and huge webbed black feet that extended forward as it made its approach. The majestic bird descended to the cloud field not more than a dozen feet in front of them, folding its large wings against its white, plumed body, its great head arching upward as it came to roost.

"This is *Alba*," Dark announced proudly, grinning briefly as he did so. "She'll take us to the Land of Dragons and faster than any ship you've ever sailed."

Aurra looked over at the old wizard for help. With a look of anticipation, he asked his companion if she was ready to depart. The small Princess looked frightfully at the monstrous bird. Had there been any other way, she would have taken it gladly, but there was no other alternative, and even though the mere thought of flying on the back of this feathered beast made her stomach churn, she resolutely announced she was ready. After all, if this half elf man can do this, then so could she.

With Dark leading the way, they moved over to the *Albatross*, and both climbed into the cockpit on the center of the seabird's feathery back. He held Aurra steady until she was comfortably secured, then he quickly cautioned her about her first flight.

"If the wind should blow you loose, don't worry…we'll get you…hopefully before you hit the ground."

Such assurances gave small comfort to the Elven Princess, who was scared enough as it was, who clutched the cockpit handrail with white knuckled grips of iron. Mephisto, seeing the girl's plight, quickly offered a small piece of ginger root as a remedy for her sickness. She ate it hurriedly. When Aurra seemed a bit more secure, the Captain of the *Albatross* then removed a long, leather-bound riding crop from beneath their feet.

"You're not going to use that to whip that poor creature are you?" the girl demanded immediately.

"Of course not…" Dark answered without hesitation, a quick smile lighting his handsome face. "This is for you, just in case you get lippy along the way." He snapped the whip sharply several times. With quick good-byes exchanged, the *Albatross* gave a long, loud and low single note, spread her great wings and rose slowly into the noon air. Petrified, the young Princess watched as the ground dropped away beneath them. After a while, the sickness she felt lessened and a feeling of heightened exhilaration began to sweep throughout her tiny body as she watched the horizon of the land below her broaden out and stretch wide apart, a spectacular panorama of cityscape, mountains and water. It was an amazing sight to behold, with the glorious noon sun shining down through a cloud-filled blue sky.

The large seabird found a path upward and climbed fast until the high-rooted walls and tall towers of Duergar seemed as small as scattered toys in the distance, and the many moored sailing boats were mere specks on the shore. Small island keys from this height, she observed, looked like lustrous pearls laid perfectly across the lapis blue of the sea. The wind whipped across them in long bursts, blowing strongly with a cooling effect of wet air from the coming storm out of the south. Dark glanced quickly over at his new shipmate, a fierce grin splitting wide his lean face. The smile he had returned was a little less than enthusiastic.

After only a few hours, the long winged *Albatross* drifted out over vast waters and far across a rolling plain of blue, navigating an invisible path flow like countless times before. Weary and still a little nauseated, the small elven woman settled next to her new companion and closed her eyes and drifted off into a sleepy haze. Their voyage took them several days to complete, and on the second day early in the afternoon, their long voyage finally came to an uncomfortable end for a grumpy Elven Princess. By late afternoon, they had reached the eastern edge of the dragon infested wasteland. From atop *Alba*, they could clearly see the whole of the valley entrance, a tangled mass of dark forests, ringed by a large range of unforgiving mountain peaks. It was a forbidding stretch of ancient woodlands, thick and heavily overgrown, containing many tree species making up the canopy, spotted with stagnant bogs and a scattering of muddy, brown swamps. There was no sign of any habitation, no towns or villages, no form of any small community or cloistered human settlement of any kind. On the whole this was a wasteland of impenetrable wilderness, dark and forbidding.

Moments later, Dark guided the *Albatross* back around and disappeared beneath a large canopy of trees. In a slow gradual descent, the giant seabird slipped through a narrow break in the dense foliage, dropping along a rugged ridgeline that fell away into the valley. Scattered clumps of trees dotted the ridge and *Alba* was brought to a rest upon a high covering of tall grass

Dark and Aurra climbed gingerly down from the bird's great back, stretching their muscles that had grown a little stiff and cramped from the long flight. After a quick command to his loyal feathered friend, the large tireless creature took to the sky once more, and once aloft, she banked right and flew steadily westward.

"What are we supposed to do now?" the Elven Princess asked curiously and a little confused.

Dark straightened himself with a slight grimace in his face. "We ride from here of course." In the next instant, the young assassin stretched forth his right arm, holding open his magically marked palm and recited the ancient words his grandfather had taught him. *"Adfer chan'r ffagla."* When the last of the words passed over his lips, a white searing fire burst forward from the sigil emblazoned on his palm, writhing and swirling like an uncontrollable tornado. The blinding intense glow spread violently outward in a brilliant field of absorbed flame, finally spiraling into a fading cone of fire leaving behind his magical mount from Hell, wreathed in the unholy fire of damnation.

"His name is Nightmare," Dark exclaimed, standing quietly before the fiery black, then lifted his head in invitation. "He's been mine since childhood, a present from Mephisto."

Nightmare came over instantly. Dark stroked the flaming neck slowly, gently and bent forward and whispered in the horse's ear. With a final word of secrecy, he swung upon the frightening beast's back, grabbing the reins in one hand.

"Well come on," his eyes sought those of the young elven girl. "Don't be afraid, he won't hurt you."

"Don't be silly…I'm not afraid," she mumbled, an uneasy trepidation sounding in her every word.

The small Elven Princess slowly came up to them and suddenly stopped. Her slim form was trembling with fear. She stood only for a brief moment, silhouetted against the afternoon sky, then hesitated only slightly once more before finally taking the assassin's arm, who lifted her up with the greatest of ease. Holding him tightly, her slender arms closed about his waist, her head fell against his back and she closed her eyes tight.

Dark and Aurra rode east out of the valley inland to an area where there still existed rulers of wind, fire, ice and water. A place where great beasts still possessed an ancient intelligence, an innate magic and born from the very primal powers from which they sprang into being. A place where the last wildernesses were marked boldly on maps with the simplest of warnings 'Here be Dragons'.

As the day wore on, the mountains seemed to loom closer above the wall of the forest in a single massive, craggy line of rugged peaks that stretched away across the whole of the Western horizon. These rugged mountain spires, called The Dragon's Teeth, extended through the wasteland, one rising above the next and offering no sign of passage nor any hint of break. With only a few hours remaining before sunset, they reached a broad, blackened pasture, once rich with verdant vegetation, but now just an expanse of charred stubble. The once lush forests of the former Elven lands that flourished with oak, chestnut, birch, pine and spruce were now a harsh rocky land with few trees and little plant life. They were transformed into a desolate wasteland with jagged outcroppings of scorched rock and burned out canyons created when a clan of Red Dragons blasted the land during the Dragon Cataclysms.

They moved on ahead at a steady pace, the eorth beneath Nightmare's flaming hooves had gone hard and cracked, but the way was clear as they followed the line of the sparse forest land. The Hell horse ran smoothly, his great body working effortlessly as he raced across the flatlands, the cooling afternoon air rushing gently over them as they rode. Dark felt a quick sense of exhilaration. He thought to himself, they were going to make it! The wasteland thinned into barren scrubs and the assassin and the elven girl at last caught sight of the broken ridges that formed the mouth of the Valley of the Döckálfar.

The incomplete thought hung suspended in his mind, when Aurra screamed. The alerted assassin jerked about, his eyes following the elven girl's fixed arm as she pointed skyward. He saw the creature almost immediately. High above them flew a huge, monstrous black shape with long, leathered wings that spanned the line of the horizon, its massive horned head lowered as it traced the mortal's path. It swept out over the blackened wasteland into the crease of the valley. Recognizing the mortal smell, it found the direction and with a shriek and a spurt of flame, it came for them.

With a sudden yell, Dark put his boots into the muscular flanks of the black horse. The beast of perdition reared up and exhaled a flaming puff through his flared nostrils in a snort of excitement, then shot back along the flatlands. Down the wasteland trail they rode, both riders bent low across the Hell horse's neck, withered limbs periodically whipping against them as they flew forward. Dark, using his keen elven eyesight, expertly guided his faithful mount with a sure hand and practiced technique past fallen obstacles and dead wood, over patches of bare, blackened ground, down one slope then up the next.

Seconds later, the dragon dove for them, falling towards them like a huge rock, plummeting to Eorth, its scaled sides gleaming red. Without warning, amid a mass of black smoke, a burning streak of fiery flame burst forward from the mythical monster's open maw. Both riders saw it come close and momentarily glimpsed the dragon fully. It was slightly bent with wings spread a mile wide, massively clawed and fanged, spewing fire and molten spittle that fell from the creases of its huge crooked mouth. The eyes of the giant reptile seemed to transfix the Elven Princess, and she felt her courage melt away.

Dark could hear the crackle and roar of scorching flame as it streaked past in fiery flashes. With a surge, Nightmare sprang into a shrub bursting with fall foliage, then broke free along a new make-shift trail and galloped on ahead, flames bursting from flared nostrils. The dragon soared on the wind, swooping and with bursting breath, unleashing its elemental rage, matching them turn for turn. On they rode barely slowing for a moment, not even for any obstacle that barred their path. The stallion's sleek black body dodged and caracoled them through a tangled mass of thick and heavy brush. Only a few hundred yards away loomed the dark forest that marked the outer fringes to the Valley of the Döckálfar. Beyond lay woods that would hide them from this enormous ancient threat, woods into which its burning gaze could not find them and its evil ears could no longer catch the faintest of whispers on the wind.

As the last light of day began to fade, the red dragon's battle howl swelled in the cool air. It echoed out across like a hiss from a vast bonfire of green logs cutting through in shrieking bursts, a noise that increased to a hateful, deafening volume that shattered the air with savage screaming, then slowly died. For an instant, they both believed they were finished, but then, in the sky a fleeting shape appeared, black against the clouds. A spurt of orange flame in the sky signaled the nearby flight of another dragon. In seconds the two dragons, one pearl white and the other a glittering red, resumed their age-old struggle, grappling, slashing and tearing at each other. White in pursuit of red, and red in pursuit of white, they writhed across the heavens like a vast fiery wheel until the sky became criss crossed with smoke trails. No bigger than a sparrow, both dragons soon disappeared over the crag like two darkened silhouettes tipped with bright flame. Then they vanished completely.

The afternoon soon faded into dusk and the darkening sky was silently slipping across the whole of the valley. The sun was lost somewhere beyond the canopy of the forest and sank down beyond the rim of the mountains. Shadows deepened and the air became cool and still they rode on in silence. The only sound that was heard was of shod hooves striking against stone and eorth that echoed eerily in the growing darkness. Behind the impenetrable walls of the mountains, the waxing moon's silvery disk was rising above the forest and one by one the stars eagerly winked into view. Within the Valley of the Döckálfar the silence began to deepen.

When at last they did stop, they were once more back on a main trailway. Dark reined in Nightmare sharply, patted the animal's muscular flanks and glanced back at Aurra with an impish grin. "Name another horse that can outrun a dragon."

The Elven Princess felt her stomach begin to settle. "None I suppose. Why are we stopping here?"

"Because we're here," he replied and quickly dismounted. His eyes alertly scanned the area for a few moments and then he frowned. "The whole city will be awake by now. Are you all right?" Dark asked softly, reaching up to take Aurra from the saddle and lowering her carefully to the ground.

The elven girl nodded wordlessly, her eyes bright with fear. "This is definitely harder than I thought it would be," she murmured, paused and glanced back at him sharply. "How are we going to get through the city once we get there? Won't they recognize us?"

"Leave that to me Princess." The light was growing steadily dimmer; the assassin glanced about apprehensively. "Stay close to me."

The air had quickly become sharply chilled with the approach of nightfall and strange sounds emanated from deep within the trees as the valley began to awaken. Donning his demonic disguise, the black garbed assassin whispered into his fiery companion's ear, then sent the steed home to Hell in a swirling blaze. Together they moved on ahead with Dark leading the elven girl through a stretch of dense forest which ran eastward. Elm trees, pine, huge black oaks and shag-bark hickories towered over them as they marched through a broad shadowed gap of tangled scrub and deadwood. The floor of the valley began to climb steadily, their footing growing less sure with loose rock littering the pathway and cracks splitting its surface. As the trail continued to rise, both Dark and Aurra stumbled and slid with each step and their pace was slowed considerably.

Then abruptly it stopped. Before them was an enormous chasm stretching out more than half a mile wide. It was a massive fissure that dropped away into a black, unforgiving emptiness. To the left water cascaded down its side in a huge waterfall with the flowing water turning into a fine mist at the bottom of a lake far below. To the right was a narrow ledge that skirted the breach, a thin crumbling pathway that would barely permit the passage of a single rider and mount.

"And then the Silver Mage, Mephistopheles, ripped open the Eorth and banished them beneath it. There the Döckálfar would forever dwell without the sun or moon, nor the rain or wind, but in the shade of darkness and eternal gloom." The words fell from her lips in a barely audible whisper, her deep blue eyes peered downward tentatively into the dim murkiness that lay at her feet.

"Beyond this entrance lies the Land of Chaos," Dark's voice came softly out of the mist. "There are countless numbers of passages, chambers and tunnels, most natural, some man-made, but all an endless maze to one who does not know the way. Soon after we enter, we will reach the Tunnel of the Damned, a tunnel inhabited by invisible spirits. They are no more than voices set to frighten weaker men. Once beyond the corridor, we will be in the Hall of the Spider Queen. These giant statues stand guard like stone sentries who keep a watchful vigil and protect the ancient city portal from unwanted intruders. Then, there will be only one more obstacle…" The half-elven assassin suddenly stopped talking, his eyes turning warily to the deep fissure. For a moment it seemed he might finish his sentence, but instead motioned the Elven Princess toward the dark sloping pathway. Aurra stood uneasily between the graying mist that surrounded them and the black yawning opening before her waiting like the open mouth of some great monstrous beast. A moment later, they moved cautiously along the pathway and down into the rift.

There was a deep, hushed stillness only magnified by the slowly dying of the wind and the echoing of their footfalls along the rocky passageway. Large webs stretched down into the darkness and far below them they could hear the faint sound of rushing water. No one spoke, as Dark led them carefully down through a series of gently winding turns. Further and further down they traveled; Dark could feel Aurra's tiny hand grip his own tightly in the blackness that surrounded them. He thought about the Elven Princess for a moment and found himself smiling. After what seemed forever, they found themselves standing before a stone stairway, and the hard to traverse slope underwent an abrupt change. Gone were the naturally formed rock walls. The stairs and surrounding passageway were now formed of stone steps, perfectly finished and beautifully massive, but unquestionably fashioned by the hands of Elves.

Still down they went for hundreds of feet; the ancient stairway wore on, endlessly bending and turning at precise angles, leveling off occasionally into small ramp ways, then twisting deeper into the darkness. The air grew pungent with an aroma of death and decay. Still they descended downward, watching as the steps wound away before them. Finally the stone steps ended. They stood within a linked network of several titanic cave systems; nearby were several areas of deep water that hid a mass of hollowed out sections of coral caves. The cave system consisted of a series of caverns and passages that stretched on for miles. Often there were too many twists and turns in a maddening fashion, forming three dimensional mazes that would discourage even the most hearty of adventurers.

From the base of the stairs, a hallway of worked stone extended north, then opened into what appeared to be a natural cavern. Lighting their way in this blackened underworld was a faint green phosphorescence that danced along the ceiling overhead. Dark hurried forward eagerly pulling at Aurra's hand, casting anxious glances over both shoulders, making certain that there were no prying eyes watching them.

The cavern stretched outward for hundreds of feet to the north, its floor broken into a myriad of ledges and tilted slabs of formed stone. Many of them were covered by a strange fungal growth that appeared to the Elven Princess to have been carefully cultivated. Clear crystal formations sprouted like broad leaves from every surface of the small cavern. Immense webs hung in dusty tatters from the ceiling and walls in white sheets, with an intricate network of webbing blanketing the entire ceiling. Dozens of long haired spiders could be seen crawling slowly around the constructed network of fine threads. Some were as small as tiny pebbles, while others were as large as a small dog.

Abruptly they came to an unsteady halt, and in the deep silence that followed the reassuring voice of the party's leader spoke gently in the ear of his elven companion. "Beyond this chamber lies the Tunnel of the Damned; pay no heed to their siren-like calls. They are no more than idle threats and whispered warnings, fear them not, for they cannot harm you."

Before she could even reply, they were moving forward again, her booted feet echoing hollowly on the cavern floor as they moved deeper into the Vault of the Drow. About twenty feet into the underground passage, they came across a heavy swinging spiked gate that barred their path. Beyond it, the tunnel continued to the northwest, stretching off into the darkness beyond.

"This gateway was intended to prevent any slaves from using this passage as an escape route," Dark announced solemnly, pointing to the iron gate. "And there are only five keys to this locked entrance in existence. Fortunately for us this poses no problem."

Within seconds, Dark and Aurra had both teleported past the spiked barrier and continued quickly through the faint green light of the narrow tunnel. This section ran for nearly half a mile, then abruptly the passage widened and grew into a massive corridor of total darkness. The smooth rock walls drew away violently and the ceiling rose and there was a total absence of light leaving the pair alone in a strange limbo of murkiness and shadow. The only reassurance offered to Aurra was the strong hold Dark had of her hand, and the belief that the world had not disappeared entirely. Showing no signs of hesitation, she was led into the blackness and gloom.

Suddenly the sounds began. The incredible banshee-like baying caught them completely off guard and unprepared, and for a moment there was panic in the small Princess. The sound grew to an enormous roar like the sound of a hundred ferocious winds that combined in both savage fury and biting force. It seemed they had joined the storied legions of the restless dead, doomed ghosts of men and women who were no longer of this world, but as yet to find peace in the other. They came in an infinity of guises; some manifested themselves as horrifying crying souls, forever screaming in anguish and torment. Others came as frightening, elusive abominations, appearing and disappearing at random, their garbled voices shrieking as they twisted in agonizing torture and utter despair. Most disturbing of all were the ghosts who came as they were left in death and not as they had been in life. Briefly they would pass by animated corpses beribboned with old tattered eorth-caked and worm ridden remnants of shrouds. Maimed and grotesquely mutilated at the moment of death, their shrieks reached a pitch far beyond the comprehension of mortals. So stunning to the ears and mind that if they listened much longer their own sanity would begin to shatter and break apart.

What seemed like an eternity had only taken a few brief minutes. In another instant, they would have been lost, but they were saved. Saved from hopelessly falling into complete and utter madness as the powerful will of the dark assassin broke through the terrifying crazed sounds to cloak them with an ancient spell of protection. The deafening screams and bellows seemed to lessen and fade almost at once, the now barely audible screeches and squeals were unable to break through the barrier erected by Dark's powerful will. Denied their easeful rest of death, the spectral malefactors returned to the grave, the power of their voices were exhausted and spent and faded away into only a deathly whisper. A moment later the passageway narrowed once again and the pair were clear of the Tunnel of the Damned.

They stepped into a small alcove, facing toward two huge stone doors laced by intricate iron bindings, the Spider Queen's Coat-of-Arms emblazoned on the door panels. The smooth rock walls and ceiling around them began to shine with a bright and steady light emitting from inscribed sigils and esoteric glyphs placed around the entranceway. With a strong push from the assassin's gauntleted hand, the massive doors swung silently open.

"The Hall of the Spider Queen," Dark's voice became only a whisper amid the calm silence.

From out of the tunnel's mouth they bore witness to a spectacular sight. High above their heads a starry sky brilliantly sparkled; a lustrous half crescent moon gleamed down upon the breathtaking setting, filling the large chamber with a soft silvery light. Flowering trees and blossoming shrubs and wild bushes circled around the entire area. Flowers bloomed everywhere and the sweet smelling perfume of jasmine, ornamental lilacs and numerous roses filled the air with a heady scent. In the center of the small cave stood a beautifully decorated dais, adorned with gold ornaments with black marble steps that lead up to a statue of alabaster surrounded by several types of wild roses. The half nude sculpture was a most alluring female Dark Elf that posed gracefully, her slender hand outstretched as if to pluck at one of the delicate flowers. There was a deep, still silence in the chamber as Dark motioned for them to keep moving toward the ancient portal. It was a stunning crafted archway made of solid adamantine set with large blue sapphires in a decorative pattern and magically inscribed with dark elven runes. On either side of the black metal portal stood two monstrous stone statues carved out of the rock and rising well over fifty feet against the dark cave wall. The statue sentries had been fashioned to appear as male Döckálfar from the waist up, with their lower portions replaced with the abdomen and legs of an immense spider. Even though their faces had been weathered by time, their eyes were wide and open as if almost alive and fixed carefully on the two mortals who stood at the very threshold of the ancient city they guarded.

"Are you ready?" Dark directed his gaze to his small Elven companion.

She paused and breathed deeply. "I think so." Aurra stared at him incredulously for a moment, shot a quick glance over to the portal, then shook her head resignedly. Too late, for Dark had already began speaking the words that would activate the silent portal! *"Baile àtha Dorcha U'drek!"*

The small Princess recognized immediately the distinct meaningful elements of the phrase just spoken. It was an ancient unit of language, a long forgotten dialect of her Elven ancestors, not spoken or heard for more than two thousand years. Simply it meant the 'City of Shade'.

The elder words that activated the portal's spell seemed to linger in the air for a moment. As the elven words faded from hearing, the archway became suffused with mystical power and began to glow softly as if illuminated from within by a bright light. One by one, brightly shining sigils appeared briefly, each symbol burning into the metal surface before quickly fading into invisibility. Instantly a pinhole of light sprang into being in the center of the arch, the energy inside swirling and twisting into a spherical vortex that exploded outward in a furious burst. An opalescent glow quickly spread out across their bodies in ripples, like water spreading out across a calm lake. Bathed in a silver green nimbus of light, their skin became imbued with a pearl-like sheen before both travelers were teleported and emerged from a second column of light a fraction of a second later.

They now stood some two hundred miles beneath the surface of the Eorth in front of an exact replica of the previous two statues and metallic arch, the light within now faded and still. Two massive iron gates marked the end of a long tunnel and the entrance to the City of Shade. Four dark figures, their features lost in shadows cast by burning torches, stood only a few feet beyond the gates, blocking the path to Aurra's sister. In an instant the black-garbed assassin's appearance was reshaped. With the Eye of Dagda hovering above his head, he now stood in the splendid purple robes of a dark Elven Archmage. In one hand he held an extremely large, black leather bound book; the other held a long walking staff. Though he had the common characteristics associated with the Drow, he also bore a ghastly feature that made most men turn away in horror. In the place where his eyes should be were now two black and burnt out voids of pure darkness.

"It seems as though your looks have improved somewhat," Aurra declared, the now familiar mocking smile appeared on her sylph-like face.

"So does this mean that our previously discussed method of payment has been…oh what is the word I am looking for… reinstated?" He gave her a roguish smile back, his behavior slightly duplicitous.

She paused, then nodded in an action of resigned consent, "Yeah don't hold your breath."

A small group of black-clad Drow guards met the pair just inside the gates to the portal, extended warm greetings to the altered assassin and his cloaked and hooded companion, and let them proceed through at once. Once past the gate, the tunnel came to an abrupt end in a cavern so large that being within it felt like you were still outside on a bright star-filled night.

In stark contrast to the ever present gloom that shrouded most of the Land of Chaos, luminescent rocks in the ceiling were aglow like shining stars onto a black, murky surface of permanent midnight, striking perfect reflections onto the water's surface. A gleaming coral reef lighted the water in several areas casting an eerie yet beautiful shadow of a deep purple light onto the walls and even into the upper reaches of the cavern. A number of sleek, ribbon-like cascading waterfalls spilled down into the placid sea from a vertical drop in the ceiling well over a thousand feet overhead.

"What do they call these arresting waters?" she smiled. "It's exquisite."

"It's called the Sea of the Fallen Stars," the disguised assassin responded, his voice sounding like that of an old scholar. "It gives one the illusion of sailing amid a sea of stars."

Then suddenly, the still and silent surface of the black lake surged unexpectantly upward; from out of the dark depths emerged a nightmare of a creature. It was somewhat serpentine in appearance, its slime covered torso raised skyward with a shriek of fury. Its massive form twisted and flexed as it reared out of the water, its deadly curved claws clutched the empty air in front of itself. Great monstrous jaws gnashed pointed teeth together in rage. The creature was completely covered with a reptilian skin that dripped with scum and blackened waste, carried from far below the black briny depths. Than as suddenly as it had appeared, it fell back into the waters amid faint traces of white mist that rose above a froth of seawater.

"Oh yeah, it might be a good idea to stay away from the water."

From one side to the other the great cavern was almost two miles wide and at least double that going north to south. Immediately in front of them was a giant causeway leading north into the very bowels of the mighty metropolis. The air here crackled with magical energy that seemed to spark from the glimmering rocks in the cave ceiling. Stalactites, stalagmites and carved columns littered the massive cavern. All of them had been worked or shaped in someway, some of the large ones being converted to castles and stately homes for Döckálfar nobles, all linked via a network of intricate stone ledges and arching bridges. At the heart of the city was a towering fortress of dark elegance, the Pillar of Woe. The castle stemmed from an enormous stalactite and stalagmite joined together to form a rare solid single column. A wide spiral staircase wound up around the outside with sweeping ramps and great terraced landings that lined the huge landmark. Complex arching bridges connected the main citadel to a thicket of stalactites, all hollowed out by slave labor, that hung down beside them.

The Elven Princess followed wordlessly as the magically altered assassin mounted the broad causeway leading to the Outer Wall. Several people passed them as they moved forward and those who looked, carefully turned to stare in horror and shock at the eyeless wizard. Peering intently toward the gates, they now were close enough to make out the lights of the sprawling city and the movements from a number of dark garbed sentries on the stone ramparts. The blind Archmage made no attempt to hide his face as he approached the shadowed faces of four armed elven guards. They made no move to stop the Döckálfar wizard or his hooded escort and no words were passed between them. Without any fear, Dark and Aurra passed beneath the shadow of the giant gateway and quickly disappeared through the mammoth gates and into the streets of the city beyond.

Within moments, the pair had crossed the courtyard and passed, once again unharassed through the Inner Wall and finally to the streets. Once more the guards positioned here stared in silent disbelief, but again did nothing to stop the travelers from entering. As the pair proceeded down the main city thoroughfare, a deadly black shadow seemed to haunt its streets with whole sections of the fabled Döckálfar settlement vanishing into this dark gloom entirely. The direction Dark guided them through was a parade route of inhospitable sceneries with less and less traffic as they made their way through several of the city's districts.

At a large intersection east of the city center, a large building stood in ruins. Its upper stories were burned out and charred black, purposely destroyed by fire. And even though the ground floor was more or less still intact, the broken windows and furniture that was left out in the street indicated it had been a great attraction to looters.

"What happened here?" the small Elven Princess spoke suddenly in a somber voice.

"Lolth has suddenly fallen silent," the half-elf impos-ter replied softly. "In Dark Elf society, the Spider Queen's will is the single most influential guiding principle and her female clerics hold on tight to the reins of power. So even though the Priestesses send their whispered pleas to the Demon Goddess, they receive no answer. They gain no spells. They gain no wisdom or even any insight. And to this day, they have no idea even if she still watches over them or has abandoned her flock altogether. Still others wonder if Lolth is even alive."

"Maybe she tests them this way," she suggested casually. "Observing her followers to see which, if any, remain faithful."

"Unfortunately the Dark Mother's slackened grip on the Döckálfar population has only brought about violent insurrections, and growing unrest among her people and moments of unbridled aspirations from the city's Archmages," continued Dark slowly, inwardly musing over the prospect. "As you can see for yourself, this silence has had catastrophic effects. Even today, the ensuing House feuds still rage, unchecked by any sense of propriety or reverence. The sooner we find your sister and get out of here the better."

The two mage travelers quickly lost sight of the large intersection behind them as they started up the slope of a high arched bridge in quick determined strides. Picking up the pace, they proceeded on and soon came to an area where larger and more elegant buildings became visible, with grand public staircases leading from one level to another. Its high stained glass windows were dark and empty, except for those on the ground floor in both the left and right wings. Dark motioned Aurra ahead of him, keeping careful watch for possible danger, peering into the shadows about them where he quickly discovered a couple dozen or so well armed guards close at hand.

The ever vigilant half-elf knew that they could be walking into a trap, just as he had silently thought to himself when they had first entered the City of Shade. His first and only inclination at this point, was to do nothing but watch, wait and see what happens and go from there. In minutes they reached the metal bound gates of the Noble district. Keeping in character, Dark blindly reached for a huge wrought iron door knocker and brought it crashing down against the gate door like thundering hammers. For a long moment there was no sound, then suddenly a low voice from the other side asked for identification. Dark gave his name as 'Solamond' and also gave a sharp command for the gate keeper. Immediately, the heavy bars were drawn back and the solid gates opened to admit two. They didn't wait long before someone with authority acknowledged them and quickly led the blind Archmage to a back room. After only a few minutes and a few gold coins, they emerged again and were permitted to pass through; several soldiers made way for them as they walked by.

"Just exactly who is this wizard that you pretend to be?" Aurra's soft voice gently drifted her question to Dark's ears. "And what if he becomes aware that you are impersonating him?"

"His name is Solamond Do' Guul, a very powerful and enigmatic Archmage who enjoys high standing in Drow society," he murmured gently. "And you need not worry about the blind wizard discovering our presence here. More than a year ago I found out he had acquired a friend of mine, sold to him in slavery. When I found him, I saw to it that he too suffered the same fate as she."

They passed under giant archways and delicate looking crosswalks that ran overhead, always guided by the Gem of Location; their final destination close at hand. The ancient artifact took them to a plateau dominated by a number of large, palatial palaces and mansions. A steep set of stairs with railings woven in a web-like pattern and spun from pure white platinum led up to the gates of a dark, yet elegant home. Its graceful arches and high towers were strangely beautiful, the very summation of what Döckálfar aesthetics were.

Aurra paused hesitantly at the bottom of the stairway that led to the Noble House, peering upward, her gaze intent. Dark once again took the lead, with the Princess following close behind, right at the assassin's heels. Together they cautiously moved up the stone steps, keeping alert for any sign of a trap. The faint light of burning torches helped cut through the darkness far above them, their orange flames flickered with energy from a gusting source of wind that came from a number of hidden openings that allowed fresh air to enter the cavern.

Once they safely reached the plateau landing, a pair of massive iron gates guarded the entrance, but one of the gates was curiously propped open. Guardedly, Dark led them past the open gateway and under a gracefully sculpted archway to a large courtyard. Before them stood a sprawling palatial palace that even a blind man could see had undergone countless additions and improvements, presumably by the last few inhabitants. On the stone walkway leading up to the mansion were two large standards, both symbols depicted were of two red eyes staring out from behind a spiked black mask.

Together they moved slowly along a stone path that led into a little garden at the side of the huge building. In quick, surefooted strides, Dark followed the guiding pulses of the large gem as they weaved between stately trees, his watchful eyes studying the enclosed palace grounds. Making certain there were no guards close at hand, they climbed a gently sloping embankment toward foliage that completely covered the wall of a new addition and melted instantly into the creeping evergreen backdrop. For long moments they remained completely invisible as they moved steadily within the camouflaged confines of the climbing vine. Pausing breathlessly within the green plant's flowering stems, the invisible intruders heard the sound of approaching voices. They waited silently, their dark forms blending perfectly with this green surroundings so that assassin and princess were totally invisible, even from only a few feet away. The guards appeared just seconds later, both still conversing in the native language of the Drow as they passed through the empty gardens and were gone.

Still cloaked in magical illusion, the pair of elven invaders crossed beneath the shadows of the new building, pausing briefly beneath a large, darkened window that was placed within a recessed alcove. With nimble fingers, Dark made quick work of the metal latch and with an audible click, the catch was broken and the window swung silently inward. Hastily, they slipped through the window opening, then carefully closed it.

They paused momentarily within the darkened chamber, making sure the window was closed and locked tightly behind them. Then giving the room more than a passing thought, Dark removed the Eye of Dagda from above his head and carefully placed it back within the now visible mouth of his demonic armor. Cautiously, and with cat-like movements, he soundlessly opened the door and peered into the lighted hallway. There was no one in sight, nor did his keen elven ears pick up any noise. Grabbing Aurra's hand, silently they stepped into the empty hallway. He followed the guiding gem to the end of the hall and turned right. The house seemed eerily empty as they followed through an open door that led into an icy corridor of dark metallic stone. The mansion's inner space was like a complex maze, featuring many twists and turns that all seemed to lead to various rooms and similar corridors.

"Stop!" he whispered the word.

Instantly the half-elf assassin turned back to face the young Princess. "There's a glowing circle of runes on the ground ahead."

Aurra stopped, she peered cautiously down the corridor, but even with her own sharp eyes, she saw nothing. Along the surface of the walls and floor were symbols of death, inscribed in many known and unknown languages. Some of these symbols and signs were magically charged with lethal capabilities, capable of slaying those who were foolish enough to try and pass them.

"Some of these engraved glyphs show signs of having already been discharged," the black-garbed assassin declared as he faced the elven girl. "Most likely by runaway slaves trying unsuccessfully to escape their cruel mistress. So just give me a second to dispel them."

He had already began chanting his divine power, shaping and transforming the energy into its arcane spell form, his eyes immediately glowing with a pale blue radiance. After a few short words of magic, the energy of the spell was released and the sigils of destruction became aglow with white brilliance. Lurid flames sprang up enveloping every dark symbol within the magical fire. And where the flame passed, nothing remained; they were utterly consumed by the fire leaving only blackened stains upon the stone.

They again moved ahead cautiously until they passed a pair of double doors emblazoned with the seal of the Red Spider. The open doors allowed access to a macabre triangular shaped room with polished marble black walls and a black marble floor. On the southern wall hung a large mural of a female Döckálfar sitting on a throne made of bones. She was strangely beautiful with skin as white as snow and both her eyes glowed an eerie red. At the right hand of the seated figure in the mural stood a second figure, another beautiful Drow woman, younger than the first, her otherwise stunning face branded red and marked with a spider insignia. Covering one of her eyes was a silver plated eye patch studded with red rubies. Below the haunting painting was a spiral staircase made from a gleaming dark stone that descended downward.

"And who are these two supposed to be?" the elven girl whispered to Dark.

"The albino witch is none other than Malice De' Sade, Matron Mother and Ruler of the House De' Sade," he whispered back, placing the glowing gemstone safely away, its magical tracking abilities no longer required. "The other next to her, Ever Syn De' Sade, the youngest of her three children. Cruel, ruthless and completely unafraid of her own death, a woman so utterly consumed with a desire for revenant power that she teeters on the very brink of sanity… and that's just the young daughter."

With a quick look back at Aurra, they started forward. Down the smooth stone steps the pair slowly moved as quiet as church mice with Dark casting apprehensive glances at what might lay below. They had descended only a few feet when they heard the sudden sound of chains clattering and clanking together. Then the sound of laughter echoed from far below them. Step by narrow step and turn by turn, the assassin descended toward the sound. As he progressed, Aurra fell into step directly behind him; the dark and gloomy stairs grew brighter until the patterns of the stonework that formed it became clearly defined. As the pair drew nearer, the sound of voices became distinctly audible in all directions.

Through the stone lattice work of the stair railings, Dark could see a small ante-chamber with a large arcane diagram filling most of the floor. Beyond the octagonal room a regal throne of bones bleached white loomed high on a black dais on the far side of the room. Rich tapestries with macabre designs hung hauntingly on the wall behind the ghastly ceremonial chair helping to contribute to its air of morbid authority. In fact most of the walls of this large chamber were decorated with enormous lurid tapestries that featured grisly scenes of death and warfare between the Drow and surface Elves. Huge spider webs stretched from wall to wall along the ceiling and within its tangled mass of sticky strands were huge multi-eyed creatures, their eyes glowing red with hate. Several Drow men, all wearing polished black breastplates and carrying gruesome looking halberds guarded the grand hall. On the wall opposite the dark Elven guards was an image of an elaborate archway carved beautifully into the stone. A path made of human bones curved from the doors in front of Dark to two nightmarish columns shaped like giant skeletons, surmounted by winged demon-like figures. Flanked on each side by these unearthly statues, and bound in shackles with an iron collar placed about the neck, was a badly beaten and bloodied female elf, above her head a small shining star that glittered and flared white. Darkness seemed to cling to everything here, the doors, the walls, even the floors themselves seemed alive somehow, like something solid draping the entire room in a living shadow. Then from somewhere beyond the void of blackness came a voice that echoed through the thick air of the malodorous charnel house.

"It seems your time here Princess has finally come to an end." There was the clatter of horse's hooves on the ancient stone floor as Dark waited expectantly at Aurra's side, his free hand held the girl's arm tightly, and in a forceful whisper warned her not to speak or move. Then the slim figure of a beautiful female elf emerged from behind a curtain of shadow riding atop a slave dressed up as a pony in modified horse tack. She had long white hair that flowed down around her slender body and she wore an exposing outfit that left very little to the imagination. Over her left eye she wore an eye patch with eight red rubies like eight spider eyes set into its silver surface. In one hand was a fine metal gauntlet, cruelly sharpened at the fingertips and at her waist hung a glowing mace made of black adamantine set with silver spikes. This was Ever Syn De' Sade.

"Don't get me wrong, I so enjoyed having you here but things have changed," she rose slowly from her human mount, still talking as she approached the restrained Elven prisoner, her sagging form held from falling only by the iron manacles locked about her hands and neck. "As I am sure you are well aware by now, our Goddess has fallen silent. Why we do not know, but because of it the City of Shade has been left in chaotic ruin. Two warring factions now fight for control of the city, the treacherous Archmages and the remaining ruling Noble Houses. Rather than abandon the worship of our Spider Queen, the surviving loyalists of Lolth joined forces…"

"You made a deal with the devil!" the Grey Elf swore with rage, her breathing harsh, her pale face bending slightly upward to face her captor.

Then with the quickness of a cat, Ever's armored hand reached outward, grasping the elf's slim throat as her fingers closed tightly about the windpipe.

"We could not just sit idly by while interlopers from other Döckálfar communities started an uprising against our regime!" She slowly released her grip on the girl's throat leaving the Princess gasping for air in ragged gulps. "The remaining refugees from the Noble Houses were too few to provide a significant challenge to the arcane brotherhood and its members, at least not without support."

"You mean Kalifen!" her breath rasped in her throat.

"So Mother turned her attention to the surface," the Dark Elf moved to a makeshift altar of decaying corpses, picking up a bone handled dagger with an insubstantial spectral blade glowing with energy. "With Lord Kalifen's help we shall form a new Empire of Shadow and finally achieve our ultimate goal, placing the Matron Mother of the House of De' Sade upon the throne of Shade."

"He'll betray you…just like he has all the others," she sputtered the words.

"Betray the Noble House of De' Sade?" the dark Priestess of Lolth gave a quiet laugh of mild amusement. "No, Nysarra, after all we have done for him and all we still have left to do…he needs us. Without the help of the Drow, his plan to raise an army of undead to lay waste to the surface world would surely fail."

Unwavering, the helpless Elven Princess tried to say something in response, but the dark daughter of Malice moved menacingly in front of her. Her sentence ended before it began in a strangled gasp as Ever grabbed her forcibly by the throat and slowly began to squeeze. Drawing the glowing dagger, she held it close to the Grey Elf's unprotected left eye. "As for you, I'm afraid the Matron Mother sees you as some sort of sign of Lolth's favor among the Döckálfar and wishes to sacrifice you as an offering to the Dark Goddess."

Nysarra's face began to turn slowly purple. "But before you go, I wish to pluck out one of your eyes as a keepsake of our time here together ."

At that moment the sharp blade from the enchanted weapon began to leisurely cut into the elven girl's skin, spurting blood, causing the gasping captive to violently burst out screaming her acquiescence.

In an instant Aurra bounded over the stone railing with the elegance and quickness of a gazelle, her sharp elven eyes cold with fury. Dark was after her with leaping strides, his one outstretched arm to stop her. In one single smooth, silent motion, the now focused female elf slid the ancient weapon of the Black Fox free from somewhere beneath her cloak, the black bow armed and drawn back.

"Get your dirty hands off my sister, you stupid filthy bitch!"

The evil cleric turned her attention from her captive to that of the voiced intrusion and met Aurra's gaze briefly, her own eyes furtive and filled with hate. Before the Drow Priestess could react, the air sounded with the deep humming of a rush of black arrows from a silent snapping bowstring, that swept through the large dim lit chamber in barely perceptible streaks.

Suddenly, a long black arrow magically appeared as her pull reached full draw-length, and for one split second everything seemed to come to a complete standstill. Then the taut bowstring was released with another silent twang, the arrow and energy stored within flew almost invisible to its intended target. As if part of the same fluid motion, the reincarnation of the Black Fox sighted down a new fitted arrow to the string and began to fire with blinding rapidity.

It all happened so fast that no one saw it coming, or even had time to react, but each caught brief glimpses of the archer's actions and the grisly scene that followed. The first arrow struck the ceremonial knife in the outstretched hand of the Drow Priestess and sent it spinning in an explosion of white bone splinters. While the suddenly astonished cleric and her bewildered group of guards were caught momentarily frozen in their tracks, the second arrow embedded itself painfully in the armored hand of the Dark Elf. The third flew through the air with pinpoint accuracy, puncturing through the gristle and exposed knee bone of the female Döckálfar who immediately gave an agonizing howl of pain. Within seconds after the first arrow struck its target, and before the third was ever fired, a dangerous looking glyph on the floor at the threshold of the huge chamber suddenly became visible with a bright flash of blue.

Behind the blinding flash, and now before the approaching elf, appeared two hulking monstrous arachnid creatures. These revolting abominations had the head and torso of a Dark Elf and the lower body of a gigantic spider. Multiple glowing eyes accentuated their pallor of death, their elongated hands and fingers were wickedly clawed, and from their mouths protruded huge fangs that dripped with venom. Each one was broad and immobile in their stance, their muscular arms raised in challenge, one great hand clutching a stone shattering flail in menacing defiance of the small elven girl that confronted them. Their shouts echoed deafeningly off the stone walls, crying out for her instant death.

Aurra paused only an instant in her pursuit to glance up at the two brutish looking distractions, their morning star maces spinning several large spiked balls on long chains high above their heads. They may as well have been statues for all the difference their unexpected appearance made to the great Elven archer, who toppled them over with two lightning-like assaults, striking both through their open maws with the metal points of the arrows protruding out the back of their skulls. When she finally did turn her attention back to her white haired quarry, the black skinned Döckálfar had slowly stepped back into the writhing darkness, using her shadow blending ability to make herself nearly invisible.

Everything was now in a state of utter confusion and mayhem, as panic stricken palace guards began screaming shouts of terror, reviling the death of the daughter of the Matron Mother and warning of the intrusion of assassins. After fighting her way past the two spawned spider creations, the few remaining guards attempted to bar the retrieval of her sister. The small Elven Princess rushed to attack. The female archer bore down on Ever De' Sade's personal guard. The Drow soldiers had drawn together with large headed halberds extended menacingly as they rushed forward. The remaining loyal Drow fighters let out a chilling cry for battle and fearlessly charged toward the female archer, their long wicked looking weapons gleaming dully. The silent arrows of Aurra felled the first rushing attacker at fifty paces, the second dropped ten paces closer, with the third crashing heavily to the ground at only twenty The last Drow fighter swarmed over her like a rabid dog but the small Princess stood firm even as his huge blade slashed her unprotected ribs.

With studied, almost mechanical precision, the blonde Elven archer let loose another of her black arrows. A moment later, the Dark Elf warrior crumpled with a shudder to the cold tile floor; the black missile had found its mark, buried deep with the man's chest and straight through his heart.

Dark, unable to stop Aurra before she could trigger the warding glyph, was engaged in a fierce battle of his own just behind them. The three guards barely had time to survey the danger before their attacker was upon them. The black-garbed assassin shoved his shadowed blade through the man nearest the doorway and was on top of the second only a moment later. The final guard dropped dead before Dark's incorporeal sword, with everything almost over before it had even started. Suddenly, a group of palace guards appeared from the forgotten stairwell. The Döckálfar soldiers, from what the dark knight could tell, numbered at least ten or twelve in all, clustered together as they rushed toward the demonic figure. He met the rush with a ferocious counterassault, his demonic eyes blazing red with flame. With unmatched speed and strength, he began to steadily cut away the number of his Döckálfar attackers. An unmistakable look of fear crossed the faces of his adversaries as he fought with the fury and rage of a demon spawned from Hell. With a final burst of magical strength, he crashed into the last of his assailants, putting his uneorthly sword into the Dark Elf up to the hilt and left it there, until it slowly faded from existence.

Nimbly, Aurra turned and found her sister chained to the skeleton pillars and threw down the bow of the Black Fox. Without hesitation, she pulled free her sword and with several deft strokes of her sharp elven blade, severed the chains and freed her sister Nysarra from her bonds. At that very moment, from out of the darkness and from the rear, Ever Syn De' Sade loomed directly over them, a black mass of twisted shadows. Reacting on instinct alone, the Elf Princess twisted desperately to one side as the huge spiked mace swung forcefully downward. Instantly Aurra felt a searing pain shoot through her left shoulder, followed by a strange numbness. Fiercely she fought to stay conscious, the pain instantaneously returning in a flood that wracked her tiny frame.

The white haired Dark Elf priestess began to circle slowly, like a cat playing with its prey before the kill. Blood streamed down the elven girl's body and she felt herself weakening. Then, the young Princess staggered heavily to her knees, sharp pain shot through her as she did so. Thinking her quarry finished, the ebony cleric lunged forward, but with one last great effort, Aurra caught the dark Priestess square in the chest, the sword biting deep through muscle and bone. Shrieking in pain, the Dark Elven Priestess of Lolth grabbed hold of the embedded blade and somehow began to stagger upward. From atop the fallen Princess, rage swelled within the crazed daughter of Malice, her grim face filled with hate. She gripped the silver spiked mace tightly in her hand, bringing the weapon around sharply until it pointed skyward. For an instant, Aurra's vision blurred, then cleared once more as she forced herself to raise the sword; then in one last desperate effort she swung her sword. The blade swept in a long sweeping arc and caught the female Döckálfar in her exposed throat. Back flew the Dark Elf, her head nearly severed from her body, her voice lost in one last gasp, the mace slipped from her hand, her eyes glazed over as her body slid slowly, lifelessly to the cold floor.

"Aurra."

The sound of her name broke the silence in a broken whisper, and the name raced through her stunned disbelieving mind as she struggled dumbly to her feet. Tears began to well up in her reddened eyes and ran down her battered face in streams. With leaden steps she picked her way over to her sister and gently cradled Nysarra's limp form to her breast.

The assassin's back was still turned to them, still working on securing the doors to the huge chamber. Finally with the entrance secured, he was already moving noiselessly through the carnage, his flaming eyes drifted to the stone archway as it suddenly began to fill with a ghostly, swirling mist. "What did one shepherd say to the other shepherd?" Dark exclaimed in earnest. "Let's get the flock out of here!"

Quickly Dark reached for Aurra, his muscular arms wrapping tightly around her thin stooped frame, bringing her face close to his own. A moment later Nysarra too felt one strong arm come around her shoulders, her terrible ordeal finally over. As the demonic assassin began to stand, bearing both elven sisters in his arms, the massive stone archway flared brightly one last time and there framed in the entryway stood the Elven figure of Malice De' Sade. Her white ivory skin was smooth and supple, her long stark white hair was neatly combed, gathered just below her shoulders in a loose ponytail. She was dressed in a light open-fronted robe of bright red, which she wore over armor forged to resemble demonic features. Malice brought her attention to behold the black-garbed assassin and stared blankly after him, hardened eyes locked together for just an instant, then suddenly he was gone.

With slow studied, mechanical steps, she threaded her way through the bodies of her fallen soldiers, stepping carefully but without looking over the tangled mass of reddened bodies that sprawled grotesquely across the center of the ancient room. Stupefied, the Matron Mother walked aimlessly, her eyes shockingly blank, her face became stricken with a terrible stunned look that screamed inwardly in silent agony. Across the floor, littered with the tangled and twisted bodies of the fallen palace guards, the eyes of the Mistress of the Noble House De' Sade found her daughter. She reached the youngest of her offspring and knelt beside her, gently cradling her still form. Then she gently laid her burden on the polished tile floor and sat quietly, her eyes flickered and her mouth moved dumbly as she fought for the words that would not come. Then, as if from far away, a terrible high pitched scream broke the silence. It grew louder and more shrill, growing and swelling into a tidal wave of agony that engulfed every corner of the room and beyond.

XII

The sound of the albino witch's long haunting laments for her daughter hung trapped in the black haze of his mind like a stray echo that threatened to envelop him. The voice seemed to carry from a great distance, floating over him through the dark, leaving him with a sluggish feeling of being bound by heavy weights. With a great agonizing effort, something or someone reached downward inside him, searching within somehow.

"Dark...Dark," the voice belonged to Aurra. He slowly sat up, forcing himself awake.

"Dark?"

She placed her hand on his shoulder, her face bent close to his, her long golden hair trailing down about her like a silk veil.

"Aurra?" he asked in a somnolent voice, his mind still clouded in darkness. "How's your sister doing?" he managed.

"She's fine, thanks to you, resting just down the hall." She smiled softly, kissing his cheek gently. "You know you have been sleeping for hours ever since we got back here."

The groggy assassin nodded his acknowledgement, suddenly aware of the pungent smell in the air. He realized immediately the familiar aroma that now permeated the entire room. Wearily he stretched the effects of a restless sleep and looked about, his mind still drugged with sleep, his thoughts still scattered. A gray, casting light seeped through the fabric of the drawn curtains, faintly illuminating the lines of his handsome face. Then the smell from a scattering of droppings left by his pet chimera brought him fully around and now more than awake. Just mere moments after finding the source next to his armor that lay folded over a plush chair, he heard the sound of subtle scratching that faded almost instantly into silence. It had come from outside the room where the culprit to the crime now stood watch. The door to his bedchamber swung slowly open, letting light from oil lamps of the hallway spill into the room. Through the opening came Baron, his heavy headed body hunched forward in lowly shame. Dark slid to the edge of the bed and looked quickly before dropping his legs cautiously to the floor.

"Don't be too mad with him," Aurra spoke softly, easing herself up from the huge feathered bed. "He stayed with you most of the night, refusing to leave his master's side even when we tried coercing him with a late night snack," she told him turning to leave. "Oh, I almost forgot. Your grandfather awaits you down stairs in the great dining hall."

He looked at her uncertainly. "Did he say what he wanted?"

"He just said it was of an urgent matter and to get your lazy arse out of bed."

"Great, thanks," he nodded in appreciation.

Then, leaving the Baron to watch over him, the Elven Princess turned and darted down the hall, glancing back momentarily and smiled inwardly to herself.

Without wasting any further time, he came to his feet and quickly dressed himself in a heavy plush shirt and pants. Pulling the door closed, and with Baron following closely behind, he made his way downstairs to the Grand Dining Hall where Mephisto had just eaten a light lunch.

The room, as always, was brightly lit by the tall candles placed along the long dining table and on decorative wall racks that hung evenly spaced along the walls. He made his way quietly to the rear of the room and seated himself in a large, leather lounging chair that sat in front of a custom built stone fireplace. Just as Dark had anticipated, his grandfather was in the process of finishing another cup of tea and smoking a long stemmed wooden pipe. He looked up idly as Dark entered the room, his face registered undisguised disappointment at the late appearance of his young apprentice.

"You're a wee bit late for breakfast," Mephisto growled pleasantly, blowing a large ring of smoke. "And how unlucky for you lunch just finished."

"I'm just a little out of sorts today," he explained quickly, then began again hesitantly. "So what is this urgent matter you have?"

"Our friend Fhaminn Dread contacted me while you were away," he smiled with a mocking grin, his tall frame straightening itself as he looked quizzically at his grandson. "He wishes to meet with you, why or what he wants I know not, but there was urgency in his voice."

"Now do you want to explain to me just why you told this STRANGER, let alone assassin anything about us?" he smiled with his own mocking grin. "I hope this person doesn't know anything about our plan." He stared intently at the old magus. "Does he know about our plan?"

The dark face of his grandfather nodded hesitantly as the old too familiar mocking smile crossed it fleetingly. "Yes, but it's not like I told him. I don't even know the man."

"Than who did?" Dark asked quietly, dumbfounded at his reply.

"It was Circe. She's obviously in love with him," he announced emphatically, he raised a lean hand to his chin to stroke his beard. "I only assume that she thought he could possible help us. And to be quite honest, he already has… more than you think."

"I don't trust him!" Dark exclaimed at last.

The tall wizard looked sharply at him, then uttered a deep low chuckle that caught his grandson a little by surprise.

"Neither do I my boy, but for now let us hear what he has to say." Mephisto turned toward him, a slight smile played across his lips. "Besides, I haven't heard from Circe for a few days and if nothing else, he should know her whereabouts."

Dark motioned for some food to be brought to him and only a few moments later an invisible servant trudged over to them, a towel thrown loosely across a phantom limb. Once his order was placed, the servant returned with a hot plate of stew, bread and cheese, and once the steaming plate was set before him, the unseen servant quickly lumbered off back to the kitchen. Once alone, Dark retold his encounter with Ever and her mother in the Land of Chaos, leaving nothing out of his narration. He finished and Mephisto stared at him wordlessly.

"And you're quite certain that's what she said?"

Dark nodded. "She said Kalifen's plan was to create an army of undead."

The old wizard shook his head doubtfully. "The only Necromancer powerful enough to accomplish such a task has long since perished, and can't possibly be resurrected. But let's not take any chances...maybe ask Dread if he's heard anything on this matter when you see him later tonight."

"All right," Dark agreed. "I'll see what he knows."

That night it began to rain. Huge black nimbus clouds rolled in from the north like dark and gloomy floating islands, and settled over the entire city. Heavy rain and gusts of wind swept across the gray skies and deep rolling thunder broke out over the surrounding valley with eorth shaking blasts. Following each ominous rumbling was a tremendous spectacle of blinding streaks of flashing lightning that laced the dark clouded sky.

It was just after midnight when Dark flew unseen from the murkiness of the blackened skies into the lighted City of Duergar. He soon entered into a section of the city with a less than inviting community. This quarter of the city was mostly a ramshackle cluster of wooden buildings, one indistinguishable from the other. The shops were rundown and neglected; the shops and taverns were a seedy lot, and the paint that colored them was chipped and faded. Many of the homes stood shuttered, with bars drawn and locks fastened tight.

He glided just above the yellow light of burning lamps of an oil based fuel source as he followed the rutted line of the cobblestone road as it wound its way through the tangle of old, dilapidated buildings. His keen elven eyes studied the small taverns and inns at either side. He flew on for another forty or fifty yards further before the invisible assassin caught sight of a small two-story hostel set further back from the other buildings within a grove of tall shrubbery. Harsh yellow lights burned through the streaked glass of the windows on the first floor, and rough loud voices echoed inside with the occasional shrill laughter from one of the many whores. The second floor, however, stood dark and silent. A window in the back stood invitingly open.

He quickly flew over the tiny courtyard that fronted the inn and glanced down. The sign indicated that the seedy establishment was called The White Hart Inn, the meeting place of his estranged abettor. Wordlessly, Dark hastened to the open window at the rear of the building and landed silently atop a sloping veranda roof. He moved ahead, eyes peering into the shadowy dimness beyond the room's open window until at last he stood at its entrance.

"Dread?" he spoke the assassin's name in a quiet whisper. No answer came. He cautiously stepped through the entry into the black shadows beyond. A faint flicker of movement registered at the edge of his peripheral vision, a movement that came from somewhere within the room. A sudden apprehension quickly swept through him, leaving him with a sense of another worldly presence. Something old, almost ancient. He stood motionless for a moment, his sight already adjusted to the dark interior; he waited and watched for something more. But there was no further movement, not even a sound betrayed the presence of the other being.

"Demon Raider?" The voice came suddenly from out of nowhere followed by a shadow that slipped from a secret door in the back of the room. Instinctively, Dark began to draw upon the powers of the Plane of Shadows forming his shadowed sword.

"Stay your hand my friend," the voice was soft yet still commanding. "I am no enemy of yours."

The shadowy form before him was that of a man; Dark could see him now, a man of medium size, standing a little under six feet. Long black robes were wrapped tightly about his lean muscular frame with the hood of his traveling cloak pulled close about his head so that not one part of his face could be seen except for the narrowed dragon green eyes that looked back at him.

"Please don't come any closer," the cloaked man whispered. "As you know anonymity in our field of work is not just a want or a need, it's an absolute necessity."

The assassin secured the window and door, drew the curtains carefully back in proper place, then turned back to stare deep into Dark's glittering black eyes and his own tightly concealed face.

"After all these years," Fhaminn Dread shook his cloaked head wonderingly, stepping forward. "The famous Demon Raider. It's quite an…"

"You asked to see me," the half-elven assassin cut him short. "Why?"

Fhaminn Dread nodded wordlessly, still slightly taken aback by the actual appearance of this icon of the underworld. Slowly he moved back to a small table and the two men took up seats across from each other. The green-eyed assassin slowly reached into his pocket and pulled out a small gray stone that suddenly began to glow red like a burning coal shining dully. "This will help keep our conversation a private one."

"I'll get straight to the point," Fhaminn Dread addressed his dark counterpart. "Circe is missing. That is why I asked you to come."

There was the faint sound of footsteps in the hallway beyond the chamber door and instantly both assassins were on their feet. Then they both paused, their faces calm as the footsteps trailed away. Each looked back at the other and sat slowly back down again.

"Where did you see her last?" Dark quickly asked, picking up the conversation .

"The last time we spoke, she was still at the Arcane Academy," he eagerly began again. "That's why I asked you here, because I can't gain access to the school but you can."

Dark nodded. "Yes I know, only those given the college's mark of entry can pass through the magical barrier that surrounds the campus grounds."

"Exactly, which is why I need you," Circe's paramour continued. "Surely the grandson of the founder of the magical institution has the mark. And with you there carrying out a thorough search of the premises, it leaves me free to investigate elsewhere."

"I don't trust you," the assassin interjected.

Fhaminn Dread became flushed. The anger and frustration he held inside was beginning to work its way to the fore. "Then maybe this will help relieve you of some of that burden of distrust you carry," he spoke softly, carefully masking any emotion as he faced his infamous counterpart. "Kalifen searches for something hidden within or around the city, what it is I know not. Aiding him in his search is a witch from the Sorrow Woods named Ouija. She is said to hold the knowledge of the unknown by some supernatural means. Longfoot frequents her in her forest home nearly twice every week, sometimes even more than that."

"Kalifen," Dark breathed the name like a curse.

"There is one more thing," the green eyed assassin began again. "Not more than three days ago, he and Lord Blackthorn set sail on three ships all heading north…that is all I know."

Dark nodded, only staring at the cloaked man without speaking.

"I know you don't trust me," he said finally. "After a very bleak and dark period in my life I met Circe…" He suddenly stopped, unable to continue. He took a deep breath and steadied himself before continuing. "There was something about her I have not since found; a sweetness, a kindness, a sensitivity about her. I know these are only just words I am speaking, but I do not speak blindly. I love her."

Dark said nothing, his black eyes intense.

"She must be found, she must…" he trailed off helplessly.

Dark's expression did not change, he only stared at him wordlessly for a moment.

"If what you say is true, then I will no longer regard you with any distrust or misgivings," he said finally. He rose, then stepped away from his chair several paces, his face partially hidden in shadow. "I will help find your paramour, but mark my words, if what you speak are lies…"

Fhaminn Dread quickly rose with him, interjecting hastily. "I promise you, the words I speak to you now are only truths. I seek only Circe."

Demon Raider did not turn. "Very well, contact me in three days time and we shall meet again. And remember, no one is to know about our meeting."

The other assassin nodded his agreement. "No one shall. And if it makes any difference or not, I only killed those who truly deserved to die."

"Yeah, me too."

A moment later Dark was through the curtained window and was gone. Fhaminn Dread stood looking at his compeer, then moved to follow.

Down a crooked road the half-elf assassin walked, his black eyes peering into the darkness about him with caution, hearing distant sounds that prowled at night. A time or two on his way, he encountered a handful of late night travelers as they walked the roadway. Cloaked and hooded, these late night wanderers passed him by in singles, pairs and small groups. Several times these transients would pause guardedly at Dark's approach. Yet as quickly as they would come, they were gone again, lost back in the surrounding blackness.

He passed at last from the gloom of the impoverished city slums into the salty air of the River Quarter. Poorly lettered signs hung from swaying rotting posts and overhead, a written collection of promises and prices beneath a maze of proprietors names. Through curtained windows and open entryways, he could see shadows of lively revelers casting from the yellow light of oil lamps and burning pitch.

It was in these taverns and inns of the River Quarter that seafaring denizens were gathered. Drinking and carousing around rough hewn tables and bars formed of boards set atop empty barrels with glasses and tankards of ale and rum. Quickly and with purpose, Dark passed by one building to the next as men and women of all races, some dressed richly while others dressed in nothing more than rags, many stumbling, others lurching as they stole their way through the darkened alleyways, and all reeked of drink. Here money clinked and changed hands quickly, often in stealth and sometimes in deadly violence. There he could see the slumping figure of a young man lying still and twisted within a darkened passage, the red liquid of life seeping from the fresh slash at his throat. All about thieves prowled the night, cut throats and brigands slinking through like silent wraiths.

A drunken vagabond accidently stumbled up against him and fumbled dumbly through his cloak. Dark shoved the inebriated man away with a deft hand. The fellow tumbled heavily to the boardwalk and lay laughing loudly skyward. The hooded assassin stared down at him a moment, giving a slight smile and hurried on. Within seconds the drunken purse snatcher's shrill and foolish laughter turned to that of cries of thievery and robbery.

He quickly started back up the roadway, studying the taverns and inns on either side. He walked only a few feet further when he caught sight of a large roadhouse covered in a red brick façade with large climbing clumps of ivy. Loud voices and raucous laughter could easily be heard, even though the crowd seemed small. He paused before entering through the lighted doorway of the large brick building, looked up and reassured himself he was at the right place. The sign read The Black Dogg Alehouse, and pulling his cowl about his face he entered.

The room within seemed cramped and thick with aromatic smoke from oil based lamps and many hemp filled pipes. A group of violent looking men and women stood clustered around a long bar at the front of the room. Prostitutes displayed their wares openly, wanting to make a quick doubloon or two off of drunken sailors. Various tables ringed by mismatched chairs filled the great room with a few being occupied by cloaked figures who kept their faces carefully hidden, hunched over tankards of ale and speaking in low hushed voices. There were several doors that led from the large hall to other parts of the alehouse, and a stairway that ran up to the second floor and a series of numbered doors.

Dark paused slightly, staring at the shadowy figures that milled behind a curtain wall. He gradually moved to the back of the room where a small table stood occupied by a monstrously fat, lumpish and unfriendly looking bearded man with his left hand missing, and in its place was a sharpened iron hook, undoubtedly used as a weapon. His companion was a stunning red haired beauty, with hair the color of blood that cascaded down her buxom bosom. The woman wore a long sleeve crimson red shirt with a sash and headband that held back her long hair. In her right hand she held an incredibly ornate silver and jade double cigar holder set with a complex inlay of gold and gemstones. She glanced up and looked at the strange newcomer, immediately concern showed in her hazel eyes.

"Hello, Eva."

The red haired woman could only stare at him. "Dark Solus, why is it you always seem to come to me like a sailor on shore leave? So what are you doing in Duergar?"

She began to rise from her chair and stared at him suspiciously.

"I need your help..." Before he could finish his sentence, the fiery red head's clenched fist solidly struck the unsuspecting assassin, snapping his head quickly to one side.

"I learned to really hate you over the last few years," her voice lowered so that the other patrons of the bar behind them could not hear.

"I never meant to hurt you," he spoke kindly, his hand reaching out to touch her soft cheek.

"I was young and foolish," Eva brushed his hand aside. "And in love. What you did to me was wrong and you know it."

"You're a big girl," his half-elven face tightened within the shadow of the black cowl. "You knew what you were getting yourself into."

"I do now. I have a new crew and the fastest ship on or above water."

"That's why I'm here, Eva." He paused. "Can we go somewhere to talk?"

Eva nodded, motioning for her massive companion to stay, then led the cloaked assassin to a back room that contained a single table with a candle and several chairs. She quickly lit the candle and quietly closed the door after one last furtive glance about the room.

"Make this quick assassin." The slender woman seated herself opposite of Dark. "I have important matters that require my immediate attention."

"Then let me get straight to the point," he declared solemnly. "Not more than three days ago Kalifen and Lord Blackthorn set sail with three ships, all heading north. I need to know where they're going Eva; so can you do this for me?"

The sailor's face was expressionless, keeping her eyes locked on Dark's own. "I'll think about it."

"I need it now Eva," Dark declared, watching the other's inscrutable face. "Right now."

The red haired beauty thought for a moment, then shook her head. "You know I just don't think I can do it…" she paused deliberately, slightly rocking back in her chair, blowing rings of smoke. "Besides my crew and I have other commitments, other places we need to be, other business which requires my immediate attention. My time is such a precious commodity, as is yours, so surely you can appreciate that."

"How much?" the assassin demanded quietly.

"Well let me see." The woman's eyes glittered. "It's fair to say that without me your plan, whatever it may be, will surely fail. So therefore you need me. And that I in turn, wish to offer you my help, willingly I might add. And that such help needs to be adequately recompensed, wouldn't you say?"

Her smile was wolfish.

"Eva, please," Dark forced himself to remain calm.

"I think I like seeing you squirm assassin," Eva interjected quickly, her smile growing wide. "Very well then, my fee... my first officer's weight in gold. A fair asking price for one in such a difficult predicament as yours. Take it or leave it."

Dark's jaw dropped and immediately he shook his cloaked head. "Have you gone mad woman? Do you have any clue how much that tub of lard could possibly weigh? The man had both his ears pierced by harpoons; even as a child he was so fat he could only play seek."

"That's my final offer, take it or leave it," Eva snapped back, brushing his words aside with a wave of her hand. "And if you don't like it, by all means seek out another captain of a ship with the ability to fly...good luck with that."

"Why you've become nothing more than a common thief, Jacquotte Eva Delahaye!" he stormed, his fists clenched at his side in anger.

"This must be really important to you Dark," she stopped momentarily and turned to look at him, her placid face dark and expressionless. "You look like you want to crack me in the jaw. I'd like to see you do it, but I don't think you're tough enough to accomplish the task. And that's Captain Blood to you."

Dark paused, choosing his words carefully. "All right... Captain, but you leave tonight, no later."

The beautiful seafaring woman smiled happily, obviously pleased with herself and pleased at the unexpected gift of gold by her estranged alliance with the black-garbed assassin.

"One more thing, I don't trust you assassin, so I require a sign of good faith on your part."

With one gloved hand, he reached slowly beneath the folds of his black cloak, fumbled about for a moment, and came forth holding a small leather pouch filled with precious stones. The scarlet haired sea captain smiled faintly and opened the pouch, pouring the stones into her open palm. She raised them and held them up to the light, admiring their brilliant glittering glow. Placing the gemstones back into the leather pouch, she rose to her feet and stood easily before the angered assassin, holding the small bag like bait before a caged animal.

"I'll contact you as soon as I find Kalifen," she said glancing back.

Dark turned away wordlessly and hastened to the window at the rear of the room and pushed it open. Without a word of goodbye or even a glance backward, he ambled through the window and dropped softly to the eorth below. Within a moment's time the cloaked figure of the assassin pulled hurriedly back becoming invisible within the shadows of the building.

He was almost back once more on the main roadway when the sound of a familiar voice rose from somewhere ahead. It was faint at first, lingering like an echo in the midst of sharper quicker sounds, yet that lone voice was more insistent. Then a new sound was heard, one that grew into an unmistakable howl, high pitched and eerie among the gloom of the darkness beyond. Silently he slipped from the protective cover of darkness and moved toward the disturbance. With the eyes of a cat he scanned the shadowed road for a few moments; in his study he found the wheel marks of a heavy wagon, the tracks still fresh.

Gazing carefully around, the silent assassin looked to see if anyone else was about, then he rose and with the ease of an acrobat, he climbed up the side of a derelict building and onto the roof. He rose and moved forward in a half crouch, running parallel to the sounds ahead in the distance. Like a shadow he slipped over the edge of the roof and dropped to a flat veranda. From its edge, there was a drop of a dozen or so feet to the ground. He bent forward and listened. The voices grew louder and more distinct and at last seemed to come from directly below his perch.

"… careful, what are you two, stupid…just lift it…"

"We are lifting it; why can't we just break it open?"

"… waste of time, we don't get any of this…"

"That's why I say we just break the lock, open it up and take what should be ours by right!"

"I agree, let's break it open!"

The voices argued on amongst themselves, whispers laced with the slurring of ale and rum, mixed with ragged breathing and wild howls. There had to be at least a dozen men out there the assassin decided. Undoubtedly it was a group of thieves and cutthroats arguing over their acquired booty. Cautiously, he eased slowly ahead, as overhead a few stars managed to wink into view, their pale white light shining down into the dark alley of the River Quarter. Gradually a large shadow began to take shape. It was a wagon, the garish color of blood caught in the reflecting starlight. The team of horses that pulled the vehicle were dead along with the driver and several armored men. Dark fell back toward the rear of the building where he was able to make out a group of dark little figures huddled next to the blood and carnage of the deadly assault.

Standing in a tight circle next to the wagon were five very large, transformed werewolves, their huge black fury bulks unmistakable even in this poor light. They were speaking with six smaller figures, considerably slighter in build, their size clearly marking them as members of the Halfling Pack. No longer cloaked, his horned helmet atop his head, the half-elf assassin edged ahead until he stood directly above the small group. He had taken no more than a few steps when a sharp cry from the same familiar voice went up behind them. Dark then made out something coming closer, a small shadow moving toward them. Gradually the shadowy form began to take shape, materializing out of the darkness and the night. Instantly he recognized the lithe form; it was the Lycan leader from a few nights past at Boddeker Stitch's tailor shop. He was a little person, smaller than an average sized halfling, dressed in dark colors with a slightly rounded face and ears only slightly pointed. His legs were short even for a hobbit and covering his large feet from his ankles down was a thick layer of brown hairy fur.

Dark studied the man for a moment with great care, trying to make out his face, and in the dim light he caught a brief glimpse of the man he had encountered previously. A small scar marked the fat face of the stranger, then the assassin caught sight of something else. A dark green cloak that had once belonged to a dwarf, flew back as he stood next to the locked chest, revealing the arm that was severed from the chest wall had indeed almost regenerated completely.

"Gather up the rest of the bodies, they still might be salvageable…but this I'll take care of personally."

The demonic assassin waited for a moment longer, watching. Then he rose upward, reached down within the open demon's mouth, making it a quick and deliberate act, and in a single motion brought forth the Halfling's severed arm.

"I believe this belongs to you," he trailed off ominously, casting down the lifeless limb to the cold hard eorth, leaving the thought unspoken. With bared teeth, fire burst from his cruel mouth and the flames of perdition engulfed his demonic eyes, giving his face an ungodly glow. Demon Raider watched as the one armed hobbit turned a bright shade of pale. Terrified, the Lycan leader seemed to undergo a sudden transformation, a chilling, uncontrollable fear surged through his body at the mere sight of this hellish, most unholy creature. For this time he knew, from out of his worst nightmares into reality, death had finally come for him.

XIII

It was a particularly cool day but Sneak Longfoot was beginning to perspire freely. The wind he found was being most stubborn, blowing his rather expensive hairpiece out of place and continually off center. And moving about without his small litter carried by his personal carriers was arduous, laborious and slow. He was hardly a model citizen of rectitude nor did he adhere to any moral principles of probity. Below his gleaming bald head, a fat face bulged, laced with an unsightly thread of tiny little veins that spoke of drink and self-indulgence. In fact he drank most of the time and at night he kept the riotous company of the young halfling pack of the city, and of course, the attention of accommodating young women were placed high on his list of eorthly pleasures. His soft, almost feminine-like hands being manicured and free of calluses showed a man who had never seen a hard days work in his life. Flaccid muscles and a small light frame lay hidden deep beneath layer upon layer of solid fatty tissue.

Belatedly he thought of the flask of scotch whiskey he had left within his home. He lumbered sluggishly along a back alley somewhere in the River Quarter. By his side was the Captain of the City Watch, a big man, blonde and bearded, his broad figure wore fitted plate mail armor and a long black cape and cowl with Blackthorn's markings. Captain Caine moved several steps ahead of the rotund halfling leader saying nothing, his eyes riveted on the horrific carnage that lay scattered about them.

"Just what were your boys up to last night Longfoot?" the tall border man asked quizzically, staring around him as he did so.

"I don't know," Sneak Longfoot shook his head. "But I'm sure as hell going to find out. And while Kalifen and

Blackthorn are absent from the city, I am the one who is left in charge, and my official title is Lord Protector and you shall address me as such."

Captain Caine came forward a step, dwarfing the small halfling leader. "Yes of course…Lord Protector." A faint mocking smile passed quickly across his lips.

The acting Dictator of Duergar edged ahead and moved forward toward the grisly scene of the slaughtered. The strange forms became more distinct after the two men had gone only a few yards. Sneak somehow managed to fight the sickening feeling creeping through his robust stomach and forced himself to keep moving forward onto the battleground. As he strode closer, the uneasiness reflecting in his eyes turned to horror. The reddened cloth heaps now became men, their still, blood soaked forms scattered on the cold ground like fallen scarecrows, torn and crumpled, their insides strewn haphazardly about the muddied eorth.

Quickly Sneak looked about, peering into the dark shadows of the back alley, searching for some sign of the thing that had done this. He saw nothing. He walked about the wagon studying the gnarled, twisted shapes about him as he went. Every last one of the pack members lay dead, their tiny bodies broken like fallen deadwood. The Guild Leader quickly felt his skin crawl. Thinking to himself, he knew what had done this. One by one, he checked the bodies until at last he found Brister, the leader of this particular pack. The small man was dead as well, his minute form limbless and gutted like a fish lay upon the ground, his roguish features frozen with a look of sheer horror. So mauled and mangled was his body that it was almost impossible to recognize.

Then he turned, listening to the roar of the wind whistling through the alleyway. A whirling sensation, almost causing him to fall, washed over him as the smell of rotting death filled his nostrils. Again he thought to himself, only one thing could have done this. He remembered the other pack members dead at the cul-de-sac in behind the Golden Eye Dragon Inn. Only one thing. It must be the demon. But how had it found them? Why was it targeting his guild, his halflings? He tried steadying himself before hastening back to the tall blonde captain, who stood several feet away, talking in private to one of his men.

"Did you find him?" he asked, his dark eyes bright. "Brister?"

Sneak nodded. "He's dead, they're all dead."

"What kind of creature could have done this? Some rival gang maybe? Or…?"

"No," the Halfling Leader shook his head quickly. "No Captain Caine. I believe I know what did this. This is the same being that attacked and killed that scoundrel Fetch and his small pack of hyenas." His rough voice quieted.

"Is it a devil?"

"No not this." Sneak glanced back at the dead upon the ground. "No this is no devil, this is a demon."

"Poor Brister," Captain Caine murmured to himself. "He finally met his match." He paused and glanced back sharply at the little Leader of Duergar. "What do we do now?"

Halfling and city guard stared wordlessly at each other, but Sneak knew the answer.

"I must see the witch."

It was almost noon when Dark awoke, feeling the warmth of the small fire that crackled and snapped with burning wood. He rose from his soft feathered bed, washed and dressed himself and made his way down stairs to eat a brief meal. He found his grandfather sitting alone at the large dining table. As Dark had anticipated, he was in the process of lighting his pipe after finishing his lunch. He waved a large hand in greeting. "You're just in time," he exclaimed pleasantly. "Come sit down and have some lunch while there's still something left to eat."

Dark walked over wearily, pulled a chair out for himself and sat down with his face towards the old wizard. His grandfather's tall frame straightened itself as he puffed on his clay smoking pipe and looked eagerly at his young apprentice.

"So tell me," Mephisto asked at last. "What did our friend Fhaminn Dread have to say?"

He told him everything that had happened since his meeting with the shadowy assassin. He spoke first of his encounter with Dread, the strange disappearance of Circe, Kalifen and Blackthorn's voyage north aboard three ships, the aid of a witch from the black forest named Ouija, and the unexpected run-in with a second Lycan leader and the violent altercation that ensued thereafter. He finished by telling his old mentor that each one of these pack members wore a tattoo of a large golden eye.

"I believe each quarter of the city is all under the control of these small gangs of hobbits," Dark announced solemnly. "And every member of these organized groups of criminals carries a mark of that particular district, somewhere on their body. And once I find one of them with these symbols, I will have found them all."

"Who would ever suspect these tiny, childlike creatures of causing any mischief," Mephisto announced shortly. "They could easily enter any city in the world by the hundreds or even thousands and no one would even bat an eye. And as werewolves, they now become a formidable army of Lycan troops. It's actually pretty smart."

Dark looked at his grandfather incredulously, his face rough and expressionless at the wizard's candid evaluation.

"Well it is," a broad smile spread slowly over his handsome features. "I certainly would never think twice about seeing a group of halflings together. Speaking of which, I was finally able to talk to Nysarra. What she had to say was quite interesting to say the least." He paused. "Do you know who Fenrisúlfr is?"

Dark seemed to stiffen at the mere mention of the name. It was a name from his childhood, an embodiment of pure terror, synonymous with all things terrible in life, real or imagined. It was a name told to him by his mother, used in spine-tingling tales designed to frighten him when he had been bad and meant to keep him out of any mischief. He looked at his grandfather's grim visage and nodded slowly.

"He is the son of Loki, said to be a monstrous wolf, and foretold to kill the god Odin during the events of Ragnarök. I believe the gods had him bound with an unbreakable fetter called Gleipnir, constructed by the dwarves from six mythical ingredients."

Mephisto's grim face turned hard. "Unfortunately these are no mere stories of myth, but of ancient truth in history. According to the Prose Edda, a compilation that comprises the major store of Norse mythology, the silken fetter Gleipnir was impossible to break…or so they thought. You see Kalifen, undoubtedly aided by the witch Ouija, found a way to do the impossible. They were somehow able to find several pieces of an extremely rare substance called Dragon Shards, crystal-like rock fragments imbued with incredible, unimaginable magical power."

"And I suppose this is when they paid a visit to Boddeker Stitch," Dark interjected quickly.

"Exactly," the old historian attested. "By his own account in the journal you found, he wrote of a late night visit from Sneak Longfoot who produced the Shards and asked for a weapon to be made from the small fragments. He told the Halfling Leader only two men on Eorth were even capable of forging such a weapon out of the tiny crystal slivers. He being the first, and the other a man who lived in the frozen far north, Weyland the Smith of Wolfdales. Regrettably he also informed Longfoot of the projectile's possible erratic behavior in flight due to the Arcane influence on the stone's immense pull on the poles magnetic fields. He regrettably then spoke of the only weapon on this Eorth with god-like accuracy, the Bow of the Black Fox, a weapon bestowed upon their champion by the Elven Gods. Unfortunately, his refusal to construct such a weapon brought about his own demise."

"And what happened to Fenrir?" Dark asked finally.

Mephistopheles looked back at his grandson thoughtfully, bowing his head slightly, he drew a few quick puffs of smoke from his pipe. "I thought about that. If true, then it would certainly explain the Halfling's ability to shape shift into werewolves. Which is why I must go there and see for myself if what the Grey Elf spoke of has any truth in merit. I'll be leaving this afternoon. I shouldn't be gone for more than a few days so try not to get into any trouble while I am gone."

His grandson hastened to nod his agreement. "Wait, I still need to get inside the Academy to find out what happened to Circe," he asked after a moment.

"No problem," the old mage acknowledged. "I shall have Gwyddien meet you at the Academy's entrance. He leads the Order now. He'll show you around the college and answer any questions you may have."

"Gwyddien, nephew of Math the Ancient?" he declared pointedly. "I know this Welsh wizard; he used to visit our home often when I was a child."

"Yes, that's right," Mephisto agreed, rocking back slightly on his chair. "Your parents and he were great friends, they even adventured together once or twice."

"And what exactly do we do about this witch from the Sorrow Woods?" he asked his grandfather at last.

The ageless wizard's head jerked up and he looked at Dark with an indomitable spirit. "Leave that Pythoness to me," replied Mephisto flatly.

The sun was barely below the horizon when Dark Solus left his floating home and moved up the walkway towards the gates that fronted the Academy grounds. The large barrier consisted of several portals of gilded wrought iron, bearing the emblems of the seven founding Mages. Flaunting the central gate were two massive pillars of marble stone surmounted by draconic statuary.

As he neared the gates, he saw that the famous enchanter was already there, hard at work tending a large flower bed. His lean frame was bent over a hearty group of perennial flowers when he saw Dark approach wearing the Order's signet pendant around his neck. As he came nearer, Gwyddien slowly straightened to his full height, one hand going to his back.

"Good evening, apprentice. Bout time you showed up."

Dark nodded. "I was in preparation for our meeting Chancellor."

"Just like your father," Gwyddien grinned, then offered his hand in greeting, looking down at the newest apprentice to the Arcane Academia. "It's been a long time and age seems to be catching up with me," the old wizard rubbed his back gingerly.

Dark nodded once more as he made his way through the front entrance; the sentries on watch nodded their greeting in turn, and he nodded back.

The Welsh wizard was a tall man with wide shoulders and long pure white hair with streaks of coal black strands that seemed to concentrate on the back part of his head. His deep set green eyes were powerful, still and unrelenting, his broad dark face looked weathered by many years beneath sun and wind. The only signs of age that showed upon his handsome face were fine grained lines that appeared around his mouth and forehead. He was dressed in clothing that seemed quite out of date to the point of antiquity. His courtly attire favored the dark color burgundy, adorned with gemstones and blood red garnets with threaded accents of gold.

"It seems your appearance has changed somewhat over the years my boy," his tone held a slight hint of mockery as he spoke. "I don't remember you being quite so...short."

This deceptive appearance had been magically altered by the intense energy from the Gemstone of Faërie nobility that held its position just above Dark's head. The illusion that the Eye of Dagda projected was the image of a youthful figure of elvish descent dressed very simply in a hooded gray robe. He seemed tiny, even by elf standards, barely taller than most women of his kind. Standing a little under five feet tall, his Elven bloodline shone through in all its celestial nature, such as silver hair, metallic eyes and attractive angular features.

"I take it you know why I'm here," Dark replied quietly.

Gwyddien grinned, then turned back and began walking down the road with a hand on the elf's tiny shoulder. "I do.

Your grandfather spoke at great lengths. I too am worried as to where Circe has gone."

"Who was the last person to see Circe before her sudden disappearance?" again Dark asked softly.

"I'll take you to see him now."

They followed the line of the roadway as it slowly wound around a few decorative statues, as well as a neatly sculptured row of green hedges. Before them, and placed in the center of the prestigious Academy, brooding and castle-like, stood the massive, ivy clad silver towering structure that was the legendary School of Magic. Merlin's Tower, so named for the greatest of enchanters and the crown of wizardry, stretched hundreds of feet into the air high above them. The impressive structure rose into a colossal central spire surmounted by four more smaller spires, situated at the cardinal points like that of a compass. Above this the central spire continued to rise into a silvery tip surrounded by seven slender floating towers that glided around its upper reaches like mounted wooden horses on a carousel.

Within the walls of the host tower hundreds of spell-casters claimed membership here in the Guild, but only less than a hundred take up permanent residence even though they are welcome to remain here. This towering edifice is the nerve center of the Arcane Order standing on the very site where the original representatives joined together and founded the organization. It had established itself over the centuries as the greatest of all colleges for wizardry. Regents instruct the apprentices and spell-casters here, where magic is taught and researched with each member benefiting from the shared knowledge and interaction from the Order.

As the pair came closer, Dark could see in more detail the tall impressive carvings and bas-reliefs depicting magical scenes and symbols with large iconic images of Merlin, Math the Ancient and Mephistopheles the Silver Mage, decorating the exterior of the structure. Another observation was quickly made, for the tower had no visible entrance except for several thin vertical apertures nearer to the top.

Still lost in thought admiring the grand spire, they were passing through the gates and up the stairway to the Tower of Merlin when a shout brought them both around.

"Chancellor, a moment of your time!"

Gwyddien rolled his eyes at the sight of a white-robed figure running toward him, the fellow's one arm waving frantically while the other clutched at the hand of a teenage boy dressed in the same attire. It was one of the Regents, a member of the governing body of the Arcane institution. His name was Doctor Thaddeus S. Venture; he was bald with glasses and had a small rusty colored pointed beard. The young adolescent was his teenage son and the large 'V' sewn into the breast pocket of his robe indicated he too was a Venture. Gwyddien waited patiently until the man and his son came stumbling to a weary halt before them.

"Good evening, Dr. Venture," he nodded. "And I see you brought your boy with you today. He just keeps getting bigger and bigger every time I see him."

"Hank's practically a man now."

"I can feel it in my bones," came the child-like response, a slight break in his voice.

"Yes, of course you can Hank," the wizard responded wryly. "Now what can I do for you Doctor?" Gwyddien queried a moment later with a charm that Dark thought only his grandfather was able to display. He glanced questioningly at the disguised assassin, then guided the doctor a few feet away in a hushed silence.

"It seems as if another one of our students has gone missing." His words were almost a whisper. "I fear that which most people here refuse to believe. There is a rise of darkness, swathed in secrecy born in the hallowed halls of this very academy. Murmurs and whispers that tell of a covert fellowship of spell-casters who dare I say dabble in the dark arts of Necromancy."

The Guild leader turned sharply glancing over briefly at Dark, then gripping the bald Regents shoulder guided him back to stand with his son. Gwyddien's eyes were fixed on those of the doctor's. "Very well Rusty, you were right in bringing this to my attention. I shall look into this matter immediately."

"Thank you Chancellor."

When the pair of father and son had turned and walked far enough away, the Welsh wizard walked back to Dark, his face seemed to have aged terribly. Sighing heavily he placed one long arm on the school's new Elven apprentice and together they moved out toward the high tower of sorcery.

It's worse that I feared," he muttered. "Not only has Circe disappeared, but now it appears that there may be a black cabal operating somewhere hidden within the school grounds."

The half-elf assassin nodded slowly to the ageless mystic. "This is why we must find Circe, find her and you'll find this black fellowship of the Dark Arts."

The broad cobblestone path they were on passed beneath an ancient construction, a monument built to honor the city's greatest guardian, the ageless Silver Dragon. Standing almost forty feet tall, this beautiful monument was a grand testament honoring the dragon guardian. Two polished dragon statues faced one another, their huge heads facing away from the gates with their wings outspread as if they were preparing to take flight. Even beneath the handcrafted globes of magical light, the statues shone almost mirror bright.

Upon uttering a few arcane words of power to release the spell, a single ring from a crystal bell began to echo through their minds. Suddenly, translucent blue notes burst outward from the tower wall, outlining a giant archway before fading away bringing into being a now visible set of doors thirty feet tall that swung slowly open. Appearing above the enchanted doorway, an ever-changing glowing sigil hung suspended as both Guild members became bathed in a white aura overlaid with a silver scale pattern that quickly faded from their skin. The heavy thick doors to Merlin's Tower closed behind the assassin, and his thoughts faded as he noted the ancient austerity of the massive awe-inspiring chamber. The fading light from outside seemed to slide down in tired streaks through the high, silver webbed windows. The floor was tiled in marble and painted with wondrous friezes located on the walls and above archways depicting the faculty of the Arcane Academy amid pillars connecting to a series of balconies and even higher galleries. Immense stone statuary resembling dragons of legend, monsters and other magical beasts of great antiquity adorned the circular interior of the walls and was illuminated in dramatic fashion with colored lights.

Among the many statuaries one in particular caught Dark's eye; an identical copy of the massive bronze lion like the one found at the Hallow's End. "What do you know about the roaring lion effigy by the stairs?" he asked abruptly.

"Nothing really. All I know is that it was here before I was made Headmaster of this academy." Gwyddien searched his memory but the graven image meant nothing to him. "Why do you ask?"

"Just wondering that's all." Dark began again after a moment.

The guard that stood leisurely next to the stairway did not question them, but greeted them cordially, both bowing their heads as the Chancellor and apprentice moved up the winding stairs. The great library was situated many floors above the grand hall. When at last they were outside its large wooden doors, Gwyddien advised Dark to choose his words carefully for the person he was about to meet was different at best.

A huge lock secured the doors to this room. The Mage fumbled for a moment at a pouch that lay about his waist until finally producing a large metal key. The intricate mechanism creaked slightly in protest; the inserted key turned the cylinder and with a loud audible snap drew the heavy bolt back and opened the door. The pair stepped inside and closed the door behind them.

The room they entered was large and brightly lit. The vaulted ceilings were painted with breath-taking frescoes, each one representing one of the many fields of the Arcane Arts. This place of private study was adorned in a classical décor and housed the library's rarest volumes that dated back to the origin of man. The room was constructed with massive leaded stained glass windows to allow in light and minimize the need for candles or oil lamps inside the repository. Just inside the Regent's library there was an inscription reading 'In quo omnes thesauri sapientiae et scientiae', which translates to 'In which are stored all treasures of knowledge and science'. And as if the gorgeous décor and impressive book collection weren't impressive enough on their own, the library also housed a unique feature known only to senior students and tenured faculty members, two secret passages hidden by book shelves and opened with replicate books.

After a quick perfunctory review of the massive chamber, the Headmaster of the Arcane Academy moved beneath an incredible beautiful two story dark wooden handcrafted arches to a wall of books to his left. He reached behind a set of huge cloth-bound books, the color of the bindings long since faded, at the end of the fourth shelf up. When he moved these two in unison, a section of the bookcase swung silently ajar. After pushing the shelving unit in, he and Dark both passed through leaving the casing open behind them.

They now stood within a small and windowless room. Against the back wall was placed small reading tables with high leather backed chairs that stood both stiff and solitary, like sentries standing at attention. An old hand-woven oriental rug lay loosely across the hard wooden floor. The fabric of the antique rug was laced with heraldic designs and bits of gold and silver patterns. Seated on a thickly padded leather stool in front of an ornate hardwood book pedestal, carved and incorporating dragons entwined with one another, was an odd sort of man. He had large piercing eyes, his hair black with streaks of gray, as was his long star shaped goatee. His odd attire consisted of black pants with gray stripes and black leather shoes with large gold buckles. His shirt was white with a vibrant red smoking jacket over top, a gold watch and chain fell comfortably in his front pocket. He wore a billowing black and red cloak made from a thick and heavy fabric of darkness with elaborate embroidery throughout. Contained on the outside and within the decorative ornamentation were large magical blinking eyes that were already alerted to the pair of intruders and were staring direfully as they came forward. The peculiar figure seemed to exude power and mystery, his dimly lit eyes shining dully beneath a dark, troublesome brow. While not physically imposing, the man had a presence about him that belied his innocuous appearance.

"Ah Professor, my dear friend. To what do I owe this unannounced but welcome pleasure?"

"I need your help Orpheus," the voice was soft but commanding.

"I am pleased to help you, what ever your need may be." His eyes stared into Dark's and the half-elven assassin found that he could not look away.

"Circe is missing," the tall Chancellor whispered. "It's like she vanished into thin air…"

"And you're certain she hasn't simply…stepped out," the enchanter cut him short. "She has been known to engage in impromptu daring do from time to time."

"No actually her paramour has been in contact with us and shares our same concern," Gwyddien was speaking again, his voice low and guarded. "Every attempt to contact her has failed … In these dark times I fear the worst."

Orpheus nodded wordlessly, still dazed by the Headmaster's unexpected pronouncement. Slowly he rose from his reading pedestal, staring incredulity first at his mentor and friend and then at the small man who followed him in.

"Oh where are my manners, Doctor Orpheus Strange, this is …"

"Wait! There's something … unusual about you my little friend … I sense … the presence of … of … mmmm … of … I cannot quite place my finger on it… Something I have never … felt … before. Something blocking me from reading your true identity…" The man's distinctive voice cried out in anguish and he showed his tendency to speak in an overly dramatic and loud tone. "He is simply…"

"Your mere apprentice, I presume," the sorcerer addressed Dark.

"We were told you were the last to see her before her disappearance, is that true?" Dark asked quickly, picking up the conversation.

"A most compelling mystery indeed," Dr. Strange continued. "Yes, I saw her no more than a few days past; it appeared Circe was engaged in some sort of investigation, but why would she abandon it in such haste?"

"What investigation, Doctor?" the Welsh wizard interjected.

"I don't know I'm afraid," Orpheus cocked his head slightly, as if considering the problem. "But I believe she has gazed upon the impenetrable, an unwilling beholder to the impossible! It appears that the sorceress believes in the prognosticated return of the Fleshweaver!"

"Shaddai Var, but how?" Gwyddien came forward, his face suddenly hard.

"I know not; it would seem only she would somehow have known," he said finally.

"If Shaddai Var truly has arisen, then we have no choice but to vanquish this pale master of the dead, or we shall find ourselves the unfortunate tenant of the devil himself! For I have touched his mind and his is the way of the serpent and the apple! He will seduce you with the poison promises of a Faustian Covenant, giving with one hand as he rips apart your soul with the other! We must stop him at once!"

"Then I fear the other disappearances must all be connected somehow."

No one said anything. Dr. Strange moved back to his stool and slowly seated himself once more. "I too am fearful that this latest disappearance has left the magical Order of the Cosmos in twain," he began again. "However, I shall endeavor to aid you in your noble quest, to right that which is wrong, and to repair the torn curtain of time itself, but I fear that this is beyond even our combined powers. We must assemble the Order of the First Circle at once."

"I find that hope a thin one, Orpheus," Gwyddien nodded, his eyes fixed on the mystic, then his head turned to face Dark. "Tell your grandfather we need to meet, the Order must be reassembled."

Dark did not turn. "As you wish." A moment later the disguised assassin was through the bookcase passage and was gone.

XIV

Dark Solus rested alone in the comfort of his warm bed and listened absently as the rain came steadily down followed by the sound of loud rolling thunder. There were still black clouds in the gray overcast sky as a storm was drifting in toward the city, a storm that hung ominously over the dark ridge line of the Sorrow Woods to the east. The clouds had screened away the light from the sun leaving another day in somber tones of dark gray. The Lord of Dark Manor yawned loudly and wearily stretched upward. He had been up all night working with many of his servants in the library, searching for any account on the Necromancer named Shaddai Var. He would have simply asked his grandfather if the old magus had been there, but he was still away for at least a few more days. Even though he was still so tired from last night's lack of sleep, he knew he needed to get up and continue his search for any texts that contained any information on the evil mage. He found himself grinning in spite of his exhaustion. A memory of his mother flashed quickly in his weary mind when she would come into his room and she would tell him his father would drag him bodily from his bed if he failed to get up in time for breakfast and his chores. He moved down in his bed as the sound of running padded footsteps brought him about. Quickly, he walked to the door and opened it. There sitting on his hind legs was Baron, the snake tail wagging viciously side to side, the three grizzled heads raised in anticipation towards his master.

"I'm up already," Master addressed his pet. "Come in if you want." He turned abruptly and re-entered his bedroom closing the large doors firmly behind them. Baron wandered in, sniffed questioningly at the strange smell from Dark's previous night attire, then apparently satisfied with what he inhaled, simply dropped to the floor after several small rounded turns of his large body. He smiled warmly at the Chimera then quickly dressed for the day's travel. Breakfast was waiting for Dark when he stepped from the hall and into the brightly lit dining hall. Being noiseless, unseen servants served their master his morning meal and within minutes cleaned the table of this burden. Wordlessly, he rose and within a few moments was dressed in the armor of the assassin known as Demon Raider. Reaching fearlessly within the magical confines of the fanged demon's mouth embedded on his breastplate, he withdrew the Eye of Dagda and placed it just above his head making his costume complete. Time, he thought, would be the greatest single factor in his attempt to find Circe, so he would begin the important undertaking of finding her upon the streets of Duergar and if he had to, he would search high and low through every inch of the city in his pursuit to find the missing sorceress. He would start by using the Gem of Location at various parts of the huge metropolis hoping beyond hope that the power held within would spring to life and find its hidden target.

It was late afternoon and like the proverbial saying, it was the calm before the storm as the rain slackened off altogether for the time being. The storm was coming, even though it appeared that the clouds were thinning out, permitting small strips of blue to somehow seep through the rolling cloud cover. Dark was seated on one of the smaller towers above the concert hall when he saw his first sign of a clearing in the clouds, momentarily diverting his attention from the task at hand. Lost in thought, he realized the threat of Kalifen and the Shadow Lord looming before him like a towering impenetrable fortress. How could he possibly hope to defeat such evil entities. Such creatures had no soul, they lived according to laws of their own making, completely foreign to the world to which he was born. They first took his parents and now with the disappearance of Circe, another was lost he thought. He must find her and bring her back, he must.

With the power of his necklace, he suddenly found himself standing in front of some stately home, its heavy doors standing closed, the metal locks looking cold and wet in the graying mist that hung suspended in the cooling late afternoon air. He turned quickly from the entryway, not wishing to be noticed by the owners of the home or their neighbors. Slowly he moved along the cobblestone road, the leaves from the trees and flowers dripping softly from the still falling rain leaving the grounds around moist and green. He moved quietly, his own thoughts as hazy and wistful as the setting that surrounded him, giving way to brief moments of sinking despair that seized him when he thought of another loss to his family and friends. For Circe had been like an aunt to him growing up, teaching him, guiding him in the Arcane Arts when Mephisto could not. She was a woman whom he looked up to and revered like his own mother and grandmother. He shook his head; something deep within himself hinted with dread persistence that he would not be able to find his friend in time, that she was already lost to him. Again he shook his head, the thoughts that crept into his brain deserving only his scorn, but still he could not shake off the gut feeling that told him she was already gone. He would need to contact Fhaminn Dread he thought to himself as the dampness closed in about him, the chill of the rain visibly showing with every breath he took.

Dark wandered aimlessly out of the residential area still lost deep in thought. Almost without realizing it, he walked out from the urban area and onto the King's Highway. The Grand Boulevard was bustling at all times of the day due to the numerous travelers constantly passing through on their way to and from various destinations, making this definitely the busiest thoroughfare in all of Duergar. The air here, even on cold and wet days, was always vibrant with the calls and cries of barking vendors, their high shrill voices yelling out prices and products.

Within the concealing shadow of his cowl, Dark Solus saw in disbelief what he thought must surely be a conjured illusion like his own disguise. She was an icon of feminine beauty; her face was perfectly symmetrical as if sculpted and cast from stone. A cloud of black hair curled down around her sweet face and she wore a golden diadem band that looped gracefully around like horizontal ribbons and joined together at the back. Her dark eyes sparkled at him and she possessed thick full lips, an attractive feature that women from other cultures often attempted to duplicate. Her dark skin was the color of melted milk chocolate; around her neck was a fortune in pearls and tightly wrapped around her was a warm heavy cloak with a panther skin draped over her shoulder. She was the daughter of Amanirenas, the one-eyed Queen of the Meroitic Kingdom of Kush and someone Dark had not seen in years. Then with the noiseless footsteps of a cat, he quickly moved behind her small lithe form and came to a silent halt next to her, the umbrella she carried shadowing wide eyes that looked up at him momentarily and then strayed to the shops beyond. The two stood without speaking for a short time as she tried to move ahead of the stranger that now seemed to follow her every movement. In the sky above, heavy clouds were still rolling in, finally covering the last faint traces of any blue as the dark of an early twilight began to show. Almost at once the rains began to fall again, now in steady sheets it mercilessly began to besiege the city streets of Duergar. Dark noted with absent relief that this night would be black and moonless.

"You seem to be a long way from home Princess," Dark spoke in an old and almost forgotten Nublin dialect. "I believe the Nubian Kingdom lies a long way off to the south."

She went almost rigid at his words, a trapped look springing to life in her frightened eyes. "Clearly sir you have me mistaken for someone else." She quickly moved ahead a few paces, trying to distance herself from this stranger and his unwanted intrusion.

"Then a thousand pardons my good woman," he said with a grand theatrical bow. "When I see her I shall explain to the one-eyed warrior queen that it was not her daughter that I saw here this day in the City of Dwarves…So I bid you good day." Dark turned slightly.

After only a moments hesitation, "No, wait! Please kind sir…"

"Sydney it's me," he cut the Princess short, speaking once again in common tongue, a large smile stretched across his face from ear to ear.

All her defenses seemed to give way, her posture now showed one of great relief. "Dark is that you?" She was angry now. "You son of a…"

"Syd!" he paused. "I see that mouth of yours hasn't changed a bit." When Dark reached for her, she pulled quickly way, stepping back from him for several long moments. Dark Solus stared after her helplessly, his smile still showing beneath his cloak.

When she did finally speak again, her voice was a harsh whisper. "You jackass, you had me scared out of my wits, did you know that?"

The disguised assassin nodded. "I just couldn't help myself, forgive me."

Quiet and composed once more, she rejoined him. With a slight gesture from his hand, Dark led them out of the rain filled streets of the city and over to stand under a canopied stall of jewelry and other common trinkets.

"I take it your mother doesn't know you're here?" Dark had drawn the Nubian Princess aside and began speaking to her again, their words hushed and secretive.

"What, are you kidding me?" she asked in disbelief, then quickly shook her head. "No, no, she would kill me if she knew I was in Duergar. She believes me to be at an old English language university in Albion attending lectures and seminars and devoting all my time in diligent study."

With night time approaching the street lamps were lit, the light revealing the familiar mocking smile as it slanted out across the assassin's lean face. "You…in diligent study?" he laughed softly. "So what are you doing here?"

"That's the best part," she exclaimed excitedly, her eyes shining bright like diamonds. "I am currently working at the

Royal Opera House, understudying one of the roles in a play called 'A Secret Garden'. Isn't that amazing!"

"Yeah, that's great, congratulations," the tall half-elf replied softly. "I know it's what you have always wanted."

"But wait, that's not the best part," the other broke in, her face aglow with great enthusiastic elation. "I am the understudy to a legendary star, the world's most famous opera singer, none other than Countess Elizabeth Bàthery."

"Who?" Dark hesitated in confusion.

The Princess paused, eyeing her cloaked friend critically. "You're kidding me right? Countess Bàthery…she's only the greatest female soprano singer on earth."

A sudden clamor from one of the vendor's a few stalls down brought both their heads around, where he was startled to see with his keen elven eyes the same limping little shape-shifting bastard from Boddeker Stitch's tailor shop. His nose was bandaged and clearly broken and he was stepping lightly through the crowd still milling about in the streets, casually pilfering cheese and even wine from the stalls. One proprietor shouted angrily at him, and he looked up in surprise. Then he boldly walked over to her and jammed his finger, making his nail as sharp as a rose thorn, right into the woman's right eye permanently blinding it.

"I have to go Princess!" Dark whispered harshly.

"Same old Dark," Sydney stated flatly. "Just promise me you'll come for opening night; everyone who is anyone will be there so you better be there. I'll leave a ticket for you with the front Manager under the same name you gave me when we first met…Dark…Dark?"

In that split second he had completely disappeared. Stolen from sight by some being of the other world that seemed to suddenly reach out and snatch the estranged assassin from her view so incredibly fast that it appeared to the astonished Princess that he had simply vanished off the face of the earth.

Dark now moved in silent concentration through the wayfaring strangers who moved about the thoroughfare, studying their faces as he moved through them. He focused his concentration on tracking his prey as he began moving mechanically about the still crowded streets, his eyes fixed solidly on the shape-shifter. Finally with his pilfering completed, he turned southward and he began strolling slowly back toward Dark, his lowered head casting sharp glances about. The ferret faced imposter led them westward for several long minutes from that point, staying close to the shadowy fringes of the back alleys and back streets of Duergar, keeping his round eyes open for any sign of any would be pursuers.

Out through dim lit lanes and into the moonless city the pretender now began to run lightly, as if to meet a lover and the unseen assassin pursued in silence. He followed the skin walker as he made his way down twisting streets and along the now quiet alleyways of the Grand Bazaar, finally halting at the gate of a walled house in the oldest quarter of the city. The gate before him seemed to magically spring open then close of its own accord.

Almost in an instant, Dark had reached the outer perimeter of the walled compound, and moving quickly, stationed himself by a tree to await events. They had come to an old abandoned church, its large windows boarded up tight so no light could penetrate in or out. The assassin moved with the lean form of the doppelganger, moving swiftly, running in a half crouch, pausing only occasionally to listen for sounds of movement other than his own. However, as he neared the little church, Dark heard snatches of music borne on the air and voices in drunken song. The Elf imposter unwrapped the cloak and cowl that closely covered his body. He glanced about quickly as he stood before the doors of the building, but there was no movement; he had made it unnoticed. He then beat a simple rhythm on the door.

The singing ceased, then the scraping of metal within was heard and after an interminable pause, the door was opened a crack. A small man with hair like wolf's fur and staring gray eyes peered out. Stammering with fear, the shape-shifter began to recite a poem.

> 'Nor Crown nor coin can halt times flight
> Or stay the dark armies of the night
> Peasant, Priest and Prince alike, man woman,
>   lad and lass
> All answer to the hour glass.'

The gray eyed halfling hesitated a moment, then with an audible grunt he let him in and bolted the door behind him.

The weather had become quite threatening during the last half hour; the once gray skies now a solid bank of rolling, blackened clouds that completely blotted out the stars and moon, leaving the churchyard in almost complete darkness. The only visible light came from the blazing fires inside the church, the flames rushing higher with the sudden opening of the massive wooden door. The storm was on its way and would be over the city before morning.

The night seemed to pass in slow minutes, and Dark moved as silent as the shadows all about him. His mind ceased to reason, ceased to wonder or think as his training now took command and his keen instincts probed the darkness once more for any hidden danger. He moved swiftly toward the church entrance, his footfalls noiseless as he proceeded forward. At length, he made his way across the courtyard and stood outside the towering walls of the halfling hall.

Within the defiled walls of this once holy church, hearths and torches blazed warm and bright and bottles of wine passed freely among the drunken members of the pack. Songs were sung that intoned the praises of their Leader, Sneak Longfoot, the Lord Protector they sang. Outside this hall of vandalism and desecration however, solitary and unseen in the cold and rain, another kind of being walked among the living. With harp music floating in the air, Dark's clawed gauntleted hands began to curl tight, and a low oath issued from his throat as he listened to the joyful songs within.

He hated these malevolent creatures. He hated them with an intensity that almost bordered on madness; a hatred that over the years had festered and grown. Now it consumed him. It was the only thing he had left. It drove him, guided him, even giving him power, and he would use that hatred to destroy all those who had caused him so much misery. These halflings! Every one of them, even if somehow he managed to kill them all, even they would not be enough to satisfy him now, not by a long shot. No, the destruction of the Halfling Guild would not be enough to heal all that he had suffered. The others, he thought, they too would, no must be destroyed as well. Kalifen, Blackthorn, the Thieves' Guild and the Assassins' Guild, all those who were a part of his parent's demise, they all must suffer the same fate. His vengeance would come not as a man but as a demon, a restless remnant born in Hell, forced by mortals of this world, bent on revenge and none shall resist its fury.

A spark of cunning formed the assassin's action, as he waited in the shadow until the singing had ceased and the glow from the blazing fires within dimmed. When the hall was at last silent and the smoke that rose through holes among the rafters no longer blew like flags in the evening air, Demon Raider struck. The attack came in a blast of flame and fire, with no more warning than a shock wave that traveled the length of the church hall. The thick sturdy doors burst open like thunder, sending out a hailstorm of tiny splinters and large pieces of broken wood. Into the dim chamber his demonic form lurched, his eyes blazing red, his nostrils flaring flames of perdition.

With a swiftness aided by his father's magical boots, Dark seized the two men nearest the door. Before either of the victims could cry out each of their throats were torn open and their spines snapped by sharpened claws. The eyes from the demon face façade upon his armor glowed a crimson red as the hatred its owner held flowed through him. And it feasted then, grasping the drunk and dreaming halflings in its fanged teeth, crushing the bodies that came near enough, tearing at their flesh and cracking their bones in its powerful jaws. The armor's gaping mouth, when it had finished, was matted with blood, and for the moment, the beast was satisfied. The same, however, could not be said for its owner.

Thus began the siege of the Halfling Guild Hall, a horror that began at the stroke of midnight, that would endure for many long days to come. On this night the demonic assassin attacked, brutally squeezing the life from halflings within the seized church. Not one hobbit could resist such supernatural strength and speed, and no weapon this night did the beast any harm. His power and cruelty towards these creatures was of a measure beyond any human experience. For on this black night, he had come prepared for butchery of his own.

At that same moment, the remaining survivors had at last changed from their diminutive frames into their Lycan forms and crept out of the shadows on four limbs, their eye slits reflecting the glowing embers. A brave few slipped into the pale fringes of the torch light, then suddenly they came at him in a rush, their clawed limbs gripping the church floor tightly as they raced toward him. Now Dark lunged forward, huge, angered and dangerous when he moved catlike as he did now. His left arm lifted mechanically, the dragon's head emerged raging for vengeance as its open mouth began to glow with a golden radiance. A blazing ball of flame shattered the darkness, bursting forth from the wand's gaping maw, a swirling mass of flaming death that rocketed towards its target and detonating in a screaming bellow around them. Smoke billowed out of the ground about the oncoming attackers, then slowly dispersed across a crispy scattering of lifeless charred bodies. But not all had fallen.

Dark, mad with bloodlust, seething with hatred for these night stalking animals, continued assaulting them in a frenzy of destructiveness. Lycan after Lycan fell dying under the silver daggers of the half-elven assassin, each wicked slash bursting in a blinding spray of blood. Terrified, the remaining survivors hesitated, but only briefly. Then, shrieking with malice and in fury, they came on, hurtling themselves at the demonic intruder. Their struggle was desperate. Finally, one last black furred werewolf sprang at Dark, its sharp claws ripping for his throat, but was warded off with a quick parry. Again the Lycan lunged at him, but once again the black-garbed assassin was quicker, pining the creature to the floor with a single thrust of his blade.

At that moment, in the deep shadows at the far end of the hall, hidden behind a wall of black smoke, something moved. Standing there, just behind the fringes of firelight, a shadow darker than the night about it edged into view. The pack leader appeared, stepping forward into the light, huge fierce and black furred, baring sharp fangs, it howled. It stood a full two heads taller than any man, small eyes glowing in its skull, its long mouth hung open as if to speak, but it uttered no sound.

A roar rose out of the monster's throat, its fanged furry face contorted with fury. With one last howl of rage, it charged into its attacker. In the battle that followed, benches crashed in pieces to the ground and glowing embers scattered setting hungry fires inside the church. The massive werewolf circled its demonic combatant, seeking some small opening for a savage strike, but Dark was too quick. Taking the beast by surprise, he eluded the Lycan's brutal bite. He locked one of its paws in his own iron grip, bending the black trapped claws back against its own wrist breaking bone. The pack leader writhed and howled in pain and tried desperately to pull away, but Dark was too strong. Aided by the magic from the Belt of Strength, Dark still held tight the monster's broken appendage, twisting sharply as the Lycan pulled. Finally the arm cracked with a loud audible snap and broke, and white bone tore through the furred flesh of the beast's massive shoulder. Still jerking it backed away. Finally the flesh ripped again and massive amounts of thick red blood gushed out in a sudden and forceful stream as the arm finally tore free. Wailing in anguish, its life's blood draining away, the werewolf stumbled out into the darkness and rain, seeking safety.

Inside the church hall, Dark stood bloodied and sweating, still holding tight the clawed arm of the were beast. Then, swinging his bloody prize over his shoulder, he walked outside to finish off the wounded pack leader. One fortunate man had somehow huddled unnoticed in the far corner of the hall. It was the little ferret-face shape-shifter, and he had somehow survived to tell the tale.

XV

It was well after midnight; the rain was still falling in a steady downpour, the night sky impenetrably black and foreboding, when a shadowy form detached itself from the darkness of the night shrouded trees in the forest. The weather had become threatening over the last hour or so; the sky had become a solid wall of massing, blackened clouds that had completely blotted out the moon and stars. The only visible light came from the lanterns of the sentries as they moved about. The silent assassin was hopeful that the rain and darkness would offer the black-garbed man a little added cover from any prying eyes. He moved down out of the shelter of the large cluster of trees, winding his way through the darkness toward a twisting rocky maze of large black boulders. The blackness of his surrounding seemed to stand like an impenetrable wall between the light from the lamps and himself; he could neither see nor hear any guards, but he knew they were there. He remained motionless for long minutes, his head cocked slightly as he listened, then suddenly he rose and like a whisper disappeared silently into the night.

The stealthy figure moved quickly, running in a half crouch, pausing occasionally to listen for any sounds of human movement. The plain was littered with small and large obsidian rocks with very few bushes to break the pattern, with two or three deformed and twisted trees scattered aimlessly about. There was no sign of life anywhere, and the only sounds he heard were the haunting howl of the rising wind and his own low and steady breathing. The fires that had formerly been just a low haze of dim light from the base of the mountains, now were spread apart into individual smoking fires covered by large wooden canopies as the assassin drew closer. He was close enough to hear the faint sounds of voices talking but he was still not close enough to enable him to make out any coherent words.

As silent as a shadow he rose to his feet, seeing and hearing nothing around, he began to move slowly westward through the wall of darkness, his long, curved knife held loosely in one hand. He wandered unchecked through the large encampment for what seemed like an eternity without finding any clue to the whereabouts of Circe. As morning was drawing nearer, he began to despair of finding anything here at all. The necklace around his neck had directed him to search this strange mountain range that consisted of loads upon loads of large black granite rocks. He grasped eagerly at the tiny heart shaped pendant; the magic it held within came quickly, flooding out like a sudden rush of heat that coursed swiftly through his veins. The necklace was a gift from his paramour, giving off a warm sensation like a first kiss whenever the two were near one another.

He wound his way through the giant encampment shielding his face from the light of the fires as he moved steadily forward, his dragon green eyes constantly searching, studying, and always looking forward. There were several times when he was certain that he had been discovered, times when he made a sound carelessly, causing him to stop, his hand holding tight the sharpened blade of his knife readily prepared to fight for his freedom at any cost. He moved through the shroud-like blackness with the speed and stealth of a well seasoned assassin, noiselessly winding his way through another maze of these razor-edged black boulders and rocks that covered the mountainside. He had not seen any sentries for quite sometime, but he knew they had to be posted close, but it was almost impossible to see anyone.

He walked for long minutes, believing he had gone too far when he suddenly heard a small noise. He froze, trying hard to locate the source, then he heard it again, a low voice from someone in the darkness directly ahead of him. It seemed a guard had given himself and his location away, and Fhaminn Dread crept forward, his movement cautious and soundless. His eyes at last were able to discover the dim outline of an armed figure standing silently, and from his size the man was clearly human. Quietly the stealthy assassin waited a few minutes longer to be certain that the sentinel's back remained turned to him, then he crept still closer at last going in for the kill until he was within just a few feet. In one fluid motion, he rose up like a solid towering shadow that fell over the unsuspecting soldier; one iron like hand gripping the sentinel's throat while the other held the steel curved blade cutting off, with a slash, the man's cry of warning before it could escape. The assassin did not pause. He threw off the cumbersome hunting cloak, already soaked through by the pouring rain and stripped the dead body of his uniform quickly wrapping himself in the heavy cloak that masked their face and most of their body. He melted back into the gloom of the forest and began moving further ahead when his eye caught sight of a small boat pulled up onto the river bank and tied to a large tree. Standing in a tight clustered circle next to the moored boat were four very large and powerful looking fiends, their huge black bulks unmistakable even in this poor light. These ogre sized demonic creatures had a thick, scaly hide, a deep blue in color, almost black. Each had four muscular arms that ended in human like hands, their thick fingers tipped with long curved claws. They gazed with glowing red eyes with a wolf-like muzzle lined with sharp teeth that seemed too large to fit into their huge mouths. They were accompanying a fifth figure, smaller and slighter in build; his robes, adorned with silver buttons and crafted of rich black velvet with strange archaic looking symbols on the front, marked him as some sort of priest.

Fhaminn Dread studied them in careful silence for a moment, trying to make out the man's face, but the dim light from the glass enclosed lanterns gave him only brief glimpses. He didn't appear to be anyone he had ever encountered before, when he suddenly remembered he had met this stranger before with Circe when he had accompanied her to the Opera House. This man was the Elven Sorcerer Famon

Fane, a small man with the noticeable narrow angular face, pointed ears and blue eyes, prominently associated with those of his race. But what was he doing here?

Then the guarded assassin saw something else, something strange. Several large bundles covered with a heavy cloth and securely tied were being lifted out of the boat and effortlessly flung over the broad shoulders of the demonic looking creatures. He studied each of them dubiously, unable to tell exactly what they were. Suddenly, to his astonishment and surprise, one of the bundles, he thought, may have moved slightly. Enough at least to convince Circe's inamoratos that there was something or someone alive beneath the thick covering. Desperately his mind raced with the thought that Circe may be beneath the fastened tarp. There were several parting words exchanged and Fhaminn Dread only caught snatches of the brief conversation, including a final comment as the boat moved out into the swift and clear waters, of a warning from the sorcerer to not be late with the next shipment.

Fhaminn Dread inched a bit further ahead and he watched as a lean man in the small boat disappeared into the gloomy darkness beyond, his oars splashing in the choppy waters. The sky was still dark and overcast with large black, nimbus clouds that still dropped a heavy, chubby rain to the eorth. He lingered a moment longer as the party of five turned from the river bank with Famon Fane's four demonic servants carrying the enclosed bundles and moving back toward the rise to the left. The hidden assassin was certain that someone had been taken prisoner by the Elven Mage. It was a feeling that came from deep inside, telling him that Circe was there, bound and held captive and that he must find out at any cost. He watched and followed as the small company moved away from him into the heavy gray mist. He was crouching now and began moving swiftly back in the direction from which he had just come, trying to stay silent and still parallel to that taken by the strange party. What if it was Circe, the thought flashed through his mind. Not only was it going to be extremely difficult to get close enough to free the prisoner, but just one of these brutes was more than a match physically for the slight assassin. And any chance of rescue depended on an escape route out of the mountains through the lines of sentries and somehow back to the city.

Fhaminn could feel the cold drops of rain strike his face as he moved, the sound of thunder rolling ominously overhead and the wind blew in force. He moved across clumps of high grass, moving steadily just behind his quarry like a black connected shadow, dodging small trees and a mass of thick brush. He passed by countless fires in his pursuit, their embers burning low and slowly dying with the closing of the night. There were tents everywhere, all marked by the same conspicuous heraldic marking as Famon Fane wore on the front of his priestly garb. At last they had reached what seemed the inner perimeter of the encampment.

He paused in a crouch just beyond the light of the camp fires, their canopied flames well fed on new wood. The cool night wind help fan the crackling flames of the large wood fires sending thick clouds of white smoke swirling out toward the hidden assassin. He watched as the small company paused momentarily at a second ring of sentries that were loosely gathered around the wet encampment of large tents. It seemed that most of the sentries were asleep, but some still standing idly about or crouching near the smoking fires for much needed warmth.

Fhaminn Dread waited a moment longer until the wind carried the billowing smoke from the glowing fires between the closest guard and himself. He rose surreptitiously, carefully selecting his entry point; he moved in a casual manner and strolled in toward the encampment. From a pouch at his waist he quickly produced two egg shaped objects and with the aim of an archer struck the flames with both tiny grenades. A wall of white smog rose steadily, blanketing his movement momentarily, masking his bulky form as he moved out of the shadows of the forest and into the ring of fires nearest him. A moment later he stood in the midst of the small party and fell in several yards behind them, unaware of their new member.

The disguised assassin pulled the patrolman's cloak closely around his head and body, making certain only his hands were visible to anyone else that may pass by. His face was only a dim shadow beneath the black hood. He glanced about apprehensively, but the sentries only continued to stare blankly out into the darkness; he had made it so far unnoticed. He shook his head of any more doubt and moved slowly forward with steady measured steps. There was no turning back now.

The small company, led by Famon Fane, was moving steadily higher and before long the woods thinned out and the party came to a path upward and climbed fast. In moments, they moved to a clearing where thickets butted up against a thick wall of black mountain rock. Their leader threw back his black hood to show a morose face, long silver hair and deep penetrating eyes. At his signal the small group came to a halt.

"Gwehyddu nid yw pryfed cop dod yma!"

Suddenly the ground beneath them began to rumble and thunder sounded throughout; a crack appeared and swept up the rock face and quickly widened. With an audible groan, a door opened into blackness, releasing a rush of chill air. Small points of light shone among the shadows. The head of the small company strode slowly through the open portal and disappeared with his faithful servants following in an orderly file. With his cloak pulled closely about him, Fhaminn Dread moved behind the small procession and in the next instant he was alone in the blackness of the shadows. When the last had vanished, the rock closed and once more became a seamless solid slab.

In a line, they started down a stone stairway, the Elven Sorcerer leading with his large sentries just a step behind. The disguised Dread trailed behind them in the shadows as they trudged steadily downward. Into the still blackness he followed, his eyes peering almost blindly, his hands groping to find the stone walls of the passage. For long moments they remained in blackness, then a new glimmering light appeared from out of the dark. A flickering, flaming torch illuminated their way as each passed beneath it. Just ahead he could see others fluttering through the impenetrable gloom.

Their descent wore on, seemingly endless as the stairway spiraled downward through the mountain. Several times they did however pass by a number of empty passageways that were tunneled out by hand through the stone. From time to time they passed isolated doors of iron, all closed and heavily locked and latched, but still they did not slow. Then a very strong and sweet odor of incense burned more strongly as they plunged lower, filling the stairwell with its pungent smell. For hundreds of feet the stairs wore on, twisting and turning, winding forever downward deep into the mountain. Large rats scurried and scattered throughout the dark, their cries faint with unpleasant squeaks of fear. Finally, the stone ended in a passageway formed of stone blocks, fashioned by hand and massive with patches of damp trails of water running down along the walls.

Then they were through the passage and stood within a great cavern, its ceiling a mass of jagged stalactites and braced with massive columns of three intertwined snakes. Strange markings were carved into the stone of the columns and walls, and iron stanchions finished with ornamental heads were arranged around a raised circular platform. Etched into the stone floor of the dais was a large pentagram, inlaid with glowing red stone that gave off a magical fiendish lambent light. Reeking of decay, a gaunt black winged monster covered in black leathery skin laid motionless in a pool of its own rank juices. A huge sarcophagus stood open in the center of the underground chamber with streams of fine mist pouring out and spilling onto the floor creating a shin high layer of bone chilling murk. Narrow book shelves filled half the walls of this foul place, with various leather bound books and ancient scrolls lining the shelving. Several unopened crates took much of the floor; one sizeable chest stood open and contained a number of glass jars for holding organs and other bodily fluids, preserving them for long periods of time.

From beneath the concealing darkness of the fallen sentinel's cloak's wide hood, the wary assassin followed dutifully the hulking sentries as they stepped into the dimly lit interior of the cavernous chamber. Then without pausing, he detached himself like a shadow from the blackness and gloom and darted silently toward cover. From behind a large crate, he raised his head cautiously, his keen eyes peered down as the black servants of Fane lumbered heavily across the mist filled floor past the platform to the far wall where a narrow band of water tumbled and gathered in a bubbling pool. Upon a quick command from their master, they threw down the bundled forms just to the right of the waterfall beside the pool into which it poured. The wizened face of Famon Fane glanced back briefly and the demonic sentinels moved toward a massive stone door that stood ajar at the far end of the huge hall. They soon disappeared beyond to another set of stairs that led downward.

A moment later the Elven Mage strode silently into the view of the hiding assassin to stand next to a large pedestal that held a basin of water, its murky surface placid and calm. He peered cautiously into the cold, black water, his eyes darting furtively about, waiting, watching expectantly for something but nothing came. Then only seconds later, the darkness was gone and in its place was the thin, black haired and haggard face of Lord Blackthorn, his cadaverous visage hard and featureless. The deep set eyes of Famon Fane were fierce as he gazed steadily into the waters of the strange basin, waiting for the commanding picture to speak.

"Have the final arrangements been made for the Cremation of Care ceremony?" the lean calculating face stared steadily back at the impassive Fane.

"Yes, Lord Xuchia," the mystic nodded obediently, quickly glancing at a glass case containing a clear opal eye and a severed human hand. "With both of the ancient remnants of the Lich King finally in our possession, we can begin preparations for fulfilling the prophecy. But without the Book of Darkness, I cannot complete the spell to affix the enchanted fragments of Vecna to my master's host body."

"I have already departed from Kalifen; even now I sail to secure the Necronomicon from the guardians of the grimoire personally," the tall gaunt usurper announced abruptly. "In just a few days time, the first of the four blood moons will signal the end of days and the coming of the Shadow Lord. For decades we have used the cloak of philanthropy to hide our revolutionary and subversive activities from the world... but no longer. For nearly eight hundred years I have been imprisoned within the Black Seal, doomed to spend eternity trapped within a ghost-like state of existence in a plane of dark damnation. For years I studied and conjured, eventually assuming a mastery of the dark arts achieved by no mortal before or since. Then, when I had finally discovered the very means for my escape, a foolish mortal mage summoned me back to this world and forced me into his servitude..." He trailed off and smiled, a faint glimmer of his plan began to form in his mind, then he looked back at the anxious face of his elven servant before continuing.

"Now I shall conquer! I have set in motion events that will grant me the power of a god. With the rising of the last blood moon, when the sun shall be turned into darkness, before the great and manifest day of the Shadow Lord, the old order will be demolished and a new order, a new world order shall take its place. And Kalifen's power, Kalifen's flesh, Kalifen's soul and even his slain bride SHALL BE MINE!"

"I live only to serve your greater glory my Lord!" Famon Fane broke in suddenly.

"See to it that you do." With a wave of Xuchia's cloak sleeve, the clear picture faded and the water once again turned murky, its surface still and silent.

Fhaminn Dread failed to pick up everything the two conspirators said, but he had heard enough. He kept his cloak wrapped tightly about him, with the shadows of the wide cowl masking his identity; he moved cautiously toward the prisoners on the other side of the huge chamber. Slowly, cautiously, he began to inch his way forward. In his hand he placed his long hunting knife, its sharp blade drawn clear from its leather sheath. Quietly, the stealthy assassin finally approached the bound captives, his face still concealed within the dark recesses of the hood, the blade extended out before him.

Silently the cloaked intruder sawed at the tough bonds with his long knife. It had to be Circe, his mind told him over and over again, it had to be Circe…it had to be. Why go through all this trouble to hide and conceal their faces and with the Elven leader being so secretive… The bonds quickly fell as the keen blade had finally severed them. It had to be her! With the ropes unbound, he threw off the large, leather satchel so the person within could finally be seen. He blinked at it. He bent over and stared astonished. In the midst of the bundle lay a small slender female. Two black eyes glared balefully up at the assassin. He backed away slowly, keeping his eyes fixed on the body before him. The assassin cringed. He had indeed rescued a woman but it was not the one he sought, it was not Circe. And this woman was dead.

Suddenly a moaning sound began to fill the air; the noise swelled into a cacophonous outcry as if a pitched battle was being waged and audibly overwhelming. The ground beneath his feet glowed momentarily with a white nimbus of crackling energy that faded away to a sickly green before disappearing completely. An instant later the mist shrouded eorth erupted in a shower of rock and dirt and a sudden movement caught his eye. He froze watching the murky ground intently. Then, slowly and inexorably, his eyes bright with fear, hundreds of stark white skeletal arms, their boney hands flexing like talons, pushed upwards towards him and sank their hard, merciless fingers into his body. And despite their ability to rise up through solid, hard packed eorth, they were no apparition.

His eyes were still bright with fear at the sight of those frightening and disgusting manifestations. He quickly pulled his arm free from the bony clasp and began to inch across the floor. And then they struck; suddenly, skeletal hands wrapped around the assassin's neck, teeth tore into his shoulder and leg. For the first time, their faces were clearly visible. Their damaged features twisted into expressions that might have been pleading. Where eyes should have been, there were only empty sockets and an oblong crater was all that remained of their nose. Their heads were little more than gleaming bone, some were still adorned with pasty shreds of flesh. No sound came from any mouth, but all around him eddied the most chilling of chanting from an invisible demonic congregation.

Pushing up and pulling out, he somehow broke the iron-like grip and reeled out of the way toward the center of the chamber. But the newly risen undead were on him in an instant, raking talons along his cheek so hard that it made his blood splatter on his neck. Strong teeth tore at his flesh; the creatures were eating his flesh! Teeth not only met flesh, but bit into bone with an audible crack. Behind him was a gleaming skeleton figure and beside it another. All around him swayed the shadowy figures of the dead, some still partially clothed in flesh, bones protruding from rags, with wisps of hair clinging to their whitened skulls. The ragged figures, clutching and grabbing, twittering and clicking their teeth and stretching their faces in gleaming grins began to close in about him.

"Hold him!...I command you!"

The loud booming voice came out of the darkness to break the stillness. Famon Fane smiled, his white teeth gleaming. The Hand of Vecna glowed a sickly green in his own hand as the hatred flowed through him. The Eleven Sorcerer paused as if waiting for something, the sharp glaring eyes riveted on the assassin's own. He stayed perfectly motionless, little more than a shadow in the pale light of the charred and rotting severed limb. With extreme effort he calmed himself, the blackened member grew lifeless again, its long, claw-like fingers stopped gesturing with the luminescent light fading to a faint, almost invisible glow.

"Tell me why it is you are here and who sent you," he quickly held up the evil artifact, holding it at the ready should his captive attempt anything further. "You have about a minute before I have your tongue ripped out of your skull and turn you over to my new cadaverous friends here."

The dragon green eyes burned into the evil mystic with intense hatred. Fhaminn Dread did not respond, but instead eyed him steadily, his mind carefully pondering the choices open to him. There was a long moment of silence as the held captive looked desperately about, the dark hidden face now ashen with fear.

"Ah, the strong silent type…no matter." The evil angular face stared menacingly at him, and in fury Famon Fane called for his personal guards. "I ought to dispose of you without further consideration, but for now I will take you to the dungeons where the others are imprisoned…When my master awakens, he'll know what to do with you."

Fhaminn Dread's eyes went wide in sudden shock at hearing the mention of the word 'others'. Just then the sound of heavy boots echoed through the stairwell, doors flew open from both sides as several dozen armed guards rushed over to take the cloaked captive. He was relieved of his weapons; his hands bound tightly behind his back. Several hands spun him about, shoving and dragging him along the misty floor, through one door, down a long flight of stairs to a long stone landing, then down another hall that wound around in a maze of twists and turns. They finally came to a sudden halt, and a set of heavy iron bolts were drawn slowly back with a loud squeaking showing the age of the iron. The door they held locked shut ponderously opened emitting a foul, rank odor of feces and decay. The hands pushed him sharply with a snicker, releasing him without warning as he fell heavily to the stone floor still bound. The door closed behind him and the bolts slid heavily into place. He was left alone with only the sound of his own breathing in the deep silence of his prison.

Famon Fane was already moving across the mist filled floor toward the bubbling pool, now surrounded by the moaning cadre of dead. He soon poised himself upon a large flat rock and then raised high a crystal bowl in the shape of an open mouth, that he bore. Into the effervescent waters he poured a liquid, green as emeralds. He watched a moment while the spell strengthened and the color deepened to a green luster.

"Hear me powers of the night!" He flung his head back and shouted. "I pray you, Father, hear my words and accept this sacrifice to honor you." He brought forth the next item he carried so carefully, and into the pool he dropped one blood red jewel. "Let my offering appease you to bring life to this empty vessel."

Then he saw an abomination in the swirling water, a green and writhing mass which crept slowly upwards. When the head appeared, it was hideous to look at, split and fanged and slavering at the mouth. Its real shape was a hideous reflection of its malevolent nature, a twisted mockery of the living forms that made up this world; ghoulishly configured sharp toothed and clawed. It was a cruel patchwork of stolen parts, goat's hooves, dog's fangs and even human faces, it stood aimlessly evil. The voice that erupted from its foul mouth was no more than a bestial howl.

"Now it is time," Famon Fane whispered.

XVI

When Dark finally opened his eyes, it was a little after noon of the following day. He found himself resting comfortably in his own large feather bed, his armor was off and arranged on an articulated wooden mannequin. On the floor next to his bed lay the still sleeping chimera, his massive legs kicked and twitched, while one head growled, one barked and the other whimpered. Dark raised himself up, his mind still drugged by sleep and he stared into the brightness of the room. Through the windows the young Lord of Dark Manor could see the sun burning brightly and patches of deep blueness behind bundles of gray clouds in the sky. Gone was the damp, impenetrable wet rain and gone was the vast dark rolling ceiling of black storm clouds that had blanketed the city for the last few days. The lands that surrounded Duergar remained soggy and scattered with tiny ponds that the saturated eorth had not yet managed to absorb.

Dark finally slid to the edge of the bed and dropped one leg at a time to the floor. He sat for a long moment in silence, his body aching with fatigue and pain of his injuries. He was bruised and battered; the Emerald Cup which sustained his life against a killing blow did not, however, defend him against all wounds inflicted. The Elven assassin had finished with his bandaging and was pulling his armor on when there was a knock at his door; it opened suddenly. Without a single word, the sound of hard heeled shoes was heard moving forward until the invisible being stood before the Lord of Dark Manor.

"I apologize for the intrusion my Lord, but Master Mephistopheles has returned and requests your presence in the dining hall," the voice of Renfield, his manservant, spoke quietly.

"Yes, of course Renfield. I'm coming now." Dark smiled wearily.

Within moments Dark was down stairs and in the great dining hall of the castle where he found his grandfather waiting. He was sitting at the large table of solid oak, his midday meal spread out before him. He was still dressed in his black riding cloak and in his hands he held open the newly published broadsheet of the day from the Guardian newspaper. Without putting the paper down he called to his grandson, who moved to the table and seated himself.

"I see you're finally back," Dark spoke quietly.

"And I see you've been busy." A faint smile crossed the tall mystic's face, his finger lightly tapping the front of the newspaper as he held it closer to his grandson. "The Death Stalker strikes again."

His grandson smiled slowly. "I've been a little busy."

Mephisto's dark gaze fixed on his grandson. "Do tell."

Quietly he told his grandfather of his meeting with Gwyddien and the eccentric Doctor Strange and his request to re-assemble the Order of the First Circle. He spoke of the disappearances of several students and a possible connection to Circe's own disappearance, and of talk from Doctor Venture of a secret black Cabal rumored to be operating within the academy and finally of the possible return of the feared Necromancer Shaddai Var.

When his grandson finished, Mephisto went completely quiet for a moment. He stared down in silent contemplation, not making a sound. Then he glanced once more at Dark, staring with uncertainty at his young apprentice, then pushed aside his plate and laid the newspaper down upon the table.

"What do you know about Shaddai Var?" he inquired.

"Well, nothing really," Dark declared after a moment. "Come to think of it, I haven't been able to find any information on him in the city or even in my personal repository, as well as your own."

"And you won't." He stopped abruptly and faced his grandson. "Not even the oldest and greatest of the archives of empires possess any knowledge pertaining to the Fleshweaver. You see almost immediately following the annexation of Shadow Moon, the hunt for degenerate works on or about the Necromancer commenced. Works were confiscated, not only from the great monastery libraries, but also from museums, from noble homes and houses, any and all sanctuaries for sacred writings, and any repositories of literature and chronicles. The works seized were stockpiled in warehouses and finally destroyed in massive bonfires by the Order."

"Why?" Dark cut in quickly. "What did he do?"

Mephisto edged his chair closer to the table and reached inside his gray robes and produced his long wooden smoking pipe. He removed a small amount of tobacco from a pouch that lay on the table, trickling strands of the substance into the bowl. With one quick burst of fiery breath he applied it to the tobacco, then took a series of shallow puffs that created a charring light. The fragrant smoke wafted gently through the air and began to take on a solid shape and form.

"A long time ago, a very long time ago, and I mean a very long time ago, like when I say a long time ago, I mean a long, long time…"

"I'm gonna punch you if you don't get on with it!" Dark interjected quickly.

"All right, all right," his grandfather smiled ruefully, as he inhaled deeply on the glowing pipe. "Just like your mother…where was I…ah yes, before the Race Wars, there was a great Mage named Vecna, who eventually assumed a mastery of the black arts, with some saying he achieved this knowledge due to the direct tutelage from the Shadow Lord. Nearly a thousand years passed and Vecna sought every means available to sustain and even prolong his own life by becoming a Lich. He found the formula for this metamorphosis in a grimoire of magical instruction, the Key of Solomon. He accomplished this means of necromancy using his own staff as a magical receptacle to store his evil soul. Now as a result of this life prolonging magic, he has a virtual eternity to research and hone his skills and inevitably become a supreme master of sorcery."

He paused, drawing in then exhaling out another large puff of the scented smoke. "Within a few short years, the Lich King rose as a demi-god of magic and ruler of a great and terrible empire centered near the modern day region of Vandringar. He saw humanity as a disease to be eradicated and sought to destroy human kind once and for all. He eventually took on an apprentice who claimed to be sent by the Shadow Lord, and pledged a vow to aid the Lich King in his endeavor. That man's name was Nago Var. And whether it was due in part to his evil nature or partly due to the lack of respect and devotion that was given to him, he decided after many years of loyal service to Vecna, Shaddai Var, taking the name of 'Shaddai' as one of the evil words of power, eventually betrayed his master. He was originally a strikingly handsome sort of fellow, and it was said the Lich King's own wicked staff whispered to Var, preying on his own vanity, urging him to slay his dark mentor and master and usurp his power. The battle ensued and it was Vecna who was slain by a great burst of light from a magical weapon that Vecna himself had constructed for his apprentice. Only his left hand and eye survived the epic struggle. The victory, however, was a costly one for Shaddai Var, who survived only as a vestige of his former comely self, costing the Necromancer the entire left portion of his body, permanently scarred and visibly hideously disfigured. Miraculously Var was saved, gathered up and brought to safety by one of his loyal and faithful servants, an Elven Militant Mage, known only as The Ghoul. The apprentice collected what remained of his master and spirited them both away to a hidden location, a lone tower set impossibly high atop a plateau accessible only through magical means. There, the disciple of Var placed his master's crippled body within a diabolical machine that was a mass of metal gears, arms, cogs and wheels that somehow turned and moved of its own volition. The device was part demon, part mechanical apparatus, infused with a fiendish essence and powered by pure unadulterated evil. So it was that within the bowels of this foul machine, the Necromancer's body became grafted with demonic flesh, his left arm muscular and sinewy with a clawed hand. His left leg became almost skeletal in appearance and heavy, leathery, bat-like wings sprouted from his back. His mutated body became covered in dissected skin, stained black in color, the kind normally associated with a frozen corpse that died due to extreme temperatures. The most hideous feature was a demonic familiar, a small obscene face with an evil expression grafted on the left side of the Necromancer's abdomen. Some say the face speaks to him, even teaches him. The wizard's face, however, could not be saved. It remained charred and lifeless, so he had it hidden behind a pale white mask bearing a perpetually evil grin."

"And this is when Shaddai Var created his army of the undead," Dark surmised.

Mephisto nodded. "Freed from the specter of a slow painful death, Shaddai Var, having obtained both the hand and eye of Vecna, now grafted the withered hand onto his arm and the hard, opal orb into his own empty eye socket. Once combining these two remnants of the evil Lich's great powers, the Necromancer transformed into something considerably more than a mere human mage. He now had amassed the power of a demi-god and the mystic might of an Archmage. With his newly created legions of undead, the Fleshweaver struck at neighboring counties, baronies and finally countries. In the wake of his army of the dead came a blackness that clung to the land and swallowed out the sun. His lands quickly grew, swallowing whole nations, until finally becoming known as the Empire of Ash. But conquest was only a means and not the ghoulish Necromancer's ultimate goal. With the conquering of Shadow Moon, Shaddai Var began to work on building a secret gate in the city, the first in a series to set events in motion that would grant him the power of a greater god.

Legend has it on that day, nine thousand, nine hundred and ninety-nine people all died, at the whim of this madman.

Shaddai Var committed this vile act to open a gateway to the bottomless pit on the lowest Plane of Hell. Ten thousand were needed, but before his purpose could be realized, the Fleshweaver was mortally wounded by Duergar, the great Dwarven King. His army of ash eventually met defeat at the hands of the Legion of Steel, but only one citizen of Shadow Moon remained alive to tell the sad tale…"

"Circe," Dark cut in quickly, his tone flat and sullen.

"She was my first student," the ancient magus replied with a faint smile. "And some even say my best…Var's protégé fled never to be seen or heard of again. As for his master, the injured Necromancer teleported to safety, only to discover his tower already occupied by the Elf King and the immortal Silver Mage. Hunted through the halls he had once considered his stronghold, he finally became cornered with no way of any possible escape. So fearful of captors and imprisoned for eternity like his master the Shadow Lord, as he breathed his last breath Shaddai Var made a pact with darker forces. In their malice, those dark forces engulfed the Fleshweaver in a bright field of magical energy and he disappeared. The gemstone ring dropped to the floor; it glowed with the essence of its master, locked inside forever."

"Then what happened?" his grandson's voice had dropped to a whisper.

Mephisto's expression did not change. "From there the cleansing began; his laboratories, his experiments, his spell books, his notes and his legions, all were destroyed. The Dwarven King then built a great city over the remnants of Shadow Moon so no man could say for certain where the Necromancer had once reigned. Secondly, at the insistence of the high priests and bishops, the King issued a sweeping set of laws and edicts to outlaw necromancy from the land forever. As for me, I took the ring and hid it on an island named Europa, where it was to be guarded by Talos, a giant bronze living statue forged by the divine smith Hephaistos himself. As far as I know the ring lies there still to this very day."

"You hope."

"We hope," the ancient historian's eyes sought those of his young grandson. "This man…this monster is so inherently wicked, so full of malice, so full of corruption and hatred, I almost dare not say his name aloud. If the evil that is imprisoned within the ruby ring were to ever be set free, it would threaten all life on Eorth as we know it." He paused, then folded his hands on the table's edge and his eyes fixed on those of his grandson. "When we are finished here, I will go on to the Sorrow Woods by myself. I believe this witch will have the answers we seek, and let's pray we are not too late." Mephisto carefully poured out a measure of the herbal tea, leisurely sipping the beverage.

"Do I even need to bother asking about Fenrir?" Dark asked quietly.

"It is as we feared," Mephisto replied, his face bitter. "Deep within the ground, I traveled to the very spot where the great wolf was bound. All that remained was the large stone slab called Grjöll along with the anchoring peg and sword that was placed within the beast's jaws."

"At least now we know for sure…" Dark trailed off, momentarily lost in thought, his dark eyes narrowed as he stared down at his feet. "Oh yeah, I acquired the fat little toad's gold state coach he uses to see the witch. It lies now in the house stables, an eight horse drawn carriage, driven by two unseen coachmen who are at the command of the person who resides within the cabin."

"That's excellent news, Longfoot's personal transport. It seems my disguise is now complete." The wizard's head lifted sharply. "How did you ever procure such a cumbersome vehicle and without Sneak knowing?"

Dark poured himself half a cup of the tasty tea, small rising wisps of steam showed it was still hot.

"I stole the carriage and horses from the Royal Mews," he replied calmly, between small noisy sips of the beverage. "It was just sitting there, nobody was around so I took it."

Mephisto smiled faintly. "And just what was it doing at the carriage house? What's wrong with it?"

"Nothing…really nothing," the grandson of the Silver Mage cocked his head reflectively. "I'm sure they fixed it; besides I checked it out myself, it's fine…trust me, I'm mechanical."

Mephisto said nothing, waiting. There was a long uncomfortable silence as the two men faced each other, Dark leisurely taking small mouthfuls until he had drained his cup dry. At last his young apprentice looked away, placing the empty cup back on the table.

Mephisto frowned. "Yes…mechanical indeed."

Within the hour, Mephisto was ready and waiting for his grandson when he finally stepped from the dining hall, and together they made their way across the castle grounds and through a large archway to the stables beyond. Wordlessly the pair followed a floral trail that took them through a small stretch of private gardens to the stable paddocks and from there to the stable entry. Oil lamps lit row upon row of stalls, and the soft, low breathy whinny of horses sounded in the stillness. Slowly, both passed down the line of stalls, their eyes shifting from horse to horse as they walked to the end and finally stopped.

"This is it," Dark pointed.

Mephisto glanced uneasily at the horse drawn carriage. The horses were all huge coal black stallions standing almost twenty hands high. They were big and good featured, built for stamina but capable of great speed over short distances. The coach was built as a traditional postilion vehicle where the coachmen rode the horses rather than driving them from the box itself. The coach was gilded and features decorated painted panels with rich gilded sculptures including four dragons on the roof. Also atop the royal carriage was a carved imperial crown and placed around the gold roof decoration were the national emblems that represented the four territories that used to comprise the vast Dwarf Kingdom.

"This will do." Mephisto studied the horses and carriage for a time, then lifted the small latch and stepped inside. The transformation was almost immediate as the tall wizard's legs and arms began to shorten and his normally thin face began to bulge with tiny threaded veins. The hair on his head began to fall out in large volumes until the mystic was left with a horseshoe head of hair around the back of his head.

"While I am gone, my young grandson," he said, his brown eyes fixed on Dark, "I entrust to you the task of finding Circe." He paused. "Find her for me."

Dark nodded; all he could do was nod for he already feared the worst for his grandfather's beloved pupil. The polymorphic spell-caster studied him a moment longer, then he, horse and carriage all vanished from view.

Mephistopheles found the Sorrow Woods to be as sinister and forbidding as the old stories had foretold. Even though the noon sky had been brilliant with sunlight when he left Dark Manor, the Sorrow Woods for the most part was a tangle of shadowed limbs in murky darkness, forever concealed from the rest of the world by ancient trees and dense shrubbery that had over the years twisted and woven around itself until there seemed to be neither a beginning nor an end to this mass of greenery. Tree trunks laid thick with moss had grown gnarled and bent, their long limbs coiled out like deadly giant snakes. Deadwood littered the valley floor, decaying slowly into the damp ground giving the whole of the place an unpleasant smell of decay and rot.

Down an old crooked trail, partly overgrown and nearly forgotten, the shape-shifting magician rode east, his ever alert eyes peering into the darkness about him with caution. There seemed to be no birds whatsoever within this dark and dingy forest; the old magus noticed this almost immediately as he traveled deeper and deeper into the deeply shaded woods. Not one species of birds would live within such shadowy blackness. In fact, there were none of the usual small woodland creatures that normally would inhabit such a place, not even common insects would live here. Once, when he had traveled deep into the shady gloom, he heard something massive moving, pushing through the prodigious entanglement of trees as if it were passing through old, dead twigs, its heavy breath huffing and puffing loudly in the stillness that fell across the forest with its passing. He could hear it, whatever it was, lumbering invisibly through the dark woods, slowly and deliberately. Whether it did not see or simply did not care to bother with the horse drawn carriage that moved along the trail, it moved on. When the sound of the creature's lumbering finally faded to silence, Mephisto signaled for the coachman to continue.

They rode on for the better part of an hour without any more sightings, keeping on the trail where the way was somewhat clear. The Sorrow Woods was a stretch of dense forests, with elms, black and red oaks and shag bark hickories that towered over a choked tangle of scrub and vines. There was nothing but blackness, deep and impenetrable. The invisible coachman guided the large carriage the whole day and as light began to slant through the trees and the shadows to lengthen, they came upon a clearing. Upon Mephisto's command, they halted at once in the concealing shelter of a cluster of birch trees. What he saw was fearful indeed, for in the clearing stood a high fence made of silvery bones and atop each fence post was an empty eyed skull that grinned with maligned intent. The gate, it would seem, was made of a criss-crossed mesh of bones, but the lock was a sharp toothed mouth that moaned and groaned, and the bolt a skeletal hand. Within the fence lay the witch's house but it seemed no one was there.

As the sun was setting, the eyes of the skulls began to glow like burning torches casting beams of firelight onto the grounds that surrounded the skeletal fence. Mephisto stayed seated inside his royal carriage, still hidden among the trees, the clearing was very still and silent. Then suddenly, he began to hear from faraway the faint sounds of small branches cracking and leaves rustling as if blown by a large gust of wind. The noises sounded nearer and nearer, louder and louder, until finally from out of the woods flew Ouija riding on her broom. She descended from the air and settled like a swallow before the unnerving gate, her long pointed nose quivering in the cool evening air.

"I smell the blood of a man," she spoke with a harsh crackling voice. "So come out, come out, wherever you are."

Wrapped in a long hooded traveling cloak that covered a silk tunic and breeches and heavy leather boots, the shapeshifting Silver Mage in the guise of the robust Halfling Leader climbed gingerly down from his royal transport and began walking off the stiffness. With a quick check of his external form, he then stepped free from the sheltering branches and bowed before the witch. "It is me, Lord Longfoot," the disguised mage spoke loudly, keeping his eyes politely lowered. "I seek your guidance and insight."

"Indeed. I knew of your coming Master Sneak," the old witch said with an unpleasant smile. "Even without the use of my divination board, I knew you would soon require my services once again."

When Mephisto lifted his eyes, he saw that Ouija looked pale and unhealthy and unnaturally thin, even for an old hag such as she was. Her eyes were glazed over and sunk deep within their sockets, and even through her semi-transparent gown the bones of her ribs and spine showed her frail, infirm form. Her weathered face was old and wrinkled, her smile a fierce and feral grin that was frightening to behold. With a single word from Ouija, the gate was unlocked and opened and Mephisto quickly followed the witch through the gate which shut behind them with a rattle of bones and a click of the lock.

As they went down the gravel walkway, the late evening sunlight could be seen seeping through the darkening screen of the surrounding forest as another day was coming to an end. Mephisto glanced unexpectedly at the small garden as he passed and was surprised to see the shrubbery, flowers and the like advancing toward him in a threatening manner and making small gestures. Keeping his rotund guise in check, he left the garden hurriedly and was almost running as he came within a few feet of the small wooden porch. Evergreens surrounded it; creeping vines banked upon stone walls stretched out everywhere. Black flowers in the shape of tiny fanged mouths snapped hungrily as they came nearer. The house itself was shadowed and still.

Mephisto slowed. Something cold seemed to settle into the polymorphic spell-caster. Still he moved ahead, brown eyes peering into the shadowy blackness beyond the open door of the tiny cottage until at last he stood at the entrance.

"Come in, come in, you're letting all the flies out!" she spoke aloud in a grating groan.

He stood motionless for a time, then resolutely he went forward, the door closed behind him and the latch locked shut. He stood for a few long seconds in total darkness, listening to the faint sound of the witch's footfalls as she shuffled slowly about the room. Then a light suddenly flared to several candle wicks. Mephisto found that he was in a small alcove, inside burnished pine from the walls and shelving filled with glass jars gleamed in the candle's bright flickering flame. Leather bound books and rich tapestries were visible even through the heavy shadows. At the far end of the room a roaring fire burst into existence, and a raised grizzled head from a large bear skin rug lay on the floor, its glass eyes stared in greeting. Ouija placed a large glowing candle on a small round dining table and turned to face the meek Halfling Leader.

"I shall indulge you just this once more, Master Sneak," Ouija's deep grating voice broke the stillness. "For next time I shall inform Lord Kalifen of your frequent visits here."

The fat Guild Leader nodded.

"Remember just this once more." The broom that the old woman had used quickly whisked itself out of sight.

Once again the disguised magician nodded his agreement.

"I think some tea is in order here." The witch was already moving across the room to a large cupboard door next to her kitchen. She opened it, looked through briefly and produced a specially decorated cup and saucer set along with an old kettle and a silver container and then closed it again. Ouija walked back across the room. "There now we can begin."

She motioned, with a nod, for the hefty hobbit to take a chair about the small table, while a second chair came scrambling over for her, seemingly alive as it moved like any four-legged creature would. The Guild Leader sat down cautiously. Ouija stared back at the portly man, hesitated, then moved quickly setting up the tea service. A cup and saucer was placed in front of her guest while the other she set in front of her. She opened the container; the alluring scent of jasmine wafted through the air, and she simply added the leaves directly to the cup. With a few words of magic, the kettle was instantly filled with water that quickly boiled to a high steaming temperature. After the hot water was poured, the kettle floated like a bird and defying gravity it stayed just above the flickering flame of the now burning fireplace. Finally Ouija threw herself into her chair, her eyes glittered.

"Now what do you seek?" she smiled faintly her voice trailing into silence. Wordlessly she flipped over the wooden serving tray, and there marked on the back were strangely written letters of the alphabet, the numbers zero to nine, the words 'yes' and 'no' along with other various symbols and signs. Her hands quickly slipped within her robes and a moment later she withdrew a polished wooden pointer shaped like an upside down heart that she used to communicate with her spirit board.

"Do you think I can have some more of this delicious tea?" Mephisto swallowed.

"Of course…" she smiled faintly again. The witch hastened forward and took from the magically altered mage the wide mouthed cup still containing a few tea leaves. The flabby face of Mephisto glanced up at her then withdrew his eyes quickly to stare down at the table, fearful of her own that burnt into him. Her hand came close before his face nearly touching it.

"Do you know what Tasseomancy is?" her voice rose as she spoke until the words rang out against the stones of the tiny cottage, echoing through the deep stillness. The witch's wrinkled face moved back from the seated Halfling, her slender hands swirled the tea leaves around the cup interior exactly three times in a clockwise direction. The wizard could feel the sweat running down his obese body.

"It's essentially a domestic form of fortune telling," her voice seemed distant now. "A simple method, to one with the knowledge, that interprets patterns in the left over sediment of the tea. The diviner simply looks at the pattern left in the cup and then interprets intuitively or by means taught to the practitioner using a standard system of symbolism. Traditionally, you read the cup from the present to the future by starting along the rim at the handle following the symbols in a downward spiral all the way to the bottom. Now those symbols of foretelling can be many things, including people, places, animals and even inanimate objects. The symbol of a flying flock of birds, for example, would be seen as a sign of good news, whereas the raven is an omen of gloom and despondency and usually a symbol of death."

She stopped as she came to stand in front of the warm hearth, the fire lit chamber became quiet, her cold eyes still fixed upon the contents of the cup. She bent her head forward, tilting the teacup about for a minute then straightening, glanced coldly at Mephisto. "Shall I tell you what yours has revealed to me?" her cruel eyes fixed on his own. Mephisto saw that the witch was toying with him.

"I don't think I want to know," the spell-caster looked uncertain.

"I shall tell you anyway!" Her voice had an edge to it that seemed to cut through the disguised mage like a knife. She turned away from the Halfling imposter, her hands slipping back within the black robe. "It seems you are not yourself today Master Hobbit," her voice was hard. "In fact you don't seem like yourself at all… Mephistopheles!"

She quickly spun around, her hand lifted and a black wand pointed. With a quick wiggle of her wand and a few arcane words, she released her spell. Instantly an invisible surge projected out where it found its foe, striking the empty chair of the wizard, exploding it into fiery chunks of wood. The witch moved forward and looked about hurriedly for him, but the Silver Mage was gone. "You are here somewhere; I can smell you wizard." The witch flung back her black robe from her gaunt frame, her ratty gray hair trailed down her skeletal shoulders, her white skin almost ghost-like in the dark.

"You are here…you are here somewhere, I can feel it in my bones," her words reached out to Mephisto, her shrieks harsh and biting. "Let me tell you old man, this nose of mine has never failed me and when I find you…you will die." She paused. "I will have your teeth for a necklace and your eyeballs for earrings."

Ouija stiffened; she sniffed the air with several deep breaths, her nose twitching erratically. The witch had come forward and now stood directly in front of the round table. "You see wizard, you just have to know where to look," her voice became a hiss. "You must have transformed back into the cockroach that I know you are…and like all cockroaches, they need to be exterminated before they can get under the floors, in the cracks and in the walls…in the woodwork…"

An umbral hand erupted from beneath the witch's own shadow and struck Ouija a stinging blow across her face. The loud sound reverberated around the room through the stillness. Ouija staggered back helplessly in surprise. Then the witch's laughter rose up sharply and unexpectedly.

"You are truly pitiful wizard…what the leaves have foretold must be true. Kalifen did not just defeat you that day on the battle field, he has trapped you somehow in an ancient enchantment with nearly half your powers lost…didn't he! That's why you cringe now before me…afraid to face me… afraid that your death is finally at hand…"

The same umbral arm came forward and struck the back of her head again before she could speak another word, so quick, so sudden was the blow that it brought an ear-splitting shriek of rage from the witch.

"Face me you coward!" Ouija's voice had a desperate edge to it now. "I will find you wizard! I will find you!" The old woman cringed in expectation of yet another heavy clout and even the familiar automated chime from her own clock made her start. As the sound of the last bell died on the air,

Mephisto's body came quickly toward her and sank hard, merciless fingers into the thin skin of her neck.

"You foolish old hag, even in my weakened state, my power is stronger than your own!" the speaker shook his head mockingly. "But you would try and change all that sorceress. You would seek to align yourself with the evils of this world and the next. In doing so, you would help resurrect a creature born of hate and raised from Hell, a villainous and vicious monster that would bring an end to both our shared domains!"

"You know nothing!" Ouija shrieked raising her left hand that still held her Hazelwood wand that now began to smolder as bolts of searing red light shot forth.

Ouija shrieked with an expression of terror and pain, the deadly bolts lanced from her glowing wand catching the magician with a glancing blow, singeing his gray robes and knocking him backwards. Before his assailant could find her target for a second assault, the tall form of Mephisto was upon her once again, grabbing her arm in desperation. The witch's face turned to look up at him for a moment, the familiar look of anger burning in her eyes, scorching fire bursting forth from her wand. Flecks of the searing fire crackled and hissed as it showered onto the wooden floor and furniture; in moments, flames began to burn, quickly spreading across the length of the narrow room. The fire spread like water, flowing down to the far corners of the cottage. Heat exploded from the pillar of fire as it rose up to lick hungrily at the walls and wooden beams that were the roof's main support.

Then a terrible shriek came from the witch's throat as hands locked and both their forms straightened with the force of their struggle. Ouija's terrible high pitched screaming broke the silence. It grew louder and shriller; her eyes glowed and her face began to contort, as if in awful agony, her lips drawn tight over yellow stained teeth. Her head jerked from side to side, glowing eyes blazed in their sockets. Suddenly, her face began to extend and expand, her mouth opened impossibly wide as if to engulf her face. Abruptly, from within the dark recesses of the witch's open maw, a venomous bright green snake with razor sharp fangs that dripped poison lashed out at the wizard's exposed neck.

Mephisto reacted with the speed of a mongoose; his hand came up to seize the creature in a vice-like grip, desperately trying to crush the life out of it. He shot a glance at his rival and she froze momentarily from his malignant glare.

"My turn."

In the next instance Mephisto's eyes began to shimmer and shine, brimming with energy, as sparks flitted among them. Static filled the air with a hissing, crackling energy and a natural conductivity was created between the two of them.

"Llucheden!"

Upon uttering the true name of lightning, the arcane energy he held inside welled up and exploded outward in a blinding flash of electricity. Ouija was instantly sent hurtling through the air, knocking her backwards with such force that she smashed violently through the front door of the tiny cottage, and she disappeared outside. But before the master magician could make his next move, Ouija's laughter rose sharply, unexpectedly.

The whole of the building itself began to shudder and shake as a massive root broke forth from the floor at his feet, and with the sound of twisting wood it wrapped tightly about Mephisto's struggling form. Upward the writhing mass surged like a huge muscular limb until it smashed through the thatched roof, carrying the struggling spell-caster with it and growing huge and towering as it reached beyond the spreading flames. Mephisto screamed. Shimmering with a blue-green energy, the monstrous root pulled its prey into its snake-like coils; the sickening crunching sound of its foe's bones breaking beneath his squeezing flesh grew both in tempo and volume. Then Ouija reappeared, floating gently downward through the smoke and haze like some ghost to stand again on the grassy ground before the constricted wizard.

"Clearly you are no match for me now wizard," the sorceress sneered mockingly, her voice filled with a cocky boldness that gave way to impudent behavior. "There was a time when I might have feared you…but now…I almost pity you." One scaly hand with stained nails stretched forth; the giant root tightened its grip and Mephisto's cries rose high and terrible.

"I thought about killing you but instead you shall be made a sacrifice of blood and bone. Very soon we shall all bear witness to the end…and very soon the world will know of the coming darkness that is the Shadow Lord. Even now the powers of Hell are already on the move, his armies shall pour forth from the place of perpetual fire to strike at you, ravaging this world and all hope of any resistance. Kalifen's minions will find The Gates of Hades…where ever it is you have chosen to hide it. Then at long last the Shadow Lord will reign over this world and it shall suffer an eternity of darkness and hell, the likes of which even you have never seen!"

"That shall not come to pass while I still live…" the battered face of Mephisto turned towards her for a moment, the familiar look of anger crept into his eyes. "I will not allow it."

Ouija came forward and now stood directly in front of the held wizard. "I have read the old books…the prophecies they contained showed me all that would come to pass," she alibied shortly. "And they show me that at the end of days the first sign shall appear in the heavens, the first in a series of four consecutive total lunar eclipses known as a tetrad. The Blood Moons serve as an omen, for the sun will turn into darkness, and the moon into blood before the great and terrible day the Shadow Lord comes. And when the Shadow Lord's way is reopened, your fate will be decided, an everlasting damnation and soon you will join the very souls you have damned. You shall hear the shrieks and see their tormented spirits, through me is the way to everlasting pain…I will fulfill the destiny that beckons me…now let my power flow through your soul."

"Power…POWER!" Mephisto's flushed angered face seemed gigantic now and his fierce eyes were wide with rage. "You forget witch…I am power! I AM A DRAGON!"

Without a word, the mage's face became covered briefly in a fine pattern of silver scales, his eyes began to enlarge and turn metallic and reptilian in appearance. A shimmering surge of bright light spread out across his skin bathing him in a white aura, and within a few seconds his body exploded with the radiance of the sun. Abruptly, the darkness erupted with a brilliant flash, and crackling blue flames wreathed around the length of the root, lighting the area in an opalescent glow, and turning it to ash. It crumpled lifelessly to the ground as soft wisps of smoke rose out from its remains.

When the fire was gone, the two spell-casters stood face to face once more, their black forms circling slightly away from one another.

"I will finish you this time old man," Ouija whispered, her eyes filled with a burning hatred.

Infuriated, Ouija shrieked with frustration and an uneorthly green flame cracked along the length of her black wand. An instant later, the spell was cast and with a roar, a jet of flame burst forth from her outstretched hand and engulfed her foe. For an instant, it seemed as if Mephisto had been consumed by the fire, but a moment later a thunderous rumble echoed from within him, his flesh hardened and his eyes gleamed. An aura of bright energy began to quickly form around him, coalescing into the shape of a semi-translucent silver dragon above his head. A sudden surge of arcane energy exploded outward in a furious blast. Immediately, deadly shards that glowed with an enigmatic power sprayed outward filling the area with the ringing sound of shattered glass. Wracked with such pain by the terrible assault, Ouija doubled over and eventually collapsed to the ground. Her hands and face were burnt and blistered from the forceful blast, her eyes clouded over with blood rendering her blind.

"I have been to Hell more times that I care to remember," the words were a chilling echo in the deep silence, his eyes frightful to behold as they blazed with new fury. "But if your wish is to see Hell witch, then I shall gladly bring you there!"

Mephistopheles started forward, his eyes seemed locked in front of him, brimming with a dark energy. He began to speak the ancient words as he now began to call upon the powers of chaos, and channeling all his hatred into binding sigils that wrapped around his indicated target. Within just a few seconds, the light from the surrounding area began to dim, and sounds of moaning filled the air. With several intricate hand motions, the Silver Mage began chanting, his eyes vanished and became shrouded in blackness and now looked like holes in the universe itself. His voice finally trailed off into a whisper as he neared the end of the spell's complex ritual. The whispers began to build upon one another, echoing in the air around them, swirling and twisting until they became a steady cacophony.

With a cruel utterance of a few foul oaths, the spell's final syllables were spoken and its terrible energy was released. An instant later, the ground erupted beneath the fallen form of his foe, shooting fountains of fiery liquid magma skyward. The faint green glow of the archaic seal flared to life, bathing the area in a sickly green light and raising up the paralyzed form of Ouija and bringing with it the stench of death. Fire flared from the ground followed by large puffs of black smoke, smelling of brimstone and burning corpses. A wave of spectral fire exploded forth from an opening in the eorth that split apart and disappeared forming an impossibly deep pit. With a deep groan, a swirling mass of writhing evil forms rushed out, their red fleshed hands grasping at the air. Over the course of a few seconds, hands came toward her and at their touch a look of mortal anguish passed over the witch's face, as her flesh began to melt away from her forehead.

Like the wax of a burning candle, it trickled down from brow to chin, carrying with it a look of pain and anguish. Slowly and inexorably, flesh fell from her fingers and oozed away from her feet. The fire died as the conflagration curled about the witch like a shroud and she was consumed. With astonishing quickness the fissure closed and all that remained was a layer of ash and pieces of blackened flesh.

"I bet you didn't see that coming, did you witch." Then the mystic turned and he walked noiselessly away through the skeletal gate and vanished by the misty trees.

XVII

The afternoon was almost gone and a multitude of clouds masked the darkening sky, hanging silent and leisurely floating high over the city. The day had gone cool at its long end and lamps had began to light within the homes of the city with lamplighters on their evening rounds lighting up the oil lamps. On the streets, units of the Night Watch began their night time patrol, marching through flickering shadows in uneasy silence.

Dark found himself trudging wearily through the Foreign Quarter, tired and exhausted, his search once again a futile one. Once the most crowded section of the city, it offered up a variety of eateries and taverns, as well as tiny, hard to find shops of many unique and rare types. It was also famous for its magnificent homes, tall towers and great architecture with hundreds of marble towers and soaring buildings that climbed higher than most keeps. Now certain sections were strewn with rubble from fallen frameworks. In these areas, destroyed structures leaned heavily against adjacent abandoned buildings. They now resembled a construction site, with dredging, excavating and grading of land, rather than city streets and were said to be populated by thieves, cutthroats and criminals or even worse.

He was dressed in his normal guise when traveling through Duergar, his tall frame wrapped in a flowing black cloak, his lean face half hidden in the loose cowl pulled close about his head, his whole appearance dark and foreboding. His trailing robe billowed slightly with a slight rush of the coming night wind. He passed by two men who had been standing rigid and aloof as sentries. These were two slim, almost shadowy figures in curious loose fitting hunting garb. He passed them quickly and only the crunch of their hard sole boots on the gravel pathway disturbed the silence as they slipped in behind Dark.

A third pursuer, slightly larger than the first two, now joined the procession. He too was silent and lagged behind the others as they walked, his head was bent in furtive concentration and there was a deep scowl on his face. Dark lapsed back into thought. He had observed the small group forming behind him, but seemed to take the situation less seriously then would those who were less prepared than he. Slowing his stride, he twisted his head to glimpse briefly over his shoulder before turning quickly back again. Dark smiled and began whistling an old song taught to him by his mother, as he hurried on. He was moving quietly past a row of empty shops, following the same gravel pathway that lead to one of the main streets, when a huge black shadow seemed to rise up suddenly, detaching itself from the wall on his left and moving swiftly to intercept him. His keen elven ears caught a barely audible sound off to his left; the cloaked assassin twisted sharply about. From behind the cover of the growing night emerged a man clad all in scarlet. It was not impossible for Dark to make out the man's features even in the dim light. Even though he was dressed in an outlandish red hunting outfit that was impeccably clean, his boots were covered with mud. He had a lean but muscular build, with fair skin, short dark hair, a round face and large brown eyes.

Dark sensed its presence looming before him like a great black viper threatening to strike at its prey. Without a word, and in the blink of an eye, the agile assassin leaped aside, a long semi-solid blade began to coalesce in his hands. Even as he crouched to defend himself, a leather edged voice sounded in his ear.

"Give us everything you have of value and maybe we will let you live."

"Why don't you give me everything you have, and maybe I'll let you live," Dark joked, relaxing his guard slightly and peered into the blackness of the figure before him in an effort to discover if this was indeed the man he sought. The voice stopped abruptly and the scarlet figure stood silent, though Dark could feel the eyes following him as he edged with cautious steps in an attempt to put his own back to the light. Slowly the cloaked assassin began to make out the others in vague lines and hardened faces. Each one looked haggard and worn, like they hadn't eaten for quite some time. Their hands and faces were covered with fresh cuts and bruises, their clothing was soiled and torn and all carried with them a foul, dungy smell that clung damply from their bodies. They had the look of a bunch of beggars, only the weapons that they held tightly in their boney hands told that they were something more.

"Look here friend, we have no time for foolishness," the voice rolled out as the scarlet figure came up to the black-garbed assassin lifting his own sword upwards threateningly. "And my offer won't be valid for much longer."

"Neither will mine," was Dark's only reply.

"You have lost this day my friend!" the stranger leaped in front of him, brandishing the long blade of his sword. The round face was distorted in sudden anger, his smile suddenly villainous. "You have no chance; there are four of us and only one of you."

"Who said I was alone?"

Almost immediately a bright clear light quickly flared from Dark's eyes, that suddenly erupted into a burst of brilliant red and yellow flame. A shimmering field of inky black energy flowed out from his body spilling out onto the ground causing the shadows cast to grow and writhe, echoing now an evil within and hissing with corruption. The channeled energy began to swirl and radiate, glowing with a dull inner light. The shadows came together with each one forming a serpentine dragon covered in thick scales, its eyes smoldering with a bright flickering fire with wisps of smoke bursting from the dragon's nostrils. It coiled in the air above their heads, twisting and undulating in response to its master's wishes.

"Wait! I know who you are," the scarlet stranger cried out, his voice edged with a harsh note of desperation, his eyes fearful as he now stared at the horrifying apparition that threatened to engulf him in flame. "You're the one from the paper…the one harassing the Halfling Pack; they called you the Death Stalker I believe."

"The name is Demon Raider." The smile was gone from Dark's face, his features hardened as he spoke, the voice cold and menacing once more. "And I know who you are Cui Tie Q'ill and I think we need to talk."

"Do I have a choice?" the debt collector asked a moment later.

"No."

It was then that Dark tied Q's hands and placed a length of rope about his neck so that he could lead without worry of escape. The Asian man allowed himself to be bound without complaining, though he was visibly distraught about leaving his friends shackled in an abandoned building. Moments later, Dark was led away from the Foreign Quarter. Cowls were drawn close about their faces and cloaks wrapped tight; they slipped through the gates and past the sentries of the Night Watch and started back toward an older part of the city. The scarlet figure did not offer any explanation as to where he was taking them, and Dark did not ask. They walked in silence, occasionally ducking in a dark alley or two with Dark a step or two right behind and Q in the lead. The assassin glanced often at the man in red, worried he was being led into another trap, but the little man gave no indication where he was going and Dark only caught an occasional glimpse of his face within the covering of the hood. And it revealed nothing.

A short time afterward, they found themselves approaching an old dilapidated church. This had to be one of the oldest buildings in Duergar still standing albeit only in part, since few sections of its original stone structure remained. It appeared to have had a square central tower with a bell in it, but that too was no longer visible. There was however some recent renovations completed, with new repairs done to the west work and probably about the same time the arcade walls were strengthened and towers recently added to the eastern corners of the church.

Q led them onto the grounds surrounding the darkened place of worship, directing them through a screen of overgrown shrubbery that bordered the south lawn. Then they made their way along a series of tall hedgerows to a small alcove and a pair of sturdy wooden doors draped in heavy shadow. Standing silently before the doors, Q tapped softly upon them in a coded succession. There was a long moment's wait, then finally the heavy door moved slightly. Inside a heavy latch was released and one of the doors swung open. Quickly Q motioned for Dark, glancing furtively about and followed, closing the door and locking it securely behind him.

They both stood for a few seconds in the dim light; a heavy set unfriendly looking woman trudged slowly about the room. She wore a blue robe and tunic with a white nurse's headdress and long apron stained with blood. A light was then struck to a candle's wick and Dark found they were in a small room, stone walls gleaming in the candle's dim flame. At the far end of the little room, soft tracings of color reflected from a few chairs and a square wooden table and a rectangular burgundy patterned rug on which they sat.

The woman placed the candle on the small work table and turned to face the pair. "I guess I'll be leaving you two alone then," the woman's deep voice broke the stillness.

The scarlet man nodded.

"Try and keep the noise down." She was already moving across the room to the single door that led to the rest of the church. She opened it, looked back briefly over her shoulder then closed it behind her.

"What is this place?"

Untying his captive, they both moved across the room, where he motioned Q to take a chair about the table drawing another over for himself.

"It used to be the Church of Foehammer; now it is a sick house for Duergar's forgotten children," Cui Tie Q'ill replied slowly, his eyes staring over at his captor. "I have answered your question, now answer one of mine. Who are you really and what do you want with me?"

That's…two actually." He paused. "I'm here for you Q. I was sent to find you, kill you and retrieve the coin cast you stole, so if you would be so kind, I'll be taking back what does not belong to you."

The small Asian man fumbled for a few seconds with the inner lining of his heavy cloak, and within a moment's time produced a custom made hardwood case with the King's insignia. He quickly opened it to show the contents were still inside and intact.

"We didn't even have enough gold to cast our own imitation coins." The scarlet man sagged heavily back in his chair. "We didn't even have enough cheap base metal for the core. I've tried selling it but nobody wants it. They think it's a forgery because the imprints used to stamp the coins don't make any sense…they simply don't exist, so they'd be worthless on the open market."

"What do you mean?" Dark asked.

"I mean the image on the obverse side is of a handsome man adorned with a great crown, but he is no King that I've ever seen before or ever even heard of." His gaze shifted back to Dark. "Featured on the back face is some sort of regal seal of a pyramid with a capstone of a large illuminated eye and below the pyramid are the words *NOVUS ORDO SECLORUM*."

"It's Latin." It was Dark who now spoke, his penetrating black eyes found those of the collectors. "It means, 'a new order has begun'."

"So what does all this mean?" Q spoke up suddenly.

Dark paused. "I don't know," he mused. Then the name finally clicked. "Foehammer…that name…Thoradin Foehammer, is that who this church is named for?"

"It is not who the church is named for, but it is who it belongs to." The scarlet man looked uncomfortable. "And he is the reason for the theft."

"What do you mean?" Dark spoke quietly. "And give me the short version."

Q looked up uneasily. "I will try and tell you in the best way I can. As I'm sure you already know, Thoradin was the leader of the Legion of Steel, the heavily armored cataphracts of the Dwarven Empire. His life as a Knight of the Crown was dedicated to combat and warfare. When the King died, he was devastated and renounced his life as a warrior and took on a vow of poverty. He then took his arming sword and thrust it deep into the rocky ground, and as he knelt before the embedded blade, he was struck with a divine epiphany. The cruciform hilt resembled that of a cross and from that moment on his life would forever change, from a path of violence and bloodshed, to that of a path of faith and one of religious belief. He built this chapel around the stone that to this very day still holds the sword of Foehammer. For years he was left alone in peace, allowed to grow his congregation for religious worship, but the last few years his fellowship withered away and diminished greatly in numbers, so he began his own investigation into the disappearances. What he found was that his parishioners were being taken and placed within an underground arena. What he saw there made his stomach churn and finally changed his mind about whether or not to lead the revolution against this repressive regime."

"And let me guess," Dark interjected quickly. "They were being fed to a giant wolf."

Q nodded in dumfounded wonder, a faint smile betraying his disgust. "Yes…Thoradin described it as a creature of monstrous proportions that would catch, kill and consume whatever was brought before it, but how did you know this?"

Dark looked back thoughtfully and bowed his head a little. "Just a lucky guess…so then what happened to Foehammer?"

"Not much more to tell really," he declared flatly. "It was just a few months ago when Blackthorn's men showed up and charged him with committing extreme acts of treason against the Sovereignty of Duergar. He was clapped in chains with an iron collar placed about his neck and heavy leg irons hammered shut around his ankles. Then he was led unceremoniously away, paraded through the streets like a common criminal to the Grand Citadel where he is most likely being kept in chains in a cell awaiting execution."

Dark thought silently for a few minutes before speaking again. "Where is this underground chamber?"

"It lies deep beneath a group of buildings in the Temple District in Duergar that now stands on land formerly occupied by the headquarters of the Knights Templar," the other acknowledged. "Located there are two of the Inns of Court and the Temple of the Light Bearer, the official residence of the Archbishop, a man named Cesare Borgia. And during this man's short reign, he has already been suspected of committing many, many crimes including adultery, incest, sodomy, theft, bribery and even murder. I have also heard that he hosts orgies inside the temple grounds that he calls the Banquet of Chestnuts. Not only is the Bishop present, but his sister, Lucretia, also is said to not only have attended this disreputable ball, she participates as well with the fifty or so prostitutes also in attendance."

Dark's head jerked up, and he looked at Q with stoic resolve, his decision firmly made. Finally he stood up, his robes gathered carefully about his wiry frame.

"Go…free your men from their bonds and spread the word of Thoradin's plight, for half the people in the free city owe their lives to him."

"We can't let him die," the scarlet man protested. "We must save him…"

"We will," the black-garbed assassin cut in sharply. "I know a way inside."

"Let me go with you," he smiled gently, almost unexpectedly.

"No I need you to do something else for me," Dark began slowly. "There are many things I wish to know, but for now I need you to be my eyes and ears. I want to know everything that goes on within Duergar, both above and below its avenues and boulevards. And not a soul comes in or goes out without my knowledge of who they are."

Q spread his hands upon the table. "These streets are like my own arteries and its buildings my bones."

Dark smiled warmly for the first time. "Good, remember what I have told you and I will contact you soon enough. When it is time we will speak further, and I shall be glad to answer all your questions then."

Both men looked at each other and nodded in agreement. The other rose silently and stood quietly as he looked back at Dark who had paused, a tall black shadow against the gray of the stone walls.

"There is one more thing that I need." One great hand reached over to grip firmly Cui Tie Q'ill's lean shoulder. "I need to cut off one of your fingers."

"You need what now?"

XVIII

Dark awoke the following morning and quickly hastened to the dining room, hoping to question his grandfather about his encounter with Ouija, but he still did not appear. He ate his breakfast hurriedly but without the old wizard's presence, he found his desire to communicate his own findings growing exponentially. After eating, he waited almost an hour for his expected appearance, but still he did not materialize and eventually, even after Dark had finally received a long overdue message from Eva by starling, long after the servants departed for the kitchen, he decided to go to Mephisto's place.

Dark left the table and within the blink of an eye, he passed through the opening to Mephisto's cave home and found the entrance unsealed and the tall magician gone. Even the great room looked as if no one had even used it recently. He made a hasty and hurried search of the area and its surrounding chambers and passages, but his grandfather was not to be found. Finally, he was forced to conclude that for some strange, unknown reason, he had left without even a parting word. As he sat in the tall, leather-backed chair before the sputtering fire in the great room of the cave, he tried to assure himself that everything was all right and his grandfather would contact him soon enough.

Dark sat in silence with only the crackling of the fire to keep him company, his thoughts concentrated on Eva's eventual contact, that is whenever she got around to it. Eventually, he grew tired and slumped down into his chair in moody silence and gazed resignedly into the hypnotic movements of the flames. In his mind he continued to ponder the details of Q's story, trying to decide what he should do next. But after an hour of quiet deliberation and extreme boredom, he soon found himself on the verge of drifting off to sleep. He hastily jerked awake and there, framed in the newly opened entry, stood Mephisto in the dim glow of the fire, his blue robes glistening wetly trailing water onto the stone floor. He emerged gaunt and pale, the angular features of his face were strained and the thin line of his mouth hard.

"Bit early for a swim don't you think?" the words slipped out before Dark could think of something better to say.

The old wizard moved forward, and with a simple wave of his hand, closed the entrance. When he turned back again, Dark could see something was clearly wrong.

"Grandfather?"

Mephisto's gaze shifted slowly to meet his own. "Dark my boy, what are you doing here?"

"A starling from Eva's ship came early this morning," was the quick retort. "So I came here to use the scrying glass… are you all right?"

"It's nothing really," interjected his grandfather quickly. "So tell me about your night."

Dark looked up with a puzzled frown. "Well…"

Suddenly, before Dark was able to finish his thought, the surface of the magic looking glass turned blue and misty at first, then gradually cleared to reveal the figures of Eva and her first mate.

"Hello Eva. It's lovely to see you again," the tall magus spoke softly. "I see you've changed your hair color."

"Do you like it?" the other replied in kind.

"Oh yes. Red is definitely your color my dear," his voice was low and masculine. "It quite suits you, and it definitely goes well with your fiery…"

"All right there Romeo," Dark's own voice was low and quick. "Do you two think we can get back to the business at hand, hmmm? Now what news do you have for me?"

Eva stared at him wordlessly for a moment, her face expressionless before she began speaking again. "Well I did as you asked and followed Kalifen," she replied firmly. "When I found them, Lord Blackthorn had boarded one of the three ships and set sail east. Where the Druid traveled to

I don't know, but the other two vessels continued north. On they sailed past the misty Island of Albion and far across plains of blue riding the frigid winds until finally we reached a place where no fish swam or barely a bird was left in the sky. Still we sailed on and within a few days we soared above a frosted continent of cracking ice and snow. Still on we flew, while Kalifen's wooden boats seemingly was somehow able to clear a path by pushing straight into ice pockets by driving the bow of his ship onto the ice causing it to break. Finally after quite some time, they were able to push ahead through the barren wasteland until we entered a river that somehow remained unfrozen."

"You have entered the Land of the Ancients," Mephisto announced quietly. "And home to the first true Kings and Rulers of the Eorth."

"It encircled the heart of this land," she continued, still smiling. "And within its confines, Kalifen and his men, who numbered in the hundreds, sought out the harsh mountains that sheltered a green and flowery valley. I sent a few of my men to closely observe, well as close as they dared to, Kalifen and his large company of men. The only thing they were able to ascertain was that scattered amid the northern mountains were volcanoes where a venerable forest grew. And there in the shadows of its enormous trees, the wizard has begun a mass excavation of gigantic proportions, the scale of which I have never seen before. Now I've done my part Dark, so I expect to get…"

With a simple wave of his hand he rendered the beryl stone silent, the image of the beautiful ship's captain faded from view, cutting her short before she could even finish her sentence.

"Don't you think that was a little harsh?" Mephisto asked quickly.

"No, because she would have gone on forever about payment," Dark exclaimed heatedly. "Trust me, I just saved both of us from a migraine."

He paused and looked directly at his grandfather. The old wizard's eyes suddenly went hard as they bored into the young man. "She's going to be furious with you," the tall spell-caster replied softly.

"She always was, she always is and she always will be." Exhausted, Dark collapsed back into his seat. "Anyway, so what is this place that Kalifen has found, and what exactly is he searching for?"

Mephisto was already moving silently about, lighting the oil lamps and candles to chase the last of the dark gloom out from the corners of the open chamber. He hesitated before the beryl stone, staring fixedly for a brief moment at the reflection of his face in the clear glass. He then sighed and turned to face Dark.

"Long ago before the Age of Kings, a large and mighty Kingdom existed in what is now the frigid far north," he began at last. "They named this place Jötunheim, the Land of Giants. And the place where Kalifen excavates now is known as the Valley of the Kings, a royal necropolis used to honor the first fallen giants and members of the Royal Family. They were buried in large tomb complexes dug deep into hillsides considered holy, to honor them as patrons of the living."

"So you're telling me that Kalifen is digging up the bodies of dead giants?" he spoke cautiously.

The ancient historian nodded wordlessly, glancing briefly at Dark and moved over to seat himself next to his grandson. "Not just any giants, but these were the largest of their kind," Mephisto answered shortly. "And they were almost unstoppable alive, so if what the witch said was true, and they do indeed have the ruby ring of Shaddai Var, then I shudder to think of the consequences if the Fleshweaver were able to raise these towering mythical creatures from the dead."

Dark was frozen, his black eyes fixed on his grandfather's, his mind still a little dazed with shock. The enormity of what he had just been told slowly took hold. The evil that had been locked away could possibly be free once more. Chaos would ensue, and in the end, a war to end all wars would begin bringing about the destruction of the world.

"How do we know what Ouija said is true?" Dark asked abruptly. "How do we even know they actually have the ring?"

Mephisto's eyes were fixed on Dark. "We don't. That is why I must travel to Europa and see for myself. And if there is any truth in what the witch told me, then we don't have much time, for with the coming of the first of four blood moons, the Fleshweaver will be made whole again."

Dark gazed despondently across the room, his thoughts hopelessly entangled by what he had just been told, unable to fathom the ramifications if the necromancer were to be brought back. His grandfather watched him in silence, only knowing what he himself must do next.

"Unfortunately I too am the bearer of bad news," Dark announced solemnly. He then told the tall spell-caster everything that happened the previous night after his grandfather had left for Ouija's home in the Sorrow Woods. He quickly spoke of his chance encounter with Q and his men, the conversation with the debt collector that followed and even the place of worship where they met to speak, the retrieval of the King's coin cast and the strange markings it possessed, of Thoradin Foehammer and his wrongful arrest and incarceration at the Grand Citadel awaiting execution. He finished by telling his grandfather about the disappearances and the underground arena below the new temple and of the Archbishop Borgia, his sister and the crimes committed by the pair, and finally of the enormous wolf they both knew to be Fenrir and the sacrifices being made to the monster.

"Thoradin…alive?" the ancient shape-shifter stared at him incredulously.

Dark nodded. "As far as I know it's all true, but of course I'll check to make sure. Now the only problem is just how do we get him out of there?"

The wizard cocked his head slightly, as if considering the problem. "Leave that to me. I'll contact King Dwaric; surely he will have the answer to your question," his grandfather answered confidently. "Let us not forget it was their kind who built the stone fortress into the side of Granite Mountain. If anyone knows of a way into the Citadel, it would be the Dwarves."

Dark leaned forward slowly. "Then I think I shall take a look at this underground arena for myself. Maybe there I might find a clue to Circe's whereabouts."

Mephisto came to his feet slowly, his eyes studying carefully the face of his young grandson. It was lined with confidence. "Be careful Dark and remember my words," his grandfather warned sharply. "Approach with the greatest of caution for that region where you wish to explore contains gold, iron and lead, including a rich deposit of Heartstone. This strange metal that pulses and beats in a steady almost hypnotic rhythm, disrupts and even cancels out the strongest of enchantments. Only relics of elder magic, which are bound and protected in ways that men and woman no longer understand, are invulnerable to the effects of this rare mineral."

"Well that's nice to know," Dark said finally. He rose, then slowly stepped away from his seat several paces, his handsome face partially turned into the shadows.

"The Eye of Dagda should still be able to serve you, as well as your armor I'm sure," the ancient historian declared in an assured manner. "Besides you have already shown me there is nothing you cannot do."

Dark nodded, inwardly pleased that his grandfather would show this kind of confidence in him. He then turned to face his mentor. "When will you leave?" he quickly asked, trying to change the subject.

Mephisto's expression did not change, his eyes dark and filled with insight. "I will leave immediately for Europa. There I will find if what the witch has said holds any truth or just merely lies."

"When will you return?" Dark asked hurriedly.

"That all depends," the wizard spoke bluntly. "Kalifen requires four items to truly resurrect the Fleshweaver and make him complete again. The ruby ring which holds Shaddai Var's essence lies just two days from here, the eye and hand of the Lich King I assume they already possess or else Ouija would have spoken of them. The last relic needed is the Necronomicon; within its evil pages and written in blood on human flesh is a spoken rite called the Ritual of Words Made Flesh. The Book of the Dead originally hung on the chapel wall of an ancient monastery where it stayed untouched for centuries. No one dared open the dark grimoire, let alone even go near it for fear of releasing the creatures its spells command." He paused. "However, the tome was recently moved to the Library of Solomon, which holds the greatest aggregation of knowledge and wisdom obtained by man. This fortress of lore lies between our world and the next, in a place where even the most fragile of works are immune from the further decay of time. Getting there will not be a problem; safely traversing the gigantic maze that surrounds the Library will consume most of my time, so I expect no less than a fortnight before my return."

"Then I shall see you in a few weeks," Dark's voice remained calm.

"Remember these words I say to you now," his grandfather now stood across from him again, his dark eyes intense. "The night of the first blood moon shall soon be upon us, and with it the resurrection of Shaddai Var. You must somehow prevent this from happening if I somehow arrive too late. You must stop this dissenting group of despots by interrupting the ritual directly or sabotage it by any means possible. This creature, this manifestation of pure evil must not be allowed back into this world again…you must stop them from completing the ritual…you must."

His grandson nodded. "I will."

"I pray you do," Mephisto's face went black.

A moment later the wizard was through the opening in the cavern wall and disappeared into the blackness beyond. Dark stood looking after his grandfather hesitantly, then moved to follow.

Silently the black specter came for Sneak Longfoot through the lethargic haze of his sleep, a demonic being created from his mind, that rose up hauntingly from out of the farthest depths of his subconscious. It was a creation of pure evil, a creature that lurked in the shadowy recesses of his mind, where his darkest, deepest fears lay hidden. Soon it would come for him like a thief in the night, with stealth and cunning, easily slipping past any obstacle which sought to block its path. He could not see the beast as it came for him; he never could, and he never would. It was like a shadow that lacked any substance; it lacked any identity; it lacked any reason. He was overwhelmed by the sense of sheer dread and terror it created by its mere existence. He ran from it now, swiftly through the crumbling landscape of his own imagination. He ran and ran until his lungs burned and his legs ached and sweat streamed down his reddened face, hoping he could somehow escape this stalking entity. But he could not. Every time he would dare to stop and turn back around, it was there almost at once closing on him, ever closing. Again he ran from it in desperation, screaming for help, anyone's help. But none ever came; there was no one; he was alone. So he ran as he always did, he ran in fear until he felt the hot and heavy breath of the thing upon the fat rolls of his neck…

He suddenly came awake with a loud start, jerking upward from beneath his blankets to a sitting position. The morning air seemed hot on his face and bulky body. Beads of sweat ran down in large streams from beneath his armpits and from his forehead, and seemingly from all about him he could hear the loud thumping sound of his own heart pounding wildly. Then there was the scurrying of footsteps in the hallway beyond and then the quick and deliberate pounding on the chamber door. It took a moment but Sneak soon realized what he had done. His nightmarish screams had brought his trusted and faithful servant, Baldrick, the last of the Baldrick family line. Slowly he went to the door, unlocked it and then opened it. He was surprised to find not only his personal attendant, but the guards on duty as well.

"My Lord Protector. Is there anything wrong?" Baldrick queried.

All who stood outside curiously peered into the chamber, but the fat Halfling Leader blocked their view.

"Oh do shut up Baldrick, and make yourself scarce." The temporary Ruler of Duergar stood silently in the open entry a moment longer, then began to close the door.

"My Lord, wait!"

"I told you to leave me," Longfoot scolded the young man sternly. "I suggest you do so now,"

Baldrick bowed mechanically, his face showing no sign of injury at the other man's words and boldly shook his head firmly. Within his dark attire, his slim form shifted uneasily as his eyes refused to meet those of his master. "But my Lord, there was someone at the door who claims to have most urgent news to tell you."

"Oh God what time is it?" Sneak asked clutching his head.

"Four o'clock," came the simple man's quick reply.

"Baldrick, I've told you before you mustn't let me sleep all day. These women charge by the hour!" There was a desperation in his eyes and on his strained, reddened face that made his voice crack. "And who would want to see me at this time of the day. What is he, new to the city?"

"No my Lord, he's a priest," his servant answered softly.

"Tell him I'm Jewish," came the sarcastic retort by the tired hobbit as he closed the door.

It was several minutes before Baldrick came running back again, his face even more troubled than previously before.

"Yes Baldrick, what is it now?"

Baldrick hesitated. "It's that priest. He still insists on seeing you."

"Tell him I know the Archbishop from the Temple of the Light Bearer…"

"I am the Archbishop from the Temple of the Light Bearer!" a tall man, almost frightening to look at, stepped forward cutting short the robust halfling's words. The Head of the Temple wore red robes normally associated with papal regalia, which included headgear with three crowns or levels, elaborately decorated and carrying the insignia of an upside down cross with an incomplete circle passing through all four lines . His robes trailed along the ground. His hair was black and he had a black moustache that connected to his long black beard that hung almost past his chest.

The Guild Leader was back in bed when the senior member of the clergy entered his private chambers. He rolled his eyes, then slipped gingerly from beneath the warmth of the bedcovers, his two female companions still deep in sleep, their naked bodies still wrapped around one another. Baldrick who had come in with Cesare Borgia was holding out a robe which his master drew about him quickly, them belted it snugly around his wide waist.

"Let me get straight down to business," his words were loud and booming. "Do you know what day it is today?"

"No I don't," Longfoot muttered ruefully.

"It is exactly one week to the day when the first of the four blood moons will be seen in the heavens," the Archbishop began again in earnest. "And on that very day, we shall also see the rebirth of the Fleshweaver, Shaddai Var. And as Lord Protector, it is your duty and responsibility to see to it that this event takes place and that nothing interferes with the ceremony."

"Yes, yes of course it is, and I have done my duty," was the little halfling's reply.

The Guild Leader crossed over to the far wall and drew the curtains aside, then pulled open several of the windows that opened onto the back of his estate. Light quickly flooded into the large chamber, the soft and sweet smell from his garden spilled into the room filling it with its fragrance. Behind him Baldrick was moving silently about, first clearing out the whores, then lighting the oil lamps to chase the last of the gloom away. The temporary caretaker of Duergar sighed and turned to face the tall prelate.

"All right Cesare, what's this all about? Baldrick said something about you bringing me an urgent message."

"The witch is dead," the Archbishop spoke bluntly, his words impacted the rotund hobbit like a hammer.

Sneak Longfoot felt his blood turn cold. For an instant, the Halfling Leader did not respond, but stood rigidly in place, his eyes securely transfixed on the speaker.

"There must be some mistake," he said at last.

The Archbishop shook his head emphatically. "There is no mistake, my Lord. Billows of black smoke signaled our soldiers to her location. Walls of ash and burnt wood were all that remained of Ouija's cottage. They were extremely thorough in their search for any remains of the witch, but all they found was a few tiny pieces of torn flesh, turned black by the fire."

The diminutive hobbit slowly turned and walked back to the open window, staring wordlessly out into the gardens below. "How is it that this thing, this creature, this cold-blooded brute can so easily bypass any protection put in place, and can somehow seemingly slip through any and all defenses. Few if any ever see this fiend coming, and it leaves no evidence or any trace of its passing. It quite literally is a shadow in the night."

"No, not a shadow, more like a demon or some supernatural being of a nature between the gods and humans," the prelate answered, clutching at his golden crucifix. "And I'm afraid my son that you are doomed. Alas, upon Lord Kalifen's return you will surely suffer a fate worse than death."

Sneak Longfoot turned sharply, glancing briefly at Baldrick, then back at Archbishop Borgia. "Not if I were to bring back this cursed creature's head on a silver platter… Fear not, for I have a plan."

Within only a week's time, the halfling natives of Duergar were soon dying in groups of tens and twenties. All over the city, blood red crosses began to appear on the doors of known establishments, taverns, inns and even homes of the small humanoid victims with the inscription, '*You shall have no mercy*' scribbled beneath. All that was left of their scattered remains were dismembered and blackened bodies that laid unclaimed in bloodied heaps. The drivers of the death carts were left to bury them. Daily, almost like clock work, they would gather up the tiny corpses, then unceremoniously dump the carcasses into mass graves on the outskirts of the city. And the cries and the moans of the dying soon eddied its way down around the robust Ruler of the Halfling's Guild.

By late afternoon, early evening on the day of the first blood moon, Dark had now reached the Temple District of Duergar. His search for anything or anyone associated with the rebirth of the feared Necromancer, Shaddai Var had so far been a futile one. His anger over the situation had grown considerably over the last few days and it was beginning to wear heavily upon him. It was still a busy hour with people pushing and shoving their way past the many small chapels, synagogues, mosques and temples that lined the roadways of this Quarter. One in particular seemed to stand out above the rest and was set like a highly prized bijou in the heart of these structures reserved for religious and spiritual activity. The Temple of the Light Bearer was a wide, multi-story stone building nestled peacefully amid a cluster of spreading trees and small gardens. The grounds were screened away from the surrounding city by a collection of high shrubbery planted closely together. The Temple itself had been enriched with the jewel-like union of glass and light that appeared facing the main street. The stain glass window was twenty feet high depicting an angel battling a god-like man in one scene. In another, it showed that the angel is felled and cast down into the Nine Hells. A sword, the fallen angel carried also plummets, landing somewhere on Eorth.

The tall iron gates were ajar, and the assassin began walking quickly toward the long stone walkway that led to the front doors of the temple. He was still approaching the decorated stone archway at the front entrance when the heavy oak door opened from within, and there, unexpectedly, was the Head of the Archdiocese. Cesare Borgia was dressed in a simple black chasuble, reaching almost to the feet and a voluminous ecclesiastical great cape with a long train proper only to Bishops. Atop his head he wore a roman hat with a wide, circular brim and a rounded rim. Covering his hands were gloves made from silk that extended partially past the clergyman's wrists that also matched the liturgical color of scarlet. He was a tall man, but his lean frame moved with the graceful ease of a big cat.

He passed in slow review before several rows of expressionless soldiers that formed the elite of the Archbishop's personal guard. They too were dressed in cardinal red, as too were a small squad of cavalry that wheeled in precise formation in front of an ornate carriage that was quickly brought up to convey the privileged party somewhere important enough to warrant an armed escort. Then the carriage came to a gentle halt, and the tall, imposing figure of the prelate climbed slowly into the carriage, his board face smiling in strange delight.

The squad captain signaled to the guards stationed near the gated entrance, and the gates to the Temple were swung open. The carriage passed through the gates and moved quickly onto the crowded Temple Way. Throngs of people who lingered in the busy streets, paused to stare curiously as the carriage, escorted by the Temple Guards, rolled speedily past them. A few even pointed or waved as they recognized the tall leader of the Temple who rode within, the bright, red colored hat he wore shadowed his closed and drawn face. Then, accompanied by the grizzled captain and several select knights, he rode purposely toward the Inner Wall of Duergar.

"Now where are you going in such a hurry?" Dark muttered curiously to himself, as he began to speculate in his own mind where the Church Patriarch would be going. His mind raced with the possibilities as to where he would be traveling to at such an hour with such an armed escort accompanying him. With no more speculation, his mind already made up, he would follow him. The sun had already passed below the horizon of the western edge of the world, its once fresh bright light now faded into darkness.

The black-garbed assassin moved in pursuit of the driven carriage with quick, easy strides, his head lowered slightly as if searching the ground before him. The trail of his quarry was readily apparent to the keen eyes of Dark. The half-elf assassin now began running hard and fast, not bothering to hide his movements any longer, and he had evidently decided on the Archbishop's eventual destination.

The great City of Duergar seemed to rush past him in short, quick flashes of buildings, streets and overpasses, all crowded with men and women of all ages and descriptions, all rushing to somewhere or from something. Both the city and its multitudes faded quickly from view as his eyes spotted in the distance the Inner Wall to the North East gates as the carriage mounted the wide avenue of the Rainbow Bridge. After the holy procession passed over to the other end of the bridge, it retained its speed towards the closed gates. From within one of the enclosures, a single trumpet sounded the arrival of the coach and its important passenger. The entryway became lined with soldiers of the City Guard, all dressed in black uniforms crested by the emblem of Lord Blackthorn and all standing in rigid salute.

Dark exited the soon to be sleeping City of Duergar, concealed by invisibility and in the midst of dozens of traders and late night travelers. Once outside the great Outer Wall, moving bits of yellow light flickered into view ahead of him from the fast traveling carriage. It rode east at a great pace passing the crest of a darkened tree-lined rise that skirted the valley rim, winding their way through the trees as the woodlands darkened steadily into night. Then, led by the procession of Temple Knights, the ornate carriage now moved north, passing by a line of tall evergreens that screened away most of what lay beyond.

Dark and grim visaged, the assassin appeared hidden amid a shelter of great trees, his wiry form wrapped in the black robes, his cowled head slightly bent against a steadily rising wind. In the next instant, the assassin stretched forth his right arm, palm held open and once again recited the ancient words, *"Adfer chan'r ffagla"*. As the last of the words left his lips, the twisted, swirling flame faded and there stood Nightmare, saddled and shaking his head with impatience. Dark mounted the big black who was wreathed in the unholy flames of perdition, then both he and the Hell Horse were riding away. The city soon became only dark shadows that faded into the mist and gloom of the northern forests and disappeared from view.

Cautiously he made his way along the forest's edge, skirting the northern borders of Duergar. Silence hung deep and penetrating, adding to the gloom of the tall forested hinterland of the Black Forest. Like ghost-like apparitions, they slipped through the darkness of the trees, his black eyes searching the night for any movements. Ahead of them, the northern peaks of the Black Mountains began to loom up darkly through the breaks of the forests. Then Dark reined Nightmare in sharply, motioning for him to be still. His keen elven eyes settled toward the fields on his right. At first, there was nothing out there he could see, only the twisted and tangled forms of branches shaded a charcoal gray in the moonlight, the total lunar eclipse not complete. A moment later, he picked out the quick movement of something vaguely like a large animal as it crept on all fours, then disappeared into the blackness beyond.

He kicked the big black's flanks firmly and urged the horse forward and into a slow trot. Nightmare snorted bright flames from its nostrils and followed anxiously. The moon's speed through the Eorth's shadow was a slow one, but he knew his time was running out, the Blood moon was upon them. The horse lunged forward at a gallop as he picked up the tracks of the carriage that moved along the edge of the forest. He now clung tightly to the Hell Horse's neck, feeling the churning muscles of the great horse beneath him as they flew into the night. Dark turned Nightmare north east and instantly put his heels to him hard. The big black snorted again and leaped ahead. The Hell Horse's great strength seemed endless, his sleek body leveling out as he raced by tall stones set in rings by unnamed ancients who once stood guard over this landscape filled with secrets.

Nightmare did not slow as he climbed a grouse moor overgrown with heath and dominated by grasses and sedges. Dark quickly became puzzled by a faint tapping sound in the distance, as if someone was knocking on a door. The mystery was soon solved when the crimson light of the moon revealed a long, fork-like shape swinging from the branches of a hangman's tree, its feet tapping gently against the trunk of a large English Elm.

The chase through the dense greenwood of the Black Forest wore on with grim determination. For the pursuing assassin, there was only the muffled whistle of the cooling wind and the steady pounding of his Hell Horse's hooves. Through the silence and dark of his surroundings, they cut between gently sloping hills and over broad grassland rises that ran, but still the distance between them and those he pursued remained unchanged.

At last rising up from the wilderness was an eerie sight that stood in stark contrast to the brush and vegetation that surrounded it. Looming out of the dark through breaks amid a green sea of trees, was the colossal, blackened clutter of enormous boulders that looked less like a natural formation and more like it was intentionally dumped there by unknown giants. This place was known as the Black Mountains. Like a series of huge solid monoliths, these bizarre mountains had long been associated with strange unexplained phenomena intertwined with dark folklore and greatly feared by the people of this region. This place was made ominous by sightings of odd and curiously strange creatures, unexplained lights and sounds, and the countless number of people whose disappearances for years were seen as part of the legend. Stories told of whole garrisons of men being dragged to their deaths within its unholy bowels by spectral hands, and shadowy ghosts never to be seen again.

The scarlet moon brightened in the night sky casting down upon the forest floor its faint red light to guide the assassin and his horse as they moved steadily forward. Then he saw a light off in the distance ahead, several fires burning through the dark like a shining beacon and he realized that he had found the Archbishop. Wordlessly, he dismounted and quickly sent Nightmare back home to Hell, then silent as a field mouse, he moved within earshot of the firelight. There he watched as the roofs of several carriages gradually began to take shape in the night until finally an entire caravan of ornate carriages stood revealed. Moments later he knelt eagerly over several sets of clearly defined footprints outlined heavily in the soft forest floor. The trail left was undisguised, leading generally north east and were only hours old, now he saw the end of the long hunt within sight. Without further deliberation, the assassin once again donned the disguise of Demon Raider and began moving northward in grim resolution.

The trail he found traveled almost in an eastward direction with the footprints growing fresher and in more numbers. The giant peaks of the forbidding Black Mountains loomed menacingly in the distance, the black boulders shaped like giant stone faces that jutted outward into the horizon. There was a sense of dread in the mind of Dark that he could not seem to shake, a fear that was growing steadily stronger as he pushed deeper into the northland.

The trail finally led him to a large encampment consisting of various sized tents and enclosures constructed on a wide open campground by a series of smaller campsites. Then he came upon it suddenly; coming down a well trodden trail he heard music from amid these tangled woods. Although a variety of trees grew within this grove, it was the mammoth Redwoods that soared to heights well over six hundred feet, piercing the canopy of the surrounding forest. These mighty giant-like trees appeared as towering sentinels, guarding the mysteries that lay within her.

Beneath his feet, the fallen twigs and leaves were still wet with a heavy dew, making a soft cushion that masked any sound of Dark's footsteps and helped to preserve his quiet approach. The trees prevented him from seeing much of anything, their great girth ranging anywhere from a few feet to well over twenty feet in diameter. The night passed in slow minutes as the black-garbed assassin wound his way through the giant encampment, shielding himself against the light of the fires as he moved steadily forward. The sun's light had finally disappeared entirely, the Eorth's shadow leaving them in blackness broken only by the pale, eerie light of the crimson colored Blood Moon.

He soon found himself gazing intently at what appeared to be lights gleaming sharply against the black horizon of a large grass covered clearing on the south bank of a thin river, beneath the spreading shelter of an enclosed grove of tall Redwood trees. Then his pointed elven ears caught the sounds of a heavy booming voice and the low hum of many voices coming from the location of light. He quickly moved close enough to determine that the curious light was caused by the burning of hundreds of small fires and the noises he heard were the booming of dozens of drums and musical instruments and the chanting of what were well over a thousand men singing in chorus through the heavy forest trees. Dark quickly moved silently off the path and into the shadows and faded into the forest.

Before him was a massive shrine with a somewhat fierce looking owl, that measured forty feet in height, standing at the head of the lake. The moss and lichen covered statue seemed to simulate a natural rock formation and served as the backdrop for this strange occult-like ritual. A large wood carving of a man in clerical robes, with his index finger over his pursed lips was placed close to the shore of the lake. Below the massive idol was built a large circular altar that was surrounded by wood heaped for burning a dead body as you would find in a funeral rite. The shrine itself was bathed in a soft, flickering light from a large stone lamp that sat right above the altar. Dark stared in disbelief.

Gathered around the altar, and all carrying torches, were what looked like thirty or so priests dressed in red and black robes, their faces painted up to resemble death. The attention of everyone however was focused on what he thought must be the High Priest, as he was the man attired in a long silver robe with a red cape and an ornate mask that completely covered his face. He stood motionless in front of the altar, then his arms extended upward and there was a long moment of complete silence before he began to speak.

"The owl is in his leafy temple; let all within the Grove be reverent before him." The High Priest turned to face his audience, with hands still held high. "Lift up your heads, O ye trees, and be ye lift up, ye ever living spires. For below here is Bohemia's Shrine and holy are the pillars of this house. Weaving spiders, come not here!"

Then the High Priest lowered his arms and moving ceremoniously he descended to the water's edge, as all eyes turned to follow. The drums banged out in steady rhythm and they began chanting louder and louder, "Hail Bohemian!" The sound was deafening in Dark's ears as he drew closer still. The brush and trees were beginning to thin out as he crept lower down the slope under their cover, but slower now, more cautious, as he kept one eye fixed on the strange ritual below. The assassin stayed close to the ground like an animal stalking its prey, his light elven frame moving soundlessly through dry fallen leaves and brittle twigs, blending into the natural terrain about him.

Wishing to move closer, the silent assassin moved forward still through a large clump of trees and crouched noiselessly on the fringe, almost beyond its limited protection. Only minutes passed when he became keenly aware of something moving several hundred feet in back of him. Immediately he sensed the unmistakable presence of someone else. The feeling that struck him made him come quickly to his feet, without a word, his shadow sword drawn as he looked cautiously about his small cover of trees. Nothing moved. He lay motionless in the brush, peering desperately into the gloom under the scarlet moon, his eyes straining to detect what lurked beyond. Then with a sudden rush of wind and leaves, a black shadowy shape rose soundlessly from a line of shrubbery just behind him, but closer than before. Its dim, lithe form seemed to rise and hang motionless, silhouetted against the faint light of the sky, then slowly moved toward him weaving ever so slightly.

Moments later the figures of a man and woman stood before the guarded assassin, both bent in stealth and clothed in woodsman's garb, their hair long and braided, their angular faces and pointed ears gave away their Elven heritage. The female elf looked at him and smiled a greeting followed by a quick wink. Dark looked quietly at her chiseled features and for a second he became lost in her beauty, then just as quick cleaned his mind and gave her a stunned look. "What are you doing here?" Dark finally spoke. "How…?"

"The same as you assassin," her gentle voice cut him short, her blue eyes soft even under the reddened moonlight. "I'm here for Famon Fane."

"You know this isn't a game Aurra; the people down there kill little girls like you," Dark volunteered abruptly.

"I assume little boys too," she smiled a bit too pleasantly.

"And who is this with you?" he stared at him boldly as if daring the male elf to answer.

"This is Tayel Sindarin," she replied, then smiled wickedly as she saw the look that appeared on his face. "And the reason we are here this night, is he infiltrated this camp and first made us aware of Fane's appearance."

The dashing elf stranger smiled happily, obviously pleased at the unexpected compliment. "I have a great talent for subterfuge and I am known to be the man of a thousand faces."

"So how is it you came to choose that ugly mug you've got now?" Dark mocked bitterly.

The irate elf started to make a hasty retort, then caught himself abruptly as their situation recalled itself sharply to his mind.

"Why Dark, I do believe you are jealous." She said it so matter-of-factly that for just a moment Dark could think of nothing to say in response. She saw him straighten abruptly, a slight degree of petulance had changed the look of his face causing him to smile merrily. "You love me," she spoke mockingly, pursing her lips teasingly.

Now it was Dark's turn to stare. "God I hate you," he said after a moment's pause

She paused, her smile wicked once more. "No you don't... you love me."

The assassin's face was expressionless. He rose abruptly and moved forward, his demonic dark face angry and set. Once again Dark's attention was drawn back to the grove floor and he watched as the High Priest and his supporters engaged in this mysterious ancient rite.

"Bohemians and Priests!" the High Priest began speaking again as all eyes focused on him. "The desperate call of heavy hearts is answered! By the power of your fellowship Dull Care is slain!" A rousing chorus of cheers rose up from the throng of Bohemian revelers, their screams echoed deafeningly off the huge redwood trees. "His body has been brought yonder to our funeral pyre to the joyous piping of a funeral march," once again the High Priest was speaking, and directed a withering glance to the left bank, his hands moving in an intricately archaic rhythm. "Our funeral pyre awaits the corpse of Care!"

A single horn sounded out, followed almost immediately by the haunting melody of a bagpiper playing a somber march. Then suddenly a lone ferry slid into view, poled by a lone boatman whose face had been painted to resemble that of a skull and his clothes favored a look of a sculpted skeletal costume. He appeared riding on an ancient flat-bottomed river styled boat with a tightly bound body upon the bow of the vessel. The anatomical size of the mummified form was that of a baby or small child, but it did not stir in the slightest. Pushing against the river bed, the death-like figure of the ferryman guided the slender craft across the water to the foot of the Shrine.

"Oh thou, thus ferried across the shadowy tide," exclaimed the High Priest who descended to the bottom of the large circular steps on which the huge image of the owl sat. "In all the ancient majesty of death, Dull Care, ardent enemy of beauty; not for thee the tender tribute of forgiveness or the restful grave. Fire shall have its will of thee! And all the winds make merry with thy dust! Bring fire!"

Several acolytes dressed in brown robes, their faces covered in shadow, now seized and lifted the bier and bundled form from the barge, holding both high above their heads, they bore it in triumph up to the pyre, accompanied by a dozen or so choristers. They laid the tiny form wrapped in black cloth onto the altar, as the High Priest kneeled down and lifted his arms to the Shrine.

After a moment Dark's elven eyes turned to see that a single torch bearer came to stand before the Chief Priest and passed him the flaming torch. "Aurra, you need to kill that Priest," the black-garbed assassin announced quietly. "He must not be allowed to set that pyre on fire."

Dark took the lead himself, searching out the softest place for the Elven archer, moving cautiously downward to a small grouping of wild brush. He motioned the pair slowly ahead until the others reached the end of their cover. Dark pointed ahead to the yards of open space that lay between them and the High Priest standing darkly beyond.

"After you hit your target, I expect all hell to break loose," he whispered cautiously. "I will then be the focus of their rage by calling attention to myself. When they rush me, move your men back into the deep cover of the forest as quickly as possible. Don't stop to look back, just keep moving."

The other two nodded in agreement and all eyes turned to rest on Aurra, who had already unstrapped the Black Fox's great bow from her back. She pulled out a perfectly balanced long, black arrow and sighted it for accuracy, then hesitated for a second, looking downward through the veiled covering of the dense brush to the unarmed priest on the altar steps. Suddenly she realized she was to kill a man, not in battle or even in fair combat, but unarmed and defenseless; he wouldn't even have a chance to defend himself. She knew instinctively that she was not as seasoned in killing as her sister; she did not possess the cold determination of Dark either. She may be brash and even brave at times, but she knew she was not a killer. She glanced back momentarily at the others.

"This needs to happen now Aurra!" Dark whispered harshly, his eyes burning with fierce determination.

She averted her face slightly in the shaded light, grim and frozen with uncertainty. She paused and Dark continued to stare at her, his patience waning.

"I can do it," Aurra announced suddenly. Without further explanation she moved forward through the clump of shrubs and crouched silently on one knee. Her blue eyes scanned hurriedly the forms of the robed practitioners below, finally coming to rest on the High Priest. The head of this strange cult stood before his followers, his small hands extended holding the flaming torch high over his head. He stood motionless before the altar as he spoke words of prayer, his face lifted towards the great horned owl. Aurra withdrew a second arrow and planted it in the ground in front of her. Then she positioned herself, coolly fitted the first arrow to the black bow and sighted. For just a split second everything seemed to come to a complete standstill, characterized by the absence of any motion by the Elven bow woman. Then without a second thought, the taut ethereal bowstring was released with an inaudible twang and the black projectile flew invisibly to its intended target. With an almost unearthly speed, as if somehow part of the same fluid motion, Aurra fitted the second arrow and drew, sighted and fired with blinding rapidity.

It happened so quickly that no one saw it coming at all. The first arrow struck the flickering torch in the outstretched hands of the High Priest causing an explosion of wooden splinters, the torch head flew upward in a shower of sparks. In the next instance, the second arrow embedded itself into the foot of the Shrine after painfully traveling through the man's masked head. The head of the strange ritual fell awkwardly in a heap to the grove floor, while the large group of revelers looked on in mixed bewilderment and apprehension at the sight of their fallen leader.

Within just a few seconds after the arrows struck their target, moans and laments of murder sang out amid the turmoil. The roar of fury from the thousand or so men that went up was frightening to hear. Almost to a man, they began to surge forward, determined to tear the heart out of the person who dared to strike their revered leader. As they charged blindly toward the trio and their sparse protection of cover, all shouting curses and blasphemous oaths, their ceremony forgotten, a familiar voice called out to the maddened horde.

"Fools! Fools! Fools!" the voice of the High Priest roared mockingly as he miraculously rose to his feet, his eyes glued to the sheltering blackness of the redwood forest. "When will ye learn that me ye cannot slay! Fools! Fools! Fools."

The angered men stopped their charging and turned to behold their Patriarch who was somehow alive and once again walking up to the altar. His laugh echoed deafeningly off the massive owl statue. Several small clusters of armed men were still climbing upwards toward Dark and his Elven companions from all directions, the foremost of which had almost reached the small crouching company.

"Both of you get out of here," Dark whispered to the others.

"We're not going anywhere," Aurra shook her head at hearing his words. "As I said before assassin, I'm here for Fane."

Then suddenly, so quickly that the trio had no time to move to deeper cover and avoid detection, a group of armed soldiers dressed in scarlet appeared from out of the wall of trees ahead of them. For a long moment everyone seemed to freeze and stood motionless, each group watching the other through the dim light. It only took a moment for each to realize, then the men who numbered twelve in all charged madly toward the small group of Elves. But even before Dark could move a muscle in defense, the Temple Knights let out a chilling battle cry and rushed toward the three, their long swords gleaming dully. The silent arrows of the witch slayers dropped five each in midstride before Dark, not to be outdone, stood firm as his flickering shadow blade cut the last two of the unfortunate soldiers in half with one great arching sweep.

Dark glanced anxiously at the others as they both watched the last scarlet figure fall, then turned back to see that the High Priest had once again reached the edge of the altar where he was apparently awaiting something. A deathly silence seemed to grip the entire grove, his black eyes looked on the dark figure who stood motionless before the huge Shrine.

Slowly the Chief Priest raised his red caped arms to the heavens and the amazed assassin saw the great owl's large and forward facing eyes shine like two beacons in the clear sky.

"O thou great symbol of all mortal wisdom, Owl of Bohemia, we do beseech thee," he cried aloud, his words clear and concise. "Grant us thy counsel!"

Then the grove floor suddenly shuddered heavily, as if some hidden form of sleeping life had just been awakened. Then the noise broke almost on top of them, thundering out of the darkness with a terrifying suddenness, both heavy and terrible. Shouts began sounding out from the red-garbed guards. Shouts filled with terror, shouts that now turned to shrieks, "Giant, Giant!" Those gathered about the clearing began to scatter, the throng of men no longer chanting ran for their very lives, old and young alike all fleeing in confusion. A scream rose high above the clamor, high and quick, dying only after a few agonizing seconds into stillness. The High Priest had lit the funeral pyre, the wrapped body instantly engulfed in red and yellow flames. Beyond the circle of the grove, something huge and dark moved in the night.

"Giant?" Dark turned to Aurra and spoke the name almost without thinking.

At that very instant the forest behind the sculptured effigy burst asunder with a thunderous thrashing of broken limbs and brush. The creature suddenly appeared from its place of concealment through a gap between two huge redwoods, pushing aside the thick wooden boles as if they were two matchsticks. What emerged was a hideous mass of enormous proportions, half decayed and partially consumed by worms, wearing the tattered remains of its burial clothes. A nightmare mutation of a living corpse re-animated through a dark and sinister magic, its long crooked legs balanced a horror to behold. Its height was such that it almost towered above the mountains and could wade through the sea. Its massive body was bent and heavy with overly long arms, stooped shoulders and a low forehead. Its gaunt facial features made it seem grim and sober with deep sunken eyes that watched without blinking. From two great, gigantic hands dangled the broken bodies of two black robed priests. It flung the dead men aside like one would discard common trash and came forward awkwardly.

"All right that ones yours," she pursed her lips teasingly, her bright eyes danced with amusement.

"No problem," Dark rose abruptly, his dark demonic face angry and set. "I've done this before."

Dark stood up slowly and advanced into the clearing, his shadow sword gripped tightly in one hand as black shapes flowed and shimmered. Aurra moved right behind him and he noted the lean figure of Tayel just within the hidden clump of trees, an arrow fitted to his bow in readiness and his quiver now strapped to his waist for easier access. The moving monolith was slow and ponderous as it took huge, eorth-shaking strides. It now towered against the night sky and shambled forward with an awkward gait through the large densely packed crown of people, swatting them aside effortlessly. A dozen or more robed soldiers met the mythical giant with spears and swords, their thrusts penetrated the creature's dead flesh but to no avail as most were simply turned aside. The monstrous zombie barely slowed at all, it reached for them, scooping up the panic-stricken men in his boney hands and ate them all where it stood.

It truly was a frightening thing to behold, a blackened, blank-eyed warrior created by men with knowledge from another time to serve the needs of its master. Its centuries old existence was preserved not only by the blanket of magic, but with bits and pieces of metal grafted to its decaying form. Even though this mountainous misshapen freak's movements were as stiff as a puppets, it was still deadly in its efficiency, swinging a recently uprooted tree in broad sweeping strokes among the scattering grove members. Its victims screamed at the impact from the huge makeshift club as it seemed the large limb was upon its helpless victims before any could move out of the way. Several groups of the robed members attempted to entangle the towering undead behemoth's legs with ropes and chains when one massive arm caught them with a glancing blow and sent them tumbling head over heels deep into the forest.

Elven longbows hummed and a rush of black arrows flew unhindered to strike at the monstrous abomination, but the giant's bones were as resistant to their sharp points as the finest steel known. The zombie did not slow, moving sluggishly over the bodies of those who had fallen. Elven archers shot again and again and still the creature moved steadily forward in mindless rage. With a muffled curse the enormous undead giant stepped forward still, leaving in its indented footprints a mass of twisted and broken bodies as it shambled up the hillside to where the Elves waited. Dark glanced hurriedly at Aurra, but the witch slayer did not see his look. Her hands were fastened around the grip of the large black curved bow, the whole of her concentration was fixed on the struggle at hand. The demonically garbed assassin now threw himself into the center of the direct line of the re-animated zombie's corpse as battle cries rang out around him. Still the living dead creature, growling with a hunger for human flesh, came forward.

At that same moment, the mythical monster broke through the tree line to the left and came slowly, shuffling up the hill with the same awkward gait in his stride toward the knot of Elves who stood before it. Then before the horrified eyes of the others, the Son of Solus stood, above his horned head was raised a shimmering sword of shadows as long as Dark was tall. With a savage scream, the colossal giant nightmare lurched towards him. Dark in turn gave his own battle cry, then moving faster than thought, leaped through the air, the huge blade gleaming dully in the reddened light of the moon and plunged the sword into the giant's black heart, so that the blood of the old one ran down the blade. With no more than a guttural moan and a spurt of blood, it barely reacted, rearing back and knocking its tiny attacker aside as if it were merely swatting a fly. Just as Dark fell to his feet with the agility of a cat, the creature brought down his immense club and for a second everything disappeared in a huge cloud of dust and debris.

It all happened so fast that no one else yet had time to act. Aurra had never seen a being of this size and proportion, a creature born from magic that apparently had somehow been hidden within these mountains for an unknown amount of days, weeks or even years. The young female elf was farthest from the battle, but moved quickly to aid her fallen comrade. At that same moment, she called for the others to help as well, and before the dust could settle, before Dark could dodge or even get a single word out, he was squeezed front and back by an unbelievably irresistible force. He flew helplessly skyward. Beneath his struggling legs, the ground dropped sickeningly away. Forest, grove and mountains whirled briefly from the corner of his eye; stars wheeled in white streaks above his horned head. Finally, the dizzying ascent skyward halted and the assassin found himself swaying seventy feet above the leaf littered forest floor.

The blow Dark received was so severe that he was knocked senseless for a few seconds and the giant animated attacker moved to finish him by seizing his tiny rival in a crushing embrace. Down his armored and straining thighs ran a network of bloody rivulets, his back had been bruised purple by the crushing blow and his body was deeply lacerated in several places. Gasping for breath, he stared into a pair of eyes two times larger than his own head and there he saw reflected in their darkened depths, twin images of himself, a tiny toy figure clutched like a doll in a ginormous fist. Only when the monster's fingers closed tighter and tighter around his body, and only when it jerked him into the air with the greatest of ease and stared through a decayed palisade of tombstone teeth into the saliva glistening, dark cavern of an eager awaiting mouth, did the hapless half-elf realize that his life may be in danger. And this instant might very well be his last.

Elven long bows hummed as a rush of black arrows, the arrow tips gleaming fiercely in the brightening moonlight, cut deeply into the unprotected flesh of the leviathan's skeletal face. Aurra and the small company of witchslayers fired volley after volley into the head of the giant abomination. It rasped in fury, not so much in pain, but in annoyance, then used its forearm to brush at the arrows and knock them loose from its blackened skin. They attacked with Elvish precision, desperately trying to get the unholy conjuration to drop its bruised and battered victim, and drawing it away from finishing another meal. Aurra and Tayel moved closer and continued to rain black arrows on the massive target. Many it seemed were harmlessly deflected by the grafted metal plating and the steel like skeleton portions of the undead giant, but nonetheless the relentless assault constantly distracted the hulking creature.

Finally, a barrage of a few dozen arrows from Aurra and Tayel blinded the towering Frost Giant in the creature's left eye. The shouts of the battle broke sharply through Dark's thoughts as he tried again to concentrate on using the Necklace of Teleportation, calling forth the magic that lay buried somewhere within it. Still nothing. The small company of Elven defenders were behind the partially blinded behemoth now, stabbing and thrusting with their weapons at its enormous legs, trying to turn it from finishing off the assassin. One massive arm swung down knocking several men sprawling and scattering the rest.

The mountainous zombie swung about, sharpened steel swords and spears hacking at its armored body and reached for the nearest thing it could find. It seized a blackened wagon and with great force hurled it through the air. The wagon fell with a mighty crash, dropping heavily like a rock on several robed men in their haste to escape, their heads splitting apart from their body as fountains of blood arched upwards. Taking advantage of its momentary hesitation, Dark, using the magic from the Belt of Heroes, pulled his left arm free and willed forth the power of the Dragon Wand. Reaching down within the very heart of the ancient artifact, he brought forth the Dragon's head through the dark hole in his palm. A brilliant blue hue of light flared up from his outstretched hand, gathered the potential within itself, then burst forward to strike at the undead monster leaving his arm trailing wisps of smoke. The blue fire crackled and hissed with robust intensity that spattered against his gargantuan foe leaving large smoking holes. Yet the creature did not release his grip on Dark, but shrugged aside the attack as if it were little more than an annoying nuisance.

Again the fire struck, singeing its huge forearm and chest. Trailing black smoke rose steadily from the zombie's blackened body but still it did not release its grip. Dark did not give in however, taking himself further into the arcane energy of the Dragon Wand, feeling its power intensify while his dwindled. The air around Dark quickly began emanating the smell of ozone, his eyes erupted and flared red, then in a flash of blinding blue light, a streaking flame lashed out at the giant. The demonic assassin struck with the full force of the Wand, the blue fire searing in long slow bursts into the creature's last good eye. Its massive eyeball exploded in flames and the behemoth's head was soon enveloped in a dazzling blue pillar of blinding light. For an instant it burned bright in the night, then detonated into ash and scattered bits of flesh and bone.

It suddenly wheeled about and a determined Dark, mustering every ounce of strength still at his command, struck so savagely and relentlessly with the shadowed blade that the zombie's hand became severed from its wrist. As the monster reared back, Dark quickly teleported and now stood solidly before the huge soulless corpse, brimming with dark energy, his flaming eyes gave off a malignant glare. A thunderous rumbling echoed from deep within him, red, green and yellow sparks flew off his body as a strong breeze began to pick up, lifting loose leaves and debris and swirling it around him with a faint glow. A quick build-up of icy blue energy centered around his hands that rapidly became an enormous bubble of frost. With a sudden burst, the icy energy was released and washed out over the landscape, flash-freezing the creature's massive legs up to its boney knees. Red glowing embers now swirled around his dark armored form. Blood seemed to pour from his eyes as the red glow grew in size, whirling around him chaotically. A surge of arcane energy exploded outward, sending a burst of red hot balls of fire that slammed against the icy walls until the creature's legs shattered from the force of the blows.

A moment later, the smell of charred flesh filled the air; its humungous body rose high within the grove until finally the broken and splintered bone gave way beneath the weight of the monstrous creature. At last, after the giant swayed to and fro in the sky, it leaned slowly eastward, gathered speed and fell toward the river. It crashed violently to the ground in an avalanche of eorth and stone, leaving huge clouds of dust and smoke that rose steadily skyward. Seizing upon his opportunity, a bright glow now emanated from Dark's eyes as he began channeling his inner energy and gathering it around him to form a prodigious second body encasing his own. This massive physical form, superimposed over his body, expanded higher and higher above him. In final form it resembled his demonic disguise perfectly, in both clothing and armor. Its movements mimicked those of the assassin, even its facial expressions were in perfect synchronization with his own so that in everyway he appeared to be imposing his will on the gigantic avatar.

Imbued with this arcane essence, he now formed into the sizeable hands of his magical avatar, a huge two-handed battle axe that resonated and hummed with immense power. With one great swing of the heavy blade, the magical incarnate form of Demon Raider completely severed its massive tattered head, leaving it on the grove floor, staring sightlessly out towards the green forest. Then Aurra was beside him. Dazed, he turned and stumbled forward to where she stood and thrust the Necklace of Teleportation into her hands. He then toppled instantly to the eorth and all went black.

XIX

The afternoon faded and shadows lengthened into the concealing light as dusk slipped silently across the cloud fortress of Dark Manor. Within his room, Dark Solus lay sleeping, still unconscious, his breathing shallow and uneven. While he slept, something blacker than the darkness just before a storm appeared, writhing and twisting, and more frightening than words could describe. Momentarily, a veil of complete and utter darkness held him. Then with a terrible howl of pain, it split wildly, torn open by the unseen force within it. Howls and shrieks from creatures of the nocturne spilled forth from the impenetrable blackness beyond, a cruel and ghastly host searching for victims among the ever intruding mankind. Their clawed limbs ripped and tore at the sudden breach, all straining towards the light.

He saw the creature almost immediately appearing out of the dark, a huge and terrible black shape that crawled, dragging itself slowly from the shadows. It had ten horns and seven heads with ten crowns on its horns and on each head a blasphemous name. The beast resembled a leopard, but it had feet like those of a bear and a mouth like that of a lion. The hideous rasping sound of its breathing was plainly audible to Dark, even from quite a distance away. Its huge feet emitted a rough scraping sound as it moved out of the profound depths and across the dark eorth.

From a few feet away its white fangs came to bare and gleamed under the night sky as it watched the half-elf intently. The two shadowy shapes faced each other in the dreaming dark, the creature still breathing in the same slow, rasping breath and the demon mouth from Dark's armor growling low and snapping at the air before it. Then with a snarl of rage from the demonic mouth, Dark sprang at the evil intruder, his own jaws open and reaching for the blackened horned head. But the leaping assassin was caught suddenly in midair by a huge claw-like limb that whipped out from beneath a billowing cloak. Desperately he struggled to break free and found that try as he might he could not. It now grabbed at his throat, then with a mighty jerk, smashed him lifeless to the ground.

Finally his eyes opened. The light from the oil lamps was harsh and bright, blinded him momentarily. He blinked in its flickering glare, disoriented and a little confused as he fought to gain some sense of where he was, and what was going on about him. Then the faint outlines of the room began to gather shape and he soon recognized the relaxing scent of lavender and the soft feel of cotton sheets and down-filled blankets wrapped close about his body. All that had happened before he blacked out came racing back in a rush, images of owls and men in black robes ran mad and muddled across his mind. The Bohemian Grove and the forty foot owl shrine; the burning of the tiny wrapped body and the attack from the giant undead zombie striking from out of the dark forest; Aurra and the Elven archers and crimson knights spread out before him; cries of pain and death then everything went black.

He twitched slightly from beneath the covers and sweat bathed his bruised and battered body. The room instantaneously sharpened before his very eyes; it was his own bedroom chamber in his manor home in the clouds. Beside him was a figure who reached for his hand and took it ever so gently in their own.

"Dark," the voice whispered almost to itself, the youthful face bent close to his own. "Thank the gods you're finally awake,"

"What happened?" he muttered, his own voice thick and dry.

"You passed out." Dark recognized the voice immediately. It was that of Aurra, the Elven Princess, her hand brushed his check gently as she spoke. "You fell after defeating that unholy abomination and you have been unconscious ever since. I was so worried..."

"How long have I slept?" he interrupted. His own hand reached to touch hers.

"Almost five days."

"Five days!"

Across the room Baron raised its many grizzled heads and opened its jaws to call out in glee, but suddenly the voracious animal's eyes met that of his masters and the tiny yelps died quickly in their throats. He glanced back again at Baron, the Chimera's many eyes fixed upon him, the small tail wagging furiously back and forth. He watched as the young beast rose, turned about several times and laid itself back down again. Dark's face once a golden glow of health was now pale and ashen with harsh lines creasing his skin giving it a drawn and weary cast. Aurra drew up short and stared, as there was a brooding look to his piercing black eyes.

The stare brought a faint smile to Dark's lips. "By the way you look at me now, I must be quite a sight to behold."

Aurra started. "You look…well…terrible…"

The arcane assassin nodded in agreement. "This unfortunately is the price one pays for invoking the mystical arts. And this is the after effect for breaking one of those laws, that so many often choose to disregard. And even the grandson of a silver dragon is subject to its dictates."

"Using magic does this to you?" Aurra looked uncertain.

Dark quickly shook his head. "No, this is the result of using magic way beyond your means." He raised himself with great effort to a sitting position. "I was taught that lying inside us all is a powerful magical essence, and if drawn upon, takes life from the user, draining strength and being. This essence is drained somewhat with every spell used, and what is lost can be recovered but slowly. So if we take too much…"

"You end up in a bed for five days looking like a dead goat's arse," Aurra broke in abruptly, her warm smile softening the mood in the room.

"Ya…something like that."

"Do you despise them so much, beyond understanding that you would do this to yourself?" Aurra asked sharply, her fragile face now flushing darkly, jerking her hand back. "Or is it that you are so driven by hate that dying means nothing to you?"

Dark said nothing at first, his eyes meeting hers then abruptly changed the subject. "I've slept too long, and in need of a bath. Opening night at the Opera House is this evening so I can't be late."

He rose and started for the door. His hand was on the latch when Aurra called out after him, her voice strangely irritated.

"Take Baron out with you. He smells worse than you."

Dark stopped and quickly looked at the lying chimera, whistled him to his side and led him outside. The door closed softly behind them.

It was evening of the same day, the allotted hour passed and those fortunate enough to have opera tickets for tonight's performance were already assembled inside the great theatre. Baron Von Munchausen sat alone in the seclusion of the grand tier, the best seat in the house, with the best view of the stage. It was a name he used when he had first met the Nubian Princess and it was the name he gave to the front manager that even now gained him access into an area normally reserved for VIP's only. Fatigue lined his face and his black eyes squinted wearily in the bright light of the thousand or so oil lamps that lit the main auditorium.

He watched from his private box way up on the top tier of the amphitheatre level and saw the room was a cavernous horseshoe shaped chamber built of oak and stone with its cathedral ceiling peaked star-like overhead and a magnificent chandelier hanging from its center. Four balconies and a top gallery surrounded the orchestra with the balconies divided into boxes scattered with gold and bright crimson draping the interiors. Each level was decorated with different stucco arabesques and was perforated by arched openings. The theatre was paneled in different types of wood to enhance the venue's acoustic qualities with each one being painted to resemble marble. The huge auditorium could seat an impressive fifteen hundred spectators, thanks to its soaring heights and was located just a few steps from the newly constructed Heroes Square and had become a major site for political gatherings and freighted with political significance.

The interior of the Royal Opera House was truly filled with magnificent splendor with imperial double-headed eagles, Chippendale chairs upholstered in claret colored damask, as new high born aristocrats leaned out from their balconies with opera glasses, hoping for a glimpse into the King's Royal Box where Sneak Longfoot was idly sitting. Burning quietly, an impassive Dark Solus smiled faintly as the portly figure of the temporary Ruler of Duergar turned to greet him, his broad face smiling in nervous delight. Disguised as a German nobleman, he stared coldly at the Guild Leader for a moment, glancing quickly at the curious servants who waited respectfully in the background. Sneak grinned quickly past the scowling assassin whose gray eyes studied him shrewdly, this time looking anxiously about as if someone were missing. Dark glanced about uneasily suddenly realizing that Baldrick was strangely absent. He knew the grossly overweight hobbit never went anywhere without his faithful manservant. Quickly he caught Dark's watchful eye.

Then, all at once, the heavy tabbed stage curtains were lifted and drawn open; the opera soon started with an overture of background music that seemed to get the onlookers attention immediately. And when several columns of performers appeared to the adagio from 'A Secret Garden', there were audible sighs of delight. The theatre was equipped with complex stage machinery intended to impress the opera going audiences with a grand spectacle. Dark watched from high atop his lofty perch as the singers moved in a choreographed sequence around the raised platform, following the golden natural light coming off the garden scene and reflected into a series of antique etched mirrors.

His mind began to wander as he stared down at the grand illusion that was taking place on stage, when all of a sudden his mind snapped back as he caught the sound of a woman's voice. A moment later the woman's mellow voice grew louder and soon the mesmeric sound of her singing filled the air in a fiery, almost wild abandon that reached into the inner most depths of the assassin's mind. It was almost as if it were bidding him to follow, to be as free as the song itself. Almost in some sort of a trance, he stared steadily on, smiling broadly to himself at the images the hypnotic tune conjured in him. From the peak of a particularly bleak hand crafted paper maché rise and down between the surrounding painted backdrop of hillocks, Dark found her flying forward, with hands outstretched that helped sell the audience the perception of flight. The created illusion by the operators was a mystery even to Dark, for it seemed they somehow could shift seamlessly from the actress's sustained flights out over the audience to quick moving hops across a reflective pond. She finally descended in a notable graceful motion to stand beneath a small flowering tree with long branches that exploded with color.

Like a spirit of the night, she came forward in deep silence, her black robes trailing from her slender form with a whisper of silk covering her ample bosom. She was absolutely beautiful, her face delicate and finely shaped and her skin so pale that she seemed almost unearthly. A tall woman, she had long black hair that fell well below her waist with a designed headpiece of fresh buds of nightshade woven into a braid. There was a timeless, ageless look to her, eternal and everlasting, seemingly somehow unaffected by the ravages of time.

One by one the stage actors fell back from her in fear as she approached and passed them without even a glance, her strange captivating eyes never leaving those of her audience who sat transfixed in her presence. Her hands stretched forth to hold them in her stare, long and slender fingers curved as if to draw them in even closer. Not one of the spectators dared speak or even make a sound, their eyes riveted on her. She looked at each of them in turn, then her pale hand passed before them as if casting a spell, her voice reaching out to hold them was both soothing and yet commanding. Finally her gaze rested on Dark. Her violet eyes burned into him and his eyes met those of the singer's and what he saw there terrified him. So compelling was her voice, that his eyes locked before her and could not draw them back again. The Countess lifted her hand and Dark felt himself grow suddenly weak, his hands stretched out toward her in a gesture of submission. Dark saw she was toying with him, trying to read his mind like alien hands probing his body; she now began moving around inside his head.

The assassin was frantic. Something was terribly wrong, but he could neither move nor speak out. Then suddenly the ancient energy that lay deep within the heart of the Faërie stone surged to life and smashed aside the barrier that held him. Without yet understanding what it was that just happened, and as he did so, he sensed something change within himself that he could not explain. Right now there was no time to give it any thought. Dark, after recovering his senses, his eyes were no longer distant as they glanced quickly at the female opera singer and then away again.

From the corner of his eye, he saw the door to the Royal Box swing open and Sneak and all six heads of his servants turned as one. Baldrick strode through, tall and forbidding in his black attire. With him was a smaller figure, cloaked and hooded, the person's face hidden beneath the folds of the cowl.

Baldrick! Dark thought at once. But who was the other one?

They both moved wordlessly to stand next to the Lord Protector of Duergar. There the personal attendant seated his companion, then lowered his dark face toward the Halfling. Almost immediately the little hobbit sat back, his face became angry with frustration lining his jaw. Baldrick paused, studying the face of his overweight employer, then turned and beckoned to the small cloaked figure. Hesitantly, the black hooded figure rose then slowly walked to stand beside the tall, long haired lackey. The rotund hobbit leaned forward impatiently, he sat rigidly in his chair, his tiny hands gripping the carved wooden arms. Slim brown gloved hands reached from beneath the thick folds of the black robe and pulled back the concealing hood. There was an instant of stunned silence as Dark's eyes became frozen with absolute certainty. It was Circe!

A raucous round of applause brought Dark's eyes back to the stage. But at that instant as he glanced down to see the light hearted operetta, something quite astonishing captured his attention. There he witnessed the Countess crossing the spacious stage in measured dramatic steps, quickly passing several times in front of an enormous mirror suspended slightly above the floor. Reflections and projected images occupied the stage and whenever a performer stepped into the space, the projection at that position changed colors that both mesmerized and captivated the onlookers. For one split second Dark hesitated, unable to believe what had just occurred, and then hastily moved to return his attention back to the equally strange sighting of Circe. But there was no reflection of the opera singer in the hanging mirror.

With unwavering scrutiny, Dark now focused all his attention on the Countess, his keen elven eyes fixed firmly in place. He saw for a moment the rosy draperies of the lady as it glowed like shards of stained glass, and the slender thread-like appendage of her delicate flowering headpiece strung throughout her hair. He also saw the sparkle and swirl of revelry, and glimpsed a shimmer on the dark surface of the pond, then observing closely, he once again bore witness to an interplay between the real and imaginary.

Wide-eyed and fearful, Dark now found himself sitting on the edge of his seat, for he had just witnessed a mythical being thought only to exist in folklore and myths, passed down through the generations by word of mouth. For the Countess Elizabeth Bàthery cast no reflection in the mirror.

He had never actually seen a vampire before, only hearing about them through ancient tales and legends told to him as a child. His grandfather once told him that painters cannot paint them, for when the portrait was deemed completed, the likeness was either black and indecipherable or somehow been rendered to look like someone else. And to anyone else, the lack of a reflection would have a more mundane explanation, where tricks and charms could cast doubt on the most basic certainties. For long moments he thought somehow that it might be a cleverly constructed hoax, such as to fool the mind into perceiving the reality that it so feared. As a practitioner of the dark arts, Dark knew first hand there were other break downs of the natural order in the world, ones ever more shocking and more intriguing.

As he watched, his mind swirled with the notion of vampirism, revenants of evil beings created by a malevolent spirit that somehow had penetrated the world of mortals. Just as his mind raced with images of corpses of the dead rising from their graves, wandering about to the terror or destruction of the living, he looked back to see the sight of his first looked upon apparition, Circe. But she was gone. Both Baldrick and the black haired sorceress were present no longer. The assassin seemed to hesitate for a moment, then stared into the private box in stunned silence, his mind racing. For a brief moment Dark and the Halfling Lord locked gazes, as if to judge each other's intentions. Dark smiled coldly at the fat Guild Leader. Still disguised as a German nobleman, he stood up abruptly and walked out of the grand theatre without even a backward glance, his cloak wrapped around his broad shoulders. Curiously Sneak Longfoot watched him go, his eyes fixed on his departing silhouette until it was lost from sight.

Within seconds, his shadowy form crouched within the bronze sculpture of the Greek god, Apollo, depicted driving his quadrige, the chariot of the gods, across the heavens by four horses. High above the portico of the Royal Opera House, hidden in his metal perch, he posted himself close to the theatre grounds, scanning the streets below, watching for any sign of his missing friend. He noticed the Opera House was well guarded by soldiers wearing the crest of the Temple

Guard, a sign he thought had no real authority in the city. It seemed to Dark that there were soldiers stationed at some of the gates throughout the quarters, all bearing the same insignia and these were strangely enough the only activated units in all of Duergar.

Now he paused momentarily within the darkened shadows of the statue and reached into the fanged mouth of his armor for the Gem of Location. He held the multi-faceted stone in his open palm, then closing his fist over the archaic bijou tightly, he stared back into the cityscape. "Find me Circe." Nothing happened.

He experienced a sinking sensation in the pit of his stomach. For unfortunately, the one thing he had feared the most had come to pass…the person he saw tonight was not Circe. Without a second thought, he tried again, concentrating on the precious stone in his hand, calling down to the magic that lay within. "Find me Baldrick, the dung-shoveller."

Reaching down deep within the heart of the magical jewel, the power once dormant, now at last brought to life. Brilliantly the light of the star flared up from his clenched hand, gathered itself, then instantly burst forward and flew off down the street. Taking flight, he chased after the shooting star and turning invisible as he did so; he flew unseen. Minutes later, with Dark following the traveling star as closely as his own shadow, he came to stand within a gathering of evergreens at one end of the temple grounds where a small side gate stood solidly chained and locked.

With the additional security moving about onto the grounds, you would not have believed it possible for anyone to reach the exterior walls without being seen by the sentries. But with his Ring of Invisibility, the assassin managed to pass without challenge. Dark seemed little more than a passing breeze, moving soundlessly, always keeping his eye close to the pulsing blue gemstone, until at last he reached a set of doors that had no window. With the help of Sleek to unlock the arched doors, he began his assault on the heavily guarded Temple of Light. He paused momentarily within the darkened room, closing the wooden door tightly behind him. He found he was in a small study, the high walls lined with shelves of books all carefully marked and labeled. He scarcely gave the room more than a passing glance as he moved to follow the guiding stone to another door at the far end. Cautiously, the half-elf assassin peered into the lighted hallway. Luckily there was no one in sight so he stepped calmly into the hallway.

Dark was not familiar with the Temple layout, having visited there on only one other occasion. At the end of the hall, he quickly turned left at a cross passage, guided by the Gem of Location. He reached a massive door that seemed to shut out the chill of the lower level when he heard voices coming from behind him. Hastily and once again with the help of Sleek, he coolly drew back the latch and swung open the heavy door and slid soundlessly inside. He quickly darted down a set of stone hewn stairs into the blackness of an empty storage cellar. Dark groped along the cold stone wall, the walls appearing solid and the molding unbroken anywhere as he probed and tapped the flooring of the chamber, certain it had to be here. At that instant his hands touched on a secret catch close to the floor which he had somehow missed.

Then he had it; after depressing the hidden lever a stone slab which covered a secret entryway was finally revealed. Grasping a large iron ring hinged at one end of the large slab, the assassin, no longer invisible, pulled upward, straining his powerful muscles. Slowly, with the heavy stone grating in audible protest, the giant slab fell back heavily on the cold flooring. He peered cautiously into the black hole that now stood before him. There was a newly cut stone stairway, wet and covered with mud, that disappeared into the gloomy blackness below. Without the need for any light, the wary assassin descended into the murky depths, silently thinking to himself he was making a mistake.

Almost immediately, after only a few short feet down, he could feel the biting chill air cutting through his armor to cling tightly to his warm skin beneath. The stale, musty air, caused him to wrinkle his nose in disgust; it was barely breathable and caused him to move down the work steps more quickly now. After quite some time, Dark finally reached the bottom of the stairs and saw there was a long single corridor leading directly ahead of him. The tunnel fell into welcomed darkness, to which his black elven eyes quickly adjusted. As he moved slowly forward, and peered ahead through the damp gloom that defied the light, he could see several iron doors cut into the solid stone on both walls and set in place at regular intervals. They were newly constructed slabs of iron, windowless and fastened securely in place by huge metal clasps.

Glancing apprehensively behind him, he realized that he could no longer see the carved opening or the stairs. The blackness that surrounded him looked exactly the same behind as it did ahead. He continued moving cautiously forward, following the steady pulses getting closer and closer together. He passed slowly down the rows of grim metal portals, carefully scrutinizing each door he passed for any signs of recent use. He started to lose count of the number of doors he had checked and the black corridor seemed to go on endlessly into the darkness.

Then, to his amazement, he thought he heard the vague whispers of human voices cut through the heavy silence. Instantly, Dark froze into a motionless statue, listening intently amid the silence, afraid that maybe his senses were somehow deceiving him. Yet again he heard it, faint but clearly they were human. Moving post haste, the assassin began to follow the sound. But as suddenly as they had appeared, the strange voices were gone. Immediately after, there came a loud grating of stone on stone, followed by a heavy thud as if an ancient tomb had just closed. Dark charged ahead, reaching the fallen stone wall and stopping short. Behind him a second grating of stone on stone followed by a second heavy thud. On either side, a huge stone slab had been closed and fastened securely, his exit to freedom barred. The half-elf stood helpless, shaking his head in stunned belief. Soon the waiting would begin.

With just a few brief words of power, his spell was complete yet nothing happened. He even tried lighting one of the torches that hung on the walls with the magic of Dragon's Breath, but that too failed to produce any results. From the belt at his waist, he used a piece of flint that he struck against the steel of his armor, the pieces of metal scraped off blazed with white light setting the combustible material at the end of the torch on fire, that gave off a soft continuous glow. Instantly, Dark saw the reason for his magical frustration. The walls of his underground prison were lined with naturally occurring veins of lead along with large deposits of the rare Heartstone. He also found strange symbols painted in gorgon's blood that completely rendered teleportation in or out of this hidden complex impossible. He must have stood for at least fifteen long minutes, motionless in the dimness of the torch light as he listened intently for any sound. Briefly he contemplated attempting to break out somehow, but quickly discarded the idea and decided to just simply wait. As the long minutes passed into hours, he began to feel that he may indeed have been truly left alone and trapped forever beneath the Temple's underbelly and with no chance of escape.

Then, far above his head, a long vertical slit of light appeared amid a falling shower of fine sand that fell about his head and shoulders. As the slit above his head grew wider, he heard the sound of metal mechanisms and hidden cables and hoists straining with the weight of the platform he stood on as it began to rise upward. Within moments all the other elements fell into place, such as the man made holes in the floor, the walls bearing numerous slots, grooves and abrasions, obviously made with great care for a certain purpose. Finally, the mechanical mechanism which propelled his ascent, came to a sudden halt beyond the wooden floor that separated the dark, stifling chamber from the airy stadium above, where a crowd of at least two thousand Halflings sat around an arena floor.

The wearied eyed assassin prisoner glanced about abruptly, and there like a roman emperor, Sneak Longfoot sat in a place of honor in an Imperial Box at the very center of the long northern curve of the pint sized coliseum where it seemed his every action was being scrutinized by the audience. The dominating feature of this candlelit circular stadium was a throne situated high behind him, carved from a single block of lead and polished to a mirror-like sheen. Surrounding him were a series of expensive tapestries depicting vile scenes of carnage that covered the chamber walls from its fine sand floor to its fifty foot high ceiling. He stepped forward slowly, his outstretched hand coming to rest on the cool handle of his shadow sword. It flickered in and out of focus, seemingly solid one second and ephemeral the next. He fingered it lightly as he pondered the problem facing him. But before Dark could act, the heretofore silent Halfling Leader strode forward and silenced the crowd who had risen to their feet, shouting wildly and uttering streams of foul oaths.

"If you're wondering if this is Dwarf made, well it's not," the Halfling Leader stated simply. "I had this arena built purely for my amusement. I must admit I did get the idea from the Republican period of the ancient Roman Empire, with a few added touches of my own. The walls and ceiling are covered by thousands of thick veins of lead as well as large localized deposits of a strange mineral known as Heartstone. An extremely unusual and even more uncommon stone with peculiar effects to anything comprised of magic, as I'm sure you're well aware of already or else you still wouldn't be here, trapped like a rat in a cage!"

For a moment there was a long period of silence as both the leader and his pack of followers alike, all stared in utter disbelief at the deceptively passive face of the lone prisoner who dared to stare down death. All the while a fleeting smile crossed Dark's demonic lips, as he noticed handsome stewards passing through the crowd carrying trays of cakes, pastries, dates and other sweet snacks, as well as generous cups of wine, which were greedily drunk.

"I have seen many assassins in my time, but somebody like you I have truly never encountered the likes of before,"

Sneak Longfoot declared quickly. "That's why it's such a pity that you have to die…I really can't let you leave here alive, now can I? So I'm afraid you'll have to die, but before you do, I'm sure you'll put forth the finest show possible to entertain my eagerly awaiting audience."

Almost disappointedly he knew this grand spectacle would begin unlike many public events in Classic Rome, without any splendid morning processions, without trumpeters, fighters, priests or any carriages bearing effigies of the gods. No, it seemed there would be only one such performer this day. For only Dark appeared in the arena and no other.

"Oh I'm sorry, I didn't quite get that," Dark admitted mockingly, the demonic face of his armor grinned wolfishly at the plump hobbit. "You see I normally don't pay attention to children speaking."

A strange silence overtook the Halfling spectators, only their eyes betrayed the unspoken outrage that lingered beneath placid facades as the fat face of this overweight leader turned from one of stone faced anger to one of impish delight. Sneak Longfoot erupted suddenly into an roar of uncontrollable laughter, holding his bulging sides in mirth. Then all around the stadium, jeers and cheers rose up, followed by loud peals of laughter that echoed throughout the domed coliseum until finally the rotund Guild Leader held up a pudgy hand calling for immediate silence.

"You must forgive me, I do wish to apologize for my rude outburst." The fur clad Lord Protector of Duergar smiled faintly down, still chuckling in delight. "You see the pack and I are not used to such bold bravado…well…from anyone really, be it man, woman or child. Our standing in Duergar is now one to be feared, unlike the days of old when my people were treated less than cordial to say the least. No we were mocked and ridiculed for our short comings…"

Dark's demonic face was distorted in sudden laughter of his own.

"Silence!" Sneak's voice rose in sudden fury, reverberating back from the stone walls, his brown eyes studying the dark face of the assassin, searching for answers that clearly were not to be found there. "Those days of living in fear are no longer, for we are the children of the night, and with each passing day, our reputation and our might grows as does the size of our pack. And soon that power shall grow even greater as we make way the path to his glory."

"You know I really should thank you," the black-garbed assassin moved forward a few feet, the constant smile suddenly villainous as anger flashed sharply in his red eyes that now flared with fire. "You really have made things so much simpler for me. For now I don't have to waste my time searching every pile of shite for you filthy little bastards one by one; you've brought them all here for me, and conveniently under one domed roof. And once I'm finished dispensing a proper justice to your pack of cutthroats and killers of women and children, I shall turn my attention to you, their faithful leader. And when I find you, I will shove the blade of my sword up your fat arse and play you like a puppet."

Sneak Longfoot backed away guardedly, glancing briefly at the faces of his followers and then stared fixedly at the demonic assassin. In an instant the bent figure of the Guild Leader snapped upright, recovered his wits about him, his sharp eyes once again cold with fury. "That's enough, you mock us all with your antics!" the Halfling Ruler went rigid, his tiny hands now gripped the edge of the railing until his knuckles went white. His eyes mirrored both anger and hate. "Let's see if you still have that smart mouth when you see what it is that all must face who enter into my arena. Bring me the beast! Bring me Fenrir!"

Then abruptly a few shouts went up from a cluster of Hobbits at the foot of the first row in a section of the stadium, joined almost immediately by the shouts and howls of others mingled in. The audience eager for blood rose uncertainly, looking quickly about for some sign of the huge creature. Dark's strong hand came to grip tightly the pommel of his shadow sword, and he tried calling forth the magic of the dragon wand, but nothing happened. He paused, standing motionless in alert anticipation, looking down at the arena floor and beyond to the walls of the domed amphitheatre, listening to the sounds of the straining pulley system as well as the low voices of the Halflings moving forward to see below.

Beneath the wooden floor of the coliseum, which was covered by sand, came the loud howling of a wolf and the scraping of sharp claws on stone below from one of many elaborate substructures of service corridors. Suddenly the innermost part of the sandy arena floor began to rustle and shiver back and forth. A hinged ramp fell downward with an audible thud and out burst Fenrir, roaring and slavering, and still tied tightly around his huge neck was the fetter, smooth and soft as a silk ribbon. A gigantic and terrible monster in the shape of a wolf with topaz eyes stepped forward menacingly on all fours. It was at least three times taller than him at the shoulder, maybe more, and its lithe, muscular body was covered in long neatly groomed black fur. It smiled broadly at Dark, revealing row upon row of sharp, pearly white fangs.

The Halfling spectators scattered back to their seats, yet the black-garbed assassin stood his ground. The beast growled again and came closer, the hackles on the back of its neck rose, swelling up until it blotted out all sight of the leaden veins of the ceiling. On its breath the great monster carried with it the reek of its birth, the stale stench of hunger and the bitter rankness of sin. In its frightful eyes were reflected scenes of carnage and mayhem, the slaughter of men, the raping of women, infants being torn from their mother's arms, then cruelly impaled on the sharpened points of bayonets.

Then Fenrir lurched forward, springing for his throat, quick and silent for one so large, its jaws gaping wide, clawed paws reaching. But Dark was way too quick. The assassin attacked with precision, striking at the unprotected flanks, between the ribs and the hip of the giant wolf, drawing the great behemoth to one side. With the agility of an acrobat, Demon Raider turned away from an awkward and backward bite, then watched as the great beast, amid a roar of applause, stalked slowly toward him, reddened jaws gaping wide with slavering hunger. The creature charged at him suddenly, bounding across the space that separated them in just seconds, launching its huge frame at the half-elven assassin's horned head. Dark brought his blade up guardedly and fell backward, blood reddened the ground from the torn underbelly of the carnivorous creature. Nimbly he rolled back to his feet, turning to face his eager attacker.

Again it came for him, its huge mouth split wide with sharp gleaming teeth, from its maddened mouth poured a stream of crimson. It began circling the assassin, occasionally barring its fangs in an angry snarl, waiting for the right opportunity to strike. Then suddenly it struck, lunging forward like a lion with huge claws ripping at his shoulders and sides, leaving Dark torn and tattered. Once again the black furred wolf circled slowly around his injured combatant, like a predator watching its helpless prey. Fenrir's ashen form darted like a shadow through the dim light in a soundless rush and lunged a third time, its bulging dark eyes fixed on the tiny figure before it. Then the creature was upon him, twisted its huge bulk and slipping beneath the arc of Dark's flickering sword, sinking its sharp fangs into the side of the assassin's heavily plated chest. Powerful jaws tore at the muscles of his chest and arms crackling like deadwood as searing pain lanced through his entire body, then suddenly he felt himself hurtling through the air. He struck the ground several feet away with stunning force, his head slamming solidly against the wood of the chamber floor and quickly disappeared in a cloud of dust; his body went quickly numb.

For an instant his vision blurred and he thought he would blackout, as chants for his death erupted from all around him, but the assassin fought off the dizziness and through the pain and somehow forced himself to rise. Dazed, he stood on unsure feet, his body ached from the force of the Lycan's attack, and even now spots began dancing before his eyes. With great effort, he somehow managed to stay erect as blood streamed down Dark's battered body in long rivulets and he felt himself weakening fast. He was losing this battle and he immediately thought it would end with his death if he did not take back control of the situation. For he would not die this day, not like this, not against some flea ridden mutt. No, he had too much to do yet, too many that still needed to pay. And they all will pay…every last one.

With renewed strength he watched as the massive wolf continued to circle, hungry snarls of white gleamed with fanged death. The half-elven assassin stumbled heavily to his knees as he tried stepping nimbly away from him. The deception worked. Thinking the fallen dark man finished, the huge beast lunged forward with murderous fury. But this time Dark was ready and waiting. He caught the monster squarely in its furred chest, the sword now twice as long and its blade twice as thick, cut deep through the bone and muscle. Shrieking in pain and howling in fury, it struck back savagely, trying unsuccessfully to crush the life out of the small form of his foe. Its black fur gaping with the ugly wound, blood ran red from the large gash, trailing a thick wetness across the sand.

It reared at first, fighting hard to escape, its back legs kicking, forelegs extended and thrusting outward as it forced down a new wave of fear, a fear it had never felt before. Both combatants were covered with blood, each one's strength ebbing from them. From atop the wounded assassin, the black furred wolf rose up howling and opening its massive jaws as wide as the gates of Hell and prepared to swallow him whole. Grimly Dark clung to the handle of his shadow sword and for what happened next, I have only the man's word which I will faithfully recount for your now.

The half-elf assassin leaped forward into the maw of the great beast. Back flew Fenrir, his voice lost in a sudden strangled gasp. As it fell to the ground, Dark moved through the body of the beast as if he crawled through a deep dark corridor, drawn only by the sound of a distant drumbeat. As he drew nearer, the pounding grew steadily louder and louder.

He finally entered what he thought was a great cavern, awash with blood and walled by white bone. He gazed ahead and there, suspended from the fleshy branches of arteries, veins and valves, was the beast's heart as alluring as a bright red garnet. Dark, unthinking, raised his arm and with a series of quick powerful tugs, he drew down the dangling heart as easily as one would plucking an apple from a tree. Within its depths, nearly drown out by the roar of the crowd above, he heard something soft and secret. He heard a final whisper of sorrow as he cradled it in his palms and crawled back out into the light again. But when he finally emerged from the belly of the beast, his arms now cradling the large organ, the ground broke beneath his feet and thunder cleared the sky. At that moment, a fissure yawned suddenly wide in the arena floor. The heart, still beating, sprang from his hands and fell into the bottomless chasm. Then as suddenly as it had appeared, the eorth trembled one last time and closed over it.

Dark stood motionless before the huge corpse of Fenrir. He staggered forward, his shadow sword no longer clutched within his hand, black eyes hard and fixed. A numbing sensation had already begun to spread through his injured body that caused him to stumble and fall to one knee. As he fell, the fat, little Ruler of Duergar, no longer staring in stunned disbelief, gathered his wits and ordered his followers to close in about the assassin and thrust their swords deep into his belly.

The walls of the coliseum reverberated with the still audible howls that rose about him, fierce and hungry for blood, his blood. Through sheer force of will, Dark awkwardly came to stand and then stood motionless for a time, his dark face impassive and showing no fear. Several dark bodies lunged from out of their seats, their bodies instantly sporting short, thick fur. Bones cracked amid howls of pain, their spines and necks became bent causing them to drop to their hands and knees which elongated into canine limbs. For an instant after, Dark's demonic eyes started to smolder, then suddenly burst into lurid flames that both stunned and silenced the crowd.

A hot mist began rising from the ground, coiling around him until it finally enveloped him in a shroud of flickering shadows.

"There are still those among you that are truly masters of enchantment," Dark straightened to his full height and grinned menacingly, his white fangs gleaming. "An elder race born of this eorth that still possesses powers that far surpass any knowing mortal that would rule this world. For coursing through my veins runs the blood of Dragons! And its powers know no bounds! For I am Demon Raider, the Death Stalker! And I am to be more feared then all those vengeful spirits left behind by the scythe of death! For I am the executioner's axe, the harbinger of doom and I bring only pain and sorrow! My hauntings, as will be told, will come to be more feared than the coming of the Grim Reaper himself! For I am here for your very souls!"

A command for repentance issued forth from his fanged mouth, carrying with it the power of the ancient spell. Shadows erupted forth and poured out from all around him, engulfing everything in its path with a black watery ichor. It sailed quickly up the curved walls of the underground stadium, out over wood, stone and flesh under fur, it curled freely in the air. In the midst were unspeakable horrors, demons of poverty, of pestilence, of starvation and of every other vice that would come to haunt mankind for ages to come.

"What spell is this?" Sneak Longfoot sputtered fearfully, his eyes wide with fright.

"This is no spell," came the woeful reply from Baldrick, stepping back slowly.

"Then what is it man?" pleaded the stout Halfling Leader, as he too backed away terrified. "What is it?"

"Our doom."

His words fell silent as the creeping shadow washed over him, the last of the light was drawn from the surrounding area, and within just a few seconds, the last of the candle light finally dimmed into utter darkness. Then the shadowed assassin struck. Unopposed, he easily slid over the arena floor, up the walls and into the seats of the coliseum. He began to fill his lungs with a swirling burning inborn energy. Then, from his demonic mouth, came a mighty exhalation that flooded the area with a powerful cone of dragon fire. Blasts of flame ignited the pillars and exploded among the fleeing spectators, causing bones to crack and then crumple to dust. Angered breath escaped from his lips with a sharp hiss as he spat gouts of searing fire in an arc that reached from one end of the werewolf advance to the other. With each exhaled blast, the bright flames swept through the ranks of Lycan attackers leaving nothing more than blackened smoldering meat and burnt ash. Howls and shrieks of pain now rose from the pack as again Dark struck, and again crackling blasts of flames leaped forth and wreathed its targets whole, lighting the area around him in a yellow glow. Blasts of fire surged outward in furious roaring bursts, disappearing in a brilliant explosion with a bright field of orange fire rising skyward to mark the end.

Huddled against the cavernous wall, Sneak Longfoot watched the fires crimson glow winking into darkness. It happened so suddenly, a final spurt of flame and then they were gone, they were all gone. All that was left to light the gloom of the chamber were the discarded lamps, their soft white glimmer faint and small. The hobbit blinked in the sudden darkness, peering blindly ahead through the shadows of the underground amphitheatre. Frightened for his very life, the corpulent Halfling Leader knew he was doomed. He was a man without any humanity, his soul was darker than the surrounding blackness and staggering beneath a burden of guilt that would never find redemption.

Dark's form was a churning channel of blackness that lurched across the plain of shadows and swallowed the light, and with arms of darkness, he reached to capture his portly foe. And for a long moment, Sneak Longfoot stood mesmerized, but his own sense of self-preservation soon spurred him into action. Ashen faced, he started to turn as a blast of hot flame took Baldrick's life, and like a fleeing coward, he ran through the dark corridors and narrow stairway of the darkened coliseum.

Dark was soon after him with a bound, leaving the writhing shadows behind him as they soon faded into nothingness. With unbelievable agility for a fat man, Sneak was already pulling frantically on the massive metal door. The half-elf assassin was halfway up the same stairs, desperately trying to stop the Halfling Leader's escape. Longfoot pushed through the partially open door to freedom, yelling for the guards, and a moment later disappeared through another doorway. From the hallway beyond, Dark, finally reaching the foot of the stairway, could hear the shrill cries from gathering soldiers. Dark raced through the open door in close pursuit; two red clad temple guards appeared suddenly from the hallway beyond, their swords drawn at the ready to confront the charging assassin. Dark moved with magical speed and struck out with a lightning assault, slicing through both armored necks as easily as a hot knife through butter. Both men were silenced before they even had a chance to defend themselves, their heads toppled and fell away, then both their bodies too fell lifeless to the marble floor. Then he heard the sharp sound of more voices from close by.

Everything was in a state of utter confusion as guards, clergymen, temple servants and visitors all milled through the panic stricken temple grounds. Shouts of terror reverberated off the stone walls; Sneak Longfoot, decrying his own death and warning of the assassin hell bent on killing him. Dark fought his way through the throngs of frightened people who seemed to be acting in a state of complete hysteria at the sight of his demonic appearance. A few brave guards sought an attempt to bar his passage, their long swords pointed in defiance. But with unbelievable fury, he heedlessly flung the unfortunate men aside with aided strength from the Belt of Heroes without pausing as he raced in pursuit of the elusive hobbit.

Then suddenly the huge stained glass window high above the temple doors shuddered under the weight of Dark and burst open with a crack and directly in front of the flying assassin was the fleeing Sneak Longfoot. The unwary Halfling Leader soon found himself struck between the shoulder blades by a heavy clawed hand, pushed face down into the dirt of a ditch, his nostrils quickly filled with the earth that soon would be his home.

Sneak's obese body was turned over and whipped upward toward the demonic assassin, the flat of his fist sharply struck the man's unprotected face, striking it in a stinging blow. The Halfling figure reeled backward, his features clenched suddenly in pain. Dark did not pause, his own strength easily holding the struggling man to the ground where his fingers closed tightly about the windpipe.

"Wait…wait, wait!" the voice choked sharply and the hobbit's breathing rasped in his throat. "I have information… valuable information…and if you spare my life, I'll gladly share it with you!"

"You're too stupid to know anything of value to me!" Dark growled menacingly, glowing red eyes surveyed the face of his captive. Moving quickly upward, he jerked the little hobbit to his feet, one clawed hand still firmly fastened on the man's throat.

"The lost City of Shadowmoon…" the voice of the Guild Leader broke slightly as the pudgy little fellow struggled to regain his senses. "I overheard Kalifen and Lord Blackthorn discussing it…they seek the Gates of Hades…they search for it day and night."

"That better not be all," Demon Raider's eyes burned into the hobbit with intense hatred and in fury, yanked the small man violently up in the air. "I ought to kill you right now."

"All I know is all of Kalifen's plans hinge on this one event," he answered eagerly. "He acts like it's the end of the world…"

The fat man's sentence ended with a strangled gasp as Dark grabbed him roughly off of the ground and began to squeeze. Sneak Longfoot's face quickly began turning purple.

"Who was the woman that came to see you at the opera house?" Once more the assassin tightened his iron grip forcing the gasping captive to nod his acquiescence. He released his grip of the man's throat; both hands dropped to seize the Halfling by the front of his tunic.

"That was no woman…" he answered eagerly. "His name is Gylifi, a shape-shifter we used to lure you out. You see we have your dark skinned partner and his paramour as well, and he told us all about her and a certain horned assassin."

"What else did he tell you?" Dark urged a moment later.

Sneak paused and looked fearfully at his captive, noting the assassin's demonic features with great dismay.

"That he and his partner searched for the girl," the pudgy Guild Leader repeated slowly. "That is all I know, I swear it! I wouldn't lie to you, that's the truth!"

"No that is not the truth."

There was a moment of stunned silence as Dark smiled easily at him. Dark was still smiling and Sneak Longfoot was caught between lies, a half smile forming on his own lips. Then with a few brief words of power, both men were propelled skywards coming to a stop some two hundred feet in the air.

"Where are they being kept?" The smile was gone from his face as his features turned hard and his voice cold and menacing. "Lie to me once more and we'll both find out if pigs can really fly."

"She lies imprisoned in the dungeon below the Citadel!" he spoke quickly, the battered face stared at the assassin frightfully. "The black man, they moved him. I don't know where…I swear I don't know where."

Then suddenly passing through the gates fronting the temple grounds, the foremost ranks of the City Guard crested the roadway leading in and the entire command moved slowly into view. Dark turned his head and watched, the demonic face of his armor gave a low guttural growl. He recognized these riders immediately, long blue cloaks bordered in black billowed from their shoulders and helmets of steel upon their heads. Each rider held a long lance from which fluttered a small crimson pennant with an illuminated eye.

The small squadron of Knights drew to a halt before the temple doors and a tall, red cloaked rider behind the military procession slowly dismounted. Catching sight of the floating pair, he passed the reins of his dray horse to another and strode forward. Mechanically, the stranger removed his wide cowl and inclined his head slightly.

"I believe you have something that belongs to me."

For an instant Dark was dumbfounded and did not respond, so surprised was he by the sudden appearance of this strange man who stood so boldly before him now. Without even seeing him, he knew who this person was, instinct alone told him this was the mystic Kalifen. He was a tall man with a cadaverous frame, a gaunt and skeletal like body with withered patches of rotting flesh. His bald head revealed sickly strips of white bone and his mouth seemed agape with incredulity, his shriveled lips were stretched back as if writhing in pain. Part of one ear was missing and a long aged scar ran from below his right ear halfway around his throat. His cloudy gray eyes fixed on Dark so hard that his eyes became locked in front of him.

"You wouldn't dare to drop me now," came the cocksure claim from the overly confident hobbit.

"You're quite sure about that are you?" was Dark's reply, a faint smile crossing his demonic visage.

"I think so…?" Sneak Longfoot hesitated in confusion, his large feet dangling high above the ground.

"Then why don't you think about that on the way down."

No sooner had the words fell from his lips, so too did the portly Guild Leader, his flabby arms flapping as if trying to fly. He tumbled steadily downward screaming laments for his most assured death. Dark's attention turned suddenly towards Kalifen, and even as he studied his nemesis, his teeth clenched in anger and his eyes burned red with hatred.

"Today I return justice to this city…AND YOU TO HELL!"

The evil face of the mystic stared menacingly at him and in unstoppable fury Dark began his spell as an inner divine energy now streamed out. What happened next was to be forever etched in his mind as if carved in stone. Then it was as if a huge burst of energy washed out over the landscape and in just a few seconds of frozen time, past, present and future were all gathered into one. There was nothing but sluggish darkness and the deep shadows that turned and fell over the landscape like a blanket of fog instantly freezing all in its path into motionless statues. Those affected struggled to move, sending all the fears and terrors they had ever known rushing through their now paralyzed forms. They could not speak, they could not move and all watched helplessly as the horned assassin flew slowly towards them. Lightning fell in long streaks and bright flashes and Dark reached down deep within himself; a quick and deliberate act, joining together his mind, body and spirit as one in a single, unbreakable purpose. Dark brought to bare the full powers of Dragon's Breath and from the dragon's maw fire exploded outward striking his foe, driving the wizard backwards. There wasn't a sound made as the space before him became flooded in an irregular red glow that engulfed everything in its path in a bright field of white, red and yellow. The flames soared high above the ground, licking hungrily at the stone and grass, crackling with unnatural life as it greedily consumed the red-garbed creature that fuelled it. Through the smoke and mist that wafted into his own burning eyes, the assassin gazed fixedly toward the glowing fire. He found himself alone with the roar of the flames and he thought at last the wizard was gone.

Then abruptly from the giant blaze ahead, a figure broke through the blinding light from the burning wall of flame, casting its shadow against the ground like a misshapen wraith fleeing into darkness. And like the mythical phoenix rising from the ashes, Kalifen strode forward, his clothing torn and burned almost beyond recognition, his hands and face only slightly singed and blackened from the heat.

"Bold words indeed," the words were a chilling echo in the deep stillness. "But such words are reserved for those with the strength to challenge me…with you I'm afraid there is no need for concern."

Dark eyed the tall mystic critically for a moment, his anger subsiding and he slowly smiled, his keen elven eyes noticing a long gold medallion hanging about the wizard's neck.

"The next time we meet, I will come to you like a thief in the night, and you will not know at what hour I will come against you!"

With those final words, both he and his tiny captive both vanished and past, present and future split apart and the seconds resumed.

The next moment, Dark and his halfling prisoner found themselves standing behind a pair of large pine trees and under the protective shelter of some low hanging branches.

"What is this place...where have you taken me?" the Guild Leader exclaimed fearfully. "And what is that loathsome stench?"

"On your feet fat boy." Moving quickly, he snatched the rotund hobbit to his feet, his hand dropping to seize the back of the colorful tunic. "This happens to be the last place you will ever see."

"Death does not matter to me demon," Sneak Longfoot spoke bravely, trying desperately to show no fear, his usually sharp wits finally coming undone. "For you forget that Kalifen now possesses the one being who can bring me back from the grave. Therefore, I shall live once more, despite what it is you have done to me. The Fleshweaver needs only a small piece of my body for me to be reborn."

"This is why I have brought you here to the Island of Turning," his tone was almost evil, as he yanked the fat man violently off the forest floor. "And to see the Harpy Sisters."

Sneak suddenly went white at the mention of these winged female monsters and an undisguised fear shot into his widened eyes.

"They literally eat everything, I'm told, including bones... they won't leave a crumb big enough for a mouse."

What the hobbit heard next wasn't so much a sniffing sound, but rather a loud inhaling noise like someone or something snuffling, sniffling and snorting and like a hog hunting for truffles in the woods. The frightened Halfling Leader knew instantly what these sounds were, and more to the point, just who was making them and why. These were obviously the Harpies. Just then, two shadowy figures stepped forward into the revealing light from the darkened shadows of the cave and came to stand before their demonic master.

"Sister can it be, our master has brought us meat to eat sister!" Aello exclaimed hungrily, her lips smacking loudly against her mouth.

"Yes sister I see, I see, a big fat hobbit!" Ocypete acknowledged eagerly to the other. "How wonderful indeed sister, a hobbit, our absolute favorite."

"But the witch told me I was to live forever!!!"

"And so you shall, you shall...for your screams will forever echo upon the winds."

Dark roughly threw the portly hobbit and the man fell crashing down to the solid earth. For a moment he watched as the two hungry sisters took hold of their chunky meal by his thick ankles, and at that very moment the awful truth of his plight now stole over him...he was about to die! Within one last glancing look, the horrified Halfling showed him the whites of his eyes and howled dismally, his pudgy little fingers clawing desperately at the ground as the winged pair dragged him towards their home.

XX

Later that same day, in the windy, seagirt Citadel of Duergar, the soon to be crowned king sat on an armchair covered in gold, his face scarlet with rage and indignation. He then raised his weary head and turned to the Captain of the City Watch who was dressed in full battle attire, his hand resting loosely on the hilt of his sword.

"Tell me Captain, when is Lord Blackthorn's expected return?" Kalifen asked soberly, then paused before his eyes turned to the knight's. "I am most anxious to learn if he was successful in the task I set out for him."

"I am told he will return within the week my Lord," Captain Caine told him quickly, the smile he gave the old wizard was faint and cold at very best. "I've also been told there is still no word on whether Master Longfoot is alive or dead."

"No matter, he was as useless as tit's on a bull." His gray eyes fixed on that of the Captain's.

"There is one more matter my Lord, that I believe requires your immediate attention."

A sudden hammering from outside the huge doors to the castle's throne room brought them all about. It was a hammering that was mixed with the muffled cries of soldiers struggling and the deep, husky growls and grunts of some wild animal about. Several of the palace guards hastened to the arched doorway and flipped clear the metal restraining latch. The wide doors flew back with a crash and a massive dark form, heavily bound and tethered was brought into the grand hall. It took forty strong men to restrain the giant creature with thick chains of irons, each long length of connected links securely attached to solid bands of steel placed around every meaty muscular limb of the gigantic beast. Fastened around the thick knot of its neck, a lockable slave collar was held by a giant of a man who was six foot four and full of muscles. Loud shouts rang out through the chamber from the beast master, with the creature being yanked roughly forward and soon the monster's face came into view.

"What have we here?" finally the rotting ruler's gaze rested on the big brute.

It was a huge, fiendishly looking troll, more than twice as tall as the tallest man. It had large powerful sagging shoulders with long ape-like arms, its hairy knuckled hands reached well past its tree-knotted knees. The beast's tremendous tree trunk-like legs ended in huge yellow clawed feet, its rough hide like bark with oily black bristles for hair that fell in a tangled mess over cold staring eyes filled with malice.

"We caught this...thing, roaming the countryside around Duergar my Lord," the regal knight addressed his sovereign, his head slightly bowed. "What would you have us do with it my Lord?"

Kalifen looked at each in turn, then finally his gaze rested on the armored man.

"Why kill it of course, and be quick about it."

"Wait!" the voice was that of the troll.

"Quiet you filth!" the big blonde trainer cuffed the monster sharply, extending a hand upward.

"I am Og, and I seek the same as you!" the great beast growled, his long fanged teeth clenched in hatred. "I too seek the one called Demon Raider!"

"You give me his name!" the wizard ridiculed sharply, his voice echoing loudly off the stone walls. "What good is a name to me...and therefore what good are you?"

"I am of great value to you, more so than gold," the mighty troll snarled his reply. "I know his scent well...so find him I can."

"Can you now..." Kalifen smiled faintly, his voice trailing into silence.

www.ingramcontent.com/pod-product-compliance
Lightning Source LLC
Chambersburg PA
CBHW071247250626
47163CB00002B/367